A
WRECKING OF
SALT
AND
FIRE

E.K. CONDOS

Edited and Proofread by Ciara Lewis @clewis.edits

Book Cover Art by David Gardias @best.selling.covers

Map by MIBLART

First Edition Published 2024

For Josh. The light in all my darkness. My northern star to guide me home. And to readers who no longer let the nightmares of the past define them.

Content Warnings

T his book contains many adult and sensitive topics. Please only read if you are comfortable with these: death, war, anxiety, thoughts of suicide, flashbacks of suicide, flashbacks to rape and sexual assault, forced consent, consensual sex, flashbacks of torture, blood, kidnapping. Your mental health matters, please reach out with any questions or concerns.

Pronunciation Guide

Places
Odessia: Oh-dys-see-ah
The Mykandrian Sea: Mee-can-dree-an S-ee
Alentus: Ah-len-tis
Morentius: More-en-tee-us
Nexos: N-ex-sos
Delphine: Dell-feen
Cantos: Cant-ohs
Xanthia: Zan-tee-ah
Lesathos: Lay-sah-th-ohs
The Manos Sea: Mah-nos S-ee
Cyther: Sigh-th-air
Skiatha: Sky-ah-th-ah
The Saron Sea: S-ah-ron S-ee
Avernia: Ah-vair-nee-ah
Aidesian: Aye-dee-zee-ahn
Voreia: Vor-ay-ah
Harrenfort: Hair-ehn-fort
Hespali: Es-pah-lee
Votios: Vote-ee-os
Tyrair: Tie-ray
Anatole: Ah-na-toll

People

Aikaterine Drakos (Katrin): Aye-kat-err-EEN-ee Drah-kos (Ka-treen)

Ember Drakos: Ehm-buhr Drah-kos

Kora Drakos: Core-ah Drah-kos

Aidoneus Drakos: Aye-don-ee-us Drah-kos

Ajax Demos: Ay-jax Day-mos

Nikolaos Kirassos I: Nee-ko-low-ss Keer-ahs-sos

Giselle Kirassos: Gee-zelle Keer-ahs-sos

Dimitris Kirassos: The-me-trees Keer-ahs-sos

Khalid Athanas: Ka-leed Ah-than-us

Zahra Athanas: Z-ahr-ruh Ah-than-us

Kohl Athanas: Cole Ah-than-us

Farah Athanas: Fair-ah Ah-than-us

Alexander: Ah-lex-an-dair

Leighton Callas: Lay-ton Cah-las

Thalia: Tha-lee-yah

Mykonos (Myko): Mee-kon-nos (Mee-ko)

Iason: Ya-son

Chloe: Klo-ee

Dolion: Dohl-ee-on

Kristos Callas: Cree-sto-ss Cah-las

Ileana: Ill-ee-ah-na

Edmund Briarre: Ehd-mund Bree-air

CONTENTS

The Binding Law of the Grechi   XVII

Part One   1

1. Chapter One   3

2. Chapter Two   9

3. Chapter Three   14

4. Chapter Four   20

5. Chapter Five   27

6. Chapter Six   32

7. Chapter Seven   40

8. Chapter Eight   47

9. Chapter Nine   58

10. Chapter Ten   64

11. Chapter Eleven   71

12. Chapter Twelve   75

13. Chapter Thirteen   81

14. Chapter Fourteen   83

Part Two   87

15. Chapter Fifteen   89

16. Chapter Sixteen   99

17. Chapter Seventeen   108

18. Chapter Eighteen   111

19. Chapter Nineteen   121

20. Chapter Twenty   130

21. Chapter Twenty-One   143

22. Chapter Twenty-Two   157

23. Chapter Twenty-Three   166

24. Chapter Twenty-Four   180

25. Chapter Twenty-Five   187

26. Chapter Twenty-Six   199

27. Chapter Twenty-Seven   206

28. Chapter Twenty-Eight   214

29. Chapter Twenty-Nine   219

30. Chapter Thirty   223

31. Chapter Thirty-One   232

Part Three   239

32. Chapter Thirty-Two   240

33. Chapter Thirty-Three   248

34. Chapter Thirty-Four   260

35.	Chapter Thirty-Five	271
36.	Chapter Thirty-Six	276
37.	Chapter Thirty-Seven	283
38.	Chapter Thirty-Eight	287
39.	Chapter Thirty-Nine	296
40.	Chapter Forty	300
41.	Chapter Forty-One	305
42.	Chapter Forty-Two	308
43.	Chapter Forty-Three	312
44.	Chapter Forty-Four	318
45.	Chapter Forty-Five	320
46.	Chapter Forty-Six	325
Bonus Chapter: The God of Shield and Storm		331
Bonus Chapter: Welcome to Hades		335
Acknowledgements		339
Kickstarter Acknowledgements		343
About the Author		345

The Binding Law of the Grechi

No god shall interfere in the will of the Fates.
Not even for the survival of one of their own.

PART ONE

στην αρχή
(In the Beginning)

CHAPTER ONE

KATRIN

"*H*elp! Please!" *Katrin screamed into the night, her voice smothered by the thundering skies. Scanning the darkened shoreline, she couldn't make out if the guards were still posted along the beach. Fires below the cliffs were doused by the pouring rain, but the men should still be there. They were always there. A moment passed as she listened for stomping boots in wet sand, for a horn to alert the castle of a threat, for anything.*

No answer came. There was no one. No one to protect her.

Thick rope dug into her wrists as her captor dragged her body down the beach. She clawed her nails into the flesh of the man, blood seeping from his skin as she squirmed. Hot breath cascaded over her ear. "Resistance is futile, Princess," the man hissed, pulling the rope tighter.

Salt from the rain slid down her forehead, blistering her eyes. Squinting through the rain, a ship came into focus, the faint outline of a six-letter word on the stern, two silver serpents with their tails curling around each other on the black sails. Images of the banners of surrounding isles shot through her mind, but this was not an emblem she knew.

Pulling at the rope to gain some balance, Katrin thrust her head back toward his face, smashing into his nose.

"You bitch," he hissed, releasing one of his hands from her wrists to cover his nose before tightening the rope. Crimson stained his palms and the coarse threads that held her tight.

"You will regret this!" she seethed.

Her captor let out a mocking laugh, one that rattled along with the thunder from the skies above. Only then did he release her from their struggle, and for only a moment, to bend down and whisper, "My only regret is not taking you sooner. Maybe I should just kill you now, save him the trouble. Although, the amount of coin he has promised me is too good to pass up." A toothy grin flashed across his face. "Eínai i katára sou."

Goosebumps rose along Katrin's bare arms. Bile began to rise in her throat as she realized he knew the Elliniká Glóssa. The language was forbidden a century ago, stripped from the books in the isles, even carved out of the murals in the ancient temples. "What does that mean? Who are you taking me to?"

Her captor laughed again. "He is your curse. Bound to you and you to him by the Grechi." His voice was as serpentine and deadly as the creatures on the ship's sails. The man bent down, meeting her stare.

Those eyes. She would never forget those eyes.

Katrin's chest heaved as a familiar copper tang coated her mouth. It rose and fell in an attempt to steady, her hands pressed deep into her thighs as she bent over. Low tide and the salty summer air burned in her nose. Sanguine and amber hues of the sun crept over the eastern cliffs of Alentus, a fair warning that a storm loomed in the distance. Rain she could manage. She would welcome the swirling tides and thrashing winds, the cooling of the air that caused the sky to rattle an unyielding call. Icy chills of her memories—that she could live without.

Hours before, she woke, the only light trailing through the gossamer curtains from the crescent moon and the constellations that dared show their spark this late in the summer. Blood trickled down her fingers, crusting under her nails. Scratches over the scars that never truly healed from years ago burned like embers crackling in a hearth.

Every night was the same routine. Fall in and out of a fitful sleep. Awake in a pool of sweat and blood, ready to hurl the previous night's dinner from her gut. Get out of bed. Slip on a pair of tight black trousers and a thin sleeveless tunic. Sneak past the guards through the hidden passage in her chambers.

It was reckless to be outside the castle alone before dawn, but she could not help it. Wind caressing her skin and the silence of the night cascading around her were the only things that made her forget anymore—forget his wretched features. Blinding red irises, crooked smile and elongated nose, raspy heated breath along her skin.

Thickened night air filled her lungs and she ran.

Ran until the scratches began to scab over.

Ran until the breath in her lungs burned more than her past.

Ran until the salt from her sweat stung her eyes.

Ran until even her bones begged her to stop.

Ran until she felt nothing.

The only people she would pass at this hour were the farmers tending their crops, although they were too busy with their hands in the dirt to notice that their princess was winding through their fields alone. Only one, a younger man, would wave to her as she passed by. Katrin would give a curt nod and he would smile, she would smile. It was the only time she felt she didn't need to force the upward tilt to her lips, jealous of the young man who could tend to his olive groves in silence and get joy from such a simple life.

Escaped tendrils of hair whipped in Katrin's face, as she took in the faint blur of three ships sailing closer to the docks below. With the sun quickly rising, the markets would be opening, and she needed to sneak back through the hidden passageway of the castle before Kohl or Ember or her mother came looking for her. Because they would, if she was not where she was supposed to be; if the guards caught wind that she was sneaking out of her chambers each night.

Then she would likely be permanently locked in her chambers, for fear she might wander off the cliff or worse be taken once more. Except she would not let anyone take her, not again. Not when she now recognized what the foggy glow in her eyes meant that night five years ago. A cloudiness in her mind that drove her to a dreamless sleep before she awoke on those shores, the gritty edges of rocks and shells scraping her feet. Recognized the smell of the drug her captor used.

Katrin could still feel the phantom hold of the coarse rope digging into her wrists. Her fingers traced the scars that were left, the scars that matched the ones on her back, the ones in her mind. Everyone at court knew about the scars on her wrists. They were easy to explain. Slashes scattered across her shoulder blades, down the center of her back—those remained her burden to carry.

Even Kohl did not know all the details of her time aboard the nameless ship. Her Fated. Her savior. Her love. Once they were married, when they were truly intimate, she would need to tell him. Right now, he would not understand. None of them could.

Tiny stars began to form in Katrin's sight, her tongue circled her mouth, dry as the sand on the beaches below. A slight tremor ran down her skin when the dusty air of the stone passageway hit her nose. Cobwebs clung to her while she made her way back up to her chambers.

Approaching the end of the passage, a faint tapping reverberated off the damp stone walls. Her hand slid to her thigh, steady and soundless she unsheathed the bronze blade, peering through a crack in the worn out wooden door. Someone was sitting in a chair facing the opposite wall, their booted foot drumming against the floor. A large hand was almost hidden against the bronze of the chair's arm, save for the white knuckles that sent a pang straight to Katrin's gut. The other hand raked through brown, waved hair.

Silently pushing the door open, the princess slipped behind him. One hand slid down his muscled chest, the other dragged the tip of her dagger along his arm. "You realize I could have stabbed you," Katrin whispered, lips grazing his ear. Turning, the man met her gaze with eyes as black as the caves in the Triad.

"You could have tried." A feral grin crossed his lips before Kohl took in what she was wearing. "Please tell me you were not outside the castle. Before dawn. Alone." Calloused hands gripped her wrist as he spoke.

"Alright, I won't tell you that." Katrin resheathed her dagger and moved around to the other side of the chair as Kohl loosened his grip, brows knitting together.

"It's not safe for you to be out there, Aikaterine." His hands slipped around her waist, pulling her onto his lap. "Nexos—"

Willing her eyes not to roll, Katrin looped her arms around his neck. "Nexos will always be a threat."

Kohl was there, the one to lift her from the seas as she clung, barely lifeless, to a piece of driftwood. Saw her sunburnt skin and bruised bones and the look of defeat in her amber-flecked eyes as Katrin wept knowing she almost did not escape the clutches of that man—the ruler of Nexos.

Stroking Katrin's back as she lay her head in the crook of his neck, the prince shifted underneath her. "You know I'd never allow anything bad to happen to you again, Katrin, but you have to promise me you won't go out between dusk and dawn alone again. Wake me up if you need to, I'll go with you."

"It's not that I don't want you there, it's just—"

"That you're having nightmares again? The guards can hear them, the screams you try to muffle with your pillow. The walls may be made of stone, but the men are well-trained."

Deep ebony eyes met hers once more, fine lines protruding from them and between where his brows were still furrowed together. Shallow breaths escaped through his clenched jaw that looked as if it was carved by the gods themselves.

"I was going to tell you, Kohl. I just didn't know how. You have so many responsibilities already, with your father's arrival and managing the Morentian fleet from an isle away. I didn't want to add to that burden."

"How long has it been happening?" Kohl's tone was deep, with a chill about it Katrin rarely heard from the prince.

"Two months—"

"Two months? We are supposed to be partners, Katrin. You need to tell me when these things happen. Last time—last time you became barely a shell of yourself. I refuse to let that happen again." Heat spread across the bridge of her nose as his rough palm cupped her cheek. "I love you, Aikaterine, even after the gods take us." He pressed his lips to hers in the lightest of kisses.

"Even after the gods take us," she whispered.

Chapter Two

Katrin

Tingling still caressed her lips, her chest still fluttering, as Katrin headed to the bathing chamber. Kohl left to attend to some morning business—what exactly, she forgot to ask. Most likely something to do with his father's impending arrival.

Even after the gods take us.

She could not remember when they started saying it to each other, but every time they parted they ended with that line. Salty tears stung the rims of Katrin's eyes. The Grechi would come and turn his mortal body to ash and dirt, but their love would remain. For those who were Fated, a bond stretched past time itself, to a realm beyond. A tether that binds even in death.

Katrin bonded to Kohl from the day he pulled her out of the swirling dark seas, from the day he fulfilled the prophecy that was told at her birth.

A newborn royal was always given a prophecy, especially one born of the gods. An old seer from the isle of Delphine came to her blessing in the temple of Alenia, the namesake of their isle. The seer reached out their frail and leathery hand, stroking Katrin's forehead, leaving a thumbprint of black ash between her brows. They spoke, in a voice that was not from this earth, neither male nor female, both old and young, ever-knowing. Thin, wrinkled lips hardly moved as they whispered the words that would haunt the princess. Mark her until she came of age.

The first daughter descended from birth and death,
From sun and stars,
Will be taken by those who only seek to destroy.
The serpent lurking in the sands will claim the maiden as his own.
Only if the man from seas and shadows
Releases her from these shackles
Shall the gift of the Grechi remain.

Katrin dipped her toe into the large limestone bath in the center of the chamber. Steam rose from the surface of the water, but the burn never bothered her. Fire and heat crept into her skin, warming a piece of her that had long since turned to ice.

Soapy water cocooned Katrin as she submerged herself, lulling her into a piercing silence. Creating a reprieve from her thoughts. Comforting her as if being curled up in a blanket by a crackling fire.

Her head floated up out of the water and Katrin leaned against the side of the bath. It was so clear to her in those days after she was rescued from the seas. Kohl literally pulled her from the shadows of the raging waves. It was him, the one to save not only her, but the power the Grechi held so dear.

Bubbles flew into the air like little crystals as Katrin splashed the water in front of her, heaving a sigh. It was too much for someone approaching twenty-five. The power of the Grechi and the peace in the isles resting in her hands, all because some old crone said so. Yet she knew the prophecy to be true, if only from the way she warmed when Kohl would look at her, hold her, kiss her. It was utterly terrifying.

Rarely in their history was a mortal bonded to someone born of the gods. So rare it was only recorded once, kept in the books at the Library of Morentius. The details so ancient, one couldn't even make out the faded names. Almost as if it were a secret, a lie no one wanted shared.

Katrin pondered this for nearing five years. Kohl was born from mortals, no blessing or magic to be seen in the Athanas family.

Then there was her, born of the Goddess of Sun and Birth and the God of Death and the Illuminating Stars of Night.

Her immortality was daunting, but she could not dwell on that now. Not today. Today all she needed to worry about was her impending birthday and wedding. When she reached twenty-five, she would finally be able to access her magic, finally be able to assume her destiny and sit upon the throne of Alentus.

A faint glow began to radiate from Katrin's finger tips, the only glimmer of her powers she showed for now. She turned over her palm, the pads of her fingertips shriveled like the fruits in the Triad Mountains after too much sun. Lost in her thoughts and the warmth of the bath water, time passed quickly and she did not realize she was no longer alone.

A soft chuckle floated through the air, and Katrin whirled around under the water line, splashing half of it onto the sea glass tiling the floors. "Ember!" she gasped.

"You know, you really should lock your door more, given everything," Ember's lilting voice drifted over the steaming room.

Katrin rolled her eyes as she shifted her body farther under the water, hiding her tattered back and shame of the past from her sister. "The guards really shouldn't let you in here without alerting me first."

She looked up at her younger sister—the spitting image of their mother—and a twinge of jealousy settled in her gut. Ember was always the more classically beautiful of the two. Hair a sparkling straw, eyes a deep golden so captivating she convinced most men her age into thinking they were in love with her.

"The guards are supposed to let *me* in anywhere I wish." Ember's hand gripped her hip, dressed in a golden gown that matched her eyes, the most stunning turquoise silken sash tied around her waist. Her foot bearing a golden leather laced-up sandal continued to tap, as she stared down at her sister.

"May I help you, then?" Katrin drawled out, finally stepping out of the bath and wrapping herself in a plush robe. Again she avoided showing her back, even to her sister. Another person she trusted, but did not—could not—trust with everything. That was a secret and a burden she alone would carry, the embarrassment too much to share.

"Mother would like to know why you weren't at breakfast this morning."

"Well mother can learn that it is none of her business." Technically very, very untrue. Kora had a right to know everything.

Ember's lips pursed shut, her golden eyes flaring with a curious flicker. "Katrin, the King of Morentius is arriving today and there is much to do. Mother just wants to make sure everything is prepared for him and his family."

Katrin wandered over to the limestone vanity and began brushing out her tangled waves. "The queen and Farah are not arriving with him. Kohl has told me they will stay behind until the wedding." Her words were too sharp as they trailed from her tongue. She closed her eyes for a second, calming the voices inside her head that told her to refuse their pity and sympathy.

Light footsteps padded behind Katrin and Ember placed a delicate palm on her shoulder. It took everything for Katrin to not recoil from the touch, one that was so close to her unexplainable markings. "It happened again, didn't it?" Ember's sweet voice was a low whisper.

All Katrin could do was nod, she did not want to dwell in that abyss of emotions any longer. She barely crawled out of it mere moments before. Only just washed the stench of shame and regret from her skin.

"I'm sorry. I shouldn't have snapped at you. I just don't understand. Why now? Why after all this time?"

"I don't know, Ember, maybe the Fates are trying to tell me something." Katrin's voice was distant, barely traveling from her lips. "I finally told him."

She turned around to face her sister. Ember was as feisty as they come, but the most loyal and caring person Katrin knew. Even if she could barely wield a sword or do much other than dance at balls and hold court. She was the first person Katrin sought after the nightmares returned, this secret at least she needed to share.

Katrin always envied her sister for more than just her beauty. Maybe it was the fact that she never needed to worry about ruling the isle that made her so carefree, or maybe it was the way her power slowly grew inside her. A gift that one day allows her to heal, to bloom. Katrin's power was only death and destruction.

"Well, I'm glad Kohl knows. It is one less secret I have to keep and he can help you, Katrin."

"I know," she whispered, putting down the sapphire comb, its handle engraved with a beautiful yet fearsome winged creature of the sea, old characters from long ago carved below the image of the crashing waves: *Αστεράκι μου.* "That's half of why I didn't tell him. We are to be married. This time should be filled with joy and blessings and laughter. Let alone the stress he already has over his father's arrival. I knew telling him would plague him with my own fears—and I just couldn't do that."

"Of course you could!" Ember took a step back. "Kohl would do anything for you. If you don't know that then you are a gods-damned fool."

Katrin's eyes widened, not at the verbal lashing her sister was giving her, but because she knew that Ember was right. She hated when her sister was right.

"I know," Katrin repeated, even quieter this time. "Just let mother know I'm sorry I missed breakfast and that I'll be down shortly, please."

Her sister nodded, turning on her heels with a whip of the golden gown fluttering behind her.

Two more months, Katrin thought. *Two more months and I will be married. Two more months and I will have my powers. Two more months and I will be queen.*

Shifting her way over to the large wardrobe, Katrin selected her finest silk gown dyed red and orange, the official colors of Morentius. A sign of respect toward her future father-in-law.

Katrin held it up and looked in the mirror, smoothing out the wrinkles. Hideous, absolutely hideous. It did not matter how beautifully the gown was made, these colors always washed out her olive skin, accentuated the copper highlight in her hair in the worst possible way.

Still, she shimmied on the gown, lifting it up to sheath her small dagger to her thigh. Again stopped, clenching her fists and willing away the faint glow radiating off them. Once composed Katrin stepped toward the doors, toward her future, toward becoming queen.

Chapter Three

Kohl

Wind howled like the wolves that sometimes prowled the mountains, the sun still in the eastern part of the sky, as Kohl paced up and down the docks of Alentus.

His father's ship was nearing closer and closer on the horizon, its red and orange banners on full display. A golden viper sparkled in the center of the mainsail, a piece of Votios, the southern continent, where his people came from centuries before. The Morentian guards still laced their swords with the lethal venom of the creatures.

Two smaller ships sailed alongside his father's, no doubt carrying some of his feared guard. They were known to be as vicious on the seas as they were in the sandy deserts, their black armor instilled a shuddering fear in all who beheld them, Kohl included.

Kohl clenched his jaw and released, gnawing at the inside of his cheek, trying to still the thoughts racing about his mind. There must be a reason why Katrin's dreams were happening again. It was too much of a coincidence that it was approaching five years since the night she was taken.

He remembered it with such clarity it sometimes didn't seem real. Perhaps it was simply a wicked dream to torture them both.

The skies were enraged every day from the time Katrin was taken. For that month, the waves grew as tall as Kohl, the winds never ceasing, but still he sailed day in and day out. He would go from isle to isle, searching every tavern and brothel and market, waiting to hear whispers of the missing princess. Week after week, there were none.

It was on the fifth day of the fourth week that he received word from his father to return home. The king's spies had heard nothing of where Katrin may have been taken. After all that time, they said, she was probably dead.

Kohl balked at the idea. There was no gods-damned way he was giving up until he had Katrin back. He pictured the princess' warm smile and quick wit. Her sparkling brown eyes and enchanting voice. The way they would race across the sandy shores of Alentus as children. There could not be a world where Kohl did not see her running toward him on the beaches again.

He let out a quiet chuckle at the memory of hurling the correspondence across the bar he was brooding in, knocking over his bitter ale he came to tolerate. Defying his father was not something Kohl did often—or ever—except that fateful day.

Kohl had left two gold coins on the counter and began to retreat back to his ship when he heard muffled chatter at one of the poker tables. A pirate from the eastern parts of the Mykandrian Sea was seen recently setting up delivery of precious cargo to the king, the voices hushed even more. He did not need to hear anymore, he knew which king it was, King Nikolaos of Nexos.

It made so much sense to him then, and Kohl kicked himself for not realizing it sooner. Nexos had been stirring with rebellion for decades. If they were just in Lesathos, then Kohl could catch up to them on the seas. *The Hydra* was faster than any ship in the isles.

For days he searched the surrounding waters until he finally found not the pirate's vessel, but Katrin, clinging lifelessly to a piece of driftwood.

When he pulled her out of the water her skin was scorched, peeling and crusted in salt. Her lips were so cracked she could barely stutter out a word except to joke that he could never have made it that long on the seas alone.

At least the spark wasn't taken from her. Kohl almost vomited at the sight of her frail body, skin hardly wrapping over bones, her eyes void of any color or sparkle he came to love when they were children. That day he vowed to destroy the King of Nexos.

Kohl was never able to act on that vow. His father stopped him. Why—he never deigned to ask. Where his father was concerned, his word was law. Not only for the people of Morentius, but his children as well. It wasn't that the king did not love Kohl, or his younger sister Farah, but in Votios affection was weakness. King Athanas did not tolerate weakness. Only control. Only power. And as Kohl was frequently reminded, but never truly believed, only peace.

Worn and weathered sides of the now docked ship took nothing away from the terror of the weaponry stacked along the rails. Soldiers lined both port and starboard with crossbows loaded with bronze darts. Toward the stern of the ship stood two catapults, ready to send oily, flaming targets toward others in battle.

The Hydra was the leading ship of the largest fleet in the Mykandrian Sea, captained by none other than the King of Morentius himself. The Viper of Votios. The terrifying, but just man.

"One day this will all be yours, my boy," the king rasped out, startling Kohl with his slick voice.

Kohl cracked his neck and took in a deep breath as his father slithered down the plank from the stern of the ship to the dock. Everyone told Kohl he was a spitting image of his father, but he could not see it. Khalid's eyes and jaw were hardened and direct, where Kohl liked to think his own eyes appear lighter, kinder. But the color was there, the same deep ebony, the same dark curly hair, now turned a peppery gray on his father, wind-blown from his time at sea.

"Hello, Father. What a pleasant surprise. You were not expected until the evening." He wrung his hands together, trying not to pick at the callouses on his palms.

Kohl needed the extra time to prepare Katrin. To ease her into his father's peculiar ways. His brute force and blunt speech. She'd met the king before, but not in recent years. Not since his demeanor declined even more after the whispers of uprising.

"The winds blessed us, my boy. It is not every day your only son celebrates his betrothal. Not every day an Acknowledgement occurs." King Athanas smiled, the corner of his lip raising up to show off his shaven teeth. Warriors in Votios all bore this distinguishing feature, reminiscent of the fangs of a viper. It was said to have originated from ancient times where the soldiers would rip out the throats of those they defeated in battle. An outdated tradition Kohl was rather glad his father never asked him to keep, although he was sure the king thought less of him for it.

He searched his father's face with curiosity, looking to see if anything showed the real reason he arrived with the rising sun. Usually the Morentian fleet only sailed under the stars for battle. Never for pleasure. Never for another isle. Especially never for Kohl. King Athanas turned from his son and pointed at one of the guards, signaling them to bring down his trunk. "And where is that bride of yours? Aikaterine did not feel like greeting me here as well?"

Kohl rolled his eyes, the first dig of many toward his princess. The king never particularly liked her for anything but her claim to the throne of Alentus. Kohl hoped that if the two of them spent more time together he would come to like her. Or like her as much as the king liked anyone.

"She was meeting with her mother since she missed breakfast." Kohl winced as soon as the words left his mouth. In the Athanas household, they were always required to attend meals.

"And why did she miss breakfast on such an important day? Does she not take my arrival seriously? The requests of her mother seriously?"

Kohl sucked in a breath and tried his hardest not to roll his eyes a second time since his father's arrival. The king was in a foul mood despite making great time on the seas. "It's not that, Father. She needed time to pull herself together. She started having nightmares again." The look in the king's eyes made Kohl instantly regret mentioning this. His look of discontent at the fact that there may be something wrong with an heir apparent. That a royal plagued by terrors at night would not be fit to lead in such contentious times.

Kohl could not believe Katrin kept this from him for two months. *Two months.* The anger started to boil again in his chest. So much so, that he almost missed the twitch in his father's eye when he spoke.

"Nightmares. That is unfortunate. Very unfortunate indeed." The king's eyes narrowed. "Has she shared details with you? Does she remember anything new about that time?" Kohl knew his father was pretending to seem interested, his gaze shifting toward the shoreline. He tucked that away for another time. He didn't want to argue with Khalid today. Not this early in the day at least.

"I don't think so. Well, she hasn't said anything to me at least. I just found out about them this morning. Why do you ask?" Kohl tried to study his father again, but the king's face stared back firm and cold.

"Just curious. We never caught the ship or the man who took her. I know I didn't let you retaliate against Nexos, but that does not mean I don't want to see those people burn as well."

The sincerity surprised Kohl, but he did not care at this point. He'd long since given up seeking the approval of his father, rather he just tried to not be an utter disappointment.

Kohl fought back rebellions in the northern continent of Voreia, learned the languages of his father's homeland, read all the books on seafaring and warfare and ruling in the Morentian Library. It would never be enough. Not until King Athanas brought peace to the entire Mykandrian isles, to the entire world of Odessia at that.

They trekked along the sands of the coast, up the rocky path to the castle set on the cliffs. His father was hushed and pondering the rest of the hike, always glancing back out at sea. Kohl watched him, trying to catch some glimmer of emotion. Trying also to not think of his tortured bride, speaking somewhere in the castle with her overbearing mother.

Continuing up and up the curved path overlooking the harbor, Kohl thought about how he now considered this isle, this castle his own. It would be one day soon. There was no chance Katrin would give up her title in Alentus to someday be a Morentian queen.

No, he would rule beside her as consort to the throne. He would be her second. Give up title and power and promise for his people, but that never bothered him. All he cared about was her. All he fought for was her. Her safety, her love, her home. To see that smile that once had been stripped from her face, the smile that he brought back to her those years ago. For that brilliant smile he would go to war. Kohl just hoped war was not the reason his father arrived early.

He had heard the whispers in the breeze, that the King of Nexos was on a warpath. But not just that, the Prince of Nexos was slated to assume the throne with no Acknowledgement. His jaw clenched at the thought. The thorn in his side since they were children. The man that threatened his kingdom, Katrin's kingdom. Nikolaos Kirassos the Second, that snide and cocky eldest son. He had not been outside of Nexos in years, hidden away until the older Nikolaos deemed him fit to rule.

"So are you going to tell me why you are really here, Father, or do you expect to keep me in the dark the whole time?"

King Athanas looked back at his son, his ebony eyes wide, and smiled.

CHAPTER FOUR

KATRIN

Dread ran through Katrin's whole body as she stood outside her mother's bedchamber. It was not that she didn't want to see Kora, but more so that she didn't want to be lectured by a very opinionated woman. She had a right to be opinionated, after all she was the queen. Not only Queen of Alentus, but Queen of the Grechi. Ruler of the gods. Katrin was raised, rather groomed, to walk in her mother's footsteps. To eat, sleep, drink, breathe royalty and grace.

Katrin never wanted it. Never wanted to be the heir to that sort of throne. Knowing that once she turned twenty-five and married Kohl she would not see her mother again, until her own first born became that same sacred age. The power that came with her line could only run in one god at a time, and when her powers fully blossomed, her mother would need to sail to Cyther, the isles of the Grechi. Spend the rest of eternity in the lush green meadows, crystal mountain tops, and shimmering seas. Relinquish her power back to the land, a price that must be paid for her years living on this earth. It was not fair that only Kora and her line suffered this fate.

Her duty, her honor, her life's mission, Kora would always tell her in the most excessive of ways. But a small part of Katrin wondered if her mother was only that way to hide her fears. Fear that she would no longer be there to protect her daughters, fear that she may simply be forgotten.

That was why her upcoming birthday was so important. At twenty-five, her powers could be accessed, but only once she bonded to her Fated would she be able to wield them fully. It was said that the two powers of each Fated would wield together, forming two halves of the same coin. Like her mother and father. Sun and Darkness. Life and Death.

Yet Kohl did not have any power. She wondered if the Fates saw something else brewing for him. If something lay beneath, in his bones, forgotten.

Katrin would need those full powers if she was to lead Alentus and Morentius in battle against Nexos. If she was going to look into King Nikolaos' eyes as she slit the throat of the man who captured her—the power of the seas be damned.

Bronze chilled her palm as Katrin traced the carving on the door of the stars and sun and lightning, her parents' symbols—her symbols—and knocked.

Peering in through the door, Katrin caught the woosh of papers being scattered across her mother's desk. If she didn't know any better, she could have said Ember snuck in and was the one sitting in front of her now, rustling about through political correspondence. But her mother's hair was now cut much shorter, the strands the color of a sparking bolt of lightning brushing just over her shoulders. Her eyes, although the same piercing gold as her sister, were surrounded by fine lines and worry.

"I thought you would stand outside that door all day," Kora's voice held in the air, smooth and sweet as honey.

"I'm sorry I wasn't at breakfast this morning, Mother."

Kora looked up at Katrin and nodded, pointing at the chaise across from her. Katrin sat down, leaning against the side of the turquoise velvet seat, knocking her arm up and resting her chin on her palm. Letting out a thin sigh, she forced a smile on her face. Kora always meant well, but Katrin knew she was about to get a verbal lashing reminding her of duties and obligations.

"Did you know, Katrin, that the King of Morentius was arriving today?"

"Did I know that Kohl's father was expected today? No, of course not," she drawled, her face going emotionless. "I just enjoy wearing these hideous colors for the thrill."

Kora glanced up from the papers through narrowed eyes.

"Sorry, Mother," Katrin huffed.

"Well then, did you also know that Kohl is currently with his father? Our scouts spotted his ships nearing the cove around dawn."

"Dawn?" Katrin croaked out.

The three ships in the distance. Not fishermen, but part of the Morentian fleet. Katrin's lungs shrunk. King Athanas was only known to sail at night if death was upon them. But they were not in the midst of war. At least not yet. Unless that was why her mother needed her so desperately this morning.

"Yes. Dawn. Which is why I requested you at breakfast, there is much to discuss before he arrives at the castle."

Kora shuffled the paper's together, signing the one that landed on top and shoved the pile into her top desk drawer. The desk was a wedding gift from Katrin's father, Aidoneus, carved by the nymphs that lived in the Triad Mountains. Its sides were adorned with gold stars, the moon, endless rivers flowing toward Aidesian, the final resting place of all living beings. Her father's kingdom.

Katrin rarely saw her father, since he was usually in the underworld tending to the lost souls of the isles. She was never allowed to accompany her father, for fear of getting entangled with one of Aidoneus' many creatures of the night. Beings that would make even the strongest of soldiers cower.

Aidoneus alone would insight a spark of fear in all, the crooked grin he flashes, the lifeless look in his dark brown eyes. Katrin wondered if someday she would look like that too. If the darkness would enthrall her. If only those closest would see the light.

"I am guessing you wished to talk about the wedding?" Katrin bit her lip, a light twitch humming in her eye.

Kora walked over to the chaise and sat next to her, clasping her hands on top of Katrin's. "Not exactly..." her words escaped in barely more than a whisper. "I know I am sometimes hard on you, it's just—it's just that I won't always be around. That time is coming closer and closer with the passing days and I just wanted to make sure you had everything—knew everything—you needed before I was gone.

"The day of the Acknowledgement, I will be summoned and I will need to leave immediately. I will have to surrender the majority of my power to the earth so they can be reborn in you and trust me, my darling Aikaterine, you will need those powers when you rule. My only wish is that I know you are happy when I leave. That you will be safe, and taken care of—not that you can't do that on your own." Kora's lips pursed into a thin line, her golden eyes glazed over with a watery film.

"Most of all, I need you to watch over Ember. I know you are barely older than her, but I now realize I coddled her far too much. I can't bear the thought of her losing me and then being thrust into war. You have to promise me, when the time comes for battle you will not let her go, that you will keep her here with you. I don't care if she leads the Spartanis, she is too young, too fragile to be put in the middle of the wreckage."

Katrin squeezed her mother's hand a little tighter. "I promise. Nothing will happen to her."

"Nothing will happen to who?" barked a voice from the doorway.

Ember's lithe frame and glowing features stood leaning against the doorway. Despite all of her sister's sass and gusto, she was only twenty-three and far too unprepared for battle. Too pretty for anyone to take her seriously as the Prytan of the Spartanis, and too stubborn to admit it.

"Must I repeat myself?" Ember drawled as she wandered over to their mother's desk, plodding herself down and kicking her feet up on top of a map still sprawled on the desk.

"You know, it is not polite to interrupt a private conversation between the queen and one of her subjects."

"It is not, but when said subject is your other daughter, I find it impossible not to." Ember flashed a grin, much like that of their father. Deadly. The one trait she inherited from him.

"I knew your father's sarcasm would appear in you both someday, I just hoped I'd be long gone before it happened," the queen laughed, and it was the first time in a while Katrin heard her mother genuinely happy. If only for a brief moment. "Katrin, remember what we discussed."

Kora slipped out of the room, leaving Katrin to handle hiding what her mother asked of her.

CHAPTER FIVE

EMBER

Wood creaked under Ember with each rock of the worn desk chair she sat in. Katrin and her mother were talking about her yet again. Talking about how she was not ready to become the Prytan of the Spartanis. Not that her avoidance of morning training, or obsession with dresses and hair styles over armor and swords told a different story.

She attended the best balls, flirted with all the men, focused on her history lessons and reading rather than dirtying herself practicing archery or swordsmanship. Then Katrin started training with Kohl, and Ember thought her sister might just take both positions. Queen and Prytan.

But that wasn't how it worked.

The Spartanis was an ancient group of soldiers tasked with preserving peace and stability not only in Alentus, but the entirety of the Mykandrian Isles. They were fierce and damning in a way even the lethal soldiers of Morentius could not be. There was only one rule. When a new generation took the throne, the second born would take their place as Prytan. The leader. An old rule, an outdated one at that, yet tradition was the backbone in Mykandria, especially in Alentus. *Without tradition*, their mother always said, *culture crumbles.*

"So...Mother is really anxious about Kohl's father arriving early. I guess I can't blame her, he gives me the creeps." A shudder released down Ember's back.

"He is not creepy, Ember. King Athanas is an honorable man." Her sister grimaced at the words she spoke.

Katrin always told her she enjoyed the company of her future father-in-law. That the violence in his eyes even when speaking to his family was traumatic, but he would protect those he loved at all costs. Protect his people. The only good thing Kohl got from him.

"Honorable or not, one slice from the Viper of Votios' sword and you're done for. Not to mention if he uses those teeth." It felt like spiders crawling all over her skin, the thought that she may need to face soldiers like the ones who made up King Athanas's army.

She heard the rumors. Teeth sharpened like knives, blades laced with venom—something few possessed the power to heal. If they all went to war in the isles, these were the kinds of monsters Ember would have to defend her people against. She could barely handle the weight of a sword, no one would want her for protection.

"You know very well that no soldier in Morentius actually uses their teeth. It is purely an homage to their people." Katrin narrowed her eyes at Ember, she never took well to insults about Kohl or his family. "Have you heard any more about the army being raised in Nexos?" Katrin questioned, knowing fully well she would not have the answers.

Ember avoided going to the barracks at all costs. Not only because of the filthy smell of sweat and what literally could be horse shit, but because of Ajax and his pompous, self-righteous, narcissistic ass. The commander was handsome, anyone could see that, but she would not be caught dead acting like the mindless idiots he kept around him. Fawning over every push-up and strike of the sword, the way sweat trickled down his shirtless body.

"Ahem," Katrin cleared her throat, lifting an eyebrow. Ember's throat bobbed. Gods, she needed to stop thinking about him and this was *not* helping. "I need you to go down to the barracks and speak with Commander Ajax. It is imperative that I have all the information our spies have gathered before any of the Acknowledgement events occur."

Sinking farther into the chair, Ember scowled. "I am not going down there to inquire. If the Spartanis knew any information they would deliver it to me directly." Technically that was untrue, she wouldn't receive direct reports until after she became Prytan. Ember should not even be told anything right now, but they seemed to give her tidbits of information as a courtesy to who she would one day be. Who she had to be.

"You *are* going down there and you will act pleasant." Katrin's voice heighted and cut like their mother's, a true queen in training. "If you want them to see you as someone in power, you have to earn their trust, and that means spending time in their world."

"But what if I don't want to be in their world?"

Katrin shook her head, shoulders drooping. "We are far past being able to decide where we want to be, sister. We both must face our fate and I will need you beside me, someone I can trust wholeheartedly."

"You can trust Kohl, and the commander is much more suited to the position of Prytan than I will ever be." Everyone knew she would fail, it was a wonder the senators hadn't pushed to rid Alentus of this outdated tradition.

"They are not blood, Ember. Kohl is too easily persuaded by love and the commander may be well-trained, but so could you if you tried. I have seen you in your history lessons—you act as though all you care for is the newest fabric for a dress, but Iason has somehow snuck in learning well beyond your years. My sister, you can do so much more than you give yourself credit for. So go, speak with Ajax, consider my words. Prove everyone that looks at you as the weaker sister wrong." Katrin stood to leave, gripping Ember's hand tightly. "And, Ember, you are right. I may need them, need the Spartanis, the senators even to help me be a successful queen, but I need *you* more."

As her sister walked through the door, Ember could not help but wonder if Katrin was right? What if she could do so much more?

Mud coated the hem of Ember's gown as she stalked through the barracks toward the commander's wing. Apparently, today was not the day to wear such a flowing fabric. An even worse day to wear her new leather slippers that were now soaked through. They cost her ten gold coins at the market, ten gold coins now worth as much as the manure that coated them.

Dark and decrepit, that was how Ember would describe the barracks—the dim lit halls and the people that frequented them. The soldiers were often gone from their normal lives for months, years even, as they trained here, foregoing their partners by law for lovers of all kinds. Courtesans usually flitted about from room to room dressed in sheer gauze, showing off all manners of *parts*. Men, women, it didn't matter who resided here. It was a permanent brothel, although the king and queen would never admit it.

Ember stepped toward the door of the commander's quarters when a tall, raven-haired girl slipped out, still giggling as she finished sliding on her diaphanous dress. Despicable. There was no point to wearing the dress when it left so little to the imagination.

Straightening her posture, Ember strutted into the room. Eyes narrow. Lips thinned. Jaw hardened.

"The lady of the hour," the commander drawled, cocking a brow at Ember. "I just finished up, but if you give me five...ten minutes I should be ready for another round."

Insufferable. He was utterly insufferable.

Ajax sat in an old reading chair by the fire, his feet kicked up on a stool, white shirt still unbuttoned, leather trousers still unlaced. Ember could not help but trail her eyes from his cropped dirty blonde hair down his lightly tanned skin, roaming over his muscular abs right down to where the tan began to disappear.

Ajax's warm brown eyes flickered with delight. "Like what you see, Drakos?" His grin widened, flashing his perfectly straight teeth in a devilish smile.

"Don't flatter yourself. You are the furthest thing from my type, Demos," Ember lied straight through her teeth, even as she felt a strange need deep in her core. Even as a light blush stretched across the bridge of her nose. "I am here on official business for the crown."

"For your sister, you mean? You know I can't share that sort of information with you yet."

Ember looked straight into those chocolatey eyes trying to discern whether what he knew was really for privileged ears, or if he was just being a gods-damned pain. She couldn't share the real reason she needed to know. That Katrin was reliving her terror of five years ago all over again. That if she did not find out for certain when Nexos would attack, she herself would go crazy. Ember envied her sister in many ways, but how she continuously fought to forget the trauma she endured was not one of them.

"Please, Commander, do not make me beg more than that." Biting down on her lips, Ember shifted her eyes down toward her feet, scraping her nails over her palms.

"As much as that would amuse me to see, I truly don't have any more information I can tell you. Our spies haven't heard more than the rumors you hear swirling about the markets. There will be an attack, it is just a matter of when."

A swift knock came at the door, before another member of the Spartanis entered.

"Commander, Princess, pardon the interruption." The soldier glanced back and forth between Ember and Ajax, at the way he so deliberately sat, clothes half on and her standing there, skin flushed and a bit sweaty from the summer heat.

Her eyes widened when she saw the mistaken look he gave them. Mortification set in as a smirk rose along Ajax's lips.

"King Athanas has arrived at the castle. I thought you would like to know."

Ajax nodded at the man and began to rise from his chair. The top of his trousers drooped a little lower down his hips before he laced them up, and gods if Ember was staring. "Do you want me to escort you back to the castle, Ember? I will be going anyway to speak with the king."

Ember shook her head and turned away without a word. She could not be near him a second longer. Not with his messy hair and raspy voice. This feeling, it was the real reason she never ventured down to the barracks, never started her training. Ajax haunted her mind. An ever present reminder of what she could never have.

Chapter Six

Kohl

Lavish orange silks and red velvet covered the guest wing where King Athanas would be staying. Kohl accompanied his father to the room, now filled with plush floor pillows for smoking and woven baskets overflowing with fruits and nuts from the king's southern lands. The servants switched out the familiar luxuries, foregoing the delicate turquoise and gold of the Drakos court.

Five years earlier, Kohl stepped into these chambers for the first time and took in their simplicity and beauty that was rarely seen in the over-done castle on Morentius. The rulers of Alentus preferred ethereal white gauzy curtains, small furnishings made of olive branches or driftwood, glass polished by the Mykandrian Sea decorating the windows. That quiet elegance was stripped away as he now roamed about the room. Now Kohl only saw reminders of a home he long since returned to. One he did not even want to see in the years since coming to this isle.

A few Morentian soldiers dropped luggage trunks off to the side of the bedchamber before his father ordered them back to the ship. King Athanas never kept a guard outside his suite. None were necessary. No one would threaten the Viper and live to tell the tale.

His father drew his curved black sword and laid it on the desk. Carvings surrounded the hilt and blade depicting an ancient battle, one that was filled with sorcery and bloodshed. One that leveled kingdoms and sunk cities. The world of the Olympi. The world his father's people fought for and failed to protect.

Goosebumps peppered Kohl's flesh despite the warm summer breeze coming through the windows as he thought of the Olympi, whose names were forbidden to be spoken. How they tortured mortals and kept them as slaves. How they raped and pillaged not only Votios in the south, but the isles here as well. How when the lands rallied together to overflow the olde gods, they sent out a burst of power, splitting the continents thereby sending entire isles to the depths of the sea, before disappearing for good.

The opposing side of the blade showed events in the wake of the Peloponnian War. It was thought that the new gods—the Grechi—were born within the caves of the Triad Mountains on Alentus, blessed by the *Mother*, Alenia, herself. Aidoneus, Kora, Nikolaos, Giselle, gods who dwelled in the northern lands of Voreia, and lesser gods who lived along the coasts of Cyther. They crawled out from the depths of the caves, each radiating with power from the Olympi. The different elemental and celestial powers were not as strong as the Olympi once were, but dangerous nonetheless. No other power beyond theirs seemed to exist anymore. The ashes and magic of the once great sorcerers of Votios vanishing into the desert never to be seen again.

Kohl remembered being a boy, grazing through the books in the Library of Morentius, reading stories of famed war heroes. How they stood in the face of sure death sacrificing themselves to protect the weak. He knew then and there that he wanted to be a soldier, a commander, a leader, fighting back in the deserts or on the high seas.

There was never a time he wanted to settle down, not until he became involved with Katrin. Now he would be consort, tasked to lead by her side, while others forged into battle. A disgrace by his father's standards, if the alliance with Alentus did not mean so much for peace.

King Athanas draped himself over one of the plush pillows, inhaling a substance from Anatole, the eastern lands. Olerae swirled around in a delicately decorated glass bottle, smoke trickled out and into his father's lungs before it was released back through his nose and mouth in a black cloud. His father was instantly relaxed, a rare sight for the king, but Kohl rarely saw his father anymore. King Athanas tipped the bottle toward Kohl, but he refused. Kohl would need his mind clear if he was to deal with the king all day. At least until he figured out what his father wanted.

"So...my...boy," King Athanas coughed out, "do you have anything to report other than your betrothed having her nightmares." Kohl rolled his eyes, hoping his father did not catch him through the black smoke. He knew that tone of voice, that quiet disdain hidden under layers and layers of court politics.

"I have not, and neither has Commander Ajax." The commander was named after one of those very war heroes Kohl used to aspire to be, although he hardly thought the man lived up to the name. *The eagle*. Ajax was skilled, Kohl would not deny that, but he was fickle with his emotions and indulged in the niceties of flesh too often. "We have spies out searching for more information on Nexos, but anytime we get close, get a lead, it disappears. Some have even found remains of people they were tracking, imprints of their bodies against the ground in a black dust." His blood boiled even thinking about that place, that kingdom, that wretched man who sat upon its throne.

"Normally, I wouldn't trust a word that comes out of the commander's mouth," the king's eyes narrowed, his tone too pointed and vicious for this conversation, "but my spies have told me the same." His father folded his hands in his lap. "King Nikolaos has a way with such dark forces even when he is locked away in that decaying castle of his. He can suffocate anyone with the shadows—and will—whether they hide information or not. A mad man made from the decline of his kingdom."

Kohl looked at his father as his face went taut, as if he was remembering something significant from the past. Not Katrin being kidnapped. No, this look was personal.

"You did not know, my boy, what they called him before the treaty? *The Bringer of Shadows*, able to manipulate the very air around you, strip the life right from your lungs before you cease to exist at all. That dark magic was forbidden among my people, the sorcerers, but a god? There were no restrictions on what they might do. The foulest man I ever laid eyes on." King Athanas spit on the ground. "May he one day rot in the dungeons of Aidesian. A spitting image of the monsters Aidoneus keeps down there."

Kohl clenched his fists, like father, like son. Nik was just as wretched as the older male. "He shouldn't be able to get away with that just because he is a god. Is that not why the people fought against the Olympi?"

"Don't be so naive, my boy. The gods, new or olde, care only for their own kind. They will destroy everything in their path to power." King Athanas inhaled the olerae once more.

"Not Katrin," Kohl's stomach turned, pinching the bridge of his nose attempting to curb the headache that formed. "She would not wish harm on anyone."

He knew it, deep in his bones. She would only use her power to protect those around her, not destroy them.

"Maybe so." The King's eyes darkened as his eyelids drooped behind the smoky haze of the drug. "Maybe she will not be a threat at all."

Kohl pondered the words his father spoke as he descended the stairs to meet Katrin in the great hall. *Maybe she will not be a threat at all*. He'd said it with such sureness. With a hint of malice. This was the worst possible time for her to greet Khalid—when there was such disdain swirling about in his father's head. It was Kohl's own fault for mentioning the nightmares to him in the first place. A breach of trust, something Katrin hadn't even wanted to confide in him as to not cause worry. Now all there seemed to be was worry. What would he tell her? Nothing. He would tell her nothing and hope that his father kept that knowledge to himself.

Approaching the wrought iron doors that led to the hall, a flash of orange and red silk caught his eye. Gods, the dress was heinous. What poor member of court was forced into—

"Kohl, there you are!" a familiar voice called. It was not a member of court at all, but his bride, somehow persuaded into wearing the colors of his people. At least his father would find that appealing, especially with the low-cut bodice and tight laces along her stomach. It gave the appearance of curves she did not have, ones that were a sign of rank and beauty in Morentius. A preference Kohl did not share with his father. He thought Katrin looked like the ideal woman, especially now that her collar and cheekbones were cut sharp against her tan skin. It made her appear older, more regal than she became in the years after her kidnapping.

"You look captivating, my darling Aikaterine." Kohl looped his hand around her waist, pulling Katrin in for a brief kiss. When he retreated from her lips, a scowl covered her delicate face.

"You know I can tell when you're lying, Kohl. The dress is atrocious, but it seems I already insulted your father by not being present at the docks. Hopefully this aids in his forgiveness of the unintended slight," she replied, hands shaking by her sides. That was not a good sign—her tremors only appeared when her anxiety was at its worst. Another thing his father would take note of.

"Yes, well—he is a very particular man as you know. He made excellent time on the seas and the servants brought him that drug he likes so much, but can rarely get from Anatole with the blockade, so he should be in a better mood than usual." Yet another lie. "Let's go in. I'm sure he is already waiting. Better we not keep him waiting any longer."

Turquoise banners with the Alentian crest were now dispersed with the orange banner of Morentius, the red viper down the center. The two colors overpowered the delicate white stone walls and marble flooring, looking out of place in such a bright and airy castle. Displays of food littered a long table in front of the dais. Unsurprisingly, Khalid was already seated, popping grapes into his mouth and sipping on a golden chalice. A small dribble of burgundy wine dripped from the corner of his mouth before his tongue shot out and wiped it away.

Katrin stepped forward, curtseying toward the king. "Your Highness, a pleasure to have you at court. I apologize for missing your arrival this morning, if I had known you were expected so early I would have been at the docks with Kohl."

Not raising his eyes to meet Katrin's, Kohl's father grumbled, "Yes, it was quite disappointing that you did not accompany my son, though he informed me of your recent ailment himself."

Narrowing her eyes, Katrin took a seat across from Khalid, keeping her trembling hands out of sight. "My ailment? I'm not sure I know what you mean."

Gods-dammit. First mistake—telling his father about the nightmares. Second mistake—not telling Katrin he knew. Her eyes were wide in disbelief, though that and the stiff kick to his shin under the table were the only signs Katrin was affected by his words. The throbbing started, though it was not in his leg, but behind his temples. Another headache to add to his many problems of the day.

Pupils widening, his father looked up to stare at Katrin. "Your nightmares, of course. Kohl says they have started once more. I have a tonic I can give you. It is rather unbecoming of a future ruler to have such debilitating tribulations, especially as a woman." He reached across the table, grabbing the pitcher of wine from in front of Kohl.

White flecks sparked in Katrin's eyes, a faint glow coming from beneath the table where her hands were fisted. "It is not a debilitating tribulation, rather just an inconvenience that does not impact my judgment as the heir to Alentus, nor my mental state as a woman."

Khalid smiled, though Kohl knew it to be disingenuous. His father did not take kindly to being told off. "You may think that, Princess, but ruling an isle takes a kind of mental clarity you do not appear to possess at the moment. I'm sure you agree, Kohl?"

Why did his father need to bring him into this? The throbbing in his head worsened, he almost couldn't think straight. "Katrin understands there will be certain duties she will rely on me for, but she is extremely capable of leading on her own." Gods, maybe he would need that tonic his father mentioned, the pain only increased with every word that was spoken.

Picking a piece of food from his shaven teeth, his father glared at him. "I guess we will see."

"Yes, we shall," Katrin sneered back.

Usually he did not indulge in spirits this early in the day, but with the continued back and forth between Katrin and his father, Kohl began to pour his favorite amber liquor and drink.

Sweat glistened on his darkened skin from the summer's unbearable heat. During this time of year the gardens were always quiet, it was why Kohl went there to think. Most of the court opted for spending time along the shores, where light breezes swept a much needed reprieve off the Mykandrian Sea. But in the corner of the garden, under the shade of one of the large oak trees, sat a small bench. The breeze whispering to him under that tree, spirits bristling their bits of wisdom and history from the leaves.

It was written that the mighty oak tree was a symbol of the ruler of the Olympi. That a bit of his power still remained in its roots as a reminder of the all encompassing control and fortitude he once had. Quite truthfully, Kohl believed it was the voices of those who passed through the gates of Aidesian, long forgotten after their death, yearning to be amongst the living again. When he first told this to Katrin she smiled and shook her head, explaining that she sat on that very bench hundreds of times and not once heard voices of the dead.

Yet, as Kohl sat there, he could hear them swirling about. Whispers of doomed fate and wars lost. Whispers of long ago.

There were too many things for Kohl to think through as he laid back against the worn bronze of the bench. His father, who never did anything without a clearly defined reason, seemed to be asking too many questions and answering too few. Arriving early, wanting to know about the dreams, prying him for knowledge about Nexos. *Maybe she will not be a threat at all.* The words repeated again and again in his mind. If his father was planning something, Kohl needed to find out what it was and fast.

A snap of a tree branch shook him out of an almost meditative state. His eyes flickered open, readjusting to the light, analyzing what figure stood before him.

"Prince Kohl, apologies if I startled you." Ajax bowed before him. "I must have a word before the isles gather for the Acknowledgement."

Post-treaty, anytime a ruler was set to inherit the throne, representatives from each isle would gather to decide—officially—that they accepted the succession moving forward. If there was not a unanimous vote, royalty from any of the isles could claim succession. Could enact the Wrecking, a fight to first blood drawn. So far since the treaty, the Wrecking never occurred and Kohl planned to keep it that way.

"Is it expected there will be an issue with succession, Commander?" he finally managed to get out.

"Not exactly." Ajax's normally stoic face loosened into one of dread. "It is Nexos, Your Highness, my spies think they are set to attack—" he inhaled an uneasy breath, "they are set to attack next week."

Kohl looked up in disbelief. Had there been rumblings of Nexos raising an army—yes—but did he expect it this soon—absolutely not. Maybe this is why his father arrived early, with two ships filled with soldiers. He could have lied, he could already know this about Nexos.

"So they are set to bring an army to battle when the rest of the isles are gathered at a stronghold? How reckless can they be? We will sink their ships before they even enter port." Kohl tried to sound confident as he spewed the words, but there was still a sinking feeling no army could defeat Nexos. Not with King Nikolaos leading the charge. Not if the old male was gaining his power back. Not if he was helped by his wretched first-born son.

"That's the thing, Your Highness, there are no signs they are bringing an army. Meaning they are either already here, or they don't seek to kill *everyone*."

CHAPTER SEVEN

EMBER

Thorns and leaves scratched Ember's skin, the bush she decided to hide behind turning out to be a bad idea. But as she strolled by the garden earlier, Kohl sat sitting beneath a tree muttering to himself about war and fear and sorcery, speaking to the shadows like people surrounded him on the bench. Several times Ember covered her mouth, for fear that her laughter would alert the prince to her spying. It was rare she ever saw Kohl drunk or under some sort of influence, he always preferred to keep his wits about him. This was a story she would have to share with her sister, not that Katrin would believe her.

Crunching of boots over the rocky path in the garden startled her, but Ember was glad she stayed hidden when Ajax's stupidly handsome face strutted right past her and over to a seemingly high Kohl.

The commander was not honest with her earlier, and now she would learn the truth. At first she did not believe the words he mumbled under his breath. Barely loud enough to hear if Ember was not an expert at reading lips. The attack was imminent. And it was not to be waged on the people. No, it was pointed. It was for Katrin.

"Training to be a spy for the Spartanis, are we, little one?" A deep voice chuckled behind Ember's hiding spot. She drew her attention away from Kohl and Ajax before she could learn anymore. Standing behind her was a broad man, face weathered from years in battle, arms lined with scars from his past, a smile that could cause the unhappiest of people to feel joy.

"Iason, hush! I am trying to hear what they are discussing." Ember raised her index finger over her lips. Iason was one of the oldest members of the Spartanis and one of its esteemed senators. He had always been a part of the Drakos court, even before he became their uncle's lover. Machius, the last Prytan of the Spartanis. Kora's younger brother. *Late* younger brother. There was not much they knew about Machius's death, only that he perished on the seas. It was where he wished to die, having always been more keen to be sailing rather than attending to his duties in Alentus.

Even though the Prytan was never allowed to marry, Iason and Machius kept their relationship in the years they served together. He was one of their own, a father when Aidon was not around to care for her or Katrin.

"You know your uncle would be proud. He always preferred the act of spying above battle."

"Maybe it's a thing all Prytans have preferred." Ember shrugged.

Iason nodded back toward the garden, over Ember's shoulder. "Not a very good spy yet, though. It looks like your lead is on his way back to the barracks—and we all know how much you hate it there."

Ember whipped her head back around, Ajax had indeed disappeared.

"I will see you at the banquet then?"

"I'll be there, little one. Save me a seat by my favorite niece, will you?"

"There's always a seat by me for you, Iason."

"Oh, I meant your sister..." His eyes squinted, lips reaching ear to ear and Ember gave him a light shove before turning around and exiting from the bushes.

"Ajax!" Ember called after him, a few times to no avail.

The commander strode away as if he could not hear her.

"Ajax! Stop being a gods-damned pompous ass. Turn around and face me right this second!" her voice not only straining with anger at the lie, but her own desperation. She could hear Iason's faint chuckle coming from where she left him.

Ajax's spine went stiff, turning around with a look of realization that Ember overheard what he and Kohl spoke of. He took a step toward her, laying his calloused palm on her shoulder, bending down so the height of those warm brown eyes met hers. "She will be safe. That I will always promise you."

Ember looked straight back at him, barely able to mutter out a whisper with his captivating gaze. "You cannot know that. You cannot promise that. Last time—"

"Last time I was barely twenty, a foot soldier if anything. Last time I was not the *Commander* of the Spartanis. I will personally see to it that she is protected at all hours, and that no harm comes to her before, during, or after the Acknowledgement."

It was true. Ember watched him grow up in the training rings, his lanky form slowly filling out into the stocky and muscular man who stood before her. He even grew a few inches, the top of her head barely made it to his chest now. In the last year, he was named commander, surpassing several candidates that out-aged him by at least ten years. Even they did not show a twinge of jealousy as he was assigned the title.

A single tear slid down Ember's paling face, her hands trembling almost uncontrollably now. "What if that isn't enough? She's been having nightmares again. It's a sign, I just know it. What if it's like you said and they are already here? What if we are just too blind to see the spies amongst us?"

Especially if it was Nexos coming again. The stories she heard around port made King Nikolaos out to be more terrifying than even the Viper. God of Sea and Shadow, deceptive and could snuff out life with a snap of his fingers. He was known for destroying all that came between him and power. Ripping into minds and leaving people wandering with no sense of where they were or even *who* they were.

Ajax shook her shoulders gently. "Snap out of it, Drakos. I'm not the only one who is different than I was five years ago. Katrin has grown into one of the finest fighters I have seen. Gods, she might be better than even me."

Ember knew he was right. She saw the way her sister trained alongside men and women down in the barracks. Her movements stealth and light with each slice of her blade. Katrin's attention to detail and form always worked to her advantage, and when swords were torn away, Kohl taught her to throw one of the most lethal punches.

"I want that." It was her breaking point, the idea that both her mother and sister could be stripped away from her. Then she truly would be alone.

"Want what, Drakos?" Ajax straightened, cocking his head to the side.

"I want to be as good as my sister. Better even. I want to learn to fight and defend myself against those who are coming. I want to start my training." Not just for if Nexos showed up at the Acknowledgement, but training to be the Prytan. To be taken seriously. To not be seen as the younger daughter prancing about the castle in her gown. To prove she was more than just a pretty face.

The corner of his mouth twitched up in a wicked grin, eyes narrowing on hers. "I thought you would never ask."

"I'm not all gowns and balls, you know. I do have substance."

"Mmm, I guess we will see. Barracks, dawn tomorrow. You show up and I will teach you all I know. You miss it, don't bother coming to me to train you again."

Ember rolled her eyes at the dramatic display of rank. Soon she would outrank him. She would be there. Barracks. At dawn. She would show him who she *could* be.

Dense fog thickened the air smelling of dew and low tide. It was quite the day to start training. When Ember closed in on the entrance to the barracks her nose crinkled, a waft of sweat or horse or something putrid burning her nostrils. A gag caught in her throat. This was a mistake. She shouldn't have come, she couldn't do this—learn to fight, be around these men who bore scars and drew blood like it was second nature.

Goosebumps peppered Ember's skin, despite it being high in the summer months. The closest thing she owned to an appropriate outfit was a thin cotton sleeveless tunic she usually wore to sleep, and a pair of tight cropped navy trousers she stole out of Katrin's dresser. Ember stood, teeth chattering, outside the main entrance waiting for the commander to grace her with his presence.

Yellow and orange hues began to spread over the cliffs as the sun broke the water's horizon. Warmth would come soon. At least Ember hoped it would.

Ajax said to meet at dawn, yet he was nowhere to be seen outside the quarters of the Spartanis. Not in the stables she poked her head into, not in the training rings she passed on the walk over, not waiting for her here at the entrance. No noise even drifted out of the doors that led to many sleeping soldiers. She hated being down here, hated walking through the gloomy low-lit corridors within the barracks even more. But her body started convulsing from the slight breeze coasting off the seas and she already made it all the way down here—what was a few more feet into the dirty place?

Ember sighed, grinding her teeth together and pushed the heavy wooden doors of the barracks open, stomping through the muddied floors all the way to the end. To the commander's chambers. She stuck her ear up to the door, making sure she could not hear any grunts or moans coming from Ajax or that raven-haired girl once more. There was nothing but the faint sound of snoring trickling through the crack beneath the door.

Once. Twice, she rapped her knuckles against the door. Still no sounds of a stirring man. She jiggled the door handle—unlocked. Ember would need to speak to him about that later.

"Ahem—" she cleared her throat, attempting to rouse Ajax from his slumber, but it was to no avail.

The commander lay face down on his pillow, dirty blonde hair shuffled about. One arm hung off the side of the bed and a foot crept out from beneath the covers. He looked exceptionally peaceful, inhaling and exhaling in deep motions. She felt guilty for waking him. Almost. Ajax was the one who said if she didn't show at dawn she shouldn't bother showing up at all.

Ember gripped the bottom of his blankets and pulled hard, dropping them down to the ground. "Oh gods!" Ember screeched.

The commander rolled over, rubbing his eyes with the palms of his hands. Ember threw up her arm to shield her own eyes, spinning on her heels in the opposite direction. Her whole body glowed a faint red as she tried to wipe the image of what she just witnessed from her head.

Now lying behind her was a dazed and confused Ajax, naked as the day he was born. It wasn't that she never thought of Ajax this way—she had—many times in fact. But seeing him actually in front of her. It was more than she could have ever imagined, and she could not let the commander know that. Could not let him see what he did to her, the want and need that clenched low in her gut.

"Drakos? Is that you? What are you doing here?" His voice was gravely as she heard him exit the bed and slide on something. She peered back. A pair of low-slung shorts. The opposite of what she needed to see.

"You weren't at the training rings, or the stables, or outside waiting for me, so I thought I'd check here." Her teeth rolled over her bottom lip.

"I didn't—nevermind. Just give me a moment." Ajax yawned, pulling a loose fitting shirt over his head, aimlessly looking through a pile of clothes on the floor for some kind of pants.

"You didn't think I would show, did you?" Ember wasn't sure why the words sent such a pain through her bones. Like someone was scraping a needle along each crevice of her insides. Honestly, Ember did not think she would show herself, but to hear the words out loud. A waft of shame crept across her skin. No one believed in her. Not even the ever-positive commander.

"Did I hope you would? Sure. Did I actually expect you to get up before the sun and traipse down here? Absolutely not."

"You told me dawn or don't try to come again." Ember locked her jaw as she sent a piercing gaze at the now clothed commander. She could not tell if she was still embarrassed or just plain pissed off.

"Gods, Drakos, I was kidding. I figured you'd just show up later, when the rest of us trained, like a normal person." His words were still groggy as he threw back a glass of water.

"Oh—right." She chewed the inside of her cheek. "Well, I am here now, so we might as well start the day." Ember crossed her arms across her chest. It was considerably warmer in his chambers, but the shock of seeing Ajax lying there without clothes, coupled with the breeze trickling in through the windows caused her breasts to peak under the thin shift she'd tossed on that morning.

The commander ruffled his hands through his hair, finally turning to face her and taking her in. Ember's chest constricted and her breath hitched as he drank her in. His gaze roamed over the curves of her body in the tight cropped trousers, how you could almost see her skin through the sheer tunic. Ajax's jaw clenched tight and his warm brown eyes took on a feral stare.

"What are you wearing, Drakos?" The sound from his lips was akin to a growl.

Her body tensed, the slight trickle of sweat dripping from her temple. He stalked closer to her, dragging one hand along her collar bone, shaking his head with a long sigh.

"I wasn't sure what to wear." Her voice trembled at his touch.

A soft chuckle escaped his throat, circling around her. "Certainly not that, if you thought we'd be in the training rings. You would get bloodied and bruised within a second. Later today we will go down to the market and get you some proper clothing. For now," he said, stepping back, grabbing a pair of thick leather boots to slip on, "we will stick to a run."

"Running...right." Ember tried to think of the last time she did any physical activity. At least any activity that made her really sweat. Maybe it was as a child, when she would prance down the sandy beaches with Katrin. But a run? Gods, she wouldn't make it a mile.

"Don't worry, *Prytan*, I'll take it easy on you."

Ember swallowed as a tiny light inside her chest began to warm and glow. Prytan. One word, and yet it carried so much weight. The scowl on her face began to shift into pure determination, eyes flickering with golden amber sparkles. "I'd rather you not."

Chapter Eight

Katrin

A week went by and Katrin barely saw her sister. Ember was avoiding her at all costs.

Honestly, it seemed as if everyone was avoiding her. Kora was nowhere to be seen, closing herself in her study, save for the occasional run-in at dinner time. Each time she tried to speak with Kohl in private, his father slithered out of the shadows and whisked him away, always claiming some important business they needed to attend to regarding Morentius. What little time she did spend with Kohl on their runs was filled with unending silence since the king arrived. Katrin knew he was stressed, knew he suffered from headaches and dizziness when he was overwhelmed, but it was happening more often than before.

She couldn't blame any of them for disappearing around her. What with all the maids running about, making sure Katrin had this dress, and this crown, and reminding her of the words she must recite at the Acknowledgement. They plied her with food and drink and practice, with little time for sleep.

Little sleep—Katrin did not mind that part so much. If she avoided deep sleep, she avoided nightmares, and if she avoided her nightmares then maybe, just maybe she would actually be prepared enough to claim her rightful place on the throne.

It was not that being in front of people frightened her, it was more the idea that the other leaders of the isles would not want her, a girl just approaching twenty-five, as their leader. Especially after Kora.

Her mother was one of the most fair and just rulers in not only the isles, but all of Odessia. Not only that, but she had ruled Alentus for the last one-hundred years. Those were shoes Katrin was worried she could not fill.

"There you are!" Katrin broke away from the maids who were showing her swatches of *more* fabric to race over to her sister. "You've been hiding from me!"

"I haven't been hiding..." Ember's eyes shifted from her sister to the commander beside her.

Mud coated her sister's face and her hands were wrapped with worn out cloth. Normally delicate styled blonde hair was now matted down to her sweaty face and neck in a tousled braid, strands falling out from every plait. Purple bags now puffed under her dimmed golden eyes.

"You were fighting!" Katrin almost regretted her surprised tone the second the words left her mouth, but Ember *did not* dirty herself. Not ever.

Once, her sister complained an entire week about a speck of dirt that got on her silk slippers. That was the whole reason her mother was so concerned about leaving them soon. She thought Ember would not be ready to be Prytan of the Spartanis, that she would never swap her schooling lessons for training, yet there she stood in fighting leathers, a sense of determination dancing behind the exhaustion in her eyes.

"Don't look so surprised, *sister*. It was only a matter of time before I traded in the fancy gowns for this lovely attire." Ember nudged the commander in the side and he smirked right back at her.

Now that was something Katrin would need to ask about once they were alone. Her sister had a crush on Commander Ajax since she was a child watching the older boys in training to be soldiers, even if she denied it every chance she got. By the way Ajax smiled, his brown eyes warming at the tiniest joke from her sister, she felt like that feeling was mutual.

A week was barely enough to learn everything you need to know to be Prytan. Even Katrin's years of training would not put her in a much better position. But Katrin was proud nonetheless.

Her heart filled with worry at why her sister became so inclined to finally start her training. Why now? Was it really because of the Acknowledgement? Or was something else the driving factor? Did Katrin's words have such an impact on her sister that it spurred her into action this quickly?

"Excuse me, Commander, but I must sweep my sister away to help with preparations for tonight. You see, she was *supposed* to be helping me for the last week, but turns out she's been spending all her time with *you*." Katrin winked at him. If she was to find out her sister's true intentions then she would need to keep things lighthearted. No accusations, no arguments.

"Of course, Your Majesty, I would never want to stand between Ember and her clothing duties." Ajax bowed to them with a smirk splashed across his face as Ember narrowed her eyes in disapproval. He turned to her then, "Princess, I will see you back at the barracks tomorrow."

When Ajax ventured around the corner, Katrin whipped around to face her sister, but Ember was already trying to worm her way through the maids and away from her.

"Excuse me, Ember, where do you think you're going?" Her sister stiffened at the words before Katrin caught up and grabbed her arm. "What is this about you starting to train, not one week before the Acknowledgement? We have been trying to get you down to the barracks for years, but this is what causes you to start?" Katrin stuck her hands out on her hips, a slight pout forming on her mouth. Ember cringed, her throat bobbing up and down.

"You found out Ajax was courting some girl and you couldn't stand it, could you? Had to tempt him to like you by showing how much of a badass you are? It's alright, sister, seeing you two together right now, well he might not say it, but the feeling is mutual," Katrin shot out in a laugh.

"It is not!" Ember protested. Although her face showed a lighter sense of worry than it did before. "I couldn't care less about that shallow heap of a man, and him toward me," her sister's voice cracked, a shallow scowl formed on her lips.

"Alright," Katrin wiggled her eyebrows at her sister, "if you say so. But truly, I am proud."

"It was your doing. You did say you'd need *me* after all." Ember rolled her eyes and she mocked Katrin's words.

"I meant it, sister. Every word."

They turned down the halls toward Katrin's chamber, followed closely by maids still flashing silks of red, orange, gold, turquoise, deep green, navy. She was supposed to choose for the ball tonight, but in reality she did not have much of a choice. It would have to be a fancier version of the hideous red and orange gown she already wore, otherwise it would be a direct insult. Even though the Alentian colors were much more suited to her olive complexion, and even though it was her being Acknowledged this week, not the Athanas family, it would be rude to wear anything else. Katrin's lungs clenched. It was no wonder Kohl always had those headaches; dealing with his family was almost unbearable.

When they entered her chambers, however, the thought of what to wear quickly vanished. Lying on her desk in the living room was a large golden box tied with a large black ribbon. No note adorned the box, neither was there one lingering beside it on the desk. Katrin slowly untied the ribbon.

"Don't open that! You don't know what's inside!" Ember screamed as she leapt across the room toward her sister.

"That's quite the reaction to me receiving a gift. Do you want one too?" Katrin laughed as she slid the last of the ribbon off.

A firm hand pushed Katrin aside before Ember opened the box instead, revealing a lovely black silk gown folded inside.

Katrin looked at her sister, brows raised. "Like I said, it's just a gift, nothing to fret over." But her sister's breath was choppy, and her brow furrowed along her usually happy face.

She pulled out the gown, its laced-up front sparkling with black and gold stitches, the sleeves narrow until they reached shoulder length then billowing out in a vee.

Katrin turned the dress around, a large delicately stitched viper in gold thread looked as if it was slithering along the back like a tattoo. Two piercing eyes were shaded in orange, its fangs and tongue a delicate red protruding from the mouth. Her eyes widened. It was beautiful—yes—but daunting as well. Wearing this was the true symbol and declaration of her alliance with Morentius. Not that everyone didn't know that she was betrothed to Kohl, but it was always *her* kingdom they would rule, *her* banner they would rule under.

Ember gasped. "That is stunning. Tell the maids to stop their search for the perfect fabric. King Athanas must have brought it all the way from Morentius, it would be rude not to wear it. Plus, it is a lot better than any of the horrendous options we've just seen."

As Katrin ran her fingers along the silk she couldn't help but worry. Worry if wearing this was proof she might take orders from others before herself, proof that she condoned whatever Kohl believed his father might be up to.

Smooth black silk wicked away Katrin's sweat despite the heat being its strongest this late in summer. The gown fit beautifully, she admitted. No tailoring was needed, it was as if each piece of the gown was pinned directly to her body and stitched on.

Spinning in front of the mirror, Katrin took in the intricate detailing once more. Her hair was fully pinned up, with braids circling into the center of a bun. Tendrils twirled down the front, framing her face and her eyes that were lined heavily with black. The deepest shade of red, matching that of the viper's fangs on her back, painted her lips. A set of gold and onyx earrings glittered in the firelight, a matching necklace engraved with the fiery sun and lightning bolt of Alentus hung at her neck.

Light notes danced along Katrin's balcony making their way through the open doors. The melody was lovely, prompting her to spin and twirl until she could not see straight. It enchanted her as she swayed over toward the doors, peering down at the people gathering below. They were dressed in the colors of the surrounding isles, the men in fine coats and shined leather boots, the women in floor-length gowns clinging to their bodies in the heat.

Although her sister usually delighted in balls more than she ever did, Katrin was excited for this one. The mark of a new era. She was not fully ready to take on being queen, but she would show everyone why she deserved it anyway. There was no more time for self-doubt. This is what she was born to do.

Ember arrived exponentially late to escort Katrin to the gardens, but looked more poised and delicate than Katrin ever could. As they entered through the archway, the music cut short, all eyes turning toward her in the long shimmering *black* gown. Her sister curtsied, picking up the corner of her simple yet flawless turquoise gown beaded with pearls, and entered first.

Out of nowhere, Kohl stepped to Katrin's side, slipping a rough palm against the small of her back. "You look beautiful," he whispered in her ear.

Katrin looked up at her love, and pure starlight twinkled in her eyes. His wavy brown hair was tied back in a sleek bun, his chiseled jaw smiled so large Katrin could hardly control the pink that spread across her cheeks. Kohl barely fit inside of the black jacket he sported, the lines of his muscular arms and back showing through the silken garb. Gold thread edged the cuffs and seams along the bottom. A similar viper to Katrin's was also stitched up his back.

A sour taste coated her mouth. Quite the ploy indeed. King Athanas knew exactly what it would show the other isles by them both arriving in these outfits. Morentius was the power in the relationship. They were loyal first and foremost to the southern ways.

In an instant, Katrin regretted playing politics and the doting bride-to-be. She wished she was in a similar gown to her sister, now glowing in the corner by the commander.

Placing her hand in Kohl's, the two began to descend the steps into the garden's courtyard. When they reached the opening on the floor below, they stopped. Ajax moved toward them in his uniform of golden leather, the symbol of the Drakos Court embossed over his heart. He bowed to Katrin and Kohl and turned toward the crowd.

"May I present Princess Aikaterine Drakos, heir-apparent to the Throne of Alentus and her future consort, Kohl Athanas, Prince of

Morentius." The crowd erupted in applause as the two future rulers walked farther into the center of the ball.

Ajax's voice rose once more and the crowd went silent. "To begin the festivities of this week's Acknowledgement, our future queen and consort will grace us with the opening dance." Again he bowed, stepping back toward Ember, who was now holding hands with Kora along the side of the garden. Iason stood next to them, permanently clutching the hilt of his sword, ready to protect the current queen if anything went awry.

Kohl grazed his lips along Katrin's cheek in a faint kiss. "May I have the honor, my sweet Aikaterine?"

Katrin laughed, "You know I hate it when people call me by that name."

"Maybe you don't like it, but I happen to love it. Almost as much as I love you." Kohl wrapped his arm around her waist, the other taking her palm in his, beginning to twirl them as the musicians started playing once more.

A sweet melody drifted toward them, one filled with romance and happiness, but also longing and unrequited love. A curious choice for the first dance of the week. Blue eyes in the crowd caught hers as they spun over the marble tiling. A familiar smile from her dawn runs. But when they turned once more, the young farmer was gone. Had she imagined the lighthearted crook of the man's lips, the tanned skin and black hair she came to recognize so well in the morning light?

Katrin let her eyes flutter closed. She must have been confused. Farmers did not attend this sort of event. Letting Kohl lead her around the dance floor, she allowed the soft notes to drift her into a beautiful trance. The hem of her gown glittered in the twinkling fire lights that lined the courtyard. So did the two vipers on their backs that seemed to spin into one in the setting sun. It was the most simple and yet magical melody that she heard in a long time and for once, a sound, not silence, made her forget the trauma of her past.

When the song finally ended, Katrin's chest heaved, breath still trying to seep into her lungs. A slight bit of sweat clung to her upper lips, but she did not care. Her eyes flicked up toward Kohl's and the rest of the courtyard disappeared. It was only the two of them there. Then the music started again and others stepped out to join them. Warm ebony eyes and a wicked grin stared down at Katrin. Kohl slid one hand down her back as the other delicately took her wrist and led her to the back of the courtyard, where tall marble pillars held up the balcony above. It was darker there, only a small torch lit the entryway back to the castle. Quiet shadows concealed their bodies.

Katrin gasped as Kohl picked her up and sat her on top of the stone wall. His hands slid up the slit in her dress and she instinctively wrapped her legs around his waist, tugging him closer by his jacket lapels. A small moan left Katrin's throat as Kohl pressed his lips to hers. Then he broke from their kiss, tracing her collar bone with his tongue as his hand slid higher and higher up her leg.

That was where they always stopped and he always let her, but the feral look in his eyes—dominating, possessive—said he might not stop this time. Katrin was not sure she could let him touch her in the ways Kohl wanted. Desire was always there, plastered on his face. The glint in his eyes, the twitch of his lips, the way his fingers dug lightly into her flesh. But after everything that happened to her, she did not know when she would finally be able to give up that part of her.

With her legs still looped around him, she could feel his want against her, threatening to break the laces on his trousers. He lifted his lips from her neck, piercing her with a devilish look. The room seemed to swirl around her and Katrin was unsure if it was Kohl, or the heat, or the glass of bubbled wine she drank to calm her nerves. Kohl knelt down in front of her, pushing back the hem of her gown. Would she need to stop him now? Was it finally time she let him have what he wanted?

"Ahem…" Katrin's eyes opened as she flashed over to the man standing by the flickering flame. A breath loosened from Katrin's lips and the fluttering of her heart began to settle, as the commander strode closer to them. "Excuse me, Princess, but dinner is about to be served and we can't start until the guests of honor are present."

Red seeped across Katrin's cheeks when she stood up, brushing the wrinkles out of her delicate gown. Kohl nodded to Ajax, no shame upon his face, and took Katrin's hand in his sweaty palm to lead her back to the courtyard. Music trickled through the air and Kohl leaned down and whispered in her ear, "I'll make sure to save some of my appetite for later."

Katrin could not find the words to tell him there would not be a later.

Lavish dishes lined the tables. Baskets of fruits and nuts. Several types of freshly baked bread with olive oil for dipping. Cheese and figs. Fresh fish caught that morning. A wild boar perfectly cooked in the center. Pitchers of wine, bubbly and still, were being served from large clay vases.

People rose and bowed to Katrin and Kohl as they walked around toward the head table, empty seats left for them to either side of Kora and King Athanas. Iason had taken a seat across from Kora, next to Ember who giggled under her palm at something the old man had whispered.

"Mother...King Athanas..." Katrin bowed to each before taking her seat. Kohl followed suit. "Thank you for hosting such a lovely party before my Acknowledgement. The food looks divine."

Katrin's smile widened at her favorite fish placed on a dish in front of her. Her mother smiled back, radiant amber eyes glittering in the candlelight. She wore an intricate cobalt blue sleeveless silk gown, dipping lower in the front than her mother usually preferred. A sheer sparkling fabric lay on top of the skirt, mimicking the crystal waters swirling on a summer's day. A delicate chain hung from her neck with a single crystal gem. A gold star, her father's wedding gift to Kora all those years ago.

Kora reached over, grabbing Katrin's hand as she sat down. Two stunning thick gold cuffs lined each of her wrists. Jewelry Katrin had not seen before. Intricate carvings of an ancient language she did not recognize swirled along them. The *Elliniká Glóssa* perhaps.

"Your Acknowledgement is quite the day to celebrate, Katrin." Her mother's smile gleamed with pride, though Katrin could not help but notice a distant look in her mother's eyes.

"And to celebrate the wedding between our two houses," the king interjected. His toothy grin unnerving despite the seemingly positive sentiment. It didn't matter how many times she saw him, tingling still inched down her spine. The king was dressed in a similar black jacket and pants as his son, except for the red stitching that replaced Kohl's gold.

"Yes, and to celebrate the wedding. A magnificent time all around," Kora added. Her eyes narrowed slightly toward the king. Iason eyed Kora, lifting his brow as if to agree with her pointed tone toward the king. He was never much of a fan of Kohl's father. He was much too harsh in his pursuit of peace. Iason, being a member of the Spartanis, preferred stability.

They used to joke about the Viper when she was little, even around Kohl. When they were not around Kohl he would tell them stories of how King Athanas would slither into his enemies' kingdoms at night and poison them all with his deathly venom. It was only a fabricated story, but most likely the reason Ember avoided the king at all costs.

Katrin was glad Iason was around, especially when her father could not be. Someone who she trusted to keep the king in line while he was here, and protect them against the harsh words that flung from his tongue. He winked at her from across the table.

For hours they ate and drank and talked and danced and ate some more. The music kept the entire courtyard lively well into the evening. King Athanas was still babbling about wedding plans that neither Katrin nor Kohl wanted to hear. Formalities and customs that were long since in practice in her court. It was not until he mentioned her sister's name that Katrin snapped out of a wine-induced haze to listen.

"You can't honestly think they will support Ember ascending to the position of Prytan, Kora. Of course, I mean no offense toward her," King Athanas turned his gaze to Katrin's sister, "but my dear, you are too small, too untrained, and much too young."

Ember's nails dug into the table so much so that Ajax took a step closer, assessing whether she would indeed lunge across the table at the king or not. Iason's jaw clenched tight, but he did not speak, only nodded at the increasingly volatile Ember.

"Excuse me, Your Majesty, but I have been training and I am taking this *very* seriously. It is my duty as it is my right to be appointed to such a title." Ember smiled right back at King Athanas.

"A few weeks of training does not make you equipped to lead one of the most highly respected legions in the isles." Venomous words. True Viper form.

"It's tradition—" she tried to continue.

"You think the men of the Spartanis will follow you? A girl of barely twenty over those who have served and fought and seen real bloodshed? Maybe it is time to see those traditions changed."

Iason's mouth opened to speak, but Ajax beat him to it. "I would follow her. I have seen her determination, her loyalty, and her skill even in such a short period of time. I have seen others more equipped, more learned, but none that have the will, the want that she does. My men would agree."

Her sister stared at the commander, her eyes wide and sparkling.

King Athanas snorted. "You might think you would follow her, boy, but that is because you are thinking with a different head."

Katrin caught Kohl slumping farther in his chair, pinching the bridge of his nose and reaching for the bottle of amber liquor in front of him. He poured a tall glass and shot it back. Again. And again.

Kora cleared her throat. "My daughter will take her rightful title, as did those in the court before her, some more trained and some less. In Alentus, traditions matter, and it will serve you well to remember that *if* our houses are to be joined."

King Athanas may have been outspoken, but he was not foolish. He would not push Kora further on the topic. Not this close to the Acknowledgement, this close to the wedding. Especially not with the threat of Nexos breathing down their necks.

"Of course, Kora. Again, I meant no offense to your daughter. We just go about these things differently in Morentius." He smiled again, flashing those shaven teeth. "If you would excuse me, I am going to take that as my time to leave. Kohl, will you join me?"

Slumping his shoulders, Kohl pushed up from his chair and nodded at his father before walking over to Katrin. He placed a simple kiss on her cheek, slurring as he spoke, "I will see you in the morning then. For training. I love you, Katrin, even after the gods take us."

"Even after the gods take us," Katrin repeated.

Chapter Nine

Kohl

The moment flashed in his eyes again, a whirlwind of emotions that was the dance, and Katrin's lips, and the feel of his fingers as they grazed her skin. How he nibbled his way along her neck and cheek and ear. How she pressed up against him, the sweetness of her skin. He could still feel the tingling of his lips even after he spoke to his father, even after he wobbled his way into bed.

Restless. Tangled in his sheets. Dreaming of her touch, her smell, her taste. Intoxicating. This person. This woman. This goddess was his and only his.

There were other women before Katrin, he knew what lay beneath the gowns and robes. But this was different. He would be *her* first. Her last. Her everything.

Katrin sitting there propped up against the wall in the courtyard filled his mind as he cared to his needs. The thought of her slipping that gown down off her body. Imagining her beneath him, arching her back to push closer to his bare skin. All the things he would do to her body if Katrin would only let him.

His control was slipping. Kohl would not make it to the wedding to have her—all of her.

Kohl woke up to the bright glittering of the sun through the balcony he left open—stupidly, he noted, as his head pained with the spirits he indulged in the prior night. The heat rolled in through the doors with a southern breeze that left him sweating rather than feel a cooling embrace.

His hand swatted at the wooden nightstand beside the bed, eyes still adjusting to the yellow rays cascading about the room. *Water,* he thought, *there you are.* Kohl clutched the jug and brought it to his lips because the small glass beside it just would not do. The now lukewarm liquid slid down his throat as he sighed from the sweet relief, his mouth no longer feeling like it was full of sand.

Kohl tried to look outside to determine the time, not wanting to leave the softness of the bed just yet to look at the sundial. He knew he would be late for his run with Katrin through the mountains, but hoped she was in a similar state to him.

When his father started discussing more in depth marital discussions, Kohl skipped over the wine and went straight to the liquor.

Then the king began insulting their traditions and Kohl no longer sipped the amber liquid, instead just tossing back full pours.

At this point, those discussions were neither here nor there. He would need to tell his father to keep his opinions to his gods-damned self. Not that Kohl would ever actually speak to the Viper that way without serious repercussions. Sometimes he wished his father was not so feared and recognized. Maybe then he would love him like a son, not use him as a way to further his agendas.

His eyes were still adjusting to the light as he persuaded his legs to move over to the wardrobe to dress for a run in the summer's heat. He took out a white cotton short-sleeved shirt and thin running shorts made from a sweat-resistant material, slipping them on as he tried to lull the pounding in his head. Today was going to have to be a light run, maybe even just a jog. He was not used to drinking that much in one night, and was not used to the repercussions it brought.

Kohl threw back the rest of the water in the jug, tied his hair back in a bun, and went to look for Katrin by the castle gates where they met each morning.

When he arrived at the gate she was already waiting, her warm brown hair pinned up in a braid, wearing the thinnest of white gauzy sleeveless tunics and the tightest of black trousers. Arms crossed, her right foot propped up on the gate behind her, she looked like wicked torture.

Kohl could not tell if he was lightheaded from the hangover or from the sight of her curves on full display after last night. As his eyes trailed up her body to her lush lips he could barely restrain himself from marching over and ripping her clothes off right there.

"You look like death came and spit you back out," Katrin chuckled as Kohl approached.

"I assure you, I feel worse than I look," he sighed back. "Are you sure you wouldn't want to take a day off and go spend it in bed?"

She smacked his shoulder as he inched closer. "Since when has the great warrior Kohl ever wanted to take a day off?" Those lush lips tilted up in a smirk.

"Since the day you started showing up wearing that, but I've been more disciplined in the past. Now I don't know what I was thinking." Kohl wrapped his deeply tanned arms around Katrin's waist pulling her in close, planting a kiss just between her brows.

"As wonderful as that might sound, the Acknowledgement is only a few days away. I need to be in tip-top shape if someone calls for the Wrecking."

"No one is going to call for the Wrecking, Katrin. The succession is not in question. You are the most fit to rule your home and the rest of the isles know that."

"Except Nexos. The rest of the Isles except Nexos. King Nikolaos could try to claim a right, he is an older god than I am, Kohl. Or his eldest son."

Kohl's jaw clenched. He did not want to think about the infuriating Prince of Nexos, the way he used to swagger around when they were children like he was better than the other boys. "No one has seen the eldest prince in years, and Prince Dimitris and their younger sister would have no claim to such a high position without their full powers and they aren't yet twenty-five."

A small chill crept up Kohl's back. The Prince of Nexos eluded both the spies of Alentus and Morentius for the past five years so no one knew what his full powers were. If they were anything like his father's, the prince could be lethal. Add in the stealth and cunning of Queen Giselle and he could be unstoppable.

Nik would be twenty-seven now, the same age as Kohl. Two years would have passed for him to learn how to harness whatever gifts trickled down from his father and mother. Small bits of it would show before then, but could be well hidden from enemies by the power of their parents, which is what Nikolaos and Giselle most likely were doing now, hiding the prince behind a shroud in Nexos, planning their strike.

"You've always been the more optimistic one, Kohl. I just have this feeling in the pit of my stomach that something is going to go wrong." Katrin leaned fully into his chest.

"It won't. I'll make sure of it, Aikaterine. Now that you have crushed any chance of me not running this morning, we should probably get to it before the sun gets too high and I decide I am no longer listening to my future queen." Kohl bowed in jest.

"Race you to the base of the Triad?" Katrin's eyebrow raised in anticipation.

"This time you might actually win," Kohl chuckled and took off. Needing the headstart with his hangover progressively getting worse.

"Hey! What a cheater!" Katrin yelled as she took off after him.

Surprisingly, the run felt good. The summer's high heat helped to sweat out any toxins he overindulged in the night before. A slight breeze swept through the trees in the forests surrounding the Triad, keeping them both cool enough to continue moving.

Watching Katrin keep pace with him the whole way was also an added treat. They never spoke when they ran together, just took in the beauty and sounds of the nature around them. The path always started at the castle, looping down toward the docks at the port where the smell of fishermen and low tide laced the air. After, they hit the sandy beaches on the opposing side of the isle, finishing by winding through the olive groves until they hit the Drakos' winter cottage at the base of the triads. All in all, it was a ten mile loop, but they would only do the five, taking horses back to the castle.

The cabin was quickly approaching when Kohl saw Katrin take off for the stables. Normally he would be able to outrun her, but his mouth had gone dry again and his breathing was still labored. When he finally caught up a minute later, she was already sipping the ice water kept in a chilled box behind the stables.

"How can you run that fast after last night? I feel like I might actually keel over and die and your father would take me away to Aidesian." Kohl reached out for the other glass of ice cold water Katrin poured and set on the small outdoor table.

"Not *all* of us drank through the Drakos liquor cabinet during dinner." The biggest smile plastered on Katrin's face. Kohl loved that smile, even here, sweat dripping down from her brow, hair slightly falling out of the braid after their run. She was absolutely beautiful—breathtaking, really.

"Well you would need to drink through a liquor cabinet too if you had to put up with my father," Kohl said and Katrin let out a light chuckle. "You know, I can think of one thing that could make me feel better though, well, other than the water."

"Oh? And what is that?" Katrin took a step closer to him.

"This..." He closed the gap between them, walking them back toward the tree the horses were usually tied to.

Kohl took Katrin's chin between his fingers, bringing her lips to his. Parting the plush pillows he dreamed about as he swept his tongue passionately in her mouth. Her eyes closed as she laced her hands behind his neck, grabbing at the hair that fell out from his bun. He slowly shifted his lips down to her neck running one hand behind her waist and the other to the spot between her legs.

"Kohl—" she barely panted out, her head shifting back toward the tree behind them, opening her neck up more for him to devour. His hand slid to the laces of her pants, pulling at them until they were loose. "What are you doing? I am absolutely disgusting after that run."

"Just finishing what we started last night," he purred in her ear.

He could feel himself harden as he took in the look of anticipation that sparkled in Katrin's widened eyes. His lips met hers again and he let her fingers wander back to where they came from. She let out little pants of breath as his thumb circled outside her trousers over and over again, causing him to only lean more into the kisses. Soon he would have those off her, would bend her over and see what glorious site begged for him to slip inside.

"Please, Kohl..." her voice cracked, "stop...please." He knew she didn't mean it, that she wanted him this much too.

"Do you like that, Princess?" Kohl whispered into her ear. He could hear her quietly swallow down a word. Katrin's eyes glazed over as she screamed.

Kohl stumbled backward clutching his shoulder. Blood seeped down the once white cotton shirt. His voice was completely stripped from his body with shock. One second they were kissing and the next he was stabbed with a dagger. And not just any dagger, but one Kohl specially commissioned.

When Kohl finally recovered from the initial shock, Katrin was gone.

Chapter Ten

Katrin

*T*he boat continued to rock back and forth with the seas. The sides of the chamber she was in shook with each smack of the waves against the ship. Two weeks. She was locked in this room for two weeks—at least, she thought it was that long. The room was barren except for a small cot with itchy wool blankets and a quite outdated bathing chamber.

She counted the meals they gave her, a small rip of bread and old cheeses and a glass of water each day. Enough to keep her alive, but barely. Although there was no mirror, Katrin could feel her ribs begin to jut out from beneath the simple white shirt they kept her clothed in.

The sun rising and setting through the tiny hole they called a window was the only way she knew that days passed. And even then, she sometimes wondered if she dreamt them. If she really was somehow in one of the deepest caverns of Aidesian, where even Aidoneus himself could not find her. If her mother also would never find her.

A knock came at the door and Katrin's stomach dropped. It would be the old woman. She knew it. Each day it was the same. The woman would come in, drop off her food, replace the wash basin, change her into the lace robe that he *liked*.

The man entered after, as he did many times before. His blood-red eyes causing chills down her entire body, still making her wretch every time he *left. The way the color trickled out of the iris in the middle like serpents writhing through the brush.*

He slithered over to her, his hot breath at her ear.

"I wonder what he would think knowing you'd be on your knees for me girl." That laughter filled her head. The same one from the first day. The same one that tormented her dreams.

The man pushed her onto the bed, easily pinning her hands up behind her. She was so frail at this point she thought they might snap beneath his large palms. His pale skin was muscular underneath his linen shirt and leather breeches. She knew even if she was at full strength he could hold her down. He did that first day—and every day since.

He slipped the other calloused hand down her front undoing the rope that held that flimsy robe together. It traveled down her body as he pressed against her, his breaches already unlaced.

When he entered her it was always hard and without regard. The first time, she bled on the sheets. The old woman never replaced them. A stark reminder that he took the one thing she had to give. The one thing that was meant for another man. At this point, she doubted that mattered. Katrin doubted she would ever see the sandy beaches of Alentus again.

Each time he would lean into her, his sweaty body dripping onto her skin, his hot breath whispering vulgar curses in her ears. How she was a whore, how no prince could ever love her. How one day she would learn to love it, learn to beg for him.

Some days, when she ate little food or water, she wondered if she would. If somehow, some way she would actually want this. Learn to need this as a break for the silence that filled the rest of her days. Katrin tried to push back those thoughts again and again.

But silence was the true curse. The waiting game. Would food come? Would they reach land? Would a storm wreck the ship and send her to the bottom of the seas in a lifeless heap? And the constant that never proved true—would someone come for her?

She tried to fight back the first few times. Not anymore. It was not worth it. She had kicked and screamed and bit him. All it did was make him want more. After the first time, he finished himself on her stomach and then beat her for her disobedience. Her black eye still crusted over, a split lip only partially healed even weeks later.

The second time he took his belt and slashed it across her back again and again. Those scars, those may never truly heal, the object laced with some poison even a god's blood could not cure. With each whip she could hear him touching himself, getting off to her pain. Once he was done leaving her skin in tethers he palmed one hand around her neck, slamming her face into the cot, entering her from behind.

He left her there after, crying and bloody, shaking on the floor. After the first few times she learned it was easier to just let him do what he wanted and leave. Let him whisper, "Do you like that, Princess?" into her ear.

Kohl did nothing wrong. She tried repeating the words over again in her mind, whispering it out into the world for no one to hear. He said those words, his hot breath against her ear and she spiraled. There was something familiar in his eyes, unlike Kohl, but still noticeable. Like she saw the look in another. In a trance she reached for the dagger, begging him to stop touching her. Then Katrin sliced the blade into the soft part between his shoulder and collar bone and she took off.

It was second nature, running through the hills, the groves that lined the base of the Triad. Salty wind flushed her cheeks as she leapt over vines and roots and she tried to forget what she just did.

Dust circled with every step Katrin took through the groves, swirling up and into her lungs. Blood coated her right hand and her thigh where she sheathed the blade before taking off into the woods. Tears or sweat stung her eyes, or maybe the wind, she could not tell. Could not focus on anything but the image of the confused and broken man who had stood in front of her.

The skies began to darken, once bright and blue now covered with clouds and haze. Fog rolled off the top of the Triad with haste, looming toward the base where she still ran. Air thickened, signaling that rain was not far behind. Katrin picked up her pace, trying to focus on her surroundings.

She'd run out this way a thousand times before, both with Kohl and without. Kohl who she was now running from. Kohl who she left bleeding out. She should have stayed, explained why she pushed away, why she reached for that dagger. But the truth would break him, maybe more than it broke Katrin herself. It ate at her insides, she needed it out, needed to tell someone, offload some of the pain that was sure to destroy her.

Drops of rain began to cascade down her skin, cathartic in a sense, the way it washed away the blood, the sins of her morning. Faster and faster she ran, not noticing the object that stood in her path in the thickly settled woods until she slammed into it. Slammed into *him*.

Instinct had Katrin's hand back at the hilt of her dagger. She hadn't even looked up at the man yet, too afraid to see what terror lurked in the storm.

"Whoa...whoa there, miss. Are you alright?" a mysterious voice drawled out, smooth as the rolling sea.

Katrin took a step back, letting her gaze rise to his. Her eyes narrowed, cocking her head to the side. It was him.

The young farmer who would wave to her in the low light of dawn as she ran. She heaved a sigh of relief at a familiar face. Looking at him this close, however, he didn't seem young at all. Fine lines framed his eyes and protruded between his brows. Lightly tanned skin reminded her of the clay in the cliffs along the caldera of Alentus, sparkling even in the rain that now fell heavily. A simple tunic and average looking breaches clung to all ridges of his tight muscular body, sending quite a blush across her cheeks, although she tried to hide it. Short waving black hair, so black it almost shone blue, was plastered against his forehead. And his eyes. Those magnificent, stunning eyes. Katrin could not place what they looked like. A swirl of the tide during a storm. Greens and blues and grays mixing together. She blinked a few times, trying to center herself.

He bowed to her slightly, lowering the basket of olives he held to the ground. "Apologies, Your Highness. I didn't mean to startle you. My name is Alexander—well most people call me Ander." His eyes swept down to her chest. "Princess, you are bleeding!"

Katrin turned away from him, gazing into the blurry skies. "It's not my blood," she said with an unnerving rasp. Her body began to shake as the winds around them swirled even harder.

A calloused hand reached out to her shoulder. Katrin looked down and it was not the dirt covering his fingers that made her lungs shrivel, but the markings along his wrist. Twins to her own.

Ander stepped closer to her. "Please, let's get you out of the rain and cold. You can dry by the fire. I promise I won't ask what happened unless you wish me to."

Thundering skies only appeared to be worsening, and she was cold, and hungry, and wouldn't be able to find Kohl in the storm anyway. It looked blacker than the night sky and any chances of using a torch to find her way back to the Drakos cabin were out of the question.

"Yes...that would be nice. Thank you, Ander."

They walked quickly to the cabin that was neatly nestled between cypress trees at the base of the first mountain. It was a small cabin, much more humble than the Drakos winter cottage she was at earlier.

Olive oil, lemon, and the salt of the sea delicately hung in the living space as she entered the cabin. A tiny table with four worn out wooden chairs sat in the middle of the room, two plush chaise lounges were nestled in front of a fireplace, their velvet fabric ripping in some places.

"Let me start a fire, the cold air came in too quickly and from the look of the skies it's not planning on leaving anytime soon. You can change into something else while your clothes dry, hopefully that will stop your shivering." His voice was light, his gaze flickering between her and the fire he was starting.

"Change into what exactly?" Katrin glanced over near the bed in the corner and only male clothes were neatly folded in the open wardrobe.

"Here." Ander crossed the small room and pulled out a navy tunic that looked like it could swallow Katrin whole. "You can slip this on for now. I have a few belts lying around that you can use to tie it with."

Katrin's limbs stiffened. A belt, blood, the dagger, Kohl. "Thank you," she whispered as she turned around, stripping out of the soaked white shirt, leaving only her undergarment remaining. The tunic fell to the floor with a wet smack.

Burning ran up her back from the heated stare she could see looking at her in the mirror. It was not a sexual gaze, but rather a wonder at why the Princess of Alentus was found wandering the woods with no escort covered in blood, why scars trailed up her back instead of smooth skin.

She slid the dry tunic on and then shimmied out of her trousers, eventually turning to face Ander, collecting the wet clothes to lay them by the fire. His face was stoic, all emotion drained as he stared back. His eyes shifted to a deeper silver, the blues and greens disappearing.

"Who did this to you?" A muscle in his jaw feathered. A crack of thunder shook the small cabin's walls.

The scars from the belt never healed. Wild slashes across her back were a permanent reminder of those weeks, matching the ones that shackled her wrists.

Ander stepped closer to her and Katrin's breath hitched. It was the way a wolf would circle their pack when an enemy was approaching, warding off all fear and evil. "It was a long time ago. I never really talked about it with anyone. If I'm being honest, I'm too ashamed," she said, hands shaking.

Rough hands clutched hers as he bent down to her eye level. It was wildly inappropriate for a farmer to be holding a princess like this, especially unprovoked, but, strangely, it put her at ease. "No one should ever feel shame over the pain others inflict on them." Warmth began to return to his eyes, his jaw softening. "The person who did this—" he traced a thumb over her wrist, "and this—" moving his other hand over the scars on her back, "they were small. They needed to see pain in others to ease their own. That is never acceptable. Never the answer."

A guttural whimper threatened to leave her throat, but she shoved it back, instead allowing only a tear to trail down her cheek. Ander reached up, cupping her cheek with his palm. "Don't cry, Princess." His brows furrowed. "The ones who cause us the most pain are rarely ever worth our tears."

Katrin was not sure if it was the fact that he was a stranger, that she would probably never see Ander again, or that the pain inside was growing from a small seed to a full grown monster, but she sat down and told him everything.

He sat next to her, eyes locked, absorbing every word she said with compassion and empathy. When she was done, the smallest amount of weight was lifted from her chest, because maybe if she was able to tell this farmer, eventually she would be able to tell Kohl.

The day drifted by well into the afternoon before the storms eventually stopped. The clouds parted, but left the cooler air in their place. When Katrin stepped back outside, it felt like a crisp autumn day, too cool for her light gauzy running shirt she had changed back into. She turned to Ander who led her over to a small stable behind the cabin where he offered her a horse to ride back.

"Do you mind if I take this?" Katrin peered over at the counter she just placed the tunic on. "I'm afraid if I ride back in just my sleeveless shirt I might catch a cold. I'll return it promptly, of course." She would not. Would most likely never venture this far into the mountains again. Their interactions would return to the half smile and passing wave.

Ander chuckled, "It would be my honor, Princess."

"The horse, how will you get him back?" She petted the side of the steed's neck.

"I'll find a way. Don't worry about that," Ander replied.

"Thank you, truly, for all the kindness you have given me." Katrin smiled at the farmer's son before turning the horse and heading back to the castle. As she gripped the reins, she noticed a small design woven into the cuff of the tunic, a matching one embossed on the horse's bridle. A sea serpent on top of two crossed swords. Her mind reeled. Something about it seemed so familiar and yet she could not place it. It was not a banner of the isles, she knew that, but she'd seen it before. Her fingers traced the marking, wondering why he had such curious items.

Chapter Eleven

Ember

When her sister arrived back at the castle gates, Ember was waiting, wringing her hands together, trying not to pick away at her fingernails—or worse, bite them. Ajax was behind her, mounted on his horse dressed in full fighting leathers.

She ran to his room the second she overheard the servants say Kohl arrived back alone and injured. Ember found Ajax there, hunched over his table sorting through letters his spies sent back on the sightings of King Nikolaos or his soldiers. The muscles in his back showed through the thin white short sleeve shirt he wore, clinging to every ripple and curvature of his upper body. A glimmer of sweat stained his arms and shone across his brow, his warm brown eyes weary as he scanned the notes.

For a second, she forgot why she went to his room, until he cracked a joke about her panting because of him not because she sprinted from inside the castle all the way to the barracks.

She begged him to hurry, to rally the soldiers to go hunt for her sister, but he calmed her. Explained that this kind of alarm a day before the Acknowledgement was not the best way to handle the situation and that he would personally go out and search for Katrin. That it was his duty as commander, he promised her that he would protect her sister at all costs.

He quickly donned his fighting leathers and slipped out to the castle to get information on what happened to Kohl, where they were before he was injured, and why Katrin was not there after. By the time he returned and grabbed his horse, the eldest princess was barreling in toward the gate.

"Where have you been!" Ember screamed as Katrin came striding in on a horse she did not recognize. She felt guilty about the harsh tone, probably the only time she did, but her sister yet again had gone missing.

With everything Ember overheard when Kohl and Ajax were speaking, she could not help but think something bad had happened. Something she could not prevent. Not that Ember could have done much.

As the fear flashed in her eyes, she realized how much she should have listened to everyone who pushed her to train earlier. She was so unprepared for what was going to happen in the coming week that she went to the commander. *She* was supposed to be the one people looked to, not him, even if she was grateful for his help in the matter.

"I was in the mountains with Kohl..." Katrin's voice trailed off. Her sister stopped the mysterious horse in front of them and dismounted, a tremor running through her hands.

"Kohl returned *hours* ago, Katrin, and with a stab wound from a Nexian spy at that, and you weren't with him. We thought something happened to you!" Katrin's brows scrunched, her head tilting to the side, swallowing down a loud gulp.

Katrin walked up to her sister and whispered, "It wasn't a Nexian spy, Ember. It was me." Ember gasped looking back over at Ajax who stood there acting like he did not overhear a thing. He might be a gods-damned pain, but he was loyal to their family, to the Grechi, and was told to have the utmost discretion with the events of today. She trusted that he would keep this secret as well.

"What do you mean, *it was you*?" Ember grabbed her sister's hand, dragging her behind one of the cypress trees that lined the walkway to the castle doors.

"I stabbed Kohl," Katrin's voice cracked, "I didn't mean to, I just—I don't know, it was like I wasn't myself—and then I ran off. I got stuck in the storm."

Ember took a step toward her sister. "There was no storm, Katrin. The skies have been clear all day."

"That's...that's impossible. Maybe it was just by the mountains, but I assure you it was pouring, thunder and lightning and all." Katrin shook. Ember thought it was best to go along with her sister. Katrin's face was worn, her eyes purple and puffy, lips chapped. She was wearing some strange blue tunic, her hair matted down on the side like she was pushed into a lake.

The sun was low at this time of day, but the end of summer heat still raged, and yet her sister stood before her with chills shivering down her whole body.

"Maybe...maybe you're right," Ember whispered.

She could still see the blood clotted on Katrin's dagger from where she stabbed Kohl's shoulder. Ember could not believe it. Her sister shoved a long bronze dagger through her betrothed's shoulder. *Kohl*, who would not hurt Katrin if his life depended on it.

She read about these things happening to victims of the kind of trauma Katrin went through. Researched for the years after her sister was taken, Kohl brought journals and books from the Morentian Library to try to find a way to get Katrin back to who she used to be. Read that sometimes, survivors would have flashbacks, terrors that seemed so real they could not tell the difference between what was happening in front of them and the past. Ember knew about the nightmares—but this—this was something else entirely.

"You should see Kohl, the healers say he will heal, that it didn't hit anything fatal."

"Where is he?" her sister asked, hands still trembling, eyes glassy.

"In his suite. They gave him a tonic of his father's to settle his nerves while they stitched his wound. Apparently it is a concoction from the spices of Votios that causes a numbness in your body. Ajax went to see him earlier to find out what happened and just as they began talking, King Athanas sent him away, he was fuming."

"Thank you—" Katrin's lips went tight. "Did he tell you it was Nexos? Or did you just guess that with the threats our spies have seen? You think

I don't know what is going on around me, but as the future queen I hear more than I let on."

Ember looked at her sister. Katrin's face was stoic, unmoving, but the tone of her voice, the way she clenched her fists, trying to settle them—that was pure terror.

"His father told us. I assume he heard it from Kohl. He was probably just trying to protect you. If the King knew you were the one to injure his son, accident or not, there would be trouble."

"Yes." Katrin's voice was distant. "Protecting me." That look on her sister had not been present for nearly five years—a look of defeat, a look of regret—as she walked away without another word.

\

Chapter Twelve

Katrin

Labored breathing came from the crack in Kohl's door. Katrin stood in front of it, unable to push it open just yet. Could she explain what happened in the olive groves? Explain everything like she just did with Ander?

There were no other noises or voices coming from inside. Kohl was alone. That was good. No peering eyes or lingering ears trying to figure out why the future consort was bloodied and healing after a routine run across the isle. At least no more people than Ember already mentioned knew.

She knocked, realizing that probably made things more awkward, more formal, then they needed to be. Yet, she couldn't bring herself to waltz in, not with the fear that he wouldn't understand. At least not fully. The fear that he would see her as damaged and unlovable. *Even after the gods take us*, she needed to breathe, remember those words, the pact they made and the love he always showered upon her. Not the strange darkness in his eyes as he pinned her against that tree earlier, refusing to stop even when she begged him.

Katrin opened the door peering in. Kohl was lying on his chaise in just the worn running shorts he wore earlier, a cold compress held to the wound that was stitched up by the healers. His eyes drifted toward her, worn and defeated, glazed over slightly from the tonic that numbed his pain, numbed his mind.

"Katrin..." his voice was raw, rough.

"Kohl, I am so sorry!" She rushed to his side, grabbing his other hand in hers. "I...I...I can't explain what happened. Are you alright? Ember said the wound would heal fine. Oh gods, Kohl," her eyes welled with tears, "I am just so sorry."

He scanned her up and down. "What are you *wearing?*" His eyes narrowed on the navy tunic, the embroidery stitched on the cuff. "That is the marking of a pirate!" His voice rose sharply, gripping her wrist with his uninjured hand and pointing at the marking on her cuff.

"What are you talking about, Kohl? It's the tonic, you must still be weary. Why would I be in a pirate's shirt?" Her brows furrowed in, breath picking up pace ever so slightly. A pirate? Ander was a farmer, not some notorious seafarer.

"That marking, that shirt, where did you get it?" He began to sit up. Katrin backed up two paces away from the chaise.

"I got this from a farmer's cabin. I was caught in the storm and my clothes were soaked through. I came across an empty cabin and took shelter while the storm passed. There were some old clothes lying about so I changed out of mine to stay warm." At this point he was pushing off the chaise stumbling a bit as he rose.

Katrin's hands begin to tremble, inching toward her dagger. The dagger that was already soaked in Kohl's blood. It was a hallucination, she was hallucinating that gleam in his eyes, the fury in the way his lips rose showing off his teeth.

"You're *lying,*" Kohl seethed.

"I am not lying!" But she was. She had the full intention of explaining everything to him when she arrived back. Well as much as she could stomach. She wasn't sure if she was ready to tell him about the scars on her back. How for weeks that man beat her bloody, leaving her to fester in her own filth. How it turned him on to see her scream in pain. But parts of it, parts of the torment she realized she wanted to share. It was freeing to speak the words out loud rather than keep bottling them down, allowing them to eat at her from the inside out. But this anger, how could she begin to explain?

He understood the markings on her wrists, understood the fear of being shoved into a small cabin, the fear of drowning on the seas when she escaped. But this? This was the one thing he wanted from her, the one thing she wanted to give to him first, but sadly she could not.

"There was a storm, I took shelter, I stole dry clothes. We shouldn't be talking about me right now, you're the one injured. You're the one *I* injured. Kohl, I am so sorry." Trying to change the subject back didn't seem to help as Kohl appeared to enter some sort of fugue state.

"Why are you lying, Katrin?" Kohl stalked toward her grabbing her wrist with a stiff grip.

"Like I said before, I am not lying!" Katrin's eyes began to swirl with the blinding fire of a newly born star. She needed to keep calm before one of them got hurt. Again.

"You are! You didn't tell me about your nightmares, you won't tell me where you went after you ran off today and why you returned in another man's clothes. You even refuse to tell me why you stuck a dagger in my arm! A dagger, Katrin! *My* dagger."

"I told you I don't know why I did it. It was like...it was like I entered some sort of trance and I thought you were attacking me." Her voice began to tremble. She could not admit why she really stabbed him. The triggering words he spoke to her.

"Attacking you, Katrin! That is the most absurd thing I have ever heard. Name one time when you have ever thought I would harm you." *Now*, she wanted to say. There was never such darkness in his eyes. Venom in his words.

"I didn't...I didn't know..." Katrin took a long breath in, trying to prevent the tears welling in her eyes from spilling down her face. "I didn't think it was you. In the moment you were someone else."

"You thought I was someone else? We were being intimate *and you thought I was someone else!* Explain that to me, Katrin. Did you think it was that man, the owner of the navy tunic." She was dumbfounded by the accusation. That he could really believe after everything that she attacked him on purpose to go have an affair with another secret man was beyond her imagination.

"I can't explain!" Now the tears started flowing openly. "I can't, Kohl. I don't know what else I can say. You have to believe me," her voice cracked as it left her trembling lips. She never lied to him before. Omitted things from the past, yes, but never truly lied. Yet now that was all she could do. To protect him. To protect herself.

"Maybe there isn't anything you can say, but maybe there's something you could *do*." Katrin tried to take a step back from Kohl but the only place back was the bed.

"What?" Her question was the softest of whispers. A hoarse breath of air more than a word.

"I said, maybe there is something you could do. To show me you're sorry, to show me you love me." Kohl inched farther toward her again, until there was no place to go, no possible escape. "It almost happened the other night, it almost happened before you *stabbed me*. You seemed more than willing to give yourself up then. Why not now?"

"Kohl...I didn't...Kohl, please." Katrin could see the glassiness in his eyes was still there. Like he didn't really know what he was saying, what he was asking her to do. A piercing pain hit in the pit of her stomach. She might be sick. It was the injury, the tonic, that made him act this way. This wasn't *her* Kohl. Her Kohl would have understood. Would have let her take care of him, not lash out with accusations and foul words. Not try to make her do *that*.

"Even after the gods take us, isn't that what we always say? I love you, Katrin. Don't you love me?" He grazed his lips up her neck trailing a warm breath to her ear. Where she used to shiver in anticipation, she did so now in fear.

Katrin's hands began to shake. "Of course I do." But at that moment she wasn't sure she meant the words. He needed to slide out of this state, back to the Kohl she knew. Back to the Kohl she trusted. Unless this was who he really was. Unless he masked his true self all these years.

"Then show me." Kohl began to unlace his trousers and push up the hem of Katrin's tunic. "Show me that you love me. Show me that you can perform the duties of a wife."

"Kohl..." She peered into his eyes, trying to pull the anger out, trying to show him the fear that she was feeling. The words didn't even sound like him. They sounded like his father. What he said at the banquet.

"Please, Katrin..." A single tear laced down his darkened cheek.

All these months, all these years, *he* was the one who protected her, who took care of her, and pieced her back into the strong woman who was set to rule this kingdom. Was it really his fault if he triggered her with words she never told him haunted her? Was it his fault that he then got angry when she stabbed him? She was still sick over the thought. What was one night? One night where she pretended. One night where she could piece him back together, not the other way around.

"Ok." She nodded. "Ok, Kohl."

He thrust his lips toward hers in a messy and violent kiss. Shoving her back on the bed, lifting the hem of her shirt up and slipping her pants down to her ankles so he could slide himself in.

Then he entered her again and again as she tried to lay as still as possible. Even though Katrin knew the person above her was Kohl, when she dared to look at his face all she could see was the man with red eyes. His evil glare, his toothy smile, his sweaty palms pinning her down so she couldn't move. *"Do you like that, Princess?"* The words she heard over and over again in her mind.

She wished it would be over fast, almost feeling guilty for thinking that. Like Kohl said, it was her duty once she was his wife, so why not try to get over her fear now? She always stopped before it got this far, always came up with an excuse. It wasn't like she didn't *want* to be fully intimate with him, it was just that she wasn't ready. Not healed enough in herself to give that part away again. She always expected him to be the one she'd be ready for. She almost was until the nightmares started again. But with it so fresh in her mind, intimacy of that kind seemed dirty and vile and wrong.

She didn't expect him to be so rough with her the first time. There was no build up, no sweet whispers in her ear. It was as if the emotion from their argument overpowered Kohl's usual romantic demeanor even after she consented. Like he was fueled by anger and not by love. Like the tonic stripped all his good qualities and emotions away. Numbed his wound and his heart.

Minutes went by before he finished and rolled off her. Placing one now gentle kiss on her cheek.

A light rap came from the other side of the bedroom door. Usually she was annoyed by Ajax's frequent interruptions, but this time she was glad. All she wanted was to be alone. To not see the conquest in Kohl's eyes. To not let him see the shame and sadness in hers.

"Excuse me, Prince Kohl, but your father wishes to speak with you. He says it's an urgent matter." Ajax knew better than to enter the room of the prince, so he waited on the other side of the door.

"I'll be back soon, my lovely Aikaterine." Kohl brushed her hair back from her face, leaving a kiss atop her head. Katrin could feel the dizziness hit, the metallic taste forming in her mouth. Regret, shame, nausea, loss—all her emotions blurred into one. She closed her eyes and nodded, trying to force a smile on her weary face. Katrin couldn't help but hope he would not return at all.

CHAPTER THIRTEEN

KOHL

Kohl entered the small study in between the guest wing where his father was staying and where his room lay near Katrin's wing. King Athanas lit small candles around the room giving it an eerie glow. His father's face was in the shadows, the chair he sat in turned away from the door. Papers were strewn about the desk in front of him, a map of the continents lay next to them. Tiny wooden ships were staged across the isles. Kohl's eyes widened, a *war map*.

"I was beginning to wonder if you were going to grace me with your presence at all. We need to discuss this," his father said, pointing at the papers in front of him.

"When you beckon in the middle of the night, you shouldn't expect me to come running," Kohl seethed. Right now all he wanted was to be back in bed with his future wife, but instead he dealt with whatever *this* was. And his head, how it was pounding from that stupid tonic. Yes, it dulled his pain in his shoulder, but it made his vision blurry, his mind cloudy. His eyes clenched shut as he tried to push out the incessant throbbing, only made worse by his father's dry tone.

"You will watch your tone when speaking to me, my boy. Remember why you are even here in the first place." Kohl did remember and he was grateful to his father to some degree, but this place was going to be his, not King Athanas's kingdom.

"Sorry, Father." One day, one day soon, Kohl would no longer feel like he was wrapped around his father's finger.

"There is much to discuss, Kohl. About you, about Katrin, about the isles." He shuffled through the papers again, looking for one in particular. "The Acknowledgement is set to take place, and there will be representatives from all the surrounding isles. Am I correct in assuming you can keep them in line? That things will go smoothly?"

Kohl looked at his father with a curious expression as he paced back and forth in front of the fire. "Are you to believe that it shouldn't, Father?"

"I believe Nexos is poised to strike and this would be the best opportunity for them to do so with no consequences." A flicker of anger flashed through the King's eyes. "If that happens, I need you to be prepared for the Wrecking."

Kohl spun around from in front of the fireplace. *The Wrecking*. It would not get to that. No one would challenge Katrin's succession to the throne. And even if they did, no one could beat her. At this point, even Kohl found it difficult to keep up with her when they would spar.

"Katrin is perfectly capable of fighting in the Wrecking, Father. I would not need to volunteer for it."

"Be that as it may, I want you prepared. We will discuss more at another hour." The king's word was always final. But not now. Not when he knew more than he was letting on.

"You will tell me more *now*." Kohl's voice echoed in the room. He was getting to the edge of patience he had for his father's secrets.

"Quiet, my boy." King Athanas's eyes washed over with ebony, the whites no longer visible in the dark study. Kohl knew that look. Knew what it meant. Knew what his father would do if he questioned him again. The prince's head started throbbing once more.

Chapter Fourteen

Katrin

Her breaths were ragged and forced, chest constricting every time she inhaled. Katrin laid awake for a time after Kohl went to meet with his father, unable to move from the spot he left her in. The sheets were stained with sweat, and tears, and regret for what she let him do. What she let herself do.

Swollen eyes from the silent tears that poured down her face during the time they were *intimate*, if you could even call it that, still burned. Kohl seemed to think those tears were ones of joy, of beginning, of love—Katrin did not know what love was anymore.

She would have to move eventually, she could not still be in this bed when Kohl returned. Katrin needed time to process what happened, what it meant for the future—*their* future.

The Acknowledgment was quickly approaching. She needed to focus on that. Her speech, what she would say to her people, to the people of the other isles that relied on her to lead. But most of all, right now Katrin knew she needed her sister. Needed her advice. Needed to confide in someone else. She could not walk back to that cabin in the mountains. Speak with the farmer's son. No, that was what caused this in the first place.

She sat up and walked over to the wardrobe in the corner. Kohl kept some of Katrin's more formal gowns in his room for the seamstresses to

---

match his jackets and breeches to. She pulled one of the more simple ones out, shimmying the gown back down until it covered everything to the floor, hiding the evidence of what transpired in this room.

The night air was still warm, yet she felt nothing but chills as she left Kohl's chamber and began the walk down the hall to Ember's wing. Servants bustled through the halls of the castle, no doubt finalizing preparations for the Acknowledgement.

As she walked closer to the corridor that led to her sister, Katrin could hear angry voices rise from inside one of the smaller studies. She inched near the door, which was open just enough for her to see the two darkened figures. One was sitting in her father's old velvet lounge chair, his hand gripping the wooden armrest. The other leaned against the desk on the opposite side of the room, his face shielded by shadows. Katrin squinted her eyes at the dimly lit room as the two men conversed.

"Quiet, my boy." She heard the man in the chair say. A pit began to form in her stomach. She only knew one man with a voice so silencing—King Athanas. Meaning the man in the shadows was Kohl.

He stepped forward into the light. "I will quiet myself down if you tell me the *real* reason for all of this." His eyes now glinted in the firelight, but they were no longer the warm ebony Katrin recognized. They were that darkened shade she saw earlier that evening, void of all emotion except anger.

"I will explain myself tomorrow, for now you just have to trust that I have the best interests of this kingdom—of all the isles—in mind. Now return to your bride, perhaps offer her a glass of wine to calm her nerves."

"Father, please..." Kohl tried to get more than the two words out before he was cut off.

"You will be wise to remember not to question the judgment of *your* king, Kohl."

"Yes, Father." Kohl began to move closer to the door before stopping to whisper something to his father that Katrin could not make out. A fresh chill swept down the corridor she was in, a strange fog creeping in through the windows from outside. She needed to get to Ember's room before someone caught her out at this hour.

Katrin quietly inched back, hoping not to alert the men that she was listening from outside the study before knocking into something hard behind her. She tried to let out a scream, but was silenced as a dark piece of cloth covered her nose and mouth and Katrin drifted into a black haze.

Sunlight began to creep in through the windows, glistening against Katrin's face. Her eyes were still heavy from the night before. She curled up to her side drawing the covers over her face, hoping to stay asleep for even a few moments longer. As she took a deep, steadying breath before facing the sun's bright rays, she recognized a familiar scent in the room. Olive oil, lemon, salt.

Katrin's eyes shot open as she remembered the events of last night, walking through the hall to see Ember, overhearing Kohl and King Athanas arguing, someone coming up behind her, that smell, that same smell, then nothing but darkness.

A noise caused her to stiffen. The familiar rocking of the ship against the waves caused goosebumps all over her body.

Her eyes narrowed and she reached down to her thigh. Her thin bronze dagger was still strapped around her leg, the silk gown still wrapped around her body. Whoever took her last night would regret not checking her for weapons.

Katrin slowly and quietly gripped her hand around its hilt as she shifted her gaze toward the creaking that was coming from the corner of the cabin. There, sitting in a wooden chair, dirty boots resting on the footboard of the bed she lay in, was a tall muscular man in dark leather breeches and a flowing white linen shirt. Her gaze met the man's. She knew that obsidian colored hair, those eyes swirling with the colors of the sea they now sailed over. Ander's eyes sparkled, the corner of his lip rising in a deadly grin.

"*Kaliméra*, Aikaterine, welcome to *The Nostos*."

PART TWO

η μέση
(The Middle)

Chapter Fifteen

Katrin

Amber flecks turned white in fiery rage as Katrin's eyes went wide. *Ander.* Her mind began to race with all the possibilities of why she was on this ship. Was it Nexos? Was it another isle that wanted to stake claim to Alentus? Was it one of the continents trying to invade and colonize their people? Ander was not a farmer's son.

A sour taste stirred in her throat. He knew *everything.* She laid herself bare to him that day in the mountains. A fool. He must have been laughing to himself as she described all the ways they broke her the last time. Gaining ideas on what she could and could not survive. What she would give up to make it home alive. That for which she would die. The first time she shared that piece of her soul with someone she trusted and it was all a lie—in vain, to an invisible enemy hiding in the shadows.

Creaking wood echoed back and forth, Ander leaned back in the wooden chair watching her. A stupid grin curved from ear to ear flashing those shiny white teeth. Katrin would have to play this carefully, hide the dagger Ander had not found on her, work her way slowly toward him, distract him with confusion or curiosity like a cat stalking its prey.

With each light step she took toward the man, she reminded herself she could not kill him yet. Not until she figured out the lay of the ship, how many men made up the crew, where they made port. Yes—she would not kill him—but a little blood wouldn't hurt.

"You have a good night's sleep, Aikaterine? I always find the crashing of waves to be a soothing melody." Ander's voice was a sweet poison sliding from his mouth like freshly made olive oil. It almost halted Katrin in place. Almost.

For just a moment she felt calmed by it, at peace, like that day in the mountains when she first followed him home. The way his eyes sparkled slightly, and crinkled at the corner when she spoke. But now he'd taken her, from her home, from her people. The audacity to speak to her with such lightness to his words. Like they were friends. Like they *knew* each other.

Katrin hacked a small laugh. "Oh do you? I generally prefer to be sleeping on solid ground. In my own bed. Not locked away on some, dare I say, pirate's ship."

The sound that left his mouth this time was again a shock to Katrin's system. His laughter filled the entire cabin with a warm and fair-weathered melody. "I don't know—you looked pretty at peace to me. I could have sworn you were even drooling."

Instinctively Katrin brushed the corner of her mouth with her free hand. It was dry. Red began to seep across her cheeks. Insufferable. This man was utterly insufferable.

Her face went numb, stripping all emotion from her eyes, her lips, her cheeks, no longer allowing them to look flushed. The same look her father was known to give those who underestimated the power of the God of Death.

"I would not test me, *Ander*, if that even is your name." She stalked closer to him, the glimmering hatred building behind her eyes. He looked nervous, that is, until he began to laugh again. Until his eyes narrowed and darkened and his grin turned pure feral.

"I do not impersonate other's names, unlike some people. But I am curious—what would you do, Aikaterine? If I *tested* you?" Sultry words replaced her threatening ones. "Come at me with that dagger of yours?"

Inches from where he sat, Katrin came to a deafening halt. His brow arched over those sea-swept eyes, as he picked a piece of dust off his shirt. "What? You think I don't know what hides behind your back? That when I brought you aboard this ship, I did not see it strapped at the top of your thigh?"

Her lungs clenched at the thought of him seeing any part of her bare again, especially that high up her leg.

"I'll admit, it is quite adorable seeing you reach for it. I like a girl who can hold her own." Ander looked around the room, flipping some strange pendant she could not make out between his fingers. "Where exactly do you think you could scurry off to aboard my ship?"

Katrin's fiery white glare held his gaze firm, the corner of her upper lip twitching. Her control was slipping, burying further down into the abyss of her soul. "I am not a rat."

"Perhaps. Fine then, Aikaterine, give it your best shot." He held his hands up, beckoning her to attack him.

Men always seemed to underestimate her. Yes, he was tall, towering at least eight inches above her. And yes, she could see his muscles through that thin linen shirt, ones she didn't even know existed. But Katrin had fought many men his size before and won.

That was one piece of her Ander did not know. Vigorous training every morning. Even when rain ripped through Alentus, or the summer's heat proved too much for the strongest of the Spartanis soldiers. She would be there, in the training ring, linens wrapped around her hands to go punch for punch with whomever dared to challenge her.

Pirates were cocky people, and Ander proved to be at the top of that list.

Katrin planted her feet, grinding them back and forth into the wooden slats below until she felt stable, a gentle bend at her knees. Then she lunged, knocking him back out of the chair and them both to the ground.

Deadly bronze held firm to Ander's throat, as Katrin clenched her jaw, the sweat on her temple threatening to drop to his skin below. With a little more pressure she could draw blood. Her breathing heightened, and she bared her teeth at the grinning man beneath her. "Is that good enough for you, Ander?"

Crimson red, only a single drop, swelled by the tip of her dagger. Sweat built farther across her forehead and brows, down the silk covering her back. Air around her thinned, and Katrin couldn't seem to catch her breath. The room became unbearably hot, skin burning with every twitch of her muscles.

Ander's tongue traced his bottom lip, eyes flashing a deep gray for only a moment before turning back to their unbearable tide swept tone. "If you wanted an excuse to straddle me, you could have just asked."

Sharp chills replaced every bit of heat in her veins. "Pig!" Katrin pushed off him, releasing the dagger from his throat.

Propping himself up on his elbows, Ander's lip twitched up. "I do love the view from beneath you."

Katrin's face heated once again. She could not help feeling a small bit of desire deep in her core. The beautiful man sprawled in front of her in his tight breeches showing off the exact size of him, *all of him*. The flowing shirt unbuttoned enough to see little wisps of hair along his chiseled chest. The golden olive skin that must fade to pale underneath his belt line.

Her eyes flared. Why was she thinking these things? Disgusting. He was disgusting. A liar and a thief and her captor. Ander gave her a knowing glance and she could have sworn she heard a faint laugh in the recesses of her mind.

"Why are you looking at me like that?" she spat.

"I was about to ask you the very same question."

Sheathing her dagger, Katrin took another step back.

It would not aid her in the rest of today's battle. She needed to figure out why she was here. What he wanted with her. This time she would be smart about her escape. This time no one would touch her or they would get a slice across their throat. Her hand still hovered over the hilt. They would have to pry the dagger from her cold dead hands.

Her mind reeled again, taking in the surroundings, the differences between this cabin and the one she was locked in before. The warmth in the craftsmanship of the chairs and the bed, beautiful branches painted on the side of them. A small desk sat in the corner, one that reminded her of her mother's, carved on one side with a mountain and wolves and the moon, the other decorated with a sea serpent at an entrance to a cove.

A velvet chaise sat in the middle of the cabin between two chairs and a low table, steaming cups of an incredible smelling spiced drink and bread and fruits spread out on top of it. Her eyes narrowed. *So poison it would be. Just like the first time. A way to drug her into a dreamless sleep.*

"Oh, what? Are my quarters not sufficient enough for a *future* queen?" Ander purred.

"Your quarters?" Katrin choked on her own words.

"Well, I couldn't stick you with the crew now, could I?"

Katrin recoiled, almost knocking over another chair. The hairs on her arms rose, her breath catching deep in her throat.

Ander leaned forward like he might reach out a hand, but then stopped. "I didn't mean it like that. No one would harm you. Trust me, you would give those men quite the competition. Leighton—" he was cut off by her sharp tongue.

"Trust you! I'm supposed to trust *you*. The man who convinced me to tell him my darkest secrets and then used those secrets and fears to kidnap me!"

"First of all, Aikaterine, I convinced you of nothing. You told me of your own free will. And second, I did not kidnap you." His words were as cold as the depths of the sea beneath them.

"Oh really, and what would you call this?" She waved her hand around his quarters. *What an insolent, narcissistic man.*

Ander stood up, placing his hands in his pockets and shrugged. "Saving you."

Katrin rolled her eyes. Livid, he was making her absolutely livid with his casual demeanor and avoidance of her actual questions.

"The only person I need saving from is *you*!"

He smirked, "I guess we will see, Starling."

Katrin snapped her eyes back to him.

"What did you call me?" Her voice went hoarse, the very air in her lungs disappeared.

"You are free to roam about the ship as you please. Just don't fall overboard, that would be very inconvenient for me to have to rescue you yet again. You'll find clothes in the dresser—don't worry, this time they are women's clothes—and the food and tea are yours to have. And before you ask, no, they are not poisoned." With that, he slipped out of the room.

Shock was plastered across Katrin's face.

Starling.

For several moments, Katrin could not move, could not shake the feeling that she'd heard that name before. Almost like it was a whisper that came to her in a dream, floating along the shores and swirling up through her window on the winds. *Starling, Starling, Starling.* A lost memory, but she could not place it.

Katrin walked over to the dresser in the corner, running her hands along the worn driftwood. Her breath caught, as if a little piece of home was there with her. That same pale gray color that filled her chambers at the castle, the same smooth lines and knots that were carved out from the sea. She opened one of the drawers, pulling out a pair of tight black cotton pants and a gauzy blue top. They looked slightly big for her, but they would be alright for now. A temporary solution to her lack of anything but a dirty gown.

Her eyes flicked around the room, searching. She could really use a bath, or just some soap and water to wash the scent of last night off her. Clean the sweat and shame that still lingered in places hidden by her dress.

A small archway sat on the other side of the chaise and table. It led to a hallway, two doors lining the side. She could hear the thumping above her, the crew must have been up and was preparing the ship to move. She could tell they were anchored for now. Spent enough time below the deck to understand what the different sounds of the waves smacking against the side meant, the graceful way the ship swayed when it was anchored in a calm cove or at port.

She cracked open the first door just slightly enough to peer in. Katrin's eyes widened as this one appeared to house what looked like a storage room. Another door lay on the other side of the room, no doubt leading to the main corridor of the ship. A large dark wooden table sat in the middle, covered in charts and small wooden figurines, each one a depiction of the banners of the isles, although she did not dare to move close enough to see which ones were displayed. The walls were plastered in weaponry—spears, daggers, long-swords, axes. The most intriguing weapon shimmered in the center of the wall. A single golden trident. Katrin never saw such a magnificent—yet deadly—work of craftsmanship in her life. At least she would know where to sneak more weapons from if she needed them.

Katrin moved on to the second door. Sweet relief filled her as she slowly opened it and took in a large bronze tub already bubbling with steaming hot water, plush towels folded next to it. An old, faded mirror outlined in gold sat above a small table with what looked like all sorts of lotions and oils. She shut the door behind her, bringing down the latch she could only hope was a lock, and breathed.

It was her first real breath since she woke and realized where she was. Deep and filling, stilling her mind and her soul. Katrin began to unlace her dress, shimmying it off and kicking it to the side. She unstrapped the leather sheath from her thigh and laid her dagger on the table to the side. Then she stepped one foot into the bath.

The heat caused tiny bumps to travel along her skin, but they quickly faded. She stepped fully into the bath, sinking her whole body straight under. Her mind went quiet, all lingering thoughts of shame and disgrace and torture leaving with each moment that passed.

When she surfaced she scanned around for something to wash herself with. Sitting next to the tub were several bottles of soap, each one a different color. She reached for the closest, opening the bottle. The scent washed over her, one of lilies and mint. It was intoxicating and relaxing. Exactly what she would need to focus herself for what was to come.

Katrin poured the soap into her hands, lathering first her body, then her hair before dipping under the water to rinse it out. She could feel the stench of regret leave her as the bubbles rinsed away. The calming scent tickled her nose once more.

She sat in the water for only a few moments longer, not wanting her fingers to shrivel. Then Katrin stepped out, wrapping herself in one of those luxurious towels in the room, its soft fibers tickling her skin.

A small table sat in the corner with a mirror. Katrin sat down, using a comb she found to detangle her hair before pinning it back into several braids.

Slipping a shirt and the cotton pants on, Katrin looped her dagger sheath around her waist to help hold the pants up. She pulled up stockings and slid on the leather boots she wore last night. Katrin took another deep breath in, looking into the mirror, attempting to center herself. All that stared back was a drawn and angular face, purplish hues rimming her eyes.

It would get better, it would have to. She would come up with a plan. Katrin would make it home.

The ship began to lean more to one side as Katrin stepped into the main corridor of the ship. It took her a moment to gain her balance, to remember how to brace her legs as she moved about the rocking ship. The long hall in front of the bedroom led from the stern where there appeared to be a set of stairs to the main deck. She walked slowly toward the stairs, taking in her surroundings, how many rooms there were, if there were grates in the floor that lead to more storage, or worse, a brig.

When she reached the end of the corridor, the light from the deck shone through so bright she squinted until her eyes adjusted. It was much different than the soft light of the lanterns below. Once Katrin fully opened her eyes she could see the movement of the main deck. Men of all sorts hurried around, tending to the sails, and cleaning the wooden planks that made up the floor.

Three large sails filled with a warm summer breeze, pushing them farther into the open seas. She breathed in the salty air, the same smell that always calmed her back home.

This was where her planning would begin.

She started to take count of how many crew members were currently working on deck, knowing that many were probably still in their shared quarters below. Katrin reached about forty when she felt the chill of someone standing behind her.

"You must be our new guest," a deep voice said.

Katrin whipped her head around, landing her gaze on a broad man. He was slightly taller than Ander with deep chocolate skin and short black hair. His eyes were a startling color, matching the emerald gem that held his gold plated armor to his shoulders.

Under the armor shone a blue tunic, similar to the one she wore that afternoon in the mountains, but made of a much finer material. A long sword was strapped to his back.

This man looked like he could pick her up and chuck her off the ship with one arm; honestly, he looked as though he could even chuck Ajax off the ship. Yet his features were soft, a lightness resonating off him as he spoke.

"My name is Leighton," he said, bowing slightly at the waist, "I am the nauarch of the ship. Ander's second."

Katrin's brows furrowed. He also knew the *Ellinikā Glóssa*.

"Don't look so frightened, Princess. I am not going to hurt you." He went to touch Katrin's arm, but she swatted his palm away.

"I am not *frightened* of you, sir," she spat back. But she was frightened. If only a little. A pirate ship filled with burly men, weapons strapped firmly to all limbs.

"Of course you aren't. The prince has told me how feisty you are," he chuckled.

"The *prince?*" Katrin raised an eyebrow. He certainly was narcissistic enough to be some foreign prince. But then why would he need her? Allyship with Nexos? Access to the trade routes?

"Yes, the prince. Our captain, Prince Alexander of the Lost Isles."

Katrin could not help but snort. "Prince of the Lost Isles? Well, he really is full of himself. Did he come up with that title all on his own?"

Leighton shifted his weight to one leg as his face lit up. "You know, I asked him that very same question years ago. He never gave me an answer."

Katrin smiled, then quickly the corners of her mouth turned down as she remembered why she was here.

"Are you looking for him? Ander?" he asked.

"No. He said I may roam the ship freely, so that is what I will do."

"Of course, Princess. Whatever you would like." He smiled again softly. "If there is anything you need, please, just ask. I will make sure it is taken care of."

Katrin was not sure why she asked this question. Whether it was the sincerity she could feel in his voice, or the pit in her stomach that would not go away until she learned.

She looked up at Leighton, a small mist forming in her eyes. "Why am I here? Why did he take me?"

Leighton's face tightened with something like pity or remorse or empathy. All things she did not want from this stranger right now.

"I am sorry, Princess, but that is not my story to tell."

Her breath caught as he lay a hand on her shoulder, thinking maybe she took it too far. Maybe she should not have asked someone else the question so soon. That he would grab her and decide to lock her back in that cabin. That she would relive the horrible weeks she spent upon that ship five years ago.

Instead, he let out a sigh and she could not help but believe a part of his words when spoke again. "Ander is a good man. You may not think that now, but you will. Everyone aboard this ship trusts him with their life. You can trust him with yours."

CHAPTER SIXTEEN

EMBER

Nausea swirled in Ember's stomach as she curled up in the bathing chambers. The Acknowledgement was approaching, and her sister just *stabbed* Kohl the day before.

She could not believe the words that came out of her sister's mouth as she mulled over what happened. Was still curious about the storm she claimed kept her trapped, the tunic that she stole from an abandoned cabin in the mountains.

Ember was worried for Katrin. Worried that these nightmares were messing with her mind even during the day.

This was different than before. She never experienced hallucinations. The nightmares, yes. Crippling anxiety to be on a ship or even near the water, yes. But illusions and twists of reality—that was new.

The sun had barely risen in the sky when Ember looked out her window. She knew she should have checked on her sister after she went to see Kohl last night. Knew that look in her eyes. Light snuffed out. Knew the darkness that Katrin battled day in and day out. Saw it years ago. Saw it when she thought her sister might wither away into nothing.

Ember eased herself up from the floor, washing away the violent hurl that left her stomach, wrapping a thin cotton robe she kept on a hook around her body, tying the sash tight. She knew her sister would be up by now; Katrin always rose with the sun, preparing herself for those morning runs through the mountains with Kohl.

She wondered if Katrin would go alone today, since he was likely still under the influence of the pain tonic. Maybe she would offer to go with her. Although Ember was not as trained as her sister, she could probably keep up with her for a mile or so. At least it would be something to keep Katrin's mind off of what she did, what she was going through.

The breeze crept in through the window, fluttering the gauzy curtains inward. If Ember was going to offer to run, she realized she better come prepared.

Ember walked over to her dresser in the corner of her bedchambers, opening the top drawer that held her lightest training gear. Ajax insisted she go down to the market and purchase everything ranging from soft, thin cotton shirts and shorts that clung close to her thighs, to thick leathers outfitted with bronze to dull a slash from a blade. She chose one of the thin cotton outfits, opting for the long-sleeve tunic instead of the sleeveless because of the light breeze off the shore, slipping them on over her undergarments.

The princess pulled a pair of leather boots from under her bed, lacing them up her calves, double knotting the bow like Ajax showed her so they did not come undone and cause her to trip.

She looked at herself in the mirror. At that new version of Ember that spurred into action the past few weeks. At the muscles forming in her once lithe arms and legs. At the determination and bravery lining her golden amber eyes.

She was proud of herself, the steps she was taking to become a better citizen of Alentus, a better Prytan for the Spartanis. She knew, once her sister saw how her training developed, that she would be proud of Ember too.

That was all she really wanted. For her sister—and her mother—not to look at her like the baby of the family, someone who needed to be coddled. Instead, she would show them that she had the strength and wherewithal to assert her rightful position as Prytan, carrying on their family's legacy.

Ember took a breath in, realizing she did have a long way to go, but this—this was quite a start.

Approaching her sister's door, Ember noticed Ajax speaking with some of the other guards down the hall. Looking at her, he ruffled his hand through his messy, cropped blonde hair, one eyebrow raised at her in a silent question.

Ember gave a soft smile back and began to turn toward her sister's door when she noticed him dismiss the other guards and start to jog over toward her.

"I thought we were skipping our training this morning because of the banquet? Although I would be lying if I said I wasn't impressed with your *eagerness*." Ember could feel the gaze of those warm brown eyes trail up her body, lingering on her heaving chest and pursed lips.

"I know we canceled our training, *Commander*, but I thought Katrin might need a running partner. You know…with everything that happened."

Ajax's expression softened at her. She knew he was just as worried about Katrin's state as she was. Maybe even more so since he knew of other terrors that may lie in the future.

"That is very kind of you. Is she awake yet? I can imagine her pacing about her chambers all night worrying about something like this. That is, if she wasn't with Kohl the entire time."

"I was just about to see." Ember knocked on the door, realizing Ajax was probably right. Knowing Katrin, she would have insisted on staying by Kohl's side until she made sure he was alright.

No sound came from within.

"Maybe she is with Kohl, then. Lucky you, you get another opportunity to skip a run. Why don't you go change and you can accompany me to the breakfast banquet. I was hoping to steal some of the good pastries before the emissaries from the other isles arrive."

The breakfast banquet. Another tradition that occurs before the Acknowledgement, when the heir apparent discusses their plans for the kingdom's future and how it will impact the surrounding isles. It also served as a place for the smaller isles to make offerings to not only the prospective ruler, but also to the gods for safe travels on the sea and prosperity over the coming years. It was not something to be missed. Dancing aside, it might even have a more lavish spread than the ball.

"I'll just knock one more time, just in case she didn't hear me."

Still nothing stirred inside Katrin's chambers. A sickening feeling settled low in Ember's gut, her intuition pulling her inside, telling her to open the door.

"Maybe I should just check inside, see if she is just asleep."

"Do you think something is wrong?" Ajax's brows furrowed and creased his forehead.

"I don't know, I just have this feeling. A tether of sorts, pulling at my mind."

"Ok, but I am going to stay with you."

Ember tried the door and saw it was indeed unlocked. Her sister never left her door unlocked unless the guards were stationed outside, and no guards lingered in front of her door. The living chambers were glowing with the early morning light, no lanterns were lit around the room. She began to step in when Ajax grabbed her arm. He shook his head, pointing at himself. She let him go inside first and she followed closely behind.

"Katrin?" Ember called with a weary voice.

No response. The door to the bedchamber was cracked open just slightly, Ajax peered in, his lips peeling out into a thin line.

"She's not there." He said, his voice low.

Ember let out a long breath, peeking around him. There was indeed no one in the room. Katrin's bed was still neatly made, no sign that someone slept there the night before.

"Like I said, she was probably just with Kohl. Making sure he was recovering."

"Yeah...you're right. I'll go check his chambers." Ember said, her voice trailing off.

"Take it from someone who has interrupted your sister and the prince many times—when they are together, it is best to leave them alone. Go change, come to the banquet and we can eat before everyone else arrives. I'm sure Katrin and Kohl will join us shortly."

Ajax put his hand gently on Ember's cheek. It was the closest to an endearing gesture he ever gave her. It made her breath catch and the hair on her arms raise as his eyes met hers.

"She's fine, Ember. I promise you that." She could tell he meant it. That he really believed she was alright, almost like he *knew*.

"Ok, I'll meet you in the courtyard then. Don't eat all the pastries before I get there." She smiled warily.

"Now that is something I cannot promise you." The corner of his lips twitched up as he ruffled her hair. "I'll see you soon, Drakos."

Ember rolled her eyes as Ajax walked off toward the courtyard, but that wary smile—now it grew.

All the dresses in Ember's wardrobe seemed too bold for the breakfast banquet, their lavish silks and glittering sashes meant for fancy balls and dancing, not gorging herself in sweets and fruits. She needed one that would not pinch her in the waist enough to make her pass out.

Flipping through the ones that were made for her more recently, she landed on a simple navy gossamer gown lined with a thin silk chemise. It was casual, but delicate, and would give in the right places if she decided to eat her weight in bread and pastries.

She switched out her leather boots for golden lace up sandals and combed out her hair from the braid she'd put it in earlier, her long blonde locks falling in waves halfway down her back.

A thin navy box lay on her dresser. She did not dare open it yet. Ember already knew what was inside. A simple golden crown, one she would wear to the Acknowledgement. Nothing like her sister's, which would be tall and spiked and decked with diamonds and topaz. This crown had no gems, only a single carved star in the center, its sides formed in the shape of lightning bolts.

The crown of the Prytan. One she would wear not only to the Acknowledgement, but everytime she would go into battle. One her uncle Machius wore until his death.

Her legacy.

She could only hope to make her uncle proud. To show her mother and her sister and her people what she was made of. That she could—and wanted to—protect her people, protect the peace.

Today she could only worry about her sister. If she was alright. If rumors of what happened in the mountains circled around the castle. Gods forbid if the rumors spread to their guests from the other isles.

King Athanas seemed to do everything to quell those whispers. To blame the incident on Nexos. No person would think he was lying. They were a threat. An attack like this so close to a sacred event was expected from a kingdom as disgraceful as theirs.

Ember noted the sun fully in the sky, realizing that she better hurry to the courtyard before the guests began to stir in their chambers or come in from the ships anchored in the harbor.

She took one last look in the mirror, smoothing out her dress and hurried out of her chambers. As she hurried down the hall to where the banquet was being set up, she took a turn too fast and slammed into someone.

"Apologies!" Ember gasped. She should not appear rushed or anxious, not when there were so many people around to question why she might be that way.

"Ember."

She looked up, the person she ran into was Kohl. Ember breathed a sigh of relief, because if Kohl was up then so would Katrin.

He stood in front of her, in what looked to be the same clothes he wore yesterday, a sling of cloth now tied around his arm and shoulder to keep it positioned to heal. There were dribbles of red blood—no, wine—trailing down his shirt. His brown hair, normally clean and pulled back in a bun, was awry around his face. His deep eyes were glazed over, his fingers circling his temples.

"Kohl? Are you all right?"

He wobbled as he tried to take a step back from her.

"Yes, yes, I'm fine. Indulged in too much of my father's wine last night." His voice was raspy and overused.

The relief faded from Ember's face. If her sister indulged in that much wine as well—she did not even want to think that. Her sister was known to barely make it out of bed the whole day, plagued with nausea and headaches that no tea or tonic could remedy. There was no way she would have been stupid enough to do that with something so important to attend this morning.

"And Katrin, did she indulge herself as well?"

"Katrin? Oh no, she did not. One of the reasons I probably drank so much. No one to share the bottle with."

"Thank the gods. Wait. What do you mean by no one to share the bottle with? Were you not with Katrin last night?" Ember's voice cracked on the last words.

"I was, but then my father called me away. When I returned she was gone. I was quite surprised considering everything..." his voice trailed off, getting lost for a moment in thought. "Again, circles back to why I indulged myself so much. Although I usually don't have this bad of a reaction to a bottle. It must have been a mix of that and the tonic my father gave me for the pain."

Bile rose in Ember's throat. Her stomach felt like it dropped straight through her.

"My sister was not with you? She's not in your chambers?"

"No?" Kohl's mind seemed to whirl behind those glassy eyes.

Ember's face went ashen and she took off as quickly as ever before.

The dining room was dimly lit when Ember entered. Her mother sat next to the head of the table, different from where she usually was on the other end of the room. Kora was whispering to her father. It was rare she saw him at home. He usually resided in their other residence. The castle in Aidesian,

the underworld. *To any other person, her father would probably be that of nightmares, his tanned skin and hair black as night. His eyes of darkness to match. When he was here, the whites around the deep brown irises showed, but in Aidesian they were a pure onyx.*

The rain pounded against the windows, thunder roaring so loudly it seemed like the walls of the castle might cave in. A storm this large could only mean one thing. The gods were angered. Not the gods that lived in this world. Not her parents or King Nikolaos and Queen Giselle of Nexos, not her sister Katrin, or even her. No, these were the gods that returned home to Cyther. The ones whose power fueled the world around them. The gods of these isles could wield their powers at will, but that power could weaken, that power would need to regenerate. The gods that were in Cyther—their power was ever flowing.

Ember walked up to her father, throwing her arms around him in a tight embrace.

"Oh it's so good to have you home! How long are you staying?"

Aidoneus's face was grave. Worry and fear plastered over the God of Death's face, something no one could say they had seen before. Her mother was silent. The whispering stopped.

A group of guards entered the room, Commander Markos with six of his most trusted men, one of which was the youngest captain Alentus had seen. Ember looked at that captain, only a few years older than she was, with terror in her eyes as her father explained what happened.

Her sister was taken from her room in the night. There were signs of a struggle down on the beaches. Remains of rope and chain were left behind or washed up on the shore. Who took her, and where they went, even the whispers of the gods could not say.

Ember threw up immediately. Her whole body shaking with confusion and fear.

The young captain approached her, with a nod from Aidoneus.

"We will find her, Your Highness. I promise." He laid a hand on her shoulder, his warm brown eyes looking directly into hers, as he kneeled before her. But only hopelessness stared back.

"There you are! I was beginning to wonder if you would miss all the good food," Ajax said as he smiled at a panting Ember. "Race over here just for the delectable pastries? I did save you one I have managed not to eat myself, although if you took much longer I may have."

Ember could not catch her breath, or maybe it was that she did not know how to speak the words out loud. That same fear and anxiety she felt in that dining room five years ago swelled in her very bones.

"Ember? Ember, what is it?"

She stood there, her very bones trembling.

Ajax took her hand, moving them both away from the table and listening ears.

"Ember, tell me what's wrong." His voice was sharp and direct.

"It's Katrin. She's gone."

Chapter Seventeen

Katrin

You can trust him with yours. Katrin kept repeating Leighton's words over and over again in her mind as she wandered on deck. How could she possibly trust Ander with her life when he was the reason she was stuck on this gods-forsaken ship to begin with? After pacing back and forth along the rails of *The Nostos* for what seemed like hours, Katrin finally settled down on an old barrel by the stern of the ship.

The crew was still mulling about, tending to the sails, washing the deck, playing games with small carved pieces of wood. She sat and she watched, tendrils of her wavy brown hair coming loose from her braid and whipping in front of her face.

Katrin breathed in the salty air, not minding the spray of the sea on her skin. It took the last few years to finally be comfortable on the water again, to be comfortable with the sounds and smells of her home by the sea. She would not lose that again.

This time she would use the air and the breeze to calm her, to center her as she plotted a way to get off this ship and back home.

Ideas raced through her mind. Everything from asking politely for them to turn the ship around—as illogical a plan as any—to jumping off the ship and hoping they were near enough to shore that she could swim. The latter was also not a good idea. She did it before, albeit with less planning, but she had almost not survived.

Her best bet was to wait until they came to port to fill up the ship with supplies and try to commandeer another ship to make it home.

"Plotting ways to kill me, Starling?" Ander's deep voice filled the air around her. He snuck up behind her, almost knocking her right off the barrel.

"Maybe. Or maybe I just like to see you sweat."

Ander grazed his hand along her back as his voice tickled her ear. "I bet you do."

Instinct had her jumping up and whipping around, her extended palm smacking across his cheek. Katrin's eyes narrowed on the captain before her. "Touch me again and you'll learn how hard I can really hit."

Ander's mouth kicked up in a grin, his hand stroking over the red mark hers left on his cheek, brushing back his waved onyx hair. "Someone is grumpy today. Did you not enjoy the bath I left for you?"

Katrin choked on a cough. He took a step closer, breathing in her scent. "Lillies and mint. A personal favorite of mine."

"Oh fuck off, Ander."

"Mmm, quite the mouth on you too, Starling."

Katrin shuddered, her cheeks warming. The look he gave her was utterly feral. "Is that what you came over here to do? To annoy me? To insult me? To smell me like some rabid animal?"

"I would never insult you, Starling. You just looked lonely, I thought I could cheer you up with my undeniable charm." He flashed a full toothy grin, wiggling his eyebrows.

"I look lonely because you *kidnapped* me and took me hostage on this ship where I know no one." Her voice was low and seething.

"Like I said before, you are not a hostage. You are free to do as you wish on this ship. And you don't know *no one*, you know me." His voice softened.

"Know you? I know nothing about you except that you find it entertaining to lie to women you meet in the woods and, oh, you apparently think yourself to be some self-appointed prince. An unlikely reality seeing as you are a pirate and pirates don't tend to have a home." Acid roiled in Katrin's stomach at the harshness of her words. But why should she care if she insulted this wretched man? All he told her were lies and delusions.

"I have a home." Ander looked away, his gaze drifting off to the sea. Katrin could have sworn the air chilled around them.

"The sea is not a home, it is a way to escape. Only a boy would hide from reality on a ship. An unworthy pirate running away from duty and responsibility, how original."

"Trust me, I am not running. If I could go home I would." His features darkened at the thought.

"Then what keeps you away?" she asked. It was curious that a man—a pirate at that—seemed so burdened by a simple question.

"You." He turned to walk back toward the door to the cabins below.

"Me? Ander!" She stepped toward him, grabbing his wrist. "You have to tell me why I am here! You say I am not a prisoner, and yet I have no way of getting off this ship. And now you claim I am the one keeping you from returning home?"

She could have sworn it was pain—pain and regret—that covered his face as he shook off her grip and walked away without another word. And for some reason, Katrin could not help feeling even more lonely than before.

Chapter Eighteen

Katrin

After Katrin and Ander spoke, the night seemed to come quickly. The winds picked up and the seas turned a deeper green and gray. A storm might not be far off. Katrin stayed on the deck for a while after contemplating why she was always destined to be swept away on the tides. A princess doomed to relive her tragic past day in and day out.

When Katrin had enough of the wallowing and self-pity—or at least grew bored enough at staring out at the expanse of sea—she wandered the edges of the ship. Circling around, but never really going anywhere. The crew would think she was a strange woman, padding about in oversized clothing, not offering her help with daily chores. To hell with them all—they must know she was not aboard *The Nostos* willingly.

Rumbling and twinges of shooting pain came from her stomach. She aimlessly wandered about the worn deck for so long, Katrin didn't realize how hungry she became. Ander left the spread of bread and fruits for her in the cabin, but she was too worried, or stubborn, to eat any of it now.

Her hand flew to her stomach as another roll let out a loud gurgling noise. It was late. There were only a few crew members manning the sails on deck. The others, she figured, were below, filling their bellies in the galley.

Katrin stepped down into the main corridor below, encountering a wisp of something delicious lingering in the air. She followed the scent to a door halfway down the hall. Glancing inside, she saw the rest of the crew sitting about the room, stuffing their faces with all sorts of things she wished to snag. Devouring mugs of ale she also wished to have—if only to turn off the unending fear that clawed at her mind.

At the back of the room, a table was filled with the spreads of food. Olive oil, bread, jams and figs. Freshly cooked fish seasoned in something Katrin could not make out. And wine. So much wine. She could forget about stomaching the bitter tasting ale and indulge in deep red liquid instead. Stepping inside the room, she made her way through the crowd of drunken men to scoop up as much unpoisoned food as she could before they noticed the only female that seemed to be aboard this ship.

A dark hand caught her shoulder, pulling her back ever so slightly. "Ah, not so fast, Princess."

Leighton spun her around before she could even throw one morsel of food into her mouth. It would be starvation then—that was this ship's form of torture.

"The captain told me I could do as I please on this ship and what I please is to have some of that food." Katrin's tongue grazed her bottom lips. Gods, she was almost foaming at the mouth to get some of that fish. Any of it, really.

"You can have all the food you want, but unfortunately, your meal is in your cabin," Leighton chuckled.

There it was. The reality setting in. She would be bound to that gods-forsaken cabin once more. Ander let her out for a day—one final day to breathe in the fresh salty air before it all went to shit. "It's not *my* cabin, it's the captain's." Her lip twitched into a scowl.

"For the foreseeable future it is yours as well."

Katrin fisted her palms at her sides, all she could hear was the pounding of her own blood boiling in her ears. "Ander told me I am not a prisoner and now you tell me I can only eat by myself, bound in the four small walls of those quarters?" Who cared if she raised her voice, no one knew her here. She would make a scene if she wanted to.

Emerald eyes widened and then crinkled at the side, matching a small smirk across Leighton's lips. "You mistook me, Princess. You will not be eating alone. The captain requests that you join him for all meals."

It was impossible not to roll her eyes for the one millionth time today. "Of course he does," Katrin grumbled. "Am I to wear some fancy gown he favors as well, or will these poor man's clothes do?" She fawned her arms over her body.

"You can wear whatever you like, Princess. I'm sure Alexander will not care either way. Now hurry along, he has been waiting."

"I'm sure he has." Katrin flipped a vulgar gesture at Leighton, before storming off toward the end of the hall. These men were insufferable. It was the last time she would let men tell her what she could and could not do.

Despite her rumbling stomach, Katrin tried to take her time wandering down the very short corridor. As she approached the door to her—to his—to their cabin, she contemplated knocking or just barging right in to demand why Ander thought he could summon her at will. She was just about to shove the door open when it creaked aside and a smirking Ander leaned against its frame.

"I was beginning to think you wouldn't show."

"As if I have a choice." Katrin pushed him aside and waltzed into the room.

Ander's features softened, the light in his eyes fading slightly. "You always have a choice with me, Starling."

She flopped down into one of the chairs. Katrin may have been forced to spend time with him, but no one said she needed to be cordial about it. "Why do you even call me that? I'm not some bird."

"You think I call you that because of some chattering bird?"

"What else could it mean?" It had bothered her all day, the somewhat familiar name lingering in the back of her mind. *Starling, Starling, Starling.* But she could not place where it was from, where she heard it before.

"That's a story for another time." Ander smirked once more, the dimple in his right cheek on display. It would help her hate him more if he didn't look so damned handsome or speak with an air of kindness in his tone. But his warmth was a facade. His way of ruining her even more. Just like in the mountains, Katrin could only trust the captain as far as she could throw him.

"You seem to say that a lot."

"Hmm...never really thought about it." Ander shrugged. He pointed down at the display of food along the low table in front of her. "The chef brought everything he made, I wasn't sure what you'd like."

Katrin wanted to scream *everything*, but she refused to indulge whatever weird fascination this man had with her and food. "I'm not hungry." She crossed her arms over her chest, hoping the pressure would ease the pangs coming from her empty stomach.

"Are you sure? The rumbling would seem to say otherwise."

She would not eat—not with this man watching her every move. Not when he refused to tell her what she was doing aboard this ship. It was probably poisoned anyway. Or drugged to put her back into a dreamless slumber.

His crystal eyes darkened, pulse throbbing the vein in his neck with a steady beat. "You need to eat."

"I do not and I will not."

He took a step toward her, reaching out his hand just slightly before he pulled it back. "You can barely fill out those clothes. How can you expect to kill me if you can't even hold a sword steady with those flimsy limbs of yours?"

Her skin went ashen. Yes—she saw it earlier, after she bathed and went to get dressed. How her face became sunken. Her normally full cheeks now sharpened like granite, her spine showing through the thin shirt she wore. It wasn't that Katrin did not eat. She had. Or more so indulged in certain sweets and loaves of bread, but those were not nourishment. Guilt would come creeping in and she would run until she felt overworked, until she threw up the unhealthy food she devoured. It lulled that pain and anxiety she housed—for a moment, at least.

"I said I wasn't hungry and I meant it." Lies. Absolute lies. The smells of the hot food in front of her were still making her mouth water and Katrin desperately wanted to eat every bite of everything on that table.

"So you would rather starve yourself than eat with me?" Ander whispered.

"I would rather fling myself off this ship and let the Fates decide my life than eat with you." A muscle in Ander's jaw feathered and his whole body stiffened. Katrin walked mere inches from him. "You lied to me! You took me against my will! You think I want to be anywhere near a person who could do something so horrible? Someone who would disregard the needs or wants of another so blatantly?"

"Fine. Have it your way." He dragged his palm over his face, shaking his head.

"Giving up that easily, are we? Aren't you supposed to be some vicious and feared pirate?"

He did not grace her with a change of emotion, no witty reply. Ander's hand gripped the handle of the door. He paused there, but did not turn back to face her.

"I left a pile of books on the shelf by the bed. I thought—well now you don't need to stare off with nothing to do all day."

He pushed the door open and slammed it shut behind him. There Katrin stood. Alone. Again.

She swallowed, almost shameful for her outburst. But why should she feel bad about the words she flung so effortlessly at him when it was how she really felt?

Saving you. What if he really thought that was what he was doing? But what would he be saving her from? Only Nexos was a threat and the only way to show them that Alentus would not bend a knee was to hold the Acknowledgement and crown Katrin as queen. The Acknowledgement that was tomorrow. One she would not be at.

Sweat began to bead along her temple even as sharp chills set up her spine. If Kohl and Ember could not find a way to postpone the ceremony someone could call for the Wrecking. That had to be why she was here. So that the succession could be in question. So that someone else could take her place.

Blood boiled in her veins, her very skin feeling like it was on fire. Katrin tried to quiet her mind, tried to control her breathing, but it was not helping. If Ander was trying to prevent her from taking what was her birthright, there was no amount of food or books that could placate her. Her nails dug into the chair as she sat back down.

Nexos. Always that gods-damned isle.

A faint glow began to hum over her skin, her eyes brightening until they were all but a blinding white. Water glasses on the table began to shake and crack. Her spirit was trying to claw its way out, trying to dull the pain and hurt and despicable feelings that swirled inside her gut. It scraped its way from the bottom of a pit within her until it reached the surface. Smoke began to rise from her palms, singing her nostrils with the smell of burning wood and flesh.

A rustling sound came from the corner of the room, over by where Ander left the books. Katrin's fiery white stare darted to the sound. Something curious sat in the corner, its yellow eyes meeting hers through the shadows. A small creature sat perched on the shelf, long white hair sparkling in the bright glow that radiated off of Katrin. Long white hair except a stripe of gray that went down the center of its head, looking like it was smudged with ash from a seer.

The animal cocked its head to the side, pointed pink ears and small pink nose twitching as it took in the surroundings. Its plush tail flapped back and forth in an almost indifferent way, like the glowing goddess in front of her was little to fear.

It jumped down from the shelf, slinking its way over to Katrin, weaving its body between her legs as she sat, still fuming with emotion. Katrin's eyes were glued to the way in which it brushed against her leg, a low purring escapings its mouth, urging her to breathe, to calm. The glow around Katrin simmered then dissipated as her hands unclenched the chair and her eyes returned to their brown hue.

Bits of her power showed over the years, but nothing like this. She never lost control, never showed her true nature so obviously. Her twenty-fifth birthday was approaching in less than two months and those who were god-born or blessed tended to get reckless with their powers close to coming of age. At least, that was what she was told.

"I'm sorry, little lady, did I startle you?" Katrin leaned down, scratching behind the cat's ears. It nuzzled against her again before turning and jumping up on the low lying table where Ander left the food.

The cat turned back toward Katrin, lifting one paw up and swatting at a plate of food. She shrugged, Katrin was pretty sure most cats did not eat human food, but who was she to tell this creature otherwise? At least she would know the food was not poisoned. Animals in the isles seemed to have a sense of this.

Another rumble left Katrin's stomach, this one even louder than before. It would be a waste to let the food just sit overnight. No one else would be eating it, the crew already ate their dinner, and the little cat surely could not eat everything on the table.

"Looks like I'll be having dinner with you, little one." Katrin stroked her hand down the cat's back, rustling its fur.

She dug into everything, from the fish to the bread to the mixed bowl of cucumber, tomatoes, olives, and a block of salted cheese. It was delectable. Days went by without her eating a full meal, and this was a much needed reprieve from the pangs of hunger she felt.

Katrin had never tasted spices like these before, wondering where the crew could have gotten them from. Trading with Anatole was halted in the last few years due to the blockade around Nexos. Even the royal families of the western Mykandrian Isles could not come by them easily.

She picked up a cup of steaming liquid and breathed it in. It smelled like bergamot and jasmine and pepper. Katrin sat in the chair eating and drinking until her stomach was so full she thought she might be sick.

"You have a good dinner too?" Katrin asked the cat.

It leapt from the table onto her lap, butting its nose into her stomach. Again the cat began to purr, sitting back on its haunches, letting its tail whip side to side.

"I'll take that as a yes."

Katrin picked the cat up and walked over to the bookshelf.

"What do you think we should read tonight?"

The cat meowed softly, trying to wiggle its way out of her arms and onto the bed.

"Not a fan of being picked up, are we?" Katrin let out a light laugh. "That's fine, you can sit right here." She placed it down by the pillows on the bed.

Katrin ran her finger along the spines of the books Ander left for her. They were all old novels of mythic romance and epics of war. She selected one, *The Odyssey*, since it looked to be the most read. The spine was worn and the pages yellowed with age. Inside the cover, in beautiful script, read

Ander,

May your life be filled with as many wonderful adventures and may you always find your way home.

All my love,

Chloe

Katrin traced the words over and over again. Someone waited for him at home. That pit in her stomach returned. Ander looked pained when he spoke of home, how he was not able to return. Here was proof, there was someone who wanted him to find his way back. Someone who needed him.

Confusion whirled in her mind and—was it guilt? For this man who took so many things from her already? It made no sense, why she should feel any sense of remorse or empathy toward this man who stripped her from her lands—except the little flutter in her heart seemed to say otherwise.

That was it. Tomorrow she would ask him again why she was really here. This time she would not take no for an answer.

The book opened with a man trapped on an island being seduced by a nymph who wanted to take him as her lover. Katrin began to read their story, the story of gods whose names were long forgotten in their world. *The Olympi.* At some point her eyes closed and she drifted off to sleep. The only sounds in the cabin were the creaking of the boat on the waves, the crackling of the lamp as the flame dimmed, the purring of the cat who slept next to her.

That night she dreamt. Truly dreamt. Not of nightmares, or horrors of her past, or present, but of a small island. One of whitewashed buildings, their doors painted a deep cerulean blue. Of flowers lining streets built of stone. Of crashing waves and a warm breeze along the shore. Of lovers hurrying off to small alleys to embrace each other. Of families sitting outside old and worn tavernas, with dancing and music and the smell of spices and sweets. Of beauty in the truest sense of the word. One she wished she could have seen.

In the middle of the night, Katrin awoke. The small white cat still curled next to her arm. Leftover food she could not finish still lingering on the table. There was no sign of Ander, but the book she read now lay shut on the night table by her bed.

Katrin slid her arms out from under the covers. Mykonos fluttered open her yellow eyes, stretching out her paws, her long tail vibrating as she yawned before making her way down to Katrin's hip and curling up again.

Mykonos, named for one of the many sunk isles of the now named Mykandrian sea. An island of culture and chaos before the Olympi ruled and attacked the lands, slowly burning and bombing the smaller cities in the continent until only a handful survived. Named for her curiosity and playfulness, though Katrin would never speak her full name. Not outside the walls of this ship. Not when doing so could be a death sentence. But even though the *Elliniká Glóssa* was forbidden and feared, the name spoke to her and remained on her tongue when she woke from her dream. A good dream for once. And when she saw the slinky white haired cat, snoring in the night's wind, Katrin knew. She would be her best companion. Her fiercest secret keeper. Her truest friend. At least for now. At least on this ship.

She looked down at Myko, scratching under her chin.

"You know, this very well may be the death of me."

Katrin shut her eyes once more, trying to block out the thoughts of where she should be, what she should be doing right now. She could not change the situation she was in, at least not yet. Kohl and Ember would find a way to stop this, find a way to delay the Acknowledgment. To make certain that her place on the throne was waiting when she returned. Because it *was* when she returned, not if. That much she knew. She could feel the tug deep in her bones. The will and the want to return to her people. To fight. To stand up for them. To assure that peace would be there for them all during her reign.

It was out of her hands now. It was up to them. Katrin opened her eyes once more and sent a silent wish out toward her sister.

CHAPTER NINETEEN

KOHL

A whip of blonde hair turned and bolted away from Kohl. Ember never ran so fast, well ever. His mind was still foggy thanks to that stupid wine his father suggested he have. Technically his father suggested he give some to Katrin to calm her down, but it was all the same. He went over the questions Ember just asked him. *My sister was not with you?* When he told her no, it was as if Ember turned into a ghost before she took off toward the courtyard.

He started picking up his pace behind her, trying to keep up but his head was still pounding, nausea still creeping up in his gut.

"Ember! Ember, what's going on?" Kohl yelled out after her, but she did not hear, or did not want to.

When they finally reached the courtyard, Kohl was panting and out of breath. He was hungover before, yesterday even, but nothing like this. Nothing that made him feel like he was in a trance. An out of body experience where he did not have full control of his limbs and how he moved.

Ember walked right up to Ajax, who was busy stuffing his face with all sorts of sweets. He looked like a bumbling idiot trying to talk to her. Kohl actually liked the commander. He thought Ajax was a strong and fair man, although he did not particularly like his choice of favorite activities for when he was not training.

He still did not understand why Ember was so frantic. She seemed on edge even before they mentioned Katrin. Then Kohl's mind went silent as she spoke the words.

"It's Katrin. She's gone."

"What do you mean she's gone?" he growled.

Ember whipped toward him. "I didn't realize you were following me." Her voice was shaky.

"I repeat, what do you mean she's gone?" Some kind of violence flashed through his eyes as Ajax took a step between him and Katrin's sister.

"Kohl, let her speak. You are not the only one here who cares about her." Ajax gripped his shoulder half to calm, and half to show he would take action if Kohl laid a hand on the younger princess.

Ajax turned back toward Ember.

"Start from the beginning. From before we ran into each other."

Ember nodded her head.

"When I woke up this morning—I don't know—I had this feeling like something was wrong. Almost an urge to go see Katrin. Ajax canceled our training this morning because of the banquet, but I wanted to see if maybe she wanted to go on a short run. You know how those help her, and she has just been so out of place recently."

Kohl's jaw tightened as he listened to Ember's words.

"Well maybe if someone told me what was going on earlier I could have helped her." Kohl began to raise his voice again and Ajax gave him a silencing look. "Sorry—continue, Ember."

"I ran into Ajax outside her room and we went in to see if she was there and when she wasn't we thought maybe she spent the night with you after everything that happened yesterday. We thought—I thought—I would just see her at breakfast. Then I ran into you and you said you haven't seen her since last night, and her bed was not slept in. There's no other explanation. We knew there was a threat—*you* knew there was a threat, and none of us protected her!" Tears began to stream down her face.

"There's another explanation," Kohl said, his voice a frightening calm.

If what he thought was true it would devastate him, but Katrin was acting differently. She was speaking out against him more. Fighting back opinions to his father. She had not trusted him with her darkest secrets, something she always did for as long as he knew her.

He looked past it yesterday. The pirate's mark, the strange tunic. Kohl pinched the bridge of his nose. *This gods-damned hangover needs to go away.* His mind was too foggy to process what he saw, what he heard. Put the pieces of the puzzle together. Make sense of the words that trailed from his mouth.

"What do you mean by another explanation?" Ajax asked.

"There's something I need to do." Kohl made to leave, but Ajax grabbed his arm.

"Kohl, if there is something you know, you must tell me. I am Commander of the Spartanis and where the Drakos family is concerned I need all the facts before I get the other soldiers involved."

"And as Katrin's future consort, I have the right to refuse you." The world was spinning around him and the future was cracking bit by bit. Pressure from his father, Katrin keeping secrets, the impending Acknowledgement that might not happen.

This was between Kohl, and Katrin, and *the owner of that blue tunic.*

"Keep this quiet until I return. Not even my father or the queen can know. Not yet."

Ajax nodded.

"Please, Kohl. Tell me where she could be," Ember begged.

"Don't worry, Ember. It's not like last time. It *can't* be like last time. I'll be back by mid-day, until then I am going to need you both to stall. Ember—explain to the guests that Katrin is feeling unwell this morning and wants to rest before the Acknowledgement. Tell them she has granted you permission to receive the gifts and honor the gods. Ajax, I insist you get me the fastest horse in the stables. We will meet back in my chambers when the sun reaches its highest. Hopefully I will know more then."

"Alright, Kohl, follow me to the stables. I will have them prepare Arion. He is our most prized horse, a favorite of King Aidon."

Kohl watched as Ajax turned back to the princess, his eyes softening as he looked deeply into hers, cupping both her cheeks in his hands.

"We will find her, Ember, I promise."

Kohl could tell the commander wanted to do more, say more, grab her in an embrace or kiss her on the brow, but that would cause questions from the guests who began to arrive. The commander and the princess. Not just any princess, but the future Prytan of the Spartanis.

That was something that could never be. The Prytan was not allowed to fall in love, was not allowed to take a partner. It would be too dangerous. Enemies could use that love toward another as leverage to bend the Prytan to their will. So Ember would remain without someone by her side until a new generation ascended to the throne. Kohl could not help but share in her pain of unrequited love.

Kohl mounted the black-maned horse, its muscles shimmered and flexed as Kohl gripped the reins. He did not know where in the mountains this cabin was. But he knew where the trail led around the Triad Mountains, where shelters could be built, where farms could be tilled. Maybe it would take him several hours, but he would find it. Find her. Kohl took the tunic that was left on his floor and showed Arion.

"This is who we are trying to find, alright?"

The horse sniffed the old shirt, taking off through the gates of the castle. Kohl understood why Ajax said Arion was a favorite of the king. The horse was swift, galloping away from the cliffs the castle sat upon toward the center of the isle. Arion wove in and out of the trees and olive groves along the base of the mountains with grace and precision. It was as if Arion knew where he was going and who he was finding.

Kohl's mind whirled with emotion. Fear that something terrible happened to Katrin. Fear that nothing happened to her, but that she *chose* to leave. Anger that he could not protect her once again, that he left her alone when he went to see his father. He wondered if it happened then, her being taken away against her will after they made love for the first time. Or that she slipped away herself, intentionally leaving him.

Katrin had seemed distant while they were intimate. Kohl knew that he was hazy because of the injury and the tonic, but it was still strange—the look that engulfed her face. Maybe she seemed distracted because it was her first time, because she was not used to the act as Kohl was. He cursed himself for not realizing he should have been more gentle with her. Maybe it was him that pushed her away, that pushed her to run. Maybe he should have waited like they originally discussed.

Or maybe it was not her first time. Kohl's chest tightened with the idea that she was lying to him this whole time. That she was having an affair with some farmer's son in the mountains. The mountains where he helped heal her. He could not focus on that now. All that mattered now was finding Katrin, making sure she was alright, even if what he found out after the fact was something he'd rather not know.

Arion began to slow, the horse whinnying as it pulled its neck to the right, signaling to Kohl. His eyes widened at what the horse found as his mind drifted. Before them stood an old cabin, its door worn and splintered, the deep azure paint peeling off.

Kohl patted the side of Arion's neck. "You really are quite the partner."

Arion huffed out a noise that sounded like an agreement.

Kohl swung one leg over the horse dismounting from the saddle, leading Arion over to a low slung branch on an olive tree nearby. He tied the reins around the branch.

"You stay here, alright? And don't get into any trouble while I'm gone."

Arion looked away from Kohl, now too distracted by trying to eat the olive leaves on the tree.

Kohl walked toward the cabin, peering in through one of the windows. It looked dark inside, even with the sun cascading through the trees. He checked around back to see if there were any signs of movement, but could see nothing. Going back to the door, he tried the handle. It was unlocked. The door creaked as he opened it slowly, one hand on the handle, one on the hilt of his sword in case someone was hiding inside.

"Hello?" he called inside, to no response. Kohl stepped inside. "Katrin? Katrin are you here?"

The cabin was modest inside. A few pieces of worn furniture in a living space, a bed and a dresser in the opposing corner, a meager kitchen area by the door. It was small enough to see that no one was there. As Kohl ran his finger along the table he could tell that not only was no one there now, but it looked like no one had lived there in a very long time. The layer of dust coming off the table was so thick he began to cough.

Maybe Arion was not as bright as he thought. This could not have been the cabin Katrin mentioned. Kohl turned and began to walk out the door when he noticed a horse's bridle hanging from a hook. He went up to the bridle and there, embossed in the leather, was the same marking that was on the navy tunic. A sea serpent with two crossed swords. This might not have been *the* cabin, but it was related.

Kohl grabbed the bridle and headed for Arion.

"Quick as you can, back to the castle. I need to find my father."

Kohl entered his father's chambers without knocking, still clutching the embossed bridle, a murderous look building in his eyes.

King Athanas sat amongst the plush velvet pillows on the floor once more, the smoke of *olerae* lingering throughout the room, but this time he was not alone. A lithe young woman with jet-black hair and skin as pale as the moon, lay sprawled across his lap. She looked to be not much older than Kohl. The gossamer of her red gown left little to the imagination, his father's hand much too close to the center between her thighs than he wished to ever witness.

"Oh don't be so chaste, my boy. I know you've seen between a woman's legs before. Maybe even your bride-to-be?" His venomous tone hit Kohl straight in the gut. His father had not heard. Ajax told the truth then, until they knew more this was to be kept quiet.

"Do not speak of her in such a way." Kohl's eyes darkened.

"And don't you forget who you are talking to, *boy*." The words felt like a smack across his face.

"Yes, Father," he replied, "I wish to speak with you privately if you wouldn't mind sending *the help* away." Kohl's distaste for hired flesh was known to everyone, including the king.

King Athanas waved her off, sending the girl to the door with a jingling pouch of coins. Reluctantly, and with a frown, she slipped out of the chambers.

"What was so important that you interrupted my private meeting?" his father hissed.

"Meeting? Is that what you call fraternizing with whores? What would mother think?"

The king's eyes narrowed. "Your mother is probably doing the same as we speak, and if she was here, it would have been her head between that girl's legs not my hand." The corner of his father's mouth twitched up.

Kohl felt the contents of his stomach start to come back up. He was not here for banter, especially about that.

"It's Katrin, Father. She is missing."

The expression on his father's face did not change, a dull gaze, except for the purse of his lips as the black smoke trailed out in rings. "Is she?"

"Yes, and if you had anything to do with it, *Father*, I don't care if you are my king. I will do what I whispered to you last night." *I will cut you limb from limb if you have a hand in hurting my Aikaterine, Father.*

His father laughed. "You will do no such thing."

"So you're telling me that you had nothing to do with her disappearance? That your plan didn't involve getting rid of Katrin right before the Acknowledgement for some self-serving ploy? That you didn't collude with these pirates?"

Kohl chucked the leather bridle at his father.

Again, King Athanas smiled, this time showing off his sharpened canines. "I can *promise* you, Kohl, I—nor any of my people—took your dear betrothed. And we most certainly didn't collude with this filth." His hands traced along the embossed symbol on the bridal.

"But this? This is not just any marking of a pirate, my boy. The sea serpent, the crossed swords, that is the banner of Skiatha."

Kohl plopped down onto one of the floor pillows. He could have sworn his hangover subsided during the ride back from the mountains, but the pounding in his skull was threatening to return. "Skiatha? The Lost Isle. That's just a place of myths."

Skiatha was a fairytale, one he read about in children's books. Once an isle of wealth and prosperity, it was overrun by a rebel army who set fires to the land. It was said that now it lays barren, its soil cursed by the gods. That the fires the army set still burn along the coastline, warning all who come upon it that they too will be cursed. It was a story parents told their children to make them behave. To threaten to be sent there, where an army of the dead—that same army that lay it to waste—will torture them and eat them.

"Ah, but that is where you are wrong. It is very real. They say the Prince of the Lost Isles, one of the most feared pirates to sail these seas, calls it home. That his fleet wreaks havoc throughout the Mykandrian Sea to the east of Nexos."

Anger crept through Kohl's veins. He was here. On their soil. In their mountains. Katrin wore this *prince's* tunic when he last saw her, the same marking stitched into the cuff.

Kohl's mind began to reel like earlier in the mountains, the pounding becoming aggressively worse as his father coughed in the background. What if she left willingly? What if she loved this man and not Kohl? What if everything was a lie? He quickly released that thought. She did love him. Always. And even more, she would never leave her people this close to the Acknowledgement. All of Alentus, not to mention the other isles, would be in disarray. She cared about them—all of them—too much to do that.

"Do you think that is who took her? This prince?" Kohl seethed.

"That is the question. It would make sense, the closest isle to where that *boy* sails is Nexos. To get to that part of the sea you would need to sail through one of the narrow passes on either side of Nexos. Perhaps he set up some sort of deal with King Nikolaos. If he gives Katrin to Nexos, they would allow him to use the passes to terrorize our part of the sea as well."

"And if this is who we are looking for, how would I find him?"

"That is something we can worry about once we deal with the more pressing problem at hand."

"This is something we will deal with *now*!" Kohl shot up from where he was seated, hands clenched firmly in fists, his eyes a menacing sweep of ebony.

The king's mouth thinned to a straight line, his jaw hardening. "We can try to delay the Acknowledgement as long as we can. In the meantime, I will send out my spies to see what they can gather on the pirate." His father's voice was firm and direct. "But Kohl—" An unnerving chill ran down Kohl's spine as he looked at his father. "If something happens, I need to know you will do what is necessary. Not only for Katrin, but for Morentius as well."

Kohl nodded. He understood. This was larger than them. Larger than him. Larger than Katrin. This was about peace. And when he found her, because he would find her again, he would not let her home be in ruin.

Chapter Twenty

Ember

M ost of the pieces from Ember's hair had fallen out of her tight braid from clawing at the strands. Her nail beds were raw from where she bit them to shreds. Tap, tap, tapping came from her sandaled feet as she paced around the room. She still wore the gown she changed into for breakfast. Sweat now seeped through the silk, sprinkles of mud coated the trim from when she ran through the castle. Even the normally calming crackling of the fire could not stop the tremors vibrating through her hands or warm the chill that clung to her bones.

Kohl said he would return when the sun was the highest, but now it almost set and she still had not heard from him. At some point she wandered from where he said to meet in his chambers down to her father's study.

She needed her father right now, but Ember knew there was no way to send word. When her father was in Aidesian, only another god of age could contact him. That would leave her mother, and although she was made aware of the situation, she could not leave Alentus while King Athanas was here.

Her worst fears crowded her mind. What if Kohl had not returned because she *was* missing, or worse, what if he found her body lying dead somewhere?

Ember wandered over to her father's desk, leaning against it with her arms crossed, trying to quiet the thoughts in her mind and the shaking of her body. Ajax came by what seemed like hours ago to inform her that Arion returned to the stables, meaning Kohl was *somewhere* in this castle. The obvious place would be his father's chambers, but Ember did not dare interrupt them if that was where Kohl was.

The king gave her a disturbing feeling, like a chill of a ghost running up her spine. He already saw her as weak, not able to take up the position that was promised to her as second-born, she did not want to give him another excuse as to why she should not accept the position as Prytan.

The incessant tapping of her foot filled Ember's head. If something did happen they would need to come up with a plan, and yet here she sat, alone, no information past this morning when she found her sister's chambers empty and unslept.

"Ajax, thank the gods! What's going on?"

Ember breathed the smallest sigh of relief as the commander entered, trailed by Iason. When she noticed that they were clad in leathers and bronze battle cuffs that small amount of relief disappeared.

If it was just Ajax, maybe she would have clung on to hope. But if he'd informed another member of the Spartanis—even if that member was someone they considered family—it had to be the worst case scenario.

"Ember—" he started, but she cut him off.

"So it's true then? She's really gone? It's happened again?"

Her lip began to quiver, as Kohl, her mother, and King Athanas entered the study behind them. She clenched her jaw, taking shaky breaths in and out, trying to prevent the tears that welled in her eyes.

"Ember, I think you should take a seat." Ajax closed the distance between the two of them. Her eyes widened.

"Is she...is Katrin dead?" Ember's skin went ashen, her voice cracking on the final word.

"She's not dead, my dear, at least from what we can discern." Kora came closer, propping herself on the arm of the chair Ember sank into. "She's not dead."

Kohl took a seat over by the fire, his eyes a deep ebony matching his father's. Angry, revengeful, but also lifeless in a way Ember could not describe.

"We think she was taken by pirates. Specifically, the Prince of The Lost Isles," Kohl spat, clenching his fists by his side. He looked tired, and anxious, and like he might throw the entire chair he sat in straight into the fire. One hand clenched the arm of the chair while the other propped up his forehead as he peered into the flames.

"The Lost Isles? But those are just myths," Ember questioned, glancing back and forth between her mother, Kohl, and Ajax. Avoiding eye contact with the Viper of Votios at all costs.

"Stupid girl. He would have everything to gain, whether you—a mere child—have heard of him or not." He flashed a wicked sneer at her before joining his son by the fire.

Ember growled at the King. His words cut deep. "I am not a *child!* And you are not to speak to the future Prytan of the Spartanis with that tone in this castle!" Ember shot out of her seat, pointing her finger at the king.

King Athanas grunted. "So she has a backbone after all." His lips crept up into a smile, flashing those shaven canines.

Iason gripped her arm lightly, flashing a look of concern at the princess who just threatened a man many considered more terrifying than Aidoneus himself. "He is just trying to taunt you, Ember. He knows nothing of who you really are," he whispered under his breath, urging the princess back into her seat.

"Attempting to console the child who was never yours, Iason? Endearing as always," the Viper hissed.

"Maybe if you cared about your children more than you care about your power, you would understand, Khalid." Iason's jaw was clenched tight, his normally indifferent gaze toward the king radiating ice.

King Athanas' ebony eyes began to darken further in the low light, the blackness seeping out into their surrounding white.

"Father, can I please just explain to everyone what is happening?" Kohl shot him a look, but it was not as fierce as Ember would have hoped.

The king's stare on the senator broke, and he rolled his hand at Kohl, his upper lip still twitching.

"From what my father has told me, this prince has been terrorizing the seas east of Nexos. He pillages the isles and the coastal shores of Anatole, leaving them in fire and ruin. Right now, Nexos has blocked off the straits on either side of the isle, meaning if this prince wanted to expand his territory, it would be a lot easier to make a deal with Nexos than travel by land and try to secure ships on this side of the Mykandrian Sea. My father thinks that he struck a deal with King Nikolaos, if he captures and provides Katrin, then he would be able to use the straits. It's the only thing to explain how he was here in the first place."

"And how do we know it's even this Prince of the Lost Isles to start?" Ember asked Kohl. "Because I found this." He chucked the bridle at her.

The leather reins landed in her lap. Ember ran her fingers over the embossed marking. "This symbol..."

"Is the same one that was on that tunic Katrin wore when she returned from the mountains," Kohl finished.

"Do you think he slipped her something then, so he could come back and take her at night? She was acting strange and muttering about a horrible storm, but the skies were clear all day here."

"That's exactly what we think."

Ember kept tracing the symbol over and over. The serpent and two swords. She recognized it from somewhere. From somewhere other than the tunic. "Skiatha. That's how you know it was him?" The image came to her. One from a book her father used to read her as a child. One of stories that were meant to scare children into behaving.

Kohl nodded his head.

"So it really is true? The island of war, the army of the dead? This prince who rules it?" Her heart began to quicken once more, feeling like someone was strangling the life right out of her.

"It is," Kohl said.

Ember looked at Ajax. He'd remained quiet since he arrived in the study. His brow was kept furrowed and his warm brown eyes paced back and forth along the floors. "You understand what this means, Ember?"

"What this means? This means we have to delay the Acknowledge-ment. Send them all home. Tell them she's sick. What this *means*, Ajax, is that we have to find her. Now!" Ember just about lost it. She wasn't ready for what he was about to ask. She was barely ready for the position she was supposed to take at the Acknowledgement, let alone assume Katrin's in her place. No, that would not happen. She could not let it happen.

"Ember," her mother looked at her, "this isn't up for debate."

"If Katrin doesn't return by tomorrow, you need to enact the Wreck-ing and volunteer yourself to ascend to the throne," Ajax's voice was crisp as he said the words. His hands were gripped firmly together in front of him. This was not a time to be concerned for a friend or a princess he protected. This was a time to be a commander, to make difficult decisions.

She knew that Ajax did not think she was ready either. She'd barely started any training with an actual weapon. Yes, Ember was improving, but she was nothing compared to the people she might have to go against. The best case scenario would be no one challenged her. The worst case scenario was Nexos.

"Why can't you just stay queen until we are able to rescue Katrin?" Ember pleaded with her mother.

"Oh, my darling, it is not that simple. Things have already been set in motion. I must leave tomorrow morning for Cyther, before the Ac-knowledgement. It's how it always has been and how it always will be."

Her mother's eyes softened. Kora stroked Ember's hair, pulling her into an embrace.

"Everything will work out, my darling Ember. You will see."

Her mother's voice was like honey, soothing her to her very bones. But she knew it was a lie. Everything would not work out. Not without Katrin. Not with the fate of Alentus in *her* hands.

The morning came quickly. After Ajax basically said she needed to be ready to fight King Nikolaos himself to protect the throne, Ember stalked back to her room and drank a sleeping tonic. Otherwise, there was no way she would have been able to fall asleep.

In the days she was training she did not even manage to complete a strike on Ajax, and she knew he was going easy on her. If she needed to go up against a true soldier, not even the heaviest of shields would protect her.

Outside, the skies were a deep gray and fog seeped onto the shores from the sea. The water was a haunting green, waves capped with white foam. Flowers and trees leaked droplets of water from a storm that came through in the night. The air hung heavy from the winds and the rain that whipped along the coast.

A knock came from her door. Ember snatched her cotton robe from the chair beside her bed, tying the sash tight around her waist before heading to see who was there.

She unlocked the door, peeking out before unlatching the final chain that crossed along the top. One could not be too careful with everything that was happening.

"Trying to keep me out, are you?" Ajax's voice slipped through the crack in the door.

"Just being cautious," Ember whispered back as she opened the door. "What are you doing here? We aren't training before the Acknowledgement are we?" she grumbled. Ember did not have the drive to endure another practice. Not this close to what she might have to do. It would only show her yet again how unprepared she was for the Wrecking. For becoming Prytan. Unless somehow, someway, they were able to delay the inevitable.

"No, not today. You may need to keep your strength."

Ajax tread over to the chaise lounge in her living room carrying a rather large box. As he sat down, the commander's eyes raked over her, over the lacey nightgown showing through the thinly veiled fabric. Ember squinted her eyes and wrinkled her nose, attempting to shield the parts of her body she desperately dreamed of him seeing. The way he might burrow his lips into her neck, pulling her hair back as he trailed up to her ear. Images that would only come in her dreams. Never a reality. Not now. "Keep your eyes to yourself, *Commander*."

He let out a soft chuckle. "I can't help it if you're standing right there. You did let me into the room in the first place."

Ember could not help the butterflies that formed in her stomach as she took in his perfectly coiffed dirty blonde hair. The way he looked in his dress clothes rather than the usual guard attire. The golden jacket fit tightly against his muscular build, a white shirt protruding just slightly from the top with a slight vee down his chest. Turquoise stitching went along the collar and cuffs of the jacket, matching the color of his pants, which were snug in all the worst possible places for her to be staring.

"Well I haven't picked out which gown I am going to wear yet. My mother had two made for me—" Ember's voice trailed off as she thought of her mother. Kora would have begun her sail to Cyther at dawn, unable to say goodbye to her children or friends. The laws around the Grechi were clear, especially for their leader. Kora must return to the sacred isle and relinquish her power back to the earth to be reborn into the new generation.

"You aren't wearing a gown, Ember. The future Prytan must represent the Spartanis in their own garb." Ajax's voice was forceful, but kind—always kind.

Ember looked over at him, a scowl across her face. She just began to get used to wearing pants and that was only for her training lessons, then she would promptly change into a dress she saw more fitting for her delicate build. "So I'm supposed to match you? That is an outfit for a man, not a princess."

She looked young enough already, but she would look like a small boy in the style of jacket and pants Ajax wore.

"No, not this, Ember. Although I am sure you'd look endearing in my clothes." He winked at her. Her whole body heated at the thought, mind wandering to her dream of the commander's room, her curled up next to him in bed wearing nothing but his linen button up. His gaze never left her as she fell asleep in his arms. It was torture.

"So that is what the box you are holding is for then?"

"Yes, that's what this is for."

Ajax handed her the large brown box. She almost dropped it, not expecting the weight in her hands.

Ember put the box down on top of her dresser, opening it. Inside was a beautifully crafted pair of fighting leathers. They were dyed a navy color with turquoise and gold threading along the seams.

Bronze and gold cuffs for her forearms glittered in the sun that now creeped through the window, along with two matching golden arm bands carved with the night sky. A navy leather baldric lay at the bottom, embossed with the banner of Alentus—her symbol—the sun with a lighting bolt piercing through its center.

The last piece in the box was one of the most beautiful pieces of fabric she ever held. A cape to hang from her back, made of a turquoise material that shimmered with gold so much that it seemed to glow in the light.

"This—this is too much—" Ember's voice cracked as she tried to keep back the tears.

"A powerful woman needs a powerful outfit," Ajax smiled, "and you are the most powerful woman I know."

Ember was dumbfounded. That he would do something so remarkable for her, it was just as she said—too much.

He stood up from the chaise, walking toward her until he stood so close she could feel the warmth radiating off his body. Ajax reached his hand forward, hooking a piece of her hair behind her ear as he whispered, "You will do great, Drakos."

All Ember was left with was a radiating buzz from where his thumb grazed her cheek.

The courtyard was filled with people from all the isles, from their leaders to their guards to even a few wealthy citizens. They hailed from Alentus and Morentius, but also the smaller isles of Lesathos, Xanthia, Cantos, Delphine, and those with no name in the written language.

Ember stood on the dais, dressed head to toe in the attire of the Prytan of the Spartanis. She would show everyone here today that she could at least look the part she was supposed to accept.

"Now that everyone has gathered," Ember began, attempting to keep her voice clear and unwavering, "it is time we discuss how to proceed with the Acknowledgement."

The whispers increased to murmurs, no doubt wondering why she was speaking and not her sister, who at this moment was not seen in the courtyard at all.

"As you all may have noticed, Princess Katrin is not present this morning. It is with a heavy heart that I must tell you all that she has fallen ill and will not be able to attend the ceremony today. However, that should not sway your votes from what we all know is the best decision. Katrin is the most fit to be Queen of Alentus; she is kind and just and has been preparing all her life to make sure the peace in our isles remains. The line of succession should not see itself broken today."

The courtyard grew louder. Ember clasped her hands together in an attempt to stop them from shaking. She could see the apprehension in Ajax's face as she spoke the words. It was what they discussed, but she could not help but feel her words would not persuade the people. The vote amongst leaders must be unanimous.

"Any who wish to speak their concerns may do so now, before the vote takes place."

A hush fell over the crowd. Everyone turned toward the eastern entrance of the courtyard. Shadows crept in through the archway, clouding around a man who appeared to be in his mid-forties. However, fine lines protruding from his silver eyes told a different story.

His hair was as black as night, flecks of white from age formed around his temples. He was dressed in blue trousers overlaid with gray leather and a bronze belt. He wore a thin white shirt over his muscled chest, leather straps crossed around him, a sparkling crystal amulet in the center. A deep gray cape flowed from his back. Bronze and silver cuffs wrapped around his wrists and calves.

Next to him stood a striking woman of similar age. She also had jet-black hair, though no white shimmered in her locks. When she blinked, her icy blue eyes were petrifying, as if they could look deep into your soul, penetrating your very insides if your gaze was met for too long.

She wore a gossamer gown, the color a deepest shade of midnight, with no slip beneath it. Silver cords enveloped her waist, holding the flowing pieces together. A silver band scrolled up both her upper arms ending in a crescent moon. A single chain with a similar crescent dangling from the center lay across her forehead. A striking sapphire amulet hung from her neck.

"Fuck." The word escaped Ember's lips.

"Well is anyone going to introduce us, or must I do everything myself?" the deep male voice echoed throughout the courtyard. No one spoke. No one could. The air stripped from the very courtyard they stood in. "Very well then, introducing King Nikolaos and Queen Giselle of Nexos. No need to bow, we know we are a bit late to the party."

Offering his hand to his wife, they descended the steps into the courtyard. There was no emotion behind the king's piercing silver eyes, and when Ember looked at the queen—she felt as if death itself would be a mercy.

Ember swallowed. King Nikolaos—and not just him, but his deadly wife Giselle. He was known for his shadows, his control of the seas; she for the moon and how it altered the tides, how it called to certain animals. It was even rumored she could morph into one of the deadly black wolves of Nexos herself.

They had not been seen outside of their isle in years. Ember flashed Ajax a look of despair. This could not be happening. Ajax took a step closer to her, his hand going for his sword.

"Not to worry, Commander, we are not here to cause trouble."

Everyone looked to Ember to say something, but this was not something they discussed last night. Although Nexos was a lingering threat, not one of them thought its king and queen would show *their* faces today.

Ember glanced over at Kohl and King Athanas to see if they could lead her in the right direction. The two were whispering back and forth, King Athanas's eyes locked directly on the queen's. It was strange the way he looked at her with more hatred than Nikolaos.

Kohl's lips thinned as he nodded at whatever his father muttered under his breath, his fingers again pinching the bridge of his nose.

It was then that Ember noticed Kohl was not in his formal attire. Usually the other leaders and nobility of the isles would wear tailored pants and an overcoat of their respective colors.

Yet, Kohl was not wearing the black set with red and orange detailing around the cuff and short collar. Instead, he wore all black fighting leathers, bronze plates covering his chest, forearms, and calves. A golden viper was engraved in the chest plate. Dual longswords were attached to his back, a curved dagger of the Southern Lands hung at his hip.

Ember cocked her head to the side. He was dressed like her, dressed to fight. She wondered if King Athanas's spies heard Nexos was coming and he wanted Kohl to be prepared. There was no other explanation for it.

King Athanas spoke next. "Not here to cause trouble, and yet you interrupt this sacred tradition?"

"You would know all about interrupting sacred traditions, *Khalid*." Nikolaos's words boomed through the courtyard again.

King Athanas laughed, the sound unnerving. His pupils dilated the same way they did the day before, the whites surrounding them until they were almost nonexistent. "Of course you would go on the defensive, *Kirassos*. And yet it was you who formulated the plot to take our dear Aikaterine, who was supposed to be Acknowledged during this very ceremony."

Voices started to rise as people realized Katrin was not sick, but worse—missing. She cursed the gods that King Athanas brought that to everyone's attention. Nexos would never admit they took her in front of all these people, especially if they were trying to capture the Throne of Alentus.

No, someone like King Nikolaos would want to draw this out. "This is the first I have heard of your lady's disappearance. Twice in a decade seems very suspicious, Khalid."

King Nikolaos stepped closer toward the dais, the crowd parting on either side as his shadows began creeping through the courtyard. "As I said, I am not here to cause trouble, just to perform my duty as a fellow leader of the Mykandrian Isles, and offer my vote." His voice dripped on the words like olive oil.

"And what of your eldest son? Is he here to perform his duties as well?" King Athanas snapped.

"You know *very well* where my eldest son is, Khalid." King Nikolaos's shadows grew thicker, as did the darkness swirling in his silver eyes.

Kohl's father just smirked. "I haven't a clue what you are implying, Kirassos." The Viper looked over at his son, giving him a nod.

Ember could not help but stare in awe at the curious interaction happening in front of her. A tinge of long-standing rivalry looming between two kings. She was so close. So close to everything not going to shit until gods-damned Nexos walked in.

Shadows began to whirl in the center of the courtyard, forming around what appeared to be another man, though this one much younger than the king. *His son*, Ember thought. As she glanced between Ajax and Kohl she could tell they both thought the same thing, each reaching for the blade at their side. But what was said next, she did not see coming. The confusion, the betrayal, it froze her standing there unable to grasp what happened. Unable to protest as the words were spoken loud enough for all to hear.

"I enact the Wrecking of the Throne of Alentus."

CHAPTER TWENTY-ONE

KATRIN

C ool air whipped about *The Nostos,* as Katrin paced the deck, Mykonos still padding by her side. She'd pulled another pair of trousers out of the dresser, these ones made of a thin brown leather. Not thick enough for a battle, but similar to the ones she wore training in the fall. Again they were too big for her, having to wrap a navy cord tightly around the top to keep from showing her skin to everyone on the ship. She paired it with a thicker long sleeve shirt, cut lower in the front than she might have liked.

Her teeth chattered as the breeze struck her skin, waiting patiently for the sun to warm her body. The skies were clear, which would help later in the day, but in the early morning light, it just meant the chill from the night lingered. At night, she curled up under the blankets in Ander's cabin. He did not bother to come back after she insulted him. She had every right to challenge him though—and his intent for what to do with her.

But this morning she intended to find him. Make him tell her exactly why she was here, where they were going. Katrin even managed to swipe one of the shorter swords from the supply room she happened upon yesterday. She flipped the pommel around in her hand.

It was only a tad bit heavier than the metals they used in Alentus. But this sword was a delicate work of craftsmanship. It depicted beautiful carvings of what appeared to be a myth, a man was tied to the mast of a ship, beautiful women with the scales of fish along their arms and wings of an eagle protruding from their backs lay on a nearby isle. It was adorned with deep blue sapphires and crystals, radiating a power that was much older than she.

Katrin paced for what seemed like hours and still there was no sign of him—or Leighton for that matter.

The sky was so clear, not a cloud or dusting of fog to be found. Only a deep crystal blue stretched out in all four directions. She knew there was a point between Alentus and some of the nearby isles that looked this way, traveled to them once as a child with her father. Maybe she was already starting to lose her mind, maybe only moments passed since she walked up to the deck.

Too many thoughts filled Katrin's mind. The Acknowledgement would be starting soon and she would not know the outcome. Deep in her gut she knew Kohl and Ember would find some way to postpone or call upon some ancient law that allowed Katrin to be Acknowledged without being there. But if they did not—Katrin shuttered to think of the state of her home if that happened. If someone managed to take her rightful place on the throne from under her, she could not imagine how bad that would be. How much worse it would be if it was Nexos.

But Nexos *was* more than likely responsible for this—*all* of this. The words of the man with the blood-red eyes replayed in her head.

He is your curse.

Maybe this *he* still was. Nikolaos.

She never saw the King of Nexos, escaped before they arrived at the isle last time. Katrin wondered if that was where they headed now. A chill creeped up her spine, not from the brisk morning air, but from a tall individual she found towering over her.

"I was beginning to wonder if you were hiding from me." Katrin turned around locking her brown eyes with his. This time an icy blue with only small flecks of green.

"I would think it would be the other way around, Starling," Ander purred.

Katrin snarled her lip, then took a deep breath, trying to compose how she would say what she needed to say. Or, technically, ask what she needed to know. Her hand kept twitching against the hilt of the sword she sheathed in her leather cross belt. A faint heat radiating off the metal, a buzz shooting up through her arm.

She kept her voice calm but forceful. It was the only way she knew he might listen to her request—given he turned her down multiple times since she woke up on this gods-damned boat.

"Ander, you say you aren't here to hurt me." She arched her head up, trying to appear bigger than her lithe frame peering up at him from below. "That I've ended up on this ship because you're trying to save me from some currently nameless enemy. I need you to tell me. If I'm going to try and trust you—which I don't know if I *could* trust you at this point—then you need to be honest. About everything."

Katrin stood firm in her place. The little white cat stopped circling her legs, instead hopping up onto a nearby barrel, sitting back on her haunches as her yellow eyes flipped back and forth between the two of them.

"Ahh, yes...honesty. Not one of my finer characteristics. But I can assure you, Starling, I have never lied to you." Ander took a step closer to her, and she retreated one.

"Again, that is not an answer. I mean it, Ander, why am I here?" Katrin scrunched her brows together, her normally plush lips thinned into a fine line.

His eyebrows cocked up, a sly grin rolling across that shimmering olive-tanned skin of his. "Fine. If you beat me in a fight I will tell you."

Katrin's mouth dropped open. "Excuse me!"

"You heard what I said, Starling. You. Beat. Me. I. Tell. You. *Everything.*"

She shifted between her feet, her hand grazing against the pommel of the stolen sword. She *was* a good fighter. The best on Alentus besides maybe Kohl and Ajax, but in the past few months she withered away into nothing more than a hollow shell.

"That's what you wanted right? A fight? Why you stole my favorite sword from the armory?"

Of course it was. "I haven't a clue what you're talking about."

The small white cat stretched out on the barrel, giving a small *meow* as if to laugh at the thought.

"The sword hooked into your belt, with the engraving of Odysseus passing the sirens." Ander pointed to her hip.

From the book Ander left her. The book from the woman named Chloe. She wondered if it was his favorite sword because it was also a gift from her.

"Oh...*that* sword." Katrin shrugged her shoulders, her face in a grimace.

"Yes, that sword."

"Fine, so if I beat you then you tell me why you brought me here?" Katrin was still wary. She did not think she could win in a swordfight, maybe a spar, but even that could be risky. When she took him down the first day aboard *The Nostos*, he all but sat back and let her.

"I'll tell you whatever you want to know. I'll even use my left hand." He bowed toward her, drawing the sword from the sheath on his back.

"Don't you dare go easy on me." Lies. More and more lies. She wished he would go easy on her. Katrin bowed back.

She flipped the sword in her hand, adjusting to its weight, holding the grip firm. Her feet were planted at an angle, knees softly bent as she held up a front guard.

Ander advanced, striking his sword low by her hip. Katrin flipped her sword down, the sound of metal clanging as they met. She drew her sword around in an arc, breaking the connection and pivoting to her left. They continued back and forth striking blade to blade as Ander advanced, Katrin having to stay light on her feet as she fell farther and farther back toward the rail of the ship. Sweat began to form along her brow and upper lip. He would give even Kohl and the Commander a run for their money. His movements were delicate and precise as he began to overpower her.

A loud hiss caused Ander's gaze to falter. Katrin made a pass back, catching him off guard. She used the slight trip in his step to lunge, knocking the sword from his hand. He stood unarmed, not reaching for one of the many daggers or the second sword across his back.

She stood across from him, chest heaving, both hands gripping her sword.

"This is the second time I've bested you," Katrin said between breaths.

"You mean the second time I *let* you best me."

Someone chuckled from behind them.

"You know that's not true, Captain. The princess has talent. As for that bargain of yours, I do believe you owe her an explanation as to why she joins us on *The Nostos*," a quiet and melodic voice swept in on the breeze.

Katrin whipped her head toward the person speaking those words. No one was there to overhear them make the bargain. No one except Mykonos.

A woman a little younger than her stood there. Her stature was smaller than Katrin's, but her presence was captivating. Long hair stripped of all color fluttered down her back, yet the eyebrows arched above her violet upturned eyes were a deep onyx. Her skin was milky white and seemed to shimmer in the sunlight. She wore a gauzy white dress held together at the waist by a leather embossed belt with flowers that matched the color of her eyes.

She reminded Katrin of the traders she used to see at port from Anatole, before Nexos cut off access to their straits. She was stunning.

Was this the Chloe that gifted Ander such beautiful things? Katrin could not help it as a pang of jealousy rolled through her as the woman reached out her delicate hand, placing it on his bicep.

"You enjoy watching me lose much too much, Thalia." Ander furrowed his brows.

Not Chloe. Thalia. How many women looked at—or wrote about—Ander with such admiration?

"It's a pleasure to meet you, Princess. It will be nice having another woman aboard the ship. If this one ever lets us spend time together." Thalia smiled.

An intoxicating and warm laughter circled the air. "I wouldn't want to see what you two would get into."

Katrin stared at her, at them both. There seemed to be something familiar about this woman, but she couldn't quite place it, as if she felt like an old friend.

The small white cat jumped down from the top of the barrel, trotting over to Thalia and rubbing against her leg.

"Is she yours?" Katrin asked, another pang of jealousy whipping through her that the one friend—if you could even call a cat a friend—she made was this woman's pet.

"In a way, yes," the sweet voice replied.

"That little spy is Thalia's *psychí*." Ander pointed at the cat as it hissed back at him.

"*Psychí*?" Katrin hadn't heard that word before. She guessed it was another of the *Elliniká Glóssa*. Ander spoke several words in that same accent. It was hard to get used to a language that was seen as a death sentence in the isles. She wondered where he learned it. Those from before the war were long dead, their books destroyed.

"Every seer has one. Their very soul personifies itself as an animal. It is thought to make up their thoughts, their personality," Ander explained.

"You're a seer?" Katrin's eyes widened at the small woman.

"I *was* a seer. Now I am just a glorified babysitter for the captain and the nauarch. Making sure the two of them stay out of trouble. But clearly this one never learns." Thalia punched Ander in the arm.

"I thought the seers were not allowed to leave the isle of Delphine except during the birth of a royal?"

"Exceptions are made," Ander cut in.

Katrin narrowed her eyes at him, throwing a vulgar gesture in his direction.

"So you're a seer, or were a seer, and Mykonos...I'm sorry, the cat is your soul?" She could not wrap her head around it. She read books about them, was given a prophecy by one, but not once heard of this *psychí*, this bond between an animal and its human. And Thalia—she was beautiful, not like the old crones she saw before.

"It's quite alright. You can call her whatever you like. Mykonos is far better than some of the names Ander or Leighton have given her."

Ander bristled. "It is not our fault you send that *daimon* to listen in on our conversations. Plus, she always leaves little gifts at my door."

Thalia rolled her eyes. "If she didn't kill the mice on this ship it would be overrun." The cat meowed in agreement.

"You can hear what is said to her?" Katrin's cheeks flushed at the idea. She spoke openly to it the night before.

"When I wish to. Don't worry, I was not listening last night. Sometimes the voices in my head can be overwhelming, and I choose to shut them off. And I decided I much rather meet you myself, make my own judgments about the coveted princess."

Katrin cringed. *Coveted princess* was not the way she wanted to be described. Ander looked away from Thalia, trying to ignore her—or avoid the little *daimon* as he called the cat. She almost giggled at the fact that he looked afraid of the small fluffy creature.

"It looks like I owe you an explanation, Starling. Seeing as you won our gamble."

"I will take that as my cue to leave." Thalia scooped up the cat. "Come on Mykonos. You are coming with me while the captain settles his debts." Mykonos hissed again, not at her human, but in a taunt toward Ander. He shuddered as he spoke to Katrin.

"You do not want to get on her bad side. And by 'her' I do mean the cat. She can be vicious."

Katrin laughed so hard she snorted. But his voice was dead serious. "A notorious pirate is afraid of a tiny white animal?"

"Trust me, that is not the only form she can take."

Her eyebrows shot up. The cat could shift? That would be an interesting sight to see. All Katrin could picture was a giant version of the innocent creature that curled up next to her last night, purring as she fell asleep. Vicious was not the word she would use to describe Mykonos.

"So, are you going to tell me why I am here now, or are you going to come up with yet another excuse?"

Ander met her stare.

"I'll tell you, Starling—but I have one more excuse. I will only tell you over lunch."

Katrin sighed, wondering what his obsession was with watching her eat. First demanding she join him for dinner, now this.

She was hungry, though. The breakfast she ate seemed to be hours ago and although the fight was short, she did not have nearly the energy she once did.

"Fine. But I get to ask *anything*."

"Well...*almost* anything." Ander smiled.

When they entered the corridor to his—well, their—chambers, he directed Katrin to an earlier door, which was the one she saw across the armory yesterday morning. As they stepped inside she could see from this view that it definitely was an armory, not a supply closet that just happened to have weapons.

Foolishly Katrin had not looked around when she stole the sword earlier. Being too afraid to be caught, she only took one step in and grabbed the nearest weapon to the door. It just happened that it was the most exquisite one, and also Ander's favorite.

He left the room briefly to grab their lunch, asking her not to snoop around, but his words were useless. Katrin had always been known for her—call it curiosity, and it often got her in trouble as a child. It probably still would cause her trouble to this day.

She took the few minutes he was gone to poke through the charts that were sprawled out on the large table in the middle of the room. She traced her fingers over the isles she knew—Alentus, Morentius, Delphine, Lesathos, Xanthia, Cantos, *Nexos*. Then she noticed two others to the east of Nexos in what was called The Manos Sea. The Manos Sea was just a myth, where Cyther and Skiatha supposedly resided. Although she knew Cyther was real—her mother would be there soon—it was not a place of this plane or realm. Instead it was like Aidesian, part of the world of the afterlife, not Odessia. Yet this chart showed it as if you could choose to sail there.

Before she could flip through any of the other charts or papers, Ander entered back into the room. The lunch he brought in was much simpler than the meals before, consisting of that same fresh salad made up of cucumber, olives, onion, tomatoes, and that delicious lightly-salted cheese as well as spiced chicken. It looked incredible.

"I hope you don't mind the food. I noticed you only ate pastries this morning and that doesn't have nearly the nutrients you need to survive." Ander laid one plate in front of her.

Katrin was trying not to drool as he drizzled a bit of olive oil on top before sitting beside her. She could eat this salad for every meal, but would not give him the satisfaction of knowing that. Ander stared at her as she began shoveling the food into her mouth like there was no tomorrow, because at this rate she really did not know.

"What?" she mumbled, mouth half full of a slice of tomato.

"You know you chew louder than any of the crew on this ship," he chuckled.

"I do not! I chew at a completely reasonable volume," Katrin said through another mouthful of food, her eyes narrowing.

"If you're an animal maybe." He cringed as she continued chomping away.

Katrin's cheeks flushed slightly and she tried to quiet, but it was difficult with such crunchy food. "Well *you* are the one who insists on eating with *me*, so I'm not sure you really have a say. Take it or leave it, Captain." She made a mocking face his way.

"I don't even know why I bother," Ander replied, shaking his wavy black hair.

Katrin shrugged. She knew she was thin and diminished almost down to skin and bone. She saw it too. What she could not understand is why he even cared in the first place.

"Why do you bother?" Katrin asked. The first question of many swirling through her mind.

"Because I don't like seeing people who have been through trauma waste away to nothing. You are a survivor, not a victim." Ander's voice seemed almost possessive as he spoke to her.

"What would you know about being a survivor?" Katrin managed to get out between chews.

Ander's eyes darkened. "More than you think."

The hairs on the back of her neck stood on edge, the air around her thickening. She had forgotten—the markings on his wrists, often covered on the ship by the sleeves of his shirts. Those markings were one of the reasons she had felt so comfortable sharing her past with him in the mountains that fateful day.

"Fine." Katrin pointed at the chart. "Why is there an imaginary island drawn here?"

"Keep your olive oil fingers off my chart!" Ander snatched it from under her greasy appendages. She flipped him a vulgar gesture before wiping her hands on her pants. They weren't *that* dirty.

The chart was beautiful, with intricate drawings of fleets and way-points across the isles. Depicting scenes straight out of the book she'd started reading, *The Odyssey*, with sirens and cyclops, and the Olympi. The marking in the upper left hand corner was familiar to her, a sea serpent, although the crossed swords that marked the horse's bridle and the tunic she borrowed back on Alentus were not there. The cardinal directions pointed out from four arrows around it.

"Sorry...that wasn't an answer. Why is Skiatha on that chart?"

"Because that is where we are going," Ander said plainly.

Katrin pushed her chair back, almost spitting out her food. "We're going to a fake isle?" She coughed. "Skiatha is just a myth, everyone knows that."

"Skiatha is as real as you and I. And it is indeed our waypoint. We must pass through Lesathos first for supplies, but then we continue on to the east."

"I don't understand. That place is just a story parents tell their children to frighten them. It's not in our books or on any maps of Odessia. How do you even know it exists?"

Ander's eyes sparkled a crystal blue, like the sea on the clearest of days. His lip twitched up into a grin, showing off one of his canines. "Because, Starling, that is where *The Nostos* takes port."

Her mind flashed back to when she first met Leighton. He called Ander *the Prince of the Lost Isles*. She thought it was something made up. A joke amongst merchants and washed-up soldiers. A way for the pirate to feel more powerful than he was.

But if they were real, if they were truly just lost and forgotten, not one of imagination, then that meant Ander led the army of the dead. Not only that, but he was one of the most vicious and corrupt leaders. One that helped lay waste to an entire civilization of people. Her eyes widened, white starting to flicker through.

"I know what is going through your head right now, but although the isle is real, those stories are not. We are a place for warriors—warriors who seek refuge from abuse of other lands. The isle is prosperous and certainly is not surrounded by a ring of flame on the coast."

Katrin's eyes dimmed back to their brown and amber tone. Her breathing evened. She was not sure why she was so quick to believe him, but she was.

No army of the dead. The idea gave her the creeps, even if her father did rule most of the dead, these warriors were supposed to be a different kind of undead.

"Well, nice to know you didn't slaughter thousands of people..." She gave a small, half-hearted smile. "Why are we going there? Why is it important that I go there?"

Ander tapped his fingers on the table. Breaking their eye contact for a moment. "Because there is a war coming, and if we don't act soon we could lose everything." His voice was grave, jaw tight.

"A war? With Nexos? I know they are a threat, but do you really think King Nikolaos would go that far?"

"Oh, Starling, King Nikolaos is the least of your worries."

Katrin's breath hitched. King Nikolaos was the only threat she had been informed of, by both Ajax and King Athanas' spies. "Then who?"

"You might want to look a little closer to home to answer that question. Don't you find it strange that King Athanas never sought retribution on the people who took you? That he even pushed Kohl to marry you in the first place, when he is neither god-born nor blessed, knowing your duty to the lands? You don't think it is strange that Kohl

just happened upon your drifting body off the coast of Lesathos? They
are the enemy."

"Don't you *dare* drag Kohl into this," Katrin seethed. "He rescued me
when I was flung about in the sea five years ago. If it weren't for him I
would be dead! We are *Fated*!"

Ander's features darkened as he strained his neck to the side. Gripping
the edge of the table. "And maybe he knows nothing, or maybe he is just
a better liar than you know."

"He loves me!" A faint glow lingered around her skin.

At least, Katrin thought he did. Their last night together was complicated, but he had always been there for her up until then. His actions had
to be pressured from his father. They had been approaching the wedding
and King Athanas always had a certain way he liked things to go. But he
would never really hurt her. It was impossible.

"Maybe so, but I have it on good authority that King Athanas has been
working with a king from Voreia for years to shake up leadership in the
isles."

"You're lying." Katrin stood up to walk out, tears beginning to form
in her eyes. "He may be known as the Viper, but all that man has wanted
is peace. You seem to be confusing them for Nexos."

He shot up from his chair, hands still clawed into the wooden table.
"They would have killed you, *Aikaterine*, if I had not taken you, they
would have *murdered* you," Ander growled.

"No, that's a lie and you know it!"

He had only called her by her full name when he spoke that first
morning. It rolled off his tongue with a taste of despair, and for once
she did not hate hearing it. When she looked at him, at his posture and
pleading in his eyes that turned a dimming gray and deep green, she could
not help but wonder if it was true. Or if he at least thought it was.

"It was the only thing I could do," his voice finally shattered. "I had to
protect you."

"Why? Why am I so important to you?" Katrin stared at him, trying
to understand, trying to see some wild point of view where the ones who
meant the most to her had been lying for years, not this man she just met.

Ander's face had softened, his eyes tracing the outline of her lips, her jaw, her neck for several moments. He finally spoke. "Because you just are."

It was not enough of a response for her. She needed an unequivocal reason *why*. But instead she asked, "Who is Chloe?" Her final question for the Captain. She didn't even know why it slipped out in the first place. Maybe because of the whirling emotions that traveled from her head to her gut. Maybe it was because she knew he would not answer any of her other questions.

"Do I detect a hint of jealousy in those words, Starling?" Ander's eyes lit up, dancing with crystal blue and turquoise green, reminding her of the waters back home. No longer the darkening color of a storm.

"Why would you think I would be jealous of anyone who thinks a brute like you is *darling*."

Ander shrugged, flashing that stupid grin of his. "Maybe because you're starting to like me."

Katrin stood up and backed a few steps up toward the door. "You *captured* me. How could you think there would be any way I could like *you*?"

"Ahh, but Starling, did I not just explain it was for a very good reason? You were in danger."

"That's if I even believe you."

Ander slid away from the table, walking over and pinning her against the wall. He leaned in until his lips were inches from hers, foreheads almost touching. She couldn't take her eyes from his as her breath quickened. Ander lifted his hand up, grazing his thumb over her lower lip.

"Oh, you believe me."

Katrin swallowed as a shiver trailed over her skin. She could feel a heat begin to replace it. But this was not the usual heat that came from anger or hatred, the one she had moments before. No—this was a fiery warmth that built deep in her center. A want. A need. A yearning for him to lean those few inches closer.

She blinked, knocking herself out of what seemed like a trance. Every time he held her stare she lost all sense of reality, purely entranced by those wandering eyes. Katrin would need to keep her wits about her. She had to find her way back home. Back to her people, to her throne, to Kohl.

"Even if I do. That doesn't change a thing." She pushed off him, breaking Ander's stare. "You took me from my home. Potentially stripped me of my birthright. I will *never* forgive you for that—protecting me or not."

Ander's jaw clenched. His tanned olive skin paling. Katrin knew he was hoping for a different response. But how could he think it was that simple? Even if she did believe him, she could never really trust him. Not after he lied to her from the moment they met in the Triad Mountains. He could have told her that day. Explained that she needed to be wary of those she trusted. She could have defended *herself* against it. No, forgiveness was not in the stars for them.

"I know you say that now—that you *can't* forgive me—but I hope someday I will change your mind. I can prove that all of this was for you," he spoke softly. "And to answer your question, Chloe was my sister."

The words struck her. He had a sister. And clearly cared deeply for her. Probably missed her more than words could convey.

Katrin again tried to send a wish out to her own sister. One that hoped she was alright. One that willed her strength and resolve through what was surely a trying time for her back home as well.

CHAPTER TWENTY-TWO

KOHL

He had not meant for it to go this far. Had not thought he would actually speak the words until they flowed out of his mouth. *I enact the Wrecking of the Throne of Alentus.* Ember would kill him, and Ajax, and Katrin. Gods—Katrin would probably kill him, have her father bring him back from the dead, and kill him all over again.

Kohl started tapping his foot. His father warned him this might happen. That Nexos might appear at the Acknowledgement poised to steal the throne. He never should have left two nights ago to speak with his father. He should have stayed by Katrin's side until this was over. Contention had been brewing in the isles for quite some time, Ajax had warned him that Nexos might already be here. They had been here, working with that lowly pirate that took his bride from him.

He hated Nexos, and King Nikolaos, and his stupid son with everything he had. When that shadowy mist began forming around another person in the courtyard he knew it was the eldest son, Nik, and the words he tried to withhold simply slipped from his lips.

Kohl would not let Ember fight him. Nexos had no sense of duty or loyalty to tradition and Ember, being the closest Drakos to the throne at present, would have the first opportunity to challenge the Wrecking. It was supposed to be a fight to first blood, but he knew Nik would make it a fight to the death if he had the chance. Yes, Katrin might be angry at him for this, but she would never have forgiven him if he did not protect her sister.

But as the shadows cleared it was not the man he was expecting. The same black hair and olive tanned skin was there, but his features were those of someone younger, the icy blue eyes of Giselle replaced the ones Kohl had come to loathe. Nik did not stand before him, Dimitris did. Kohl growled, the youngest son had the same insolent smirk as his father, as Nik, plastered across his face.

"My son, Prince Dimitris of Nexos, second in line to the throne," King Nikolaos announced to the courtyard. Dimitris bowed toward Ember. Ajax stepped in front of her, drawing his sword and pointing it toward the ground by his feet.

"As much as we all love your introductions, King Nikolaos, we must continue with the ceremony," Ajax spoke with a feral sense of protection.

Kohl watched him turn toward Ember, her eyes now welled with tears. He would have to apologize later for why he did this. Why he called the Wrecking. Ajax whispered something in her ear, but she shook her head, wiping the tears from her eyes and readjusting her posture, her Alentian fighting leathers showing her status as future Prytan of the Spartanis.

Again Ajax spoke. "As tradition has it, we first ask the heir apparent if they wish to accept the Wrecking. Ember, seeing as Katrin is not present, you may choose to accept or defer to the other isles."

Ember's face went grim as she stared down Kohl. Her golden eyes glimmered and darkened. "I accept the contest of the Wrecking."

Her words were sharp and clear, but Kohl could not understand. She had been training, but did she really think she had a chance against him? All this would prove was that she was not ready to accept her own position as Prytan. Give his father more reasons to strip that birthright from her.

"Ember, don't do this," Kohl begged.

He could hear King Nikolaos chuckling from the other end of the courtyard before he, Queen Giselle, and their son disappeared in a cloud of black.

"We will now give the two contenders time to prepare for the Wrecking. When the sun reaches its peak the battle will begin."

The crowd went up with a roar of cheers. Kohl saw Ajax try to quickly shuffle Ember off, but she stalked directly toward him.

"Not here," he heard Ajax yell over the crowd.

Ember tried to break his grip, but the commander would not let go.

Kohl quickly stepped out of the courtyard, going back to the study where they met last night, his father surprisingly nowhere to be seen since Nexos disappeared.

"How dare you!" Ember screamed as she burrowed through the door.

She stalked right up to him, shoving him back. It would have been cute to see a young woman, barely reaching his shoulders, try to push him over had pure hatred not laced her words.

"What would Katrin think! You couldn't even protect her and now you mean to steal her throne!" Ember spit on Kohl. His gut reacted as he flashed the back of his hand across her face. She stepped back, clutching her palm to a now red cheek. Ajax's brows narrowed as he reached for the hilt of his sword.

"I would think very carefully about what you do next, *Kohl*," Ajax growled through clenched teeth.

Kohl flashed his eyes between the two of them. Betrayal was written all over their faces. He had not wanted this to happen. Kohl dragged his palm down his face, sighing as he sunk into the chair nearby.

"I'm sorry, Ember. I'm so, so sorry. For all of this. I saw him and I thought it was Nik and I just acted. I wanted to protect you, protect what is your sister's." His voice cracked as he spoke.

"Protect what is Katrin's? No one had called the Wrecking, Kohl. No one but you. It never occurred to you that this is what Nexos wanted? For us to look weak and indecisive even between allies? You didn't *think* at all." For a younger woman not trained in politics, she was making a very good point.

"But if they had declared, he would have killed you."

"You don't know that—"

"I know Nik! And my father warned me this could happen. His spies heard they might try to usurp us," Kohl cut her off. His hands were shaking now. Where was his father? He needed him here to explain why Kohl would even float the idea, why it had been no question when Nexos arrived that he would protect them all at all costs.

"That was not your decision, Kohl. It was Ember's and hers alone. And now look at the situation—two allies competing for something that wasn't even theirs in the first place." He had never seen Ajax this furious. Kohl didn't understand, Ajax should have wanted him to enact before Ember had to face some insolent male from another isle.

Ember continued pacing around the room. Kohl was used to Katrin being this hot-headed and fueled, but Ember had always been the light-hearted younger sister. Showing a flair for the dramatics, yes—but only when it came to choosing which dress to buy or ball to attend. The way her brows quashed together and her hand clenched he could have sworn it was as if part of her sister flowed through her in that moment. The fury of their father, not the lightness of their mother's power.

"You must yield. That's the only way to come back from this. I understand why you did it. You thought you were protecting me from Nik, or from Dimitris, or whoever King Nikolaos had thought to throw against us. But that isn't happening now. Now it is you and me, and what Katrin would want is for her people to be ruled by her family, not one of the other isles. Especially not one influenced so much by the Viper, father or not." She stopped pacing and looked Kohl head to toe before giving a vicious smile and exiting back to the courtyard, Ajax following closely.

Kohl sunk farther into the chair, his head throbbing. What had he gotten himself into?

When Kohl returned to the courtyard just before the peak of the day, the center had been outlined in a ring—their sparring grounds. His father stood nearest the archway by his chambers, speaking with one of his guards.

Kohl pushed through the people of the isles—those who would watch him battle his future sister-in-law—to get to the man who started this mess in the first place.

"Where have you been!" Kohl said through clenched teeth.

His father's eyebrows arched up, those ebony eyes flickering with amusement.

"I went to alert my guards that Nexos may try to strike again. King Nikolaos can move a fair distance in his shadows, but he can't make it off this isle. And I doubt the only reason he was here was to introduce his youngest son."

Kohl's nostrils flared. As savvy as King Athanas was in battle he was a gods-damned pain in his ass. "You told me to do whatever was necessary and now look what a mess I'm in, Father! Ember is furious, I know Katrin would be if she were here."

His father cut him off. "But she is not here. And do you really think your future bride would want to return knowing her younger sister was named queen? Had stolen the title that was rightfully hers? Or, would she rather you—the man who was always supposed to rule by her side—take up that position so that when we do rescue her, she is able to resume her rightful place?" King Athanas showed off that toothy smile, causing even a shudder down Kohl's spine.

His father did have a point. If—*when*—he rescued Katrin, this would be the easiest way for her to become queen. Just as she would have had him rule equally beside her, he would have Katrin.

"You really think this is what she would want, Father?" Kohl faced King Athanas again, needing that final bit of validation before he entered the ring, his mind too cloudy to think straight.

"What Katrin wants is the best for Alentus, my boy. A man who was raised to become king is much better suited to lead this land to peace and prosperity over a young girl, who up until a few weeks ago skirted her own responsibilities to this court. Ember is kind and she is beautiful, but she is not ready—nor may ever be ready—to be a queen."

The words were harsh, but Kohl knew they were true. Today Ember may be dressed like a ruler, but she was never raised to be one. She did not understand the inner workings of appeasing allies, or monitoring trade routes, certainly not the financial undertakings of the throne.

If he yielded to her, not only would he appear weak in front of the other isles, and his father, but he would be putting the people of Alentus in danger of war. He could not—would not—do that to Katrin's people. *Their* people.

"Then I will not yield."

King Athanas nodded his head, and for the first time in a long time, his father looked proud.

As he entered the ring, unsheathing his sword from behind his back, Ember stood silently on the other side. They would only be like this for a few moments, until the sun reached its peak and the shadows disappeared. Whispering to Ember, Ajax covered his mouth so Kohl could not make out the words. She still wore the same navy fighting leathers embossed with the symbol of Alentus. Ember grasped her lithe hands in Ajax's, looking him straight in the eyes. *Thank you*, Kohl could see her say before also stepping into the ring.

Her hair was pinned back even tighter than before, to keep the long blonde strands from blocking her line of sight. She unsheathed a thin bronze sword with a delicate turquoise leather wrap as a grip, a matching bronze and turquoise shield was attached to the forearm of her left arm, her wrist cuffs still prominent, protecting a fragile area. The simple crown of the Prytan of the Spartanis sat upon her golden locks, shimmering in the high sun.

As the sun inched closer and closer to its peak, the crowd around began to hush. The tradition was simple, fight until first blood. It was then common for the person who was struck to yield. No vote would occur after. The Wrecking of the Throne was binding.

Again the commander spoke, his voice much warier than earlier in the day. "Through the blood that is spilled on the sands of our people, so shall our leader rise." He raised his hand over the center of the ring, letting sand from the shores of Alentus trickle down. "May the Grechi give their blessing." He bowed to each challenger as was tradition before exiting the ring.

Kohl locked eyes with Ember, bowing to each other as well. His shadow inched its way back to his body.

"Begin!" Ajax's voice rang clear throughout the courtyard. No one dared to murmur as the Wrecking commenced.

Kohl stared Ember down as she took a fighting stance, one foot slightly back from the other, knees bent, shield up protecting her chest, sword gripped tightly in her right hand. He began to circle the ring, dragging his sword in a line through the sand. He felt bad for taunting her, but he would need to put on a bit of a show. Not only for himself, but to convince the crowd that Ember possessed some skill, some fighting chance to one day lead the Spartanis. She followed his movements closely, weaving her steps in the same manner, her breathing calm and still.

Beads of sweat began to creep down Kohl's neck before either of them had even taken a blow, neither wanting to be the first to strike. Ember's eyes faltered to her feet just once, for only a moment, and Kohl took the opportunity to lunge. Metal clashed against metal as Ember planted firm through her legs, blocking his blow with her sword. Again he struck, this time she took the force with the shield, his edge slicing into the leather strip that went across the bronze circlet.

Ember pivoted, lunging the tip of her sword toward his bad shoulder. The same one Katrin had injured. The one that had miraculously recovered in a matter of days. Kohl's eyes narrowed, thinking back to that day, to Katrin and how she had lied to him. Ember had taken advantage of that, of his emotions when she struck. He spun quickly, avoiding the blade, and sliced across her left arm, drawing blood. The warm red liquid trickled down, glistening on the cuffs she wore.

"Yield!" Kohl yelled.

For a second, Ember clutched the cut along her upper arm, wincing from pain. Sweat dripped from her brow and along her lip, her breathing labored. She lunged at him, screaming, sword connecting with sword once more. She struck one, two, three times, inching him toward the corner of the ring. It was enough of a display of skill that the people of the isles would be impressed.

Kohl blocked her fourth strike, but missed as the blade quickly came back toward his face, a thin cut sliced across his cheek. That was the last time a Drakos woman would get him. He swung his blade out behind her, cutting the back of her thigh. Ember staggered back.

"Yield, Ember!" He did not want to hurt her, but he had to fight until she yielded. It was the way of the Wrecking. If he just stood there he would look weak, which would only entice Nexos to attack, or try again to steal what would soon be his position of power. His thoughts were dizzying as he followed the princess in front of him.

"I will not!" Ember's hair was now matted against her skin, the golden hue streaked with red from each attempt to brush loose strands from her face.

He struck again with more force, hitting against her shield and knocking her from her feet. "Don't do this, Ember. It's over."

She stood up, limping toward him as she raised her blade in a fighting stance, even with the pain of the two blows still lingering on her face.

It was embarrassing. A warrior of many years battling a young princess. Kohl could see his father's distaste as he mouthed the words, *End it.*

He swung once more, knocking the sword from her bloody palm. "Yield!" he repeated.

"I. Will. Not. Yield." Her voice was raspy through her gritted teeth.

Dust and sand swirled around her on the ground. Her wounded arm trying with all its might to hold the shield above her as Kohl's sword came down.

He glanced sideways at his father again, his ebony eyes darkening to an emotionless abyss. He kicked her shield and it went flying out of the ring. "If I have to repeat myself again, Ember, you will not like what happens next. Now, yield!" Kohl yelled, his voice ricocheting off the stone walls of the courtyard.

Her chest heaved, tears starting to well in the base of her amber eyes. She clenched her hands into fists, ready to go punch for punch with him. "For Katrin, I will not yield."

That was it. His undoing.

"This is for Katrin," he seethed.

Kohl lifted his sword driving the hilt into the side of her head.

All in the crowd went silent. All but Ajax, whose blood-curdling scream could be heard across the Mykandrian Sea. Kohl stepped from the ring, leaving a motionless Ember lying behind him.

Chapter Twenty-Three

Katrin

The wind had picked up aboard *The Nostos*, sending the ship swiftly toward its first port. While they continued on their journey to the isle Lesathos, the seas began to turn. The usual calm and crystal waters around Alentus churned, turning a deep green hue. Waves peaked with white foam crashed against the sides of the ship.

For a few days it had been this way. The rocking back and forth, the sea flooding over the deck causing many to lose their footing, the constant nausea swirling in Katrin's stomach.

She'd set sail on many ships, but only the nameless one from her past had ever sailed across rough seas as these. It was not the rolling water below, or the howling wind causing the ship to sway incessantly back and forth, that made her feel like she might hurl her breakfast. It was everything else.

The reminders of her previous captor, his hot, seedy breath, the way his sweaty palms would push her down. The fear that her sister and Kohl had not found a way to delay the Acknowledgement, that someone else now sat on her throne. The idea that she may never return home, that Ander was lying to her when he told her of the threat to her life.

The sun had risen and set five times since the Acknowledgement would have happened. Each night, while Katrin lay wide awake under the blankets in the captain's quarters, a wave of guilt and horror would wash over her. She couldn't escape it, the feeling that she had abandoned her people. Even if it was not true. Even if she had not left of her own free will.

When she would eventually drift away into sleep, it was never the sweet embrace she craved. Instead, she had visions of her sister lying lifeless on the ground. Her sparkling blonde hair dulled and crusted with dirt and blood. A shadowed man stood above her with a bloodied sword. She could never make out his face. Only her sister's. Still. Helpless. Beaten. Just as Katrin had once been. She would try to run to her, try to help, to stop the man that stood there as he crashed his sword into Ember's skull, but she never could. Her sister just drifted farther and farther away.

Katrin would wake sweaty and thrashing in the bed, blankets tossed from her, chest heaving. The nausea would roll in again causing her to sprint to the bathing chamber. Nothing came up. Nothing ever did. She would just kneel there, coughing nothingness into a black abyss, panting and desperate to be rid of it all. Five nights. Five nights she wished for her old nightmares. Wished to relive her own trauma so she did not see her sister like that one more time.

When she would return to the bed, Mykonos would curl up by her neck, nuzzling her whiskers against Katrin's clammy skin. She had told Thalia she did not need the creature as company, but each day the seer refused, allowing Mykonos to stay in Katrin's quarters rather than by her side.

Sometimes Katrin wished the seer would stay to talk, not just her *psychí*. For so long, Katrin kept her trauma trapped inside, eating away at her very soul. She missed having another person around, someone with whom she could confide in. Someone who would not judge her for the past tragedies she faced. Thalia seemed like that person—not divulging what horrors she herself had faced before coming aboard this ship.

Ander had stayed away since the day of the Acknowledgement when he had explained that her husband-to-be and his father might want her dead. Still, she had been unable to process any of it, more consumed by her visions of Ember than accepting that truth or lie, or whatever it may be.

Sometimes she would catch him staring at her from across the ship as she read, his hair always windswept, rubbing the back of his neck with a pained gaze. When they would lock eyes she would quickly turn away, not giving him the satisfaction of knowing she might have been staring too.

On the sixth morning, when Katrin stepped outside it smelt different. The salty air of the sea had turned sour, a blend of days old fish and sweaty men. Instead of an endless rolling sea, a small isle now lay before them. Its port was lively, with merchant and fishing ships lining the docks. People were selling goods directly from the ships all the way into the village where the market sat.

Katrin heard the stories of Lesathos, how it was ridden with crime and seedy characters, brothels at every corner, ale houses and dens filled with the smoky black drug *olerae* from the Eastern Plains. But also of its rich spice and textile market. The soft leathers and exquisite silks that the women who were not in the trade of selling their bodies would weave and cut.

She had always wanted to visit to experience the unknown. Her parents always forbade it. Even with her skill in battle, the isle was too dangerous. Too unpredictable. Yet here she was, looking over its coast as *The Nostos* neared closer and closer to the docks.

"We will only be here for one night."

Katrin jumped, startled by that deep and brooding voice she had not heard for days. Ander stood next to her in a slim fitting long-sleeved jacket, its color matching that of the midnight sky. He looked at her intently, words dancing on the tip of his tongue. But he never spoke.

"And I'm what—supposed to stay locked in my room so I can't escape?" Katrin narrowed her eyes at him, but Ander met her gaze. The subtle blue and green swirls of his eyes flickering in the morning sun, tracing every inch of her face.

"How many times do I have to tell you that you are not a prisoner aboard this ship?" His words were sharp as knives. Something had set him off today. Katrin couldn't imagine what. "Lesathos is not the place for a beautiful woman to wander about, especially a princess."

Katrin tried not to blush at the fact that he called her a beautiful woman. She knew she was pretty, but most preferred her glowing younger sister to Katrin's harsher features and demeanor. And Ander, as much as she might loathe him, could have someone far more beautiful than she would ever be. That gut-clenching jealousy hit her once more. It was infuriating. Even more so because she felt like someone as ruined as her did not deserve to be called beautiful.

"So I'm not a prisoner, but I am also not allowed to leave the ship." Katrin stuck her hands on her hips, tapping her foot. If Ander could have a pissy tone, so could she. It was pathetic, immature even, but she didn't care.

He sighed, running his hand through his rich black hair. "Please, Starling. You just have to trust me on this." His lips drew out in a fine line, jaw clenching like stone.

Katrin arched up one brow. "Trust you? Like I'm supposed to trust you on everything else?"

"Yes. Because it's the truth. Because unlike you think, I have always had your best interest in mind."

"I'm sure you think that." A pinched expression grew on her face.

"I have to go dock the ship. Leighton, some of the crew, and I will be going into town to gather supplies for the rest of the journey. Please just stay here. Read your books. Play with that devil cat you seem to like so much." Mykonos hissed from next to Katrin's legs. She had not even noticed the light-footed creature creeping up next to them. "Just don't venture off, you never know what is lurking in the shadows here."

"Whatever you say, *Captain.*" Katrin gave a mocking bow. Ander shook his head as he walked back toward the ship's wheel to bring *The Nostos* into port.

"You can always spend time with us while the rest of the crew is in town," a delicate voice said beside her. The small framed seer stood there, now holding a purring Mykonos. Her long white hair, usually pinned back or in a braid, lay stick-straight down her back despite the heavy winds that brought them into port. She had also swapped her usual leathers and tunics for a beautiful deep violet gown that matched her eyes.

Katrin needed to stop being so startled by people sneaking up on her aboard this ship. Especially Thalia, who was as silent as—well, as the white cat she now held when approaching.

"And what exactly do you plan on doing?" Katrin asked softly. She *had* been eager for the company.

Thalia let out a soft chuckle, "Gossiping of course. It is a lot more fun when I share it with someone other than this ball of fluff." She ruffled her hand through Mykonos's fur as the cat's pupils narrowed and she let out a hiss. "Oh shush! You are such a drama queen." The cat wiggled loose from her arms, plopping back down between the two of them.

"After the few days I've had, I think a little gossip would be nice." Katrin's lips tipped up into a smile for the first time in days.

"Wonderful, come by my room after we dock. I'll even sneak one of Ander's good bottles of wine from the storage room. He locks it, but I've always had a knack for picking locks. Must be the claws." She flashed her elongated nails painted a sparkling black.

"For nice wine, I'll definitely be there." Katrin tucked a piece of her tangled brown hair behind her ear. "Should I wear a dress as well?" Her eyes scanned the seer's gown once more.

"If you'd like. Sometimes I need to remind the crew there is a lady aboard. They are absolute animals otherwise. Plus, you never know who might be looking." She flicked her eyes back toward the helm of the ship, where both Leighton and Ander stood pretending they had not just been gaping at their interaction.

"I don't need—or want—to impress Ander." Katrin twiddled her thumbs together. "But maybe it would be nice to pretend everything is normal, even for one night." Katrin bit her bottom lip, trying not to overthink what had happened the past week. Or what might be happening back in Alentus.

"Whatever you say, Princess. I'll leave some options to try on in your chambers." Thalia smiled wide. The young seer began to pad away toward the door to below deck. She turned back, a soft expression glowing on her face. "Katrin—" her words became less playful and more gentle, "I'm really glad you said yes."

Katrin nodded her head at the seer as the ship began to dock. She would meet Thalia later, yes. But after—after she would find a way off this ship and a way back home.

Watching the crew dock *The Nostos* in the main harbor of Lesathos, Katrin pretended to read *The Odyssey* while she was really staring at Ander. The way he smiled at the crew when he gave orders rather than shouted at them, the way he joked about, peering at the nearing shoreline with as much intrigue as a little boy.

His eyes were always a warm and glittering blue with hints of crystal green while sailing. The colors of fair weather and a calm breeze. Quite unusual for a hardened pirate, or so she thought. She had not spent any time with them besides the red-eyed man, although she was fairly certain he was something much worse than a pirate.

When they were fully secured at the dock, Katrin ventured below deck to get ready for her evening with Thalia, and to pack a small bag for later that night. She could only hope the men would come back from the "market" too drunk to notice her sneaking off the ship.

A few pairs of clothes, some bread and fruits, a satchel of coin she found stored in Ander's desk drawer, and the book she was reading would all go in a leather bag she found in his quarters.

She would leave a note apologizing for the latter two. The money she did not feel horrible about—he was a pirate, he was probably rolling in it—but the book, that had sentimental value to him. It was just that Katrin had become quite engrossed in the characters, seeing the world of the Olympi she was never allowed to learn more about. The way they were wrathful and vengeful like she was taught, but also fierce protectors of the mortals.

When she entered the chambers she saw Thalia had indeed left several gown options to wear. It had been more than a week since she felt the smooth touch of silk against her skin. The gowns were each intricate, no doubt sewn by the very textile workers that lived on these shores.

One stood out in particular. In the lantern light of the bedchambers it sparkled a golden hue. The sleeves were made of a sheer material billowing down until the cuff, which was again the golden silk material. It reminded her of something Ember would wear. The others were lovely as well, but this—this dress was one of a kind.

She bathed first, washing off the smell of the ship with that lovely lily and mint soap. Katrin took her time pulling half her hair back, twining braids around the side and pinning them up, leaving a few tendrils falling out at the front. She used makeup in one of the wooden drawers in the bathroom, black to line her eyes and a shimmering bronze shadow for the lids, a delicate rose paint for her lips. Curious that Ander would have makeup, most likely it belonged to the woman he seemed to ponder over so often. It was silly to doll herself up for a night staying on the ship with the seer she barely knew, but it gave her a feeling of home, and right now that was what she needed.

When Katrin returned back to the room, a necklace lay on top of the gown. A golden gemstone hung from a chain, carved into a fiery sun on one half and a moon on the other. She wondered if Thalia had a piece of jewelry ready for whichever gown she had picked, and how she knew it was the gold one. Katrin looked around to see if Mykonos had been spying, but if the small white cat had been there, she was no longer.

After she dressed, Katrin made her way down the hall to what she had learned was Thalia's room. She went to knock, but the door flew open. The seer stood before her looking how Katrin assumed the Olympi would have appeared. Young, but wise beyond her years. Her delicate frame was draped in a white gossamer gown, only what looked like skimpy undergarments lined the dress, not a usual slip one might see in Alentus. The panels were held together by a thin silver chain that looked like the threads of a vest. It dipped together down her chest and pinned at the waist with a violet stone.

"I didn't realize you would change again. You look lovely, Thalia." Katrin stepped through the threshold into a room that looked—well a lot like Ander's. She didn't know why she thought the rooms on the ship would be more personal. This was where they supposedly spent the most time.

"Oh, well I am rather fickle with my outfits. Plus it ruins all the fun if someone's seen you in it." Thalia smiled as she waved her hand through the air. "Welcome to my humble quarters." Mykonos meowed from a nearby plush velvet chair.

Yes, everything looked similar to Ander's chambers except the colors. Where his were ones of deep navy and forest green, Thalia's were crisp beige and lilac and lavender. Not to mention hers just smelled better. Although Katrin realized Ander had not been spending much time in the room, if at all, of late so the smell was probably her own.

"I had Leighton bring us in some food before they left for—what did they say they were doing? *Going to the market.* Have as much as you'd like, otherwise the little one will gobble it all up."

Mykonos sat back on her haunches and yawned, her sharp white teeth glowing in the dim light of the room.

"So they really aren't going to the market for supplies?" Katrin asked.

Thalia half sat, half leaned on one of the lilac chaises by the table. Katrin was surprised she was not falling out of the gown altogether. "They'll get supplies, yes, but the men tend to spend some extra time in town when we come to port at Lesathos." Thalia plucked some berries from the table, dropping them into her mouth as she spoke.

"Even the captain?"

Thalia arched one of her dark brows up as she grinned. "Yes, even *the captain.*" Katrin blushed. The seer had caught her glancing one too many times up at the helm the last few days. "You know, he's not a bad person, Princess. Quite the opposite, actually."

Katrin rolled her eyes. She got it. That's what Thalia said, what Leighton said, what the rest of the crew said, and definitely what Ander said. It was not that she did not see that person sometimes, it was the reason she caught herself staring, wondering if this was under different circumstances if she would feel any different. If he had not lied to her that first day and just laid it all out there.

"We met, you know, before he captured me or whatever you people are calling it." Katrin slumped down in the chair across from Thalia and Mykonos not even caring if she ruined the silken dress.

Thalia nodded.

"If he'd just told me then. Warned me. I could have protected myself, I could have warned my guard. But instead he *saved* me. Didn't give me the chance to do the same for Ember, or Kohl, or *my people*." Her voice cracked, tears welling for the thousandth time that week.

The seer picked at a berry seed that had gotten stuck in her teeth with her claw-like nail. "I understand his ways were, shall we say, flawed, but his intention—that is what matters. That he cared so much he put us all at risk to protect *you*." Her words were sweet. Like she felt a similar sentiment to Ander. Like she also wanted Katrin safe.

"Again, that's what no one will really tell me. Why me? Yes, there was a threat to my life, but why should he care? Why should you care?"

"I'm not sure I should be the one to share that with you." Her eyes softened at Katrin. She could tell Thalia wished she could, but it was not her place. Apparently, it wasn't anyone's place. "Let me tell you something else though. Maybe—well maybe then you might look at him differently."

She uncorked a bottle of a deep crimson wine, pouring them each an unusually large glass. Katrin did not mind. She took small sips and picked away at the food as Thalia sat up, took the small white cat in her lap, and breathed a deep and soothing breath. She turned, pulling her hair away from the nape of her neck. What Katrin saw—she almost dropped the crystal wine glass, her limbs freezing at the site. Burned into the space between the bottom of her neck and her shoulder blades were two intertwined snakes.

"You were right to question how a seer could be so far from Delphine."

Katrin began to reach for her dagger. *That mark, that mark, that mark.* But Thalia's face was dull and her chin began to tremble. Not in anger. Not threatening. Just sorrow. Katrin slid her hand back to the glass, shaking as she brought it to her lips.

"Two years ago I was requested to join a group to give a prophecy to a baby born in Voreia. It was strange a seer of my age would be allowed to leave the isle without a guide. Usually the younger acolytes kept to the temples, offering sacrifices and prayers to the gods. But he was supposedly sick, and I had shown promising healing ability much beyond my years, so I went. As you could guess, I never made it north. Instead I was taken here by the Lernaean Legion, a group from their lands who traffic and sell women and men into slavery. I was brought here, to Lesathos to be sold to one of the many brothels. A maiden seer. I was on the market for quite a fair amount of coins. But when I was given over to my new *owner*..."

Katrin could see the twitch in her neck as she remembered.

"I never expected it to be him—Ander. I was petrified. I assumed he had purchased me for the same reason, but instead he wrapped me in his cloak, brought me to the ship, fed me, gave me this room—and time. Time to process. Time to come to terms with what the men did to me those days between Delphine and here. When I finally was able to be around people again—gods, it must have been a month—he told me I was free. He would take me back to Delphine or anywhere else in the world I wanted to go. But I couldn't go back, not after what I lost, and I hadn't known anywhere else. So I stayed on *The Nostos,* and Ander and Leighton and the crew, they became my family. All because he saw me and thought I was worth saving."

"How did you do it?" Katrin's voice was raspy.

"How did I do what, my dear?"

"How did you forget? What they did to you..."

The seer sat up on the chaise, moving over toward Katrin. "Oh, Princess...I will never forget. You *should* never forget. But I can not change what happened and I can not let my life be consumed by that pain. Otherwise, what hope do I have for love? For happiness?"

Katrin began to sob, tossing her arms around the small seer. Her brown hair became entangled in Thalia's white. She sat and she cried and the seer let her, until her eyes were dry and the black streamed down her face. Until a little piece of her put itself back together.

"Hush, hush, Princess. Let me take you somewhere you can forget, at least for the moment." Katrin cocked her head to the side, still wiping the tears from her rosy cheeks. Thalia's violet eyes twinkled. "You didn't think I would let the men have all the fun, did you?"

Thalia led Katrin by the hand into a seedy looking tavern in the middle of the market. Disheveled sailors and fisherman lined the worn wooden tables within the dining space, the floor so sticky Katrin had a hard time lifting her boots. The smell of stale mead and piss and sweat filled her nose. If this was Thalia's idea of fun, she was not sure she wanted to hang out with the seer again. The old men whistled at them as they slid through this room to a smaller one, jingling their small purses of coin at them like they were prostitutes.

In a smaller room sat a thin young man dressed in red and green with a feathered mask. He clacked his long nails against the table where he sat.

"*Láthe biósas,*" Thalia whispered to the man. He nodded at her before she pulled two masks of her own out of a small satchel she carried. One was covered in a deep violet silk, edged in black lace, its sides curling up in swirls, tied together by a silken black ribbon. The other was a sparkling gold, not made of fabric, but carved straight from some pliable material Katrin had not seen before. It sparkled in the light, catching every flicker of the flame in that small room like a star glowing in the night sky.

"Put this on, Princess. We wouldn't want the crew to catch us." She winked before tying the violet mask around her own face. Thalia looked devilish behind it, her eyes narrowing to just the slit of her pupil in the low light, her lips painted a bloody red in contrast to her moonlight skin and hair. Katrin took the golden mask in her hands and lifted the delicate material up to her eyes.

"It's remarkable, but where are we going?" Katrin asked.

"We are going somewhere where you, Princess, can be anyone." Thalia ticked up a feline grin, taking her by the hand once more as the man pushed a single book on the shelf behind him and a hidden door slid open. "Welcome to *Hades.*"

Katrin gazed in front of her at the stark difference between the tavern they just walked through and what lay before them. The room was dimly lit with torches surrounding the outer walls. A small orchestra of musicians playing in the corner. The music fluttering from the stringed instruments was intoxicating and sensual, as were the individuals dancing in the center of the room. Each person wearing a different mask, a different persona, as they hid their true identity. Wine and liquor were flowing openly into chalices by women dressed in tight, lacey garments, their black feathered masks like ravens in the night.

Small, low-lying tables lined the perimeter of the room, surrounded by lucious and pillowy chaises and chairs also colored that dark as night black. Sumptuous velvet curtains draped in front, with a sheer material hiding details from onlookers. Both men and women inhabited those dark corners, indulging in activities that sent a rosy hue across the bridge of Katrin's nose.

One blocked-off section in particular caught her eye. The sturdy male that leaned back against a mountain of pillows, clad in dark leather, his shirt unbuttoned at the top. The woman with fiery red hair cascading down her back and lucious lips grazing against his neck as his hand inched slowly up her silken dress. Those swirling tide eyes that locked with Katrin's as he ticked up a feral grin, the red-haired woman shifting her body against his thigh.

"Come, I want to dance." Thalia knocked her out of her daze.

The lithe seer dragged her through the crowd until they reached the center, staying there for hours dancing and drinking and laughing. All the while, her eyes kept glancing back at that man as he became further enthralled by the red-headed woman. Curiosity built low in her stomach.

Katrin hadn't been that free, without burden, in some time. Her body swayed with every note as she sipped from her drink. Her eyes closed as she took in the swirling colors of the people around her, spinning and spinning until she felt like a leaf caught in the wind.

Air escaped her lungs as a hand slid delicately around her waist to her stomach, pulling her tightly back against a muscular body. Every hair on her stood on end as a warm and soothing breath tickled her neck and soft lips grazed her ear.

"You didn't think I'd let the most ravishing woman wander about alone all evening, did you?" That predatory voice enchanted her. She was not sure if it was the heat, or the music, or the many glasses of wine she drank, or simply what Thalia had told her, but she leaned fully into Ander's embrace. "Care for a dance?" His lips tickled her ear.

He whipped her around until her body was planted firmly against his, her chest heaving in that tight golden gown. The grip on her lower back softened as he took her hand in his. The orchestra began to play another song. This one was not as sensual as those prior. It did not make you lust after an idea of someone. It was not intoxicating and vengeful. No—this one was sad and dark, bringing forth every emotion all at once. It made you long for something you never had. Like your entire world was there sitting in front of you, but just out of reach. A feeling of loss for a person that would never be yours.

Katrin did not dare look Ander in the eyes. His stare could be felt over every inch of her as they moved about the dance floor. If she did, if she looked into those captivating crystal irises, she might lose it. Might melt into the ground they swayed upon. She was lost. Lost in the music. Lost in her mind. Lost on the seas, never to return home. And for a moment—just this one fleeting moment—she did not care. She wanted to be lost. She wanted to forget. Because forgetting was better than the world that surrounded her.

The reverberating string melody came to a close and just then did she allow herself to really look at the man in front of her. His black waved hair, his sea-torn eyes, tan olive skin hidden behind a navy scaled mask. The way his lips parted just slightly as he leaned down toward her. She did not stop him as he brought those lips to her cheek and kissed her gently. When they parted his face looked pained, his eyes darker, his full brows narrowed in. He opened his mouth to speak, but closed it once more and began to turn. Ander strode away one pace before he halted, clenching a fist so tight Katrin could see the vein pulse. He looked back over his shoulder.

"Thank you, Starling, for the dance. You can leave—you can go home."

He knew it was her. She knew from the second his words grazed her ear. They had pretended. For that song they were not a pirate and a princess, captor and captive, enemy and victim. They were—well, Katrin could not quite describe what it was. Her fingers brushed over her cheek, still tingling from the kiss. She wished it was her lips he grazed.

Katrin looked back up wanting to reply, but Ander disappeared into the crowd.

Thank you. It had not been for the dance. It had been a good-bye. What she asked for this past week. The ability to return home. He was giving it to her, just like that. No explanation, no anything. She had to take the opportunity, even if right now she did not want to leave. Even if she wanted to ask him more. How he knew the people that had taken her. How he had fought against them to set Thalia free. If he would have done the same for her.

Right now none of that could matter. She was going home. To Ember. To Kohl. To her rightful place on the throne. Katrin lifted her skirts and ran. Ran toward the docks, ran toward the sea, ran toward Alentus.

CHAPTER TWENTY-FOUR

KATRIN

When Katrin reached *The Nostos* she went straight for Ander's quarters, where she had packed away her small satchel of necessities. She now had enough money to book passage back to Alentus, and in a week's time she would step on her shores once more. What was waiting for her when she returned, she did not know.

He had let her go. This whole time Ander kept saying over and over how this was what was best for her. To stay here. Then he told her they would travel to Skiatha and see what army was growing to defeat those men in Voreia. The same men who had supposedly been conspiring with King Athanas.

It was not that she did not believe Ander. After everything she had learned, she did. She trusted he thought he was doing the right thing. But if King Athanas had really been plotting against her, Kohl would have known, or her mother would have known. They would have seen right through it. And if Kohl *had known* and not said anything—well, that was not an option. He loved her. He had always loved her. And she had loved him back.

She needed to be home, to learn what had come of the Acknowledgement. To return to her people and lead. If a war was coming they would need to prepare and she would need the support of Morentius and the other isles behind her.

Katrin opened the door to the quarters. She would need to be swift, before Ander changed his mind. The satchel was lying on the desk where she had left it and on top was Mykonos, sitting up with her yellow eyes peering straight into Katrin's soul.

"I'm sorry, little one." Katrin lifted her off the satchel. The cat hissed. She would miss the little white feline. The company she gave Katrin in her worst moments aboard this ship. "Tell her I'm sorry too," Katrin whispered as she put the small creature on the ground.

She'd needed Thalia's story. To hear she was not the only one that had suffered silently for acts they could not prevent or control. Needed to hear it would get better. That it never left you, but it also did not need to consume you.

Mykonos knocked her head against Katrin's leg. She reached down, giving the cat its last pet before taking off into the night.

She'd heard some of the crew mention a merchant ship that sailed between here and Alentus regularly. They offered passage aboard their ship for a small amount of coin and assistance with the cooking. Katrin was a princess, but she had always been fascinated with food when she was young. She had helped the cooks whenever she could sneak away from her lessons.

For a way home, she would do it again.

The docks were empty of people this time of night. Sailors either sleeping or drinking in taverns by the market. That was where she would start her search, the small taverns closest to the water. Every street and alleyway was low lit, the only light coming from the windows of homes that were peppered through the market and the thin crescent moon in the night sky. Katrin wrapped the cloak she had grabbed tighter around her as the night's chill caressed her skin.

She remembered one particular tavern that many had talked about. One would need to walk up the main street and turn down the small corridor on the fourth right from the dock—or had it been the third?

Katrin could hear voices coming from ahead. That was a good sign, one that meant she was closer to a tavern and to finding that merchant ship.

The princess turned the corner and as she walked toward those voices the light around her began to fade. Only the moon's whitish glow provided a path, the shadows along the buildings arcing up toward the sky. She spun around to walk back to the main road, clearly having taken a wrong turn, when several men surrounded her.

They were obviously quite intoxicated, well, at least three of them were. The other few looked more aware of their surroundings.

"And what's a lovely lady like yourself doing wandering around Lesathos alone at night?" one of the more sober ones said.

Katrin smiled. She learned what to do in these situations, she could hold her own, and if it came down to it she knew how to kill. How to pull her dagger and show force. She had never done it before, but this close to finding her way back to Alentus, to home—she would do whatever it took.

"I must have just taken a wrong turn. I was meeting a friend of mine at one of the taverns. He told me how to get there, but I must have miscalculated. If you don't mind I'll just be going." Katrin went to take a step when the man's hand found her wrist.

"Well, I'm sure I could help get you there." A disturbing smile spread across his ruddy face.

"I really am quite alright. He will be expecting me any moment."

The man chuckled. Low and raspy. His companions followed suit. One of the more intoxicated ones slipped behind her. "I don't think anyone is expecting you, lady. It looks like you were on your way from someone, not to them." He cocked his head at the satchel. "Take it." He spoke firmly to one of the other men.

A tall, thin man with long tied-back blonde hair stepped from the shadows and went for Katrin's satchel. She gripped his wrinkly hand using the other to unsheath her dagger from her hip. "I wouldn't do that if I were you."

The men started to laugh again. They always did. One look at her thin body, her young demeanor, and she was quickly underestimated. All it took were three swings, one across his arm to catch him off guard, the other behind his left knee to have him writhing on the ground. The final—across his throat.

The leader of the group smiled. "That's alright, I like my women *feisty*." He beckoned the other men.

Katrin stood her ground against them, slicing away across limb and gut, injuring a few. She kept it up for a while, but she was only one person and they were now four. Eventually she grew tired, and it was at that moment one of the men snatched the dagger from her hand, chucking it down the alley back toward the main road.

"Not so dangerous now, are you?" the leader said, his ruddy face sweating and bloody. "Now you'll get what is coming to you." He swung at her face, landing a right hook across her jaw as two of the other men held her arms back. Katrin stumbled a little, spitting blood on the ground. She glared up at him, her body boiling, feeling as if she might explode from the heat, from the pain, from the exhaustion. One of the men holding her back screamed, clutching his hand that was now covered in blisters.

"What are you?" the man gasped.

Katrin smiled—wicked and villainous. "Your nightmare." But her skin cooled just as quickly, and another man took his place. Her power was not truly formed yet. It had come in bursts when her emotions were heightened, but she was tired, and beaten, and, quite truthfully, drunk.

The ruddy man came at her again, and this time his fist hit her eye. Again and again he punched and kicked, until she lay on the ground panting.

"And to think, if you had just given us your bag we would have left you alone." He kicked her in the stomach, sending bile straight to her mouth.

Through her coughs and pants Katrin managed to rasp out, "Men...like...you...never...do." She wished it would end. That her vision would blur and her mind go black. It was not that she couldn't take the punches and kicks. No—she had endured much worse on that boat five years ago. The physical pain had never been what hurt her most. It was the mental pain that lingered long after the cuts healed and the bruises faded that she could not let go of. The constant reminder that she was too weak, too fragile, not good enough. That if she could not protect herself against evil, she could never protect her people.

Fog began to linger down the alley, swirling around the four remaining men.

"Is this one of your remaining tricks, witch?" She could see the ruddy man's eyes narrow through her swollen lids, his lip twitch up in a snarl.

"A witch?" a voice trailed down the alley with that fog. In the distance Katrin could hear thunder crackle. "Well that's new."

Katrin was in and out of consciousness, but she could see his outline. The dark leathers he still wore. His jet-black hair slicked back, still in that scaled mask. "Now what do we have here?"

She could have sworn that the leader of the men shuddered at the approaching figure. "Just a whore—she tried to steal our money after we sent her away. Killed one of my men in the chase."

"Is that so?" Ander hissed, cocking his head to the side.

The man clawed at his throat like an invisible hand was wrapped around it. He coughed and coughed, eyes widening, before he dropped to the ground. The other men tried to run, but they did not make it far, falling to their knees, hacking breath after breath as their lungs gave out. It was as if life was sucked right out of their souls as the fog swirled around them. Their bodies lifeless on that dirt alley.

Katrin could not tell if she was hallucinating it all. If she had taken one too many blows to her head. Warm, steady arms wrapped around her as her body still shook. Calloused hands cupped her cheek, thumb grazing beneath her swollen eyes, wiping away the tears. Despite the blood, despite the dirt, he held her. Silver storms swept through his eyes. "You're safe. You're safe. You're safe." Not a reassurance, but a promise. A vow even the gods could not break.

Ander carried her all the way back to *The Nostos*, past the crew who still drunkenly trickled onto the boat. Past Leighton whose worry was plastered on his face, and Thalia, whose terror and guilt shown on hers. Down and down until they reached his quarters.

He lay her on the bed, hurrying off toward the bathing chamber. Katrin was still in shock, her eyes swollen shut, lip split and bloody, bruises and cuts covering her from the attack. When he returned he carried a damp cloth and a small vial, the latter poured into her mouth.

"Drink, it will help with the pain." Katrin nodded, wincing as she tried to swallow the burning liquid. It lit a fire within her, coursing through her blood as she felt like she might truly explode.

"Why did you let me go?" Her voice was hoarse and raspy, but she did not care. The bruises along her arms and legs sent sharp pains down to her bones. It only took a moment before the tonic Ander had given her started to help. Before the burning flame in her veins turned to a numbing icy chill.

Sleep was approaching quickly, but she needed to know. He had come for her. He had saved her. Not once, but twice now. He had saved her, he had taken her, he had let her go.

"You really don't see it, do you?" Ander sighed, sitting down on the bed next to her. He took a cool cloth to her face, wiping away the sweat and dirt and blood from the alley. Continuing down her neck and her chest and her arms. All while his face slowly blurred in her vision. "All I want is for you to be safe and to be happy. I saw how you were these past few days. It's why I kept my distance. I thought maybe after you had time to process why you were here things would change, but you still longed for home, for your sister, for *Kohl*. So I let you go. Go back to them. I didn't want you to hate me anymore than you already did." Ander looked away from her, gazing out through the window into the starry night sky.

"I never hated you," Katrin whispered.

"I shouldn't have let you go. I should have begged you to stay, to understand. If I had—those men—those men would have never laid a hand on you. You asked me once why I spent my days on the sea. It was because I had to find you." She could have sworn a tear began to form in his eyes. But she was fading fast and her imagination began to warp reality.

Katrin was back in that cabin, the tattered sheets below her. The man had left hours before, but she still lay clutching her feeble arms around her. Her hair had turned stringy, plastered to her face by sweat. All that covered the princess was the itchy woolen blanket, but it was the only thing that stood between her skin and the chilled autumn air. The only thing that stopped the chattering of her teeth.

Pain stung low in her gut and Katrin could not tell if it was from hunger or the fist that had landed there before the man buried himself inside her. The blood stained sheets still lay below her, scratching at her skin from where they had crusted over.

A hand grazed down her cheek and her whole body stiffened. He was back. He had never come back, not on the same day. "Shhh, asteráki mou, I'm here." A gentle voice caressed her ear. Katrin dared to lift her gaze toward the speaker, but the face did not match that of the man. The speaker had piercing blue eyes, and hair dark as night, a tear coursing down his cheek. "I will get you out of here. I promise you that."

Katrin noticed the chains around his wrists, on his ankles. He was a prisoner too. The voice was deeper, but that face—she remembered it from somewhere. The light smile, even in the darkest of times. The twinkle in his eyes as he tried to calm her. "I know you might not remember me, but this is not the end. For you. For us."

Then the voice disappeared, there was no longer a man by her side. A hallucination, a way to imagine her pain was not near to breaking her. Her eyes fluttered, stinging with tears that would never come.

In and out the princess went. Dream. Reality. Dream. In her daze, words floated through her mind, a soft whisper against her mental walls.

"You were my northern star. The reason I kept hoping, kept believing. The thing I knew would lead me home."

Katrin shifted closer to Ander, letting the smell of lemon and olive oil fill her lungs. Let it lead her into that final stage of sleep. He stroked her broken lip with his thumb, lingering where the man had caused a split to form. *"Asteráki mou,"* she whispered, "what does it mean?"

He smiled softly, a breath catching in his lungs. "It means my little star."

Katrin blinked a few more times, no energy left to respond, before fully drifting off to sleep. A memory of a young, black-haired boy holding out a silver and sapphire comb filled her mind. *For my Starling,* he had said—the engraved words she forgot the meaning of over the years. A smile caressed the boy's face as she accepted the gift. The hope, light, and excitement of it all shining in his eyes.

Chapter Twenty-Five

Ember

B linding light of the morning seeped in through the blinds in her chambers. A searing pain still lingered, shooting from her right temple to the center of her head. Ember tried rolling over, but the bruises and slashes on the rest of her body prevented anything but small movements. Bandages were wrapped tightly around her thigh, arm, and forehead. The faint smell of eucalyptus and mint trickled up into her nose. Her tongue lifted to the roof of her mouth, grazing over her lips. Dry as the sand on the beaches in the height of a drought. Water. She needed water.

Only air flowed out of her mouth when she went to speak. No more than an inaudible rasp. How long had she been knocked out? Silky sheets grazed against her bruised skin. Someone had changed her out of her leathers and into a rather skimpy nightgown.

Not someone—Ajax. Her whole body heated as a low snore came from the chair next to her bed. He was dressed in breeches and a light shirt rather than his uniform, but his long sword still lay across his lap, one hand gripping the hilt even as he snored away.

The last thing she could remember was being in the courtyard, how she had taken blow after blow from Kohl, until she ended up on the ground. He had gone almost feral at that point of attacking her, but she would not give up. She would not let the people see her as weak. For

Katrin—for her family—she fought. Right up until she saw that bronze and silver blade coming down toward her head. Death should have come for her. Or maybe it had, and this was all an illusion.

Ajax stirred in the chair, his normally neatly textured dirty blonde hair instead a disheveled mess; his smooth skin now covered with short stubble.

"How long?" she managed to rasp out through labored breaths. He stirred again as his head began to nod awake. "How long?" Ember fought out once more, her words feeling like acid as they left her throat.

The commander jerked upright, gripping his sword tighter. His eyes flashed toward the still locked doors, then back to her. "Princess! You're awake."

Water began to well in his warm brown eyes. He put his sword down on the chair, rushing to her side, running one of his hands over her cheek. Ember winced at the soft touch. Not because she did not want it, but because her whole body felt like it was on fire and water was out of her reach.

"I—we thought we lost you." His brows knit together as he looked her over. Checking each bandage. Replacing them with new cloth, rubbing that eucalyptus and mint balm over each cut and bruise. Oh gods—if he was doing that now, that meant he did them before. That he really was the one to strip her clothes and change her and, by the lack of sand and dirt on her skin, *bathe her*. Ember was horrified at the idea. Embarrassed and horrified. This was not how she wanted any man—especially Ajax—seeing her naked for the first time.

"How long?" she repeated, this time a little stronger.

A painful gaze locked on her, and Ajax tightened the cover on the balm. "Five days."

"Five days?" Ember screamed. She didn't know she even had that much of a voice left and would probably regret it later. "I was out for five days?"

"Yes. The physician—well he said it would be a faster recovery, really your only shot at recovery if we kept you sedated. He had a tonic brewed to keep you in dreams until the swelling in your head resided. The King—he insisted." This time Ajax winced at the words.

"The King?" Ember's voice lightened as she tried to push up to a seated position. "My father is here?" She knew he did not mean King Athanas. That frightening old man would probably have let her rot if given the chance. Did not think she was worthy of the title she was promised, and certainly would not have thought she was worthy to be queen in her sister's place.

A small smile began to spread across her bruised face. Someone had gotten word to her father down in Aidesian. He would be able to fix all this. He would rally people to go looking for Katrin. Aidon always made everything better.

"Not your father, Ember. *Kohl.*"

"Kohl!" Ember screamed again. She really would regret this later. She tried to push herself up again, through the pain and hurt of it all. "He is no king of mine." She could not believe it. Her sister was gone. She was basically useless in bed. Her future brother-in-law had tried to kill her and now he stole her family's throne.

Ajax sat down beside her on the bed, attempting to get her to stop trying to stand up. He sighed, cocking his head just slightly to the side. "Technically—well, technically he is not king yet. The coronation has not occurred."

She looked at him with a hatred in her eyes she had never felt before. "Then call the isles back! Call a vote! Make them *choose.*" Kohl could not do this to them. He came here as a friend. As a protector of her sister and these people, and then he turned his back on them. She did not understand why he had gone to those lengths. He was never a violent or power-hungry man before. His father, yes—but Kohl, he was kind and gentle and always put Katrin above all. Yet, he would hurt Ember in the name of all that. It was a gods-damned lie if she ever heard one. She would get to the bottom of it, even if she was remanded to her bed.

Ajax shifted, slipping his hands away from the princess. It must have been difficult for him. His loyalty always lay with the Drakos family, but the Spartanis was supposed to be loyal to Alentus. To whatever ruler sat on its throne. Now that ruler may very well be Kohl, but instead he was here with her. Making sure she was safe and cared for, while she lay unconscious for days. Maybe the commander really did have a heart.

Maybe she did stand a chance to earn his affection. To be like Machius and Iason. Together in all ways, but the official oath.

"You know that's not how this works, Ember. Tradition states that if the Wrecking is called no vote is necessary." He seemed to stiffen at the words.

"Then screw tradition! Isn't that what *the Viper* was saying just the other day? I will not have the blood of Morentius sitting on my sister's throne, regardless of whether they were to be wed or not." It was probably Kohl's father who poisoned him with this idea anyway, his words oily and deceitful. That same shudder she felt every time she thought of that man trickled down her back. She had seen the way King Athanas whispered in Kohl's ear. Sowing dissent. But Kohl had never seemed to listen to him before.

Rough fingers gripped her chin, making her stare directly at Ajax. "You don't mean that. Tradition is the backbone of this isle, your family, your people. I know the result is less than ideal, but I don't know what other choice we have."

"I want to speak with him." She clenched her jaw through the pain. Her breathing became more ragged. Even just a few moments of anger and speaking after she woke was draining all the energy she had left.

"I don't think that's such a good idea," Ajax said. "You are angry. You need time to process."

"Need time to *process?* Ajax, I thought you of all people would understand. I thought—I thought we were friends."

"We were—*are* friends. I just think we need to focus on what is best for your health right now. You need time to get better, to heal. And we need time to find your sister. We can't be battling from within." He was right. Of course he was right. It did not change how she felt though. She was beyond angry. She felt like she lost something—a piece of her. A piece of her home.

Ember's voice cracked, "He tried to *kill* me, Ajax."

"I did no such thing." A voice trailed in from her now open door. Kohl stepped through in all black pants and slim jacket, the red and orange viper stitched on his breast pocket.

"Well we can see where your loyalties lie," Ember spat, turning away from Kohl. Ember changed her mind. She did not want to speak to him. Did not want him anywhere near this castle. For all she cared, Morentius could pack their bags and slither back to the southern isle. "You slammed the hilt of your sword into my skull, Kohl. How exactly is that *not* trying to kill me?"

Kohl stepped farther into the room, trying to move toward Ember.

"Don't take another step." Ajax stood between Kohl and the bed. His jaw clenched tight.

"Remember who you serve, *Commander*." He was really trying to pull that line so early.

"As Commander of the Spartanis my loyalties lie with *its* Prytan, not you," Ajax growled. Technically he was right. As commander he would report to the Prytan, but she would then report up to the king or queen. To *Kohl*.

Kohl rolled his eyes, stalking forward anyway. "I'm just here to talk. To explain. See? No weapons." He showed the inside of his jacket. "No sword, no dagger, nothing hidden there or anywhere else." Ember did not care, she simply did not want to speak with the terrible, lying, stealer-of-her-lands man.

"You have no right to be here. Go slither back to your father, traitor," Ember bit out. She really wanted to scream at him, beat him, make him hurt like he did to her. But what good would that do?

A loose sigh left Kohl's lips, his broad shoulders shrugging. Ember looked at him then. Really looked at him. His ebony eyes had large circles under them, the light that usually showed in them muted. He looked worn, older almost.

"You need to understand, this is the last thing I wanted. I haven't slept in days. You wouldn't yield—and Ember—if I hadn't knocked you out they would have made me kill you. The people were cheering for it. They were bloodthirsty. That is the nature of the Wrecking. I did what I had to do so that you survived."

Ember began to laugh. The sound was menacing and disturbing with her crippled voice. "That—that is how you let me survive. I still almost died, Kohl. I can barely move even now. You could have just stepped down. All of this could be avoided."

"You know that's not true," Kohl scoffed. "You only just started learning the politics of these isles. When Katrin returns, her position remains. If you were crowned, there would be no way to reverse it. You'd be queen and she'd be nothing."

Ember cringed at how he spoke. Her sister would never be *nothing*. It was true, she did not know the politics that well, but there was no precedent for this. If the heir was not present. The Wrecking hadn't even happened since the time of the Olympi. Who was he to decide what happened in her family's lands?

"You mean she would be nothing to *you*. Your father's plans would cease to exist. Is that all you care about? Katrin is not away on some trip, Kohl. She is missing. She might never return." Her voice went soft. It was the first time she really acknowledged that possibility. A week had passed and yet none of the spies had found a trace of her.

Kohl's expression darkened, his lip twitching as she spoke. He shook his head. "She will return. I'll make sure of it." They both glanced at the commander.

Ajax nodded his head as well. "We have an entire legion out looking for clues of where she could have gone. It's only a matter of time before we catch a lead." Ajax rested his calloused hand on her arm. It calmed her a little, but Ember was still furious with Kohl.

"And what are you doing to find my sister? You say you love her so much and yet here you stand, in front of her lowly sister rather than out fighting for her!" Kohl began to pace back and forth. "Well? Are you going to do anything or not?" Her words were as bitter as stale basil in her mouth.

Kohl looked like he was going to speak, then stopped. He did this several times, running his hand through his dark brown hair. "My father thinks I shouldn't leave until after the coronation. He thinks it leaves too much up in the air."

"Your father is a manipulative pig," she snapped. His father was not a leader or an advisor on this isle, he should not have been dictating what happened. "I'm sure he'd rather my isle burn than give up the sway he seems to have over you."

"Ember, please. Remember who our real enemy is. Remember who we are fighting. You have to trust me. This is what's best for you, and for the people of this isle."

"You want me to trust you again? After you almost killed me? Fine. Swear me in. Swear me in as Prytan of the Spartanis and maybe—just maybe—I can begin to forgive you for this." She was done talking, done playing games. If she couldn't convince him to do the right thing, maybe she could at least get him to give her this. Her rightful position.

Kohl cracked his neck. "I can't do that, Ember. My father is worried it will make us look weak. We can't have two transitions of power at once with Nexos on the move again."

"I don't give a gods-damned care what the Viper of Votios thinks anymore. This is not the south. Two transitions of power at once? That's a bull-shit excuse from a man with an agenda. They always occur at the same time. Swear. Me. In."

Ember had managed to finally sit up and lean against the back of the bed. Her breathing continued to be labored, a layer of sweat clinging to her skin. She was done being the weaker sister. The one people associated with parties and men, not politics and leadership. She may have been behind in her training, but she would prove to all of them that she was a force to be reckoned with. Even if the first step in that was standing up to King Athanas. That was a thing more frightening than war.

Ajax smiled beside her and Ember melted. His warm brown eyes pierced right through to her soul. He helped her gain that confidence these past few weeks. Treated her like she belonged.

"She has the full support of not only myself, but the entire Spartanis. King Athanas would find it wise not to taint the relationship the Spartanis have with this kingdom."

"I will take it under advisement." Kohl bowed as he backed toward the door. "And, Ember, I really am sorry." All she could think to do was give him a vulgar gesture as he exited her chambers.

Ember slinked back down under the covers. She was exhausted. Every tiny bit of energy stripped from her body. "I really have the support of the entire Spartanis?" she asked. Ember found it hard to believe that the men would prefer her to some Morentian soldier.

Ajax gave a small laugh. "Those men adored your sister. Feared her, really. And after they saw what Kohl did to you—there was no other choice. For the Drakos family and for Alentus." He wrapped one arm around her, leaning so close their noses almost touched. "And most of all, for *you*. The warrior that the world didn't see coming." Her whole body seemed to heat as he grazed his lips in a light kiss on her cheek. "Now get some rest, we need you healthy for when you officially accept your title."

"Thank you, Ajax. For believing in me when no one else would."

It had been two days since Ember first woke up. She was finally able to walk around the castle, even if the stipulation was Ajax following her like a shadow. He was acting like an overprotective dog. Everytime she would step outside her chambers, there he would be waiting in full uniform, as if someone was going to come and threaten her life. Even if it seemed there was little chance that would happen again.

Despite the annoyance of never being alone, with Kohl lingering around, supposedly trying to make amends and explain again and again why he did what he did, Ember felt better with the commander by her side. Kohl was the last person she wanted to see or hear or talk to, and Ajax seemed to be keeping him at bay.

Until now. Until she was forced to speak with him because her entire future was at risk. They were meeting in the great hall to discuss the position of Prytan.

It was absurd that it was even in question. A tradition so ingrained in the history of Alentus, Ember could not fathom how they would reverse it. Yet, here she was, about to beg for what was clearly supposed to be hers.

A few weeks ago she would have given the position away. Gladly, even. But she was tired of always being second, never being enough to truly impress her parents like Katrin always had. And most of all, she needed to do this for her sister. So when they found her, *she* would have the full support of the Alentian army, not Kohl.

Again she wore those beautiful leathers Ajax had made for her. The soft navy with turquoise and gold threaded accents. The baldric with the Alentian banner. *Her* symbol. The simple gold crown with lightning bolts hooking the ends. One she would not give up so easily.

Ember ran her fingers over the leathers where the blood and dirt had been washed out. Places where the seamstress had patched over cuts from Kohl's blade. Her sister's fiery spirit raged through her and she finally understood the fear that Katrin sometimes felt for her powers. Ember followed in her mother's footsteps. Her power would be light for healing. The power of the sun and the earth. Katrin was fueled by the light that shone in darkness like their father. A festering that sometimes creeped into Ember. If it was not kept in check it could be consuming and spiraling. The way she hated Kohl right now, it was sending her down that fine line.

"Are you ready, Prytan?" Ajax looped his fingers through hers, giving them a tight squeeze. He smiled softly, his words meant to be reassuring. That the Spartanis wanted *her*.

Ember nodded her head, even though she was not, could never really be ready for the responsibility and power that would be thrust upon her today. But the gods be damned, did she love it. The idea that she finally was more than a pretty face to her people. That she could help further her sister and her family's legacy on the isle that gave them so much.

The sun was nearing its peak when Ember and Ajax stepped into the Great Hall, no longer gripping each other's hands. Kohl sat on the throne at the end of the hall. Her mother's throne. Her sister's throne. One with gilded foil and designs of the Alentian people. Its sides with intricate carvings representing the Triad Mountains, arms embossed with lightning, sun, and stars. Their symbols. Their power. Not his.

Leaning forward, Kohl sat with his elbows propped upon his knees, hands clasped in front of him as if he had sat upon that sacred dais his whole life. A smug grin splashed across his face, pairing well with the obsidian and burgundy of his tunic. A stark contrast to the turquoise, white, and gold of the Alentian banners that lined both sides of the room.

"Ember, Commander, so nice of you to finally join us." She had not noticed the Viper as he slithered out from behind the dais. Kohl's father would have been quite attractive if it was not for his hardened features and terrifying grin. Ember would—could no longer be afraid. Ajax told her over and over again this morning that someone like King Athanas only responded to power. If she believed she was strong enough and worthy enough to be a leader, then show it.

"I wasn't aware we were late to anything," Ember spat back. This meeting was to be between Ember, Kohl, the Commander, and the five elected senators of the Spartanis. Outside influence had never been allowed to attend a vote. "What are you doing here anyway? This is a closed meeting." Her voice was forceful and unwavering. She was tired of cowering in front of powerful men. Especially those who belittled individuals who they considered less than.

King Athanas laughed, deep and wicked. "Clearly, *Princess*, you have not been taught enough about your own traditions. Not only the heir apparent to the position is allowed to be present at this vote. Any who wish to offer their opinion or recommendation of another can attend and make their case." His lip curled back flashing those elongated and shaven canines. The five senators all muttered to themselves behind her. Two were the younger guards—Remus and Linard—between her and Ajax's age, the next generation of the Spartanis. Two were generals—Asterios and Paris—older in age and seasoned in battle. The last, a man who should have been well past his prime, yet he still walked and fought with the same grace he did fifty years before. Iason.

Ember looked up at Ajax, who gave her a swift nod. He had spoken with the five senators again this morning. Every one of them had been in support of her claim to the sacred title. "I am well aware of *my people's* laws, King Athanas. That does not change the fact that the ruling has already been decided in my favor." She smiled back at him sarcastically. He would not win this round. Ember had made sure of it.

The Viper circled around by his son's side. Clacking his fingers on the arm of the throne, lifting a brow at Kohl. "Is that so?"

Kohl straightened, shimmying in the seat until he sat with a straight back at attention. "I agree that a member of the Drakos house should have a place at all times. It wouldn't look very good for political relations between the isles otherwise. Like I have said over and over, I am sitting here because of my Aikaterine—for her, until she is found. I would like the people in the Mykandrian Isles to know that unlike Nexos, Morentius does not intend to steal their lands." As much as Ember loathed him right now, she was grateful Kohl did not push back further on the matter. "However, as law dictates, we will hear my father out."

And then he messed even that bit of forgiveness up.

"Thank you, my boy." Ember guessed that was probably the first time King Athanas had ever spoken those words. "We all know that this position means a lot to the Drakos family, the young princess included, but in these times we need someone who can truly *lead* the people, not a pretty figurehead."

Ember was seething. She was more than just a symbol. She had started to fight. Had shown at the Wrecking that she did not relent even when the odds were stacked against her. She would not bend.

The Viper continued, "My spies have confirmed the worst of our fears. That the day of the Acknowledgement was not the last we would see of King Nikolaos. It is no longer a question of if Nexos is raising an army, but rather when that army will grace our shores. They will come soon and both of our isles need to be led by someone who knows how to command an army, not a girl barely over twenty. I request you consider another for the position."

Ember wanted to go straight up to Kohl's father and punch him in the face. The useless, manipulative snake.

"My father makes a convincing point," Kohl started.

"You lying piece of—"

Ajax gripped Ember's arm. "Breathe, Ember. It will be fine." She rolled her eyes, but did not finish her sentence toward Kohl.

The king smiled again. "She has a fiery spirit, just like her sister. But she is not Katrin. She has not trained for years to accept this role. I nominate Ajax, your current commander, to assume the position of Prytan." Ember went sheet white.

Ajax would be a better fit than her. He was seasoned and determined and one of the finest strategists the Spartanis had probably ever seen. *The Eagle*, they called him. A majestic predator on the battlefield. She could feel the senators bristle behind her, along with Ajax's widened eyes and shaky hand. King Athanas never liked him, and made that clear on more than one occasion. Yet, now the king nominated him for this position. Why?

"Ajax would make a fine Prytan of the Spartanis." She almost passed out when Iason began to speak. "But you may remember, Khalid, that many had the same concerns about Machius when he first took the position." Ember could see the loss flood into Iason's eyes while speaking of her uncle. It had been years since his death, but the pain still lingered. "She is young, yes, and has a lot to learn. But her will and determination outweighs each of those shortcomings. When faced with an adversary well beyond her years, she did not yield. That is a quality any one of us would be lucky to have in a leader. Of the Spartanis or of this isle."

She attempted to keep tears from forming in her eyes, but one slid down her cheek. It was rare that Ember felt so worthy, so loved, so supported for anything other than her looks. But these men, these strong and powerful men of the Spartanis stood there in full support of her.

"So that is your vote then?" King Athanas sneered. She could tell he thought the senators would mull over his nomination a bit more.

"It is. As is the vote of all the senators." The other senators nodded behind him.

The Viper's eyes begin to darken, the ebony center wiping away the white surrounding it. "And what of your vote, my boy?"

Kohl's fingers began to dig into the arms of the throne, his jaw clenched tight. His father's stare pierced through him. Ember could see it took all of Kohl's will to go against his father. "I vote to induct Princess Ember Drakos as Prytan of the Spartanis."

Ember reached for Ajax's hand, but he pulled away. She scrunched her brows together. Was he not happy for her? This is what they talked about. What he had told her just this morning he wanted. But the commander just stood there, now a step out of her reach.

CHAPTER TWENTY-SIX

KATRIN

*S*alt water poured into her throat over and over again. She couldn't get her bearings, what was up and what was down. The storm came fast in the night, rocking the ship side to side as waves crashed against it. It beckoned to her, a caressing call in the moonlight. To wake from her dreams. To walk toward the door. To jump from the ship.

They forgot to lock her door that night. The men aboard the ship had yet to be so careless. But Katrin had little left to her, skin barely stretching over bone. What energy remained she used to concentrate on dulling the pain of starvation. With each day that passed it became harder and harder to do. She could feel the powers of the Grechi slipping from her.

The hallucinations had gotten worse. Her hope had faded, dreams blurring with reality. One night she could have sworn she was visited by a raven haired boy, not much older than she. That he whispered to her and promised her she would not die. That he would protect her at all costs, even if it meant slaughtering the crew one by one. But he never returned. Only a figment of her dazed imagination.

Then she heard the deep voice in the storm, and followed it to the stern of the ship. "Jump," it beckoned. "Jump and I will keep you safe." But the voice had turned shrill, no longer that of the boy, but of a treacherous creature. It was too late. One foot was already off the rail, and Katrin's balance *faltered. Down and down she fell into the storming seas. Her nightgown caught around her.*

She had been a fine swimmer once, holding her breath for minutes as she dove under the caverns of Alentus. But much had changed since then. Bubbles trickled out of her nose as she decided which way she should swim. Even under the water the tumultuous waves seemed to crash against her.

The reflection of the ship pulled away, its name blurred on the stern by the tides. But a mirror image also lingered below her. Six letters. Six letters. Six letters. Where to swim? Where to swim? Where to swim? She clawed at her throat as she tried to kick. Propel herself toward the surface, toward the air of the night. Willing herself to keep going for just a moment longer. But with each kick, the water's break seemed to get farther and farther away.

She would not make it, and Katrin wondered if it would be easier to just give up. The water poured into her mouth. She was drowning. She was dying. She was already dead.

Katrin coughed and gasped and clung to her throat. Over and over she rasped breath after breath, not knowing where the next one would come from.

"Shhhh..." she heard that voice whisper. The boy from her dream. No, not from her dream at all, but from her memory. Ander had been there. He had seen her. He had tried to protect her. Like he was now, sitting beside her on the bed stroking her long, tangled brown hair.

Ander had been willing to let her go. He had kept saying again and again that she was not a prisoner on this ship, but she never thought he meant it.

What would you know about being a survivor?

More than you think.

Her breathing was labored as she tried to focus again—what had been memory, what had been present? Her throat and ribs and bones burned, much like they had during those days floating on the sea. When she had not known if she would ever reach land or eat or see another person again. When she had not known if she would live.

"It was only a nightmare, Starling. You're safe now. You're safe here." His voice was soft and light. A stark contrast to the one she had heard in the alley last night as he slaughtered the remaining men.

"It wasn't a nightmare," she rasped, the salty taste of the sea still lingering in her mouth. More likely a taste from the sweat that dripped past her lips. "It was a memory."

Katrin could feel Ander's chest rise and fall against her. Normally she would have pushed him off—replied with a sarcastic quip. She was too tired, and honestly too lonely to do that now. How many times would awful men take pieces of her? She fought tooth and nail and it was still not enough. She was *never* enough.

Ander gripped her chin between his thumb and forefinger, his deep turquoise eyes staring straight through her, like he really *saw* her, like there was more behind those muted, lifeless brown irises. "Do you want to tell me about it?" he asked.

She shook her head. She did not want to talk about it. Did not want to add the mental pain to the pain she physically felt. She kept thinking about the nameless ship. She never made out what it was. "Where did *The Nostos* get its name?" A ship's name was always very personal, a lover or a place that was dear to one's heart.

"Questions again? The ship may be new, but the name is from the time of the Olympi. It was my father's ship's name once, and his father's before that. It is supposed to represent a journey home." Ander sat up a little, cradling his hands behind his head. Katrin nuzzled her head into the nook by his shoulder. She needed to be close to someone. Anyone.

It absolutely, unequivocally, did not have anything to do with the kiss he left on her cheek last night, or him carrying her to safety from the alley, or his intoxicating scent of lemon and the sea.

"A journey home. I like that." She hated that she loved the sound of his voice, what it did to her insides. The heat that formed in places that made her blush and cringe and *yearn*. "Tell me about them." She flicked her eyes to meet his, feeling his breathing hitch as she placed her hand on his chest.

He smiled at her, soft and kind. "About who? My father? My grand-father?"

"No, about the Olympi. We were never taught their history in Alentus. Not more than them destroying much of the Olde World before being defeated in the Peloponnian War."

"The Olympi..." Ander's jaw twitched, like he was thinking deeply about what he could and could not say. It was forbidden, yet they spoke the language aboard this ship. Maybe it was not fear then that halted his words, but wonder. Wonder of why she had asked in the first place.

"Were they like us—well, like me?" *Us*, like Ander was somehow also born of the gods. Katrin vaguely remembered how the men had been killed last night. But it could not be. She must have misheard him, delusion already fabricating the images in her mind. Or blurred that memory with another. This mysterious prince who hailed from a hidden isle had no power to his name.

Ander took her hand in his. "Were they like you? I would say yes. They were strong and feared, but they were also fiercely loyal and could love deeply. There was Poseidon, God of the Seas. A moody bastard at will, but a friend to the sailors. I think he would have favored you. Always having an eye for beauty. Then there was Zeus and Hera, the king and queen. Zeus with his wandering eye and Hera with her unrelenting jealousy. Athena, goddess of wisdom, often came to those in need during war as an owl, she was always my favorite as a boy. I often ran about at night in the woods by my home looking for the mysterious and wise winged creature, my mother would hate it. I usually only encountered wolves and that would become a whole other argument for why I should not be alone at night.

"Let's see, then there was Aphrodite, born of the sea, the goddess of beauty—" his sweet smile turned feral, "and sex." Katrin swallowed, feeling Ander's muscled chest under her palm. "There were the twins Apollo and Artemis, god of healing and goddess of the hunt."

"And what of my father's position? Was there a god like him? Of death?" Her curiosity peaked.

"There was. But right now we need to get you bathed and fed. If your wish is still to return to Alentus I can personally get you passage on a merchant ship back." His words were melancholy. He'd said it last night that he should not have let her go. If he hadn't, then she would have been safe, unbruised, and unburdened—at least from those horrors.

"We can discuss it after I have bathed then." Katrin went to sit up, wincing at every move of her body.

"You're going to need help." Ander slid his hand behind her back to try to guide her up and off the bed. This time Katrin swatted him off.

"Excuse me?" she gasped. "Need help with what?"

"With bathing, you can barely sit up, your injuries are healing quickly since you are nearing coming of age, but you can barely lift your arms. How do you expect to wash yourself?" He said it so matter of factly that she cringed.

Ander was right, but she would rather sit in filth than let him bathe her. Well—let him bathe her again. She could still feel the shivers that went through her as he took the damp cloth to her skin the night before. And now he wished to do that to her again. While she was naked. Katrin's whole body glowed a bright red.

"What? It's nothing I haven't seen before." He had probably been with many women before based on that red-head last night. But this was different. Yes, she had half-stripped in front of him before. But that was in the cabin, when he had been a stranger she would never see again. A distant stare, not his hands this close to her bare skin. "I can get Thalia, if you would prefer another woman?"

No. She could not bear to have someone else see the scars on her back. To explain why they never healed. To relive those moments on the bed or why she always flinched when someone mentioned a belt. Even the seer. Even someone who had gone through the same pain. "It's fine. Just...just try not to stare."

"I'll try my best." She could feel his eyes rake over her, even as she looked away.

He gently gripped her under both arms as he helped to lift her from the bed. Her balance was uneasy, the pain in her ribs still flowing deep through her core from where those men had beat her. Kicked her as she lay on the ground bleeding, no power left, no fight left. The vein by Ander's temple twitched each time they took a step closer to the bathing chamber, no doubt pledging to kill those men all over again. She was honestly surprised he did not just pick her up and carry her like he did last night. Maybe he wanted to give her some semblance of control knowing she had little else to herself at the moment.

The bathing chamber felt warmer than usual, even though the autumn's crisp air was beginning to trickle in on the winds.

"May I?" Ander asked, running his hands along the edge of her silk chemise like he had not changed her into clean clothes after she passed out last night. Katrin nodded, and he helped her slowly lift her arms, sliding the shirt off first. Then slipping her shorts down until they dropped to her ankles. She gently stepped each of her feet out and there she stood, bare and ruined and broken in front of him.

Katrin tried to take a step into the bath, but her knees seemed to give out beneath her. He brushed his hand down her arm. "Please, let me help." His gaze met hers, but she did not hold it. She only let Ander lift her body into the soapy water. She could not dare to see the judgment in his eyes.

But he did not look away. Despite his many prior vulgar comments, this was not a sexual gaze, nor was it one of pity. It was sorrow and regret and it burned more than the scalding water he lifted her into.

"Thank you," Katrin whispered as she let herself sink below the water. She had almost drowned once, and yet underwater was where she felt the most at peace. It was silent, and calming—a good place to feel alone. Maybe Ander was right. Maybe the now dead sea god would have favored her.

It felt like minutes that she sat under the layer of bubbles, pushing the memories of the night from her mind. Centering herself, if she could even do such a thing anymore. When she surfaced, Ander was there waiting, cloth in hand.

"You don't need to do that. I just needed help getting into the bath." She reached for the cloth he held and sucked in a sharp breath as her healing arm writhed in pain.

"It's fine, really." His words again soft against her ears as he dipped the cloth under the water, beginning to wipe what dirt and sweat and blood remained on her skin. "Just let me know if I am hurting you, alright?"

Katrin took a deep breath, still unable to meet his eyes. "I will." So there they sat in silence as he moved the cloth over her back, her chest, her legs. Ridding her of any trace of those men. Of the shame she felt for killing a man, even if he had attacked her.

He poured soap through her hair, washing away the tears and snot that lingered from her sobs last night. Then Ander lifted her back out of the bath, drying her with one of the plush towels he kept stored in the room, until he was left kneeling before her.

She swallowed and heated as his eyes trailed back up her body, lingering on places she now wanted him to touch.

Ander blinked, a rosy hue she had never seen on him bridging across his nose. "Let me go get you a clean gown." He quickly stood wrapping her in the towel.

"Yes..." Gods was she embarrassed. Her mind had gone blank and she could not think of anything to say. He began to open the door back to his chambers—*their* chambers. "Ander?"

"Yes?" He turned, flooding with hope and longing, back toward her.

"I'll stay. I can't sit back and let the evil of the world win. If there is a war to fight, then my people will fight it. And if we must go to Skiatha to make that a reality, then we will." Katrin's voice was soft, but steady. She meant it. She could not let one more man take from her. Not let these people from across the seas ruin what her family had built. The peace they now desperately craved. "That is, if you'll still have me."

Ander smiled. "It would be my honor, Starling."

She nodded. "Then it is settled. This afternoon we sail for Skiatha."

CHAPTER TWENTY-SEVEN

KATRIN

The sun began its descent in the later half of the day when Ander helped Katrin up to the deck of *The Nostos*. He'd said she needed fresh salty air for the salve he had covered her body in to work. She thought he wanted to keep an eye on her as they left port. Make sure she didn't slip away back into her nightmares and self-loathing.

He had clothed her in a loose skirt and a thin knit sweater to combat the slight chill in the autumn breeze. The baggy clothing an unexpected grace, the materials soft against her healing wounds. Those would take only a day between the salve and her power slowly fueling itself back to life. She was only a month from her twenty-fifth birthday, and those flickers of power that surged through her would be her saving grace.

The internal wounds would take longer to heal. A week or so between her powers and the concoction that Ander had her drink. It tasted repulsive, but anything that would help to get her on her own two feet again she would try. Katrin hated that she was this reliant on another person's kindness to move, to bathe, to eat. She hated that it was him, even more than she longed for his gentle touch as he guided her toward the stern of the ship.

Then there were the mental wounds. The ones she tried again and again to piece back together. She was not sure if she would ever really be able to heal those fractures in her mind. Like the scars on her back, they would be with her forever. Katrin only hoped one day she would see them as the marks of survival and determination, not shame and regret. That she'd be able to move forward with processing everything that happened as Thalia had mastered.

The seer let Mykonos stray near her, and Katrin was glad for the silent company. The little white creature spent its time either gently lying in her lap curled up in a ball, or threading in between Katrin's dangling feet. She tried not to laugh when at one point Mykonos darted after a scurrying rat. The rodent did not stand a chance. She half hoped the cat would drop her prey off by Ander's feet like he explained she did sometimes. He hated it apparently, but it would cause a smile for Katrin.

He'd told her it was a long journey to Skiatha, the first part thankfully calm while her bones healed, but the second he could not promise. Tempests often swept through, nearly crashing ships on the jagged rocks of smaller isles, and creatures much more treacherous than those aboard this ship hunted in the seas and near the rocky coastlines. Ander traveled these shores many times, so Katrin was less inclined to worry. She was more intrigued at this side of the world that she'd never experienced before, either in real life or in word.

The way he described it sounded like pages out of *The Odyssey*, which she was nearly through. An adventure with sea monsters, cyclops, and sirens. Though the Olympi would no longer be there to protect them—or seek to destroy them.

Ander and Odysseus were kindred spirits, the way they were both always trying to return home, but never could. One to his wife and child, the other to his father and sister—or possibly a woman as well. He never told her why he could not sail himself home. Or had he last night? *You were my northern star.* No—just another hallucination. Still, the melancholy that washed over him as he stared out at the vast and empty sea left her wondering—what was keeping him away?

She wondered if her sister looked out at the sea that same way. If *Kohl* did. If he was searching for her again, thinking those evil men held her once more. Not knowing that she now decided to stay willingly.

It still pained Katrin how things were left between them. The day in the olive groves, the stabbing, the actions that followed. Even after these weeks spent away, she still didn't know how to feel about him. For years he had been her partner, her confidant, her everything. What she wouldn't do to just be able to simply sit and talk to him like they used to. But all of this would have to wait. For now, they sailed the journey to the lost isle. The one of treacherous myths and legends.

If the journey was to be two week's time, Katrin would need to find another one of Ander's forbidden books to read. She could not keep looking out at the sea, contemplating the mess that spiraled in her head. But she would need help to do that. Ander and Leighton were both at the helm, steering *The Nostos* out of port. She wouldn't bother them.

She looked down at the little white cat, who was now chasing around some imaginary bug across the deck. "Little one, would you be able to get your—" Katrin did not quite know what to call her. Owner, mother, human, body. None of those seem to fit the relationship between Thalia and her *psychí*. Mykonos stared back up at Katrin, her little white face cocking to the side, yellow eyes widening. "Oh, you know what I'm asking, just go get your other half."

She could have sworn the cat let out a laughing sound as she padded off toward the lower deck. Katrin wished she had something like that, a way to turn off her mind and let her body drift somewhere else. To seemingly live carefree if only for a few moments. But most of all, to know she always had someone there. Even in her darkest days, a living being that would not shy away and run scared. That would stand by her, sharing in the pain and the emotions, easing the burden just enough to keep it bearable.

Katrin sat curled up in a blanket on the chaise in the captain's chambers. She was able to move about on her own now. It had taken a week for her bruises and bones to heal. She was still sore as she meandered about the ship, but it was better than needing a constant shadow to even relieve herself in the bathing chamber.

In that week she devoured not only what had to be all the food on the ship, but also a shelf of books. They were all about the warriors and heroes of the Olde World and the stories of the Olympi and their—dare she say, scandalous—lives.

Then there was the book she was currently reading. This one was something else entirely. The hardback cover had been utterly unhelpful, a plain pale blue in color, its pages well read. Ander was sitting across from her, on one of the plush velvet chairs, sipping wine and just *watching* her with a devilish grin.

Ander arched one brow. "Are you enjoying your new read, Starling?" he purred, his expression slightly cloudy from the alcohol, but his stare caused a light blush across her cheeks.

"Did you really read this?" Katrin's voice was hoarse. The things it described—gods, it made her ache. Even worse so, since Ander seemed to be eating up every expression she made as she read. She was always terrible at hiding emotion and this book—well it drove the best kinds of emotion out of her.

Ander chuckled. "I don't need to read about those things, Starling. I would rather just live them. You know, I could teach you much more than that book ever will." Katrin gulped. She still couldn't stop imagining the way his eyes had raked over her body a week ago. The way she had wanted him to take her all in, wanted *him* in a desperate way she had not felt before.

She chucked a piece of bread at him. "Don't flatter yourself, Ander." Her words not coming out as sharp as she intended, because, gods, she did not mean them and he knew that.

Shrugging, he leaned back, continuing to sip his wine once more. "Whose book is it then, your sister's?"

Ander flinched, his face turning sour. "Well you certainly know how to kill the mood. The last person I want to think about reading that *book* is my sister. It's most likely Thalia's. She has a thing for *those* kinds of novels." Katrin's eyes went wide. She had always heard the seers of Delphine were chaste and bound their life and body to the gods. "I'm sure if you like that one, she has a handful of others you could borrow in her quarters."

Katrin peered back down at the novel, her whole body heating now. Despite the joking, she did enjoy it, and hated to admit that she sometimes pictured Ander as the harrowing male the author described. The way that he served at the pleasure of the princess. Wondering what it would be like if his hands slid up the gown she now wore, his fingers gliding over her wetness.

The sound of stuttering breaths filled the room as Ander choked on his wine. "Do you need me to leave?" His stare was piercing, looking at her now trembling hand. A knowing gaze lighting his eyes.

A shiver went down her spine at the thought of him imagining what she might do to herself if she were alone in the chambers. The way her fingers might travel down her body. "I think...I think I need some fresh air. If you'll excuse me." Katrin marked the book and put it down on the table, curtsying before she quickly scurried out of the room. If she had not embarrassed herself enough, that really put her over the edge.

As Katrin stepped on the deck she wondered how she was going to make it another week confined to just this ship with him.

The seas had become rough over the past few days. It was what Ander had warned of, why he had hoped her wounds would heal quickly. Katrin often woke in the night thrashing along with the waves against the sides of *The Nostos*, but her mind would be blank.

Ander was there, watching her, lulling her back to sleep. Every morning looking weary-eyed, his face weathered, gaze distant, like he felt every inch of her pain and confusion. He would rush off to the helm of the ship, leaving Katrin to her books and her breakfast like nothing had happened. Leaving her more confused than ever. But when she would fall back asleep, it would be dreamless. No nightmares clawing their way through.

During the day, she continued wandering the deck. Even as the rain poured for three days. Even as the crew took refuge in the cabins below. Even as the thunder crackled in the distance and lightning threatened to strike. The bolts etched across the night sky, devouring the stars in their wake. She watched, unafraid of the symbol of her people.

The Grechi had been angered. Angered to a degree she had not experienced in years, if the storms were to be this harrowing and consuming. It reminded her of that night, when she escaped the seas, when she had almost given in to death. Perhaps that was why Katrin stayed above. Maybe she wanted to feel every drop of rain, hear every perilous clap from the sky. Remember why she cowered that day. Remember to never feel that way again.

She would not break this time. She was stronger. Or at least, she was trying to be.

Katrin stood by the stern of the ship, looking out to where the storm had broken, where the skies cleared to a starry night sky. Each one twinkling in succession, like the beat of a song she had heard once long ago. Then the voice came. Soft at first, like a whisper behind her ear. "*Come find me.*" Words danced around her. "*Come find me and you will be safe.*" Where was it coming from—this delicate, beckoning call?

"*Come join me and I will protect you.*" The lilting voice turned deeper, meshing with one she recognized. "*Come join me in the depths of the sea.*" It was his voice—Ander's voice.

"Ander?" Her eyes glazed over as she ran her hand along the ship's rail, its weathered shellac peeling off.

"*Come find me. Come find me. Come find me.*"

His voice was a gentle coaxing, luring her to the salty abyss beyond.

Katrin gripped the rail tight, hauling herself up until she stood on its slippery surface. Whipping at her face, the storm raged as she held onto a beam across the stern. He was there, hiding in the star-filled sky reflected in the calm seas in the distance. She had to go to him.

"Starling? Starling, what are you doing! Starling!" Katrin's gaze flipped back and forth. The sounds. They were coming from everywhere at once. "Starling, please!"

"*Come find me. Come find me. Come find me.*"

She took one step off the side of the rail, ready to let go, the salty air filling her lungs with every breath she took.

"Aikaterine!"

As her hand lifted from the crossbar, she was yanked back down into the ship, landing against something hard. Her eyes cleared, now stinging with the piercing rain and wind.

"Didn't you hear me? You almost—you could have been killed." His voice was shaking as he gripped her arm tightly. The grip wasn't one of force or malice—rather a yearning to know she was there, that she was safe.

Katrin stared back at him with disbelief. "I—I did, but..." His voice was there. She swore it was his. Rising from below the swirling tides. Then it was behind her. Then from all sides. She couldn't tell what was real and what was in her mind.

"You're not supposed to be up here! The storm along these shores is not one of the gods, but of creatures much more deceitful. Come, let's go below before their song starts once more." He began leading her back toward the stairs to the cabins below, careful to not let her slip on the soaked deck. Katrin could see Leighton taking over at the helm, hands gripped tightly on the wheel, steering them farther into the storm, farther from the calm waters she just witnessed. There was something in his ears. *Wax.*

"Sirens?" she whispered. "They're real?" The creatures from his book. Beautiful, wicked beings that drew sailors to their death with their melodic songs.

"I thought you would realize by now that many things you thought were not real exist in our world." His voice was soft.

"But it was you. I heard *you.*" Katrin was still overcome with shock. It was the same voice in her dreams, in her memories, in the waters tonight. *He* called for her. Ander called for her.

Ander froze, glancing back at her, his eyes turning silver and deep green. The same color of the seas she heard him beckoning from. The voice had been dark and wicked and inviting, but this stare was nothing of the sort. It was shock, and torment, and something Katrin could not quite discern. "You heard me?"

She nodded.

"I—" Ander glanced back away. Something wasn't right. Something more than the fact that she had almost jumped to her death for a second time. "I—I should have realized it would affect you. You aren't of age yet. I should have known."

Katrin came to a halt. She noticed Ander had no wax in his ears, and yet the voices had not seemed to plague his mind. "Why do you not hear them? Why were you able to stop me?"

He opened the door to their chambers. The warmth of the room filled Katrin after being out in the storm. "There are many things that make you immune to a siren's song. Being born of the gods is only one of them." He shrugged his jacket off, hanging it by the fire in the corner. "You should change into dry clothes, and put this in your ears." He handed her two small pieces of wax. "We haven't passed them fully yet."

She began to rustle through the wardrobe, looking for warm pants and a knit shirt to shake the cold. "You didn't answer my question. Why do *you* not hear them?"

"Trust me, Starling, this time it is better that you don't know." He stripped his shirt next, reaching for a dry one on the bed. That's when she saw them. The jagged lines along his shoulder blades, down his muscled back. Scars not unlike her own. And above them all was a brand. Two snakes intertwined. The same mark as Thalia. The symbol of the nameless ship.

Chapter Twenty-Eight

Kohl

Kohl's father had been angry. For a week he stalked around the Alentian castle, taking his rage out on the innocent staff. He locked himself in the guest chambers at night with an assortment of women from the seaside brothel, smoking that gods awful black substance. His temper grew worse and worse as the days inched closer to the coronation.

Kohl had known his father would never stand for Ember being crowned Prytan of the Spartanis, but it was all he could think to do to show her that he was sorry. He needed to prove that even though he had hurt Ember, he was doing this all for Katrin, for her people. Now they would be his people.

Envy had followed him everyday since arriving on this isle, of what the Drakos family had, the love and support they gave each other. How proud Kora and Aidoneus had been of their children. How different it had been from his mother and father.

Yes—he enacted the Wrecking to help protect Ember against the threat of Nexos, but he could have stepped down. He could have yielded to her, a rightful heir in the Alentian succession. But he had not wanted to. Kohl wanted to prove to his father that he was as ruthless in war and battle and politics as the Viper of Votios. That he could lead one of the isles, just as King Athanas did.

And that driving jealousy and lingering feeling of never being good enough landed him here. King apparent. Those who had become his family hating him. Katrin definitely would when she returned. For harming her sister. For stealing her throne. He would have to think of a way to make her understand. Show her that nothing would be different. Except that was not true. Kohl would be creating the laws and enacting them. He would choose where and when to go into battle. He would rule the people of this land, not her. Katrin would only sit dutifully at his side, like he was supposed to do.

Maybe that was the true reason he wanted this so badly. Kohl thought he could give it all up for her. The power. The title. The need for more. But she squashed those dreams and wants that day in the groves by the mountains. When she stabbed him. When she *lied* to him. His father had been right. She was indeed nothing more than a means to an end. But he still loved her. At least a part of him still did. Still longed for her acceptance, her touch, her kiss. The way it had been in the years before all this happened. When he was her everything.

Maybe if he found her, if he rescued her again they could return to those two people. The ones who laughed and held onto each other like there was no tomorrow. The children who had raced through the Triad Mountains, swam in the depths under the Alentian caves. Had wanted all that was good in the world.

So he rebelled against his father. Gave Ember the position—that was truthfully hers to begin with—as a last shred of hope that things could be different. That they *could* get back to those people. The final thing he clung to with all the strength he had.

Kohl swore he'd had a perpetual headache since the Acknowledgement, one that only worsened in his father's presence. One he was sure would not relent with the coronation looming mere hours away. Especially with his father banging down his door. It seemed as though Kohl would not have a moment of peace today.

"Are you avoiding me, my boy?" his father rattled off as he entered Kohl's living chambers. King Athanas was already dressed in the traditional dress of Morentius, a silken black overcoat with a short collar, the viper stitched on the left chest and up the back of the coat in red and orange with matching pants that had red and orange trim along the bottom. He had trimmed his beard short so when he spoke the shaven canines were on full display. The gall his father had to suggest he was the one skirting duties, or avoiding the other the past days.

Taking a deep breath, Kohl shut the door to his chambers. This was *his* day, not his father's. He was the one who would be crowned King of Alentus. "Of course not, Father. There is just much to do before the coronation. I need to use this time to get ready, not bicker with you."

His father's eyes narrowed, gleaming dark obsidian. "You would not need to bicker with me if you had just listened to me in the first place. Instead, you chose that weak girl for one of the highest honors in our isles."

"Ember is not weak. I think she proved that during the Wrecking." It was the same conversation every day for the past week. There were times when Kohl thought he might be persuaded to change his mind, just so that his father would leave him be, but he could not give up that one piece of lingering hope for forgiveness. Not yet, at least.

King Athanas paced the room, his hands clenching, avoiding eye contact with Kohl. "She is not a warrior," he seethed.

"She doesn't need to be. Not yet. The other members of the Spartanis can hold their own. For now she is merely a figurehead. A bit of familiarity to the people of Alentus." It was the same song and dance every time with his father. Eventually, King Athanas would huff and sneer and walk off.

"You say you want to protect your *beloved's* sister. Then listen to me, boy. If you will not induct the commander as Prytan, then choose someone else. War is coming, sooner than we think. The Spartanis will need to be at the forefront of the battle, leading the charge against Nexos. We cannot have a girl who is not even of age leading our soldiers."

"Enough, Father. I am tired of repeating this conversation. I have made my decision and it is final," Kohl growled. He rarely ever—actually never—stood up to his father. "It is the will of the king."

"You are not a king yet, boy." His father looked at him, a blinding stare. "Do not forget your place, your loyalty."

"Is that a threat, Father?" Kohl's jaw clenched.

"Not a threat, merely a reminder." His father smiled. "Remember where you came from. How you got here to begin with. Now, if I can't change your mind, it would seem it is my time to go." King Athanas walked away, the shimmering viper on his jacket seemed to give a deadly stare as he exited the room.

A chill ran down Kohl's spine as he pinched the bridge of his nose. Another gods-damned headache. If they did not let up he would need to invest in some sort of tonic to make them go away. He couldn't focus when they plagued his mind. Could barely think or even see. Kohl took a large sip of his amber liquor, hoping it would dull the pain long enough for him to make it through the coronation.

He would no longer wear his father's colors—the colors of Morentius. Instead he would don a turquoise overcoat, its cuffs adorned with gold, interlocking stitching. The symbol of the fiery sun and lightning bolt was delicately embroidered up the back. Matching flowing pants of the same turquoise material were covered in stitched gold stars. But the most intricate piece was the crown. The center had the symbol of Alentus engraved in the solid gold relic, three spikes sat on either side, each of them ending in a five pointed star entirely crusted with diamonds and jewels.

Kohl lifted the crown to his head, his dark brown hair left down, grazing just above his shoulders. He looked like one of them, like the family he had always craved. Now he would be part of their world forever, even if Katrin decided not to forgive him.

It was finally time. Time for him to accept the role he fought for. The role he had yearned for since stepping on these shores many years ago.

He headed out of his chambers, dressed as the royalty he would become, and toward the courtyard, where the men and women of Alentus had gathered to see him crowned king and Ember sworn in as Prytan.

As he entered the cheering began, the people clapping, and screaming out their praises. Kohl drank it in, that acknowledgment of who he was—who he was becoming.

Kohl walked up to the dais, where a priest in flowing white robes stood with two golden and jeweled chalices. One for him and one for Ember. Katrin's sister stood to his right, her long blonde hair braided tight behind her back. Her clothes were an inversion of his, the material golden with turquoise stitching. A single bronze, curved sword hung from her hips, the delicate and simple golden crown of the Prytan sat upon her head. Her normally warm amber eyes were still and violent, as were her blood-stained lips. Kohl had to admit that she looked lethal.

He ascended, standing on the opposite side of the priest. The people in the crowd began to hush over. Ajax and the five senators remained behind them. Ready to strike if there was a threat. Kohl could see his father toward the back of the courtyard, his ebony eyes encompassing all the white. It had always been strange how his father's eyes darkened in such a way, how Kohl's eyes could as well, sucking the life and light right out of them.

The priest began to speak, his voice old and raspy. "We are gathered here to swear in these two individuals to their rightful positions. When they speak the word of the Grechi they accept the immense responsibility to protect those of Alentus from the wrath of others. Our King, Kohl Athanas. Our Prytan of the Spartanis, Ember Drakos."

Ember would speak first. She stepped up to the priest, kneeling in front of him, leaning her head forward. "From the blood of the gods I drink. From the bones of the gods I eat. For power, for peace, for prosperity." Taking a sip from the first chalice and a piece of fleshy meat from the second, Ember accepted her responsibility. The priest nodded and she rose, stepping back toward her side of the dais.

Kohl followed suit, kneeling before the priest, saying the sacred and binding words. Sipping the warm, thick red liquid, eating a piece of the bloody flesh of a beast killed in the mountains. Lifting his hands toward the clear blue sky, the priest declared, "Let the Grechi bless their humble servants."

Just as quickly as it started, the ceremony was over and Kohl Athanas was king.

CHAPTER TWENTY-NINE

EMBER

A giant feast occurred following the coronation as expected, even with Katrin still missing. Tradition stated that you must honor the new king or queen with a lavish assortment of food, liquor, song and dance. But now it was over, and Ember was seething.

Not once had Kohl mentioned her sister during his speech to the people of the isle, no gratitude, no empathy at her loss, no mention of a plan to find or rescue her. Instead, he let young women fawn over him, no doubt vying for the position of royal mistress.

She had sat across from him, reluctantly shoving the spread of food down her throat as she glared at the new king, her mother's crown now atop his head.

At one point, Ajax had even leaned over to beg her to change the angry expression crossing her usually perky face, and to possibly stop chewing her food so loud that everyone could hear her jaw crunching. Ember had not even noticed that she had been that loud or looked that distasteful, but instead of agreeing she flipped him a vulgar gesture.

The commander could go rot in the dungeons of Aidesian for all she cared. He had been a complete ass to her since the meeting with Kohl, his father, and the senators—ignoring training sessions, avoiding her in the halls. Ember did not understand what she had done wrong. The entire time since she had decided to begin training he had been so supportive of her, then King Athanas nominated him for *her* position and everything changed.

Yes, Ajax would have made an exceptional Prytan with his extensive knowledge of battle and years of training. It was clear he was a better option on all fronts. But he had never voiced that he would like to assume the role, that he personally thought he was better suited for the position than her, or that he disagreed in any way with the succession.

If he wanted to ignore her, then Ember would pay no mind. She could just as easily ignore him.

But Ajax's disappointed stare was not half as bad as what she saw at the end of the night, Kohl walking away with one of the many women who had fawned over him. A golden-haired girl who looked around Ember's age, her blue eyes sparkling in the light of the flames around the courtyard.

"That gods-damned fool!" she yelled to no one in particular. Her sister was *missing* and he was happy to spend the night with some other woman. She started after them, avoiding Ajax's hand as he attempted to stop her.

"Don't do it, Ember. It's not worth causing problems tonight," Ajax pleaded.

"Oh, and now you care, do you?" She took off behind the newly crowned king and the *whore*.

"Kohl! Kohl, get back here!" she shouted after them. The murmurs of the guests leaving the courtyard still lingered, but she knew he was choosing not to hear her. "Kohl! Kohl, I need to speak with you!" He continued ignoring her as she chased after him down the hall. "Kohl Athanas, you stop right there or I swear to the gods!" Her breath was heavy as he finally stopped, turning toward her.

"What, Ember? What could you possibly want at this hour?" he replied flippantly.

Apparently, all the men in this castle were keen to act like narcissistic pigs. The young woman looked frightened as she stared back at the angered leader of the Spartanis. "You can run along, *miss*. His highness won't be needing you tonight." The woman took off as quickly as she could back to the courtyard.

Kohl rolled his eyes. "You're joking right? You have no place to send away a guest of mine."

Ember stepped closer to him, looking up at his pissed off expression. "You realize my sister has been taken and you have done *nothing* to find her these past few weeks except steal her place on the throne?" Her jaw was clenched so tight she thought she might burst.

"I told you, Ember. We needed to wait until after the coronation. Tensions are too high in the isles right now. We couldn't risk an attack with no one on the throne." The same words he had repeated to her day after day.

"And waiting until after the coronation involves bedding some whore? You claim to love my sister and yet you forgo your duties to *her* for that girl."

"Don't be so naive, Ember. You really think one night will make a difference?"

Ember's blood began to boil, and in that moment she wished she had been gifted her father's power, not Kora's. Wished she could wipe that smug grin off Kohl's face, shroud him in fiery starlight and choke him with darkness. He was a liar and a traitor.

"My son is right, one night will not make a difference." Ember jumped. The Viper slipped out of the shadows, still dressed in his black overcoat and trousers. She had not even heard him approach. "However, now that he has assumed the crown he will take a small unit of soldiers to follow the leads we have hunted down these past weeks. He sails for Lesathos in the morning."

"Yes, I will set sail tomorrow with my crew. Is that sufficient enough for you, Ember, or do you still think I am not doing enough to find my love?" Kohl might have spoken the words, but Ember could tell this was the first he was hearing of that plan. "And while I am gone, I leave my father in charge of all diplomatic decisions." King Athanas smiled.

Ember's jaw dropped. He could not be serious. The next in line if the king or queen was incapacitated or away was the consort, and seeing as there was no consort, the next person down the list was the Prytan, not a foreign king. "That's not going to happen. I am fully in my right to rule in your absence."

King Athanas' eyes narrowed, the whites almost entirely gone once more. It petrified Ember when that happened. With the shaven canines he looked like a monster from her father's underworld. "You may have just been crowned Prytan, girl, but the fact remains, you know nothing concerning war or the politics in these isles. This is not the time for a child to lead."

Ember almost stuck her tongue out at him, but realized what little good that would do given the insult he'd just thrown at her. "Kohl?" she gritted through her teeth.

"I have made my decision, Ember. My father will step in as regent. I am sorry, but that is what is best for Alentus. Now, if you'll excuse me, I must retire to my chambers *alone.*" His hands were clenched tight and the snarl that ticked on his lip terrified Ember, reminded her of the Viper, not the Kohl she had known since she was a small child.

Ember could not tell if that was an insult for sending that woman away or at his father for not wanting to speak any longer. She did not care either way. Her chest clenched in rage, air not easily passing to her lungs. The next day she would begin planning. Over her dead body would she let someone as vile as the Viper make any decisions for her people.

CHAPTER THIRTY

KATRIN

Fiery shadows danced along the cabin where Katrin remained until they passed the jagged coastline of the sirens. Only then did the half woman, half bird creatures living on shore disappear into specks, their lilting voices fading as well. It was the second time she had been fooled by the wickedness of their song.

If what she read about sirens was true, she could not think of how she remained out of their clutches when she fell into the abyss of the seas the first time. She had woken to the blistering sun, draped over a piece of driftwood, no jagged shores in sight, no cruel women luring her to her death. Maybe she really was favored by Ander's God of the Sea. She certainly knew King Nikolaos had not used his powers of the deep unknown to help her.

She could feel them entering the waters around Skiatha. Shimmering magic tingled along her skin as they passed through the wards, deeming them worthy enough to step upon that sacred, protected land.

Katrin peered out the window, taking in the beauty of an isle that looked much like her own. It was not surrounded by a ring of flames, its land scorched and abandoned like the myths they were told as children. Instead, sparkling crystal waters swept against soft white sands. To the east of the isle, tall cliffs cut from an orange colored rock stood over-looking the bright skies. Small whitewashed homes were built into the cliff's side, narrow roads running down to the shore. In the distance, an outline of a small mountain stood against the sapphire sky.

It reminded her of home, pushing an intense feeling of longing for the cavernous shores of Alentus. For her runs through the Triad Mountains. For whispers in olive groves.

The door to the captain's quarters creaked open and Thalia poked her head through. "We've just set anchor in the harbor. Ander said you can join us on the deck. There's—well there's something he wants you to see."

"Thank you. I'll just change and will head outside." She smiled softly at the seer dressed in a long silver diaphanous gown. She wondered what Thalia was getting up to if she was dressed in such finery as that.

Katrin stripped out of her night clothes, leaving them in a pile by the bedside. She was not sure if they would be staying on the ship now that they reached their location, but she would pick them up another time. Shimmying on a pair of trousers and a linen tunic, Katrin wondered what Ander could possibly have to show her. Maybe it was just the beautiful isle that lay before them. Or maybe he had gotten her something in Lesathos that he kept secret for these two weeks they had sailed.

She slid her feet into the pair of leather boots she had come aboard the ship with and headed for the deck. Soft chatter came from above as Katrin walked up the steps at the end of the corridor. Two men were talking, one she knew was the captain. The other, his voice also seemed familiar, low and raspy and calming. The man stood in front of Ander, his black cloak billowing out in the wind. His hair was dark as the Stygian River, his skin the same lightly tanned olive as Katrin. When he glanced back at her, his eyes, so brown they were almost black, warmed at the sight of her.

The God of Death and the Illuminating Stars of Night. The King of the Underworld. Aidoneus. Her father.

Katrin sprinted from the stairwell, flinging her arms around him. "Father! How? Why? What are you doing here?" The answers did not really matter. He was here. She had not seen her father in well over a year, his duties as ruler of Aidensian taking precedence over being in this realm. He was only allowed out at times of crisis, or on occasion celebration, and for a single week of the year to visit her mother.

"Whoa there, little one. Let's take this one question at a time." He hugged her back, a firm but loving embrace. "I have missed you," he chuckled in his booming voice. "I swear you have grown since I last saw you."

"Father, I am almost twenty-five. I have not grown, and I am not your *little* one anymore. I am a lady now." Her smile beamed almost from cheek to cheek. The light in her eyes a sparkling amber and brown.

"You will always be little to me, Kat," her father said, ruffling the top of her hair like she was still a young child.

Ander snorted beside them. Katrin flashed him a narrow glare. He would not ruin this moment for her. He held his hands up in front of his chest, backing off a step. She rolled her eyes back, this man really knew how to annoy her.

"But really, Father, why are you here? And with *him* nonetheless." She pointed at Ander who now sat up on the rail on the ship, one foot knocked back.

"How about we get to shore, and then we can have that talk. There's much to discuss, my little one." Her father gave a small smile and flashed a—was it concerned?—look toward the captain. Katrin knew better than to argue with her father, and she was just so happy he was here. That little piece of home and familiarity easing the pain in her heart from being absent from Alentus all these weeks. Still, she could not help but think it strange that her father would be on this shrouded isle, be allowed to leave his sacred realm, and most of all be working with a pirate.

Now it was Ander's turn to speak. "You can leave all your stuff on the ship. The crew will pack it up and take it to shore on the row boats. You can join your father, Leighton, Thalia, and I on the first one out."

Katrin bit her lip. She had left her night clothes in a heap on the floor, and now some member of the crew would be bundling it up. Ander only had thin silk slips when she had come aboard the ship. Katrin had not minded it until now. It was what she had always preferred at home when the weather had not chilled off for winter yet. But thinking about what the crew would say when they found this little measly thing on the ground. Oh gods—they would think there was something between them. But was there?

"Something bothering you, Starling?" Ander purred, sneaking up behind her.

Katrin jumped. "What? Nothing is bothering me." He gave her a wicked glare, like he knew what was causing the princess' skin to tingle, stomach to clench, cheeks to flush.

Her father glared over at them and Ander apparently took that as his sign to walk away toward the rope ladder hanging over the side of the rail. How was Thalia supposed to get down that with her dainty little dress? Katrin was glad she had opted for something more conducive to climbing down the swaying ladder.

"Ladies first," Ander said as he gestured toward the side of the ship. She slid up onto the rail of *The Nostos*, swinging her legs over to get her footing on the wooden dowels hanging down to the raft below. The last time she had been this close to the rail, this close to the water, she had almost jumped to her death. The hair on the back of Katrin's neck stood as she slowly lowered herself down. It was over. The sirens were gone. Her father was here now. She was safe.

"Let me help you, little one." Her father reached for her hand as she took the last few steps down into the raft. The boat was small, but still enough to fit six people—the five of them and a burly looking man tending to the oars, rowing them to the coast. He looked somewhere in his fortieth years of life, cropped black hair and piercing blue eyes, or at least they would have been. One was muted, a jagged scar tracing from above his eyebrow to his cheek. Katrin did not want to know how he got that scar.

Leighton and Ander followed next, quickly scurrying down the rope. Then came Thalia, her gown billowing in the light breeze of the isle. Katrin knew she would have fallen flat on her back if she had tried to descend wearing that, and yet Thalia was graceful as—well, graceful as a feline, as she stepped back into the small row boat. Mykonos was not far behind her, leaping from the rail of the ship and landing lightly in Thalia's lap. Katrin leaned over, giving a little scratch to the purring creature.

It was a short journey to the shore; the sea floor dropping off close enough that *The Nostos* had been able to sail most of the way in. Leighton directed them into one of the smaller whitewashed buildings on the coastline, its door painted a deep azure, the color of the sea beyond them.

"We'll stay here before we journey to the training grounds at the base of the mountain. Thalia can show you to your room afterwards, but first we eat," Leighton said, gesturing toward an intimate dining room.

A worn wooden table sat in the center with just enough room for six chairs. A small fireplace was placed in the corner, already ablaze, countering the chill in the air from the early autumn breeze. Elegant paintings hung on every wall, their bright colors adding a sense of warmth and life in the whitewashed rooms.

"It's lovely here." Katrin glanced around at the other rooms. A living space stood through an archway from the dining room. Plush, velvet beige couches and chairs sat in an arc around another fireplace, a low lying table standing in the center filled with water marks from drinks shared. It reminded her of her family's winter cabin in the woods. It looked like a *home*.

"Thank you, it was my mother's." Ander smiled softly as he ran his hand along a wooden cabinet in the dining room. "I think she would like you, Starling. She always was the feisty one of the family. You have the same spitfire she does."

Katrin locked her eyes with his, a simple longing behind them. "You really think so?"

"She would love you, little one," her father butted in.

"You know Ander's mother?" Katrin whipped her head around.

"I know many people, being a god and all." Aidonius chuckled. Katrin rolled her eyes at her father. This was the closest he'd ever been to attempting a joke.

"Are you all going to keep talking or are you going to actually join us for food?" Leighton quipped, his mouth half stuffed with bread from the table. A spread from *The Nostos'* chef had been brought in—breads and fish and boiled vegetables. It smelled incredible.

"If you don't sit soon, Leighton might have eaten it all," Thalia laughed as she grabbed a bottle of white wine from the center of the table.

Leighton would get along great with Ajax, the commander also loved to
stuff his face with food.

They all sat down at the round table, digging into the food while it
was still there.

"So, are there no docks in Skiatha?" Katrin directed her question to
Ander, although it was her father who responded.

"There are, but only on the far side of the isle. If the wards protecting
Skiatha were to fall then it would give the people enough time to escape.
The waters on the far side are much more treacherous than these. Only
well-trained sailors would be able to navigate around the deadly shoreline." Her father's raspy voice was just like she remembered.

"But the wards can't fail, can they? Ander told me they were powered
by the Grechi." Katrin looked curiously between her father and the
captain.

"These specific wards were cast by two of our gods. But our powers
are not nearly as strong as those of the Olympi. It would not be easy, but
if one of them used their power, the protection would fall." Her father
looked worried, a small sweat building by his temples. This was not a
look Katrin had seen much—if at all—on her father. Little concerned
the God of Death.

Katrin choked on a sip of wine, blinking at her father. "But the
Olympi were destroyed in the war." How could one of them take down
the wards if they were all dead? Unless—

"You didn't tell her everything then?" Aidonius asked Ander, his
brows raising.

"I thought you might want to be the one to tell her this part. I wasn't
sure she would believe me." Ander cringed, reaching for a glass of wine
no doubt to take the edge off.

Katrin scoffed. "You didn't think I would believe you? I'm here aren't
I?"

"My daughter has a point. Clearly she trusted you more than you
thought." But had she? Yes—she was here now—but when Ander had
given her the choice to leave she had taken it. It was not until the attack
and the way he cared for her after that she chose to stay. Chose to fight.

"Yes, *your daughter* always seems to have a point." Ander bristled and Katrin did not want to see what type of vicious glare her father threw back at him.

"I will tell you a story, Aikaterine, one that is no longer allowed to be written for fear that our lies will come crashing down. There once was a beautiful maiden, Persephone, who often joined her mother Demeter, the Goddess of Harvest, in the fields to pick flowers. Her hair was blonde as the light that radiated from her smile save for a shimmering strawberry hue, her skin soft and pale, and as she picked the flowers an entrancing melody would dance from her lips. One day, Persephone strayed from her mother, finding herself lost in the dark woods. There she came upon a man dressed in a black, velvet cape, his hair dark as night, his eyes a shade one could not describe as anything other than the color of death, on a large black steed. Hades, the God of the Underworld sat on his beast, watching the young maiden to see if she would cower and run, but she did not."

Hades. Katrin's mind flashed to the night of the masquerade.

"*'Come with me,'* he had whispered. *'Come with me and I will keep you safe.'* And Persephone did. Taking his hand, she was pulled up on the winged horse. But he did not lead her to safety, instead he whisked her to the underworld through a chasm in the ground. What the maiden did not realize was that Hades had known she would be in those woods, had lured her away from her mother with the lovely smell of the narcissus flower. He had become obsessed with Persephone and her delicate nature, something he did not experience in the dark kingdom he ruled. Hades forced her into a marriage, but his brother Zeus interfered. See, Zeus was the king of all gods and had answered Demeter's calls to save her daughter from the wicked place. But Hades would not give her up so easily, sealing her fate with four pomegranate seeds with which he laced her wine. Four seeds for the four months she would be bound to spend with him in his kingdom of endless night. At the sign of first frost, Persephone would descend to the underworld to live the colder months with her captor. It is ironic that Hades now lies confined to a place he cannot stand to be."

Katrin stared at her father in disbelief. He was the God of the Underworld, not this Hades. And yet, the lilting voice, the blonde hair and pale skin, born from a goddess whose powers were of harvesting, of growth—the woman he described sounded like her mother, like the earthly powers she possessed. "Is mother—is she Persephone?"

"Not fully. When the final battles occurred, some of the Olympi were truly destroyed, their magic returning to the earth to be reborn in others. Your mother, she was given many powers, one of which was from Persephone, the Goddess of Growth." Her father's eyes deepened as he spoke, his jaw becoming tight. "Some gods, however, were merely captured. Some of their powers left them, but enough remained, keeping them alive in gold-plated stone tombs, even with the blood magic that ensnared them all those years ago. I filled the role Hades left when he was entombed, but the wicked god still lives, and some people believe those captured gods should be set free. Whether they wish to wreak havoc on the world or be owed a favor from the wickedest of the gods, I cannot say."

Katrin could feel the food she had just eaten rise in her stomach, the sour taste of bile lining her throat. "And who wants Hades to be set free?" Clearly, she was the only one who seemed concerned about this. Ander, Leighton, and Thalia all sat sipping wine from their cups and biting down on more food like they did not comprehend the gravity. Or maybe they were so desensitized from hearing the story over and over that nothing seemed to frighten them.

"There is a king in Voreia who seeks the power that would come with releasing the Olympi. But that takes a kind of blood magic that is no longer practiced. He has been hunting for a key, for an individual from a very powerful line of sorcerers that was lost after the war. But believe me, Aikaterine, when I say, if this king finds who he is looking for, not only are the isles in danger, but all of Odessia." Her father was not frightened by much, God of Death and Night and all things most people find terrifying. But this—the grave look he held in his face—that was pure unadulterated fear.

"Why is this kept hidden from the people? How is it that you, nor mother, have ever told us?" Katrin was worried, but she was also angry. That meant her parents had been lying to her for her entire life.

"Many don't remember. Our memories were wiped clean when the powers of the Olympi who were destroyed seeped into our veins. But gradually I began to experience dreams, flashbacks of sort, to the end of the war. To being in a golden cage, and the memories flooded back.

"And where exactly are these golden cages? Where are the Olympi entombed, Father?" Katrin's hands shook as she asked the question she already felt she knew the answer to.

"They are held in the mountains of Cyther."

CHAPTER THIRTY-ONE

KOHL

When Kohl departed Alentus, he felt only partially guilty for leaving his father in charge of ruling. Except for the fact that Ember was young and not politically inclined and could very well cause the entire isle to implode before he was back, hopefully with Katrin in tow.

He *had* to wait, at least that was what Kohl kept telling himself. Delaying the search for Katrin had nothing to do with him being afraid she had left him or that she may lie dead at the bottom of the sea. It had entirely been about the fate of her home, her people.

Yet, in the moments Kohl had alone the past few days, sailing toward the precocious isle of Lesathos, he could not help but acknowledge that it really had been so much more. Kohl wasn't sure what he would do if he found her, how he would explain that he had almost killed her sister, that he had taken her throne, that he had put his desire for power above the need to rescue her. He would maybe leave that part out. After all they had been through, he could only hope Katrin would forgive him.

Kohl had hated this gods-forsaken isle, the way it smelled of piss and regret. The useless brawls that broke out in alleyways spilling from the taverns. But this is where his father's spies always found their information, where he had heard of the ship that took Katrin last time.

Lesathos housed all sorts of oily merchants and men who made their trade in things that were not allowed to be spoken. No doubt the home of the black market where his father obtained that smokey drug *olerae*. It was the only port trading in goods from the Anatole. Merchants had to travel along the dangerous coastal road on the main continent to reach the Port of Thesea on the peninsula of Voreia. From there, ships would cross over to Lesathos with hopes they were not raided by pirates roaming near the shores.

A direct waterway from Anatole to any of the Mykandrian Isles had been sealed off by the blockade surrounding Nexos. It was truly the only thing that made Kohl nervous, not being able to broker the ship through the blockade if Katrin had been taken past that looming isle. King Nikolaos had been adamant that only ships that bore the wolf and crescent moon, his banner, would be allowed passage. And if Katrin was being held on Nexos—well, he would need much more than the small crew of soldiers to rescue her.

His father had given him twenty of his best men for the journey. Men of which Kohl himself was almost frightened. They were the true warriors and sailors of Morentius, originally hailing from Votios. Much like the king, their canines had been shaven down into sharp fangs, their bronzed brown skin shimmered in the sunlight but their ebony eyes made them look deadly. The blades each warrior carried were laced with the venom of the viper, deadly to all who dared to challenge.

Kohl had wanted and also not wanted to be one of these men all at once. He wanted his father's respect and pride and yet, these men slaughtered first and asked questions later, all under the guise of peace. But he was certainly pleased that this elite team was on the journey to find the princess, especially if some pirate who terrorized the eastern isles was responsible for her capture.

The pirate would pay. Kohl could only hope he would be the one to slit his throat, because when it came down to it, he loved her. Loved Katrin more than he could ever describe. Even at their worst moments, she was still the sun he revolved around. Even when his ambition clouded his judgment, it was always to benefit her.

The Hydra had been docked at Lesathos since morning. They had sailed through every night, each member of the ship taking a shift manning the wheel and the sails. A trip that would normally take a week had only taken them five days. It would have been faster had the winds not died out on day three and the current not pushed against them for several hours.

Now, the crew aboard waited for the group of spies King Athanas had sent before *The Hydra* to return. They needed that initial information the spies collected in the taverns and at the ports around the isle before they could start devising a plan. A plan that would most likely involve some less than approachable characters.

One of the soldiers knocked on the door to Kohl's quarters where he was fumbling through old reports his father possessed on the Prince of the Lost Isles. The man at the door was broad with deeply tanned skin. His hair shone the same color as Kohl's, but he kept it braided long down his back. "Excuse me, Your Majesty, but it appears the spies have returned. Would you like me to send them to the war room?"

Kohl fumbled through the papers again, searching for any description of this prince, but he had no luck. "Yes, let them know I will be right in," he said as he waved off the soldier. There was nothing. This Prince of the Lost Isles was a mystery. Not his age nor the color of his hair, or even from where he originally hailed was recorded. No man could have actually been born on this island that most thought to be merely a myth. The prince had to have come from somewhere, and Kohl would figure it out even if he had to interrogate people. He had always despised that part of war—torture. His father was proficient at it, but Kohl had always preferred other methods to gain the truth from people.

The war room on *The Hydra* was massive. Larger than most of the non-merchant ships that sailed the Mykandrian Sea. Although their ancestors hailed from the deserts of Votios, the Athanas line had quickly taken to the seas.

Their fearsome soldiers and rigorous training tactics built Morentius into the fiercest naval force, however their size never stood in comparison to that of Nexos or the Spartanis of Alentus. That would change now that an Athanas sat on the throne of Alentus. The two fleets would easily outnumber King Nikolaos's naval forces if it was not for his power to control the seas. That same power that made it so easy to blockade the straits to Anatole and the seas beyond.

Kohl entered the war room, positioning himself at the head of the long mahogany table. He leaned over a chart one of the soldiers had laid out. It was similar to the ones he had grown up studying; however, in the north-eastern corner lay an inlet from the Mykandrian Sea he did not recognize. The inlet had the words Manos Sea scrawled over a depiction of waves and fog. There lay two isles, Skiatha and Cyther. The mythical lands that Kohl had only just learned existed.

"So we have a chart to guide us, but how do we know this is real? How do we expect to cross through the straits to either side of Nexos?" He glanced around the room at silent faces. The thin and oily men his father usually sent out to do his dirty business seemed to have nothing to say. "Did you all not bring this to me under the guise it held the secrets we need? Or is this just another piece of useless information?" Kohl pointed at the chart. It had been weeks and the spies had found nothing. Nothing except this apparently.

"It is useless, Your Majesty," a seedy voice piped up. Kohl looked among the men and landed on one in the far corner, standing in the shadows opposite the door he had entered.

Kohl cracked his neck, his jaw clenching shut. "Then why exactly have we all gathered here?"

The man who spoke stepped closer into the light surrounding the table. He was shorter than most of the soldiers his father employed, his skin paler and face ruddy and sweaty. He looked like the kind of man who would lose to you in a bet then try to steal your coin anyway.

"You are one of my father's spies?" Kohl questioned the man.

"No, Your Majesty. My name is Dolion. And I have a personal vendetta against this prince you are after." One of Dolion's hands gripped the side of the table so hard his knuckles went white. The other grasped around a velvet pouch. "He slaughtered my men as well as my brother outside a tavern only two weeks ago. And it just so happens I know exactly how to find him, I only need a crew to take me."

Kohl would have cringed at the way the man spoke, his voice causing a need to recoil in his bones, but if he had more information about the Prince of the Lost Isles then Kohl had no choice. "I thought you said that chart was useless."

The man smiled. "It is. Without this of course." He allowed the device in the velvet pouch to drop onto the table.

Kohl scoffed. "A compass? We're on a ship, we have enough of those." This man was really all the spies could come up with? He would have done a better job searching for answers himself.

Dolion chuckled. His booming laughter filled the room in an un-savory way. "I am sure you do, Your Majesty. But this is no ordinary compass. It came from one of the ancient temples before the war. A gift from the god Poseidon himself. It is said to hold a drop of his power, enough to let you mask yourself to a foe on the seas. Enough to fool the wards around the Lost Isles into letting you pass."

Kohl's eyes widened. The soldiers around began murmuring to one another in hushed tones. Poseidon. An Olympi they had been forbidden to learn about, all knowledge of him vanished or burned save for the spo-ken lores. And if you were ever caught speaking one of those forgotten myths it was grounds for execution, a punishment written into the treaty between the isles after the Peloponnian War.

"And what was this Poseidon the god of exactly? Why would his power allow these things?" Kohl questioned, leaning in. Gazing at the chart, the details seemingly changed. As if the parchment itself shim-mered around the depictions of the isles. Taking in the smaller markings, Kohl noticed the movement of a ship, a symbol of a sea serpent and two crossed swords hovering above it. Saw as it entered past the perimeter of the wards and disappeared. *Katrin.*

Dolion held everyone's ear as he spoke. "He was the God of Sea and Storm, of course. It was his magic that warded Skiatha from its foe. From anyone who might seek to harm his line of succession."

"Nikolaos," Kohl whispered. Of course. His father had thought Nex-os was working with this pirate, but now they knew for sure. "How do we know this compass is real? That someone did not con you into a fake, or lie about the story?"

"Oh, it's real. See for yourself, Your Majesty." Dolion slid the bronze compass across the table toward the king.

The whites of Kohl's eyes began to flicker black as he took hold of the instrument. A faint heat radiated against his palm, feeling *something* else.

He couldn't quite put a finger on what it was, but this was certainly no ordinary device.

"And what do you want? For letting us use this compass? For leading us to Skiatha? Gold? A ship?" Kohl was expecting a hefty price. The man looked like he was one to gamble away all his fortunes. A typical disgusting man of Lesathos. But he did not care, Kohl would give Dolion whatever he desired. To find the pirate. To find his bride. No amount of coin was too much.

The ruddy man laughed again. "All I want is to watch as that pirate dies."

Kohl smiled back at him, the ebony color retreating back to the center. "Well, I'm sure we can arrange that."

PART THREE

στο τέλος
(at the end)

CHAPTER THIRTY-TWO

KATRIN

C yther. Her mother likely sailed there the morning of the Acknowledgement, unable to interfere with tradition, whether it was postponed or not. If the Olympi were entombed there, held against their will until they were released to aid these northern dissenters, what of the Queen of the Gods herself?

Aidoneus could no longer sense his wife, something they could do since they became Fated after the Pelopponian War. A permanent buzzing that hummed through the deepest cells in his mind, that type of bond could be felt even in the furthest and darkest dungeons of Aidesian. For him not to sense Kora now—that could only mean one of three things. She was shrouded. She had burned out. Or she was dead.

A few of the soldiers from the mountain traveled to the shore; they would shepherd the party to the training camps located deeper into the isle. They had gathered in what used to be Ander's mother's home, confined to a tiny room underground with dim lighting and certainly not enough space for the large warriors of Skiatha. They stood shoulder to shoulder muttering about why this young princess was in their midst. She couldn't help but wonder if the look they gave her was one of fear. But not fear of death, none cowered from Katrin's father, or the fate he brought them—fear from an untapped power that lived inside her, wild and untrained. As if she might explode at any moment, reducing those around her to ash and dust.

Or perhaps it was fear of the little white creature sitting atop Thalia's lap by the door. Each man had shuddered as they stepped below into the damp underground room. As if they had previously seen the *daimon* she could become. Her true form. No longer the little spy, but the adaptation of Thalia's *psychí* that haunted even the likes of Ander and Leighton.

The captain and the nauarch stood next to Katrin in front of the burning hearth. Droplets of water trickled down from the ceiling onto their skin as they waited for the men to quiet.

Ander cleared his throat, "As some of you may have noticed, we have a new guest in our presence, Aikaterine Drakos, Princess of Alentus." Thus began the murmuring once again as Katrin smiled lightly at the men. She was not afraid of them, at least she thought she need not be. Her father was there, as well as *The Nostos* crew and she trusted them. Her gut trusted them. But the broad shouldered and tattooed men had an air about them. One that signaled they had seen despair and death in its truest form. That they would slaughter those who stood in their path without hesitation.

The men began to hush once more. "I expect everyone to treat our *guest* with the utmost respect and care. If you don't, it will not be me you have to answer to, but her father." He nodded to Aidoneus standing in the corner, half hidden in the darkness and shadow of the flames that were posted haphazardly about the room. Looking terrifying in this moment, her father with deep brown eyes piercing, firm jaw clenched, held his lips in a snarl. Gods help them. She had not seen her father look that overbearing or protective in—well, in five years.

An older man stepped out of the crowd of ten soldiers, his eyes weathered, but his stocky frame was still built out with muscle. His skin was a deep brown hue like Leighton's, his irises a similar striking green, an unusual feature. A black tattoo circled up his bicep, extending to his neck—a sea serpent releasing from water, its wings flaring from his shoulder across his chest and back.

"You don't need to worry about us, Captain. No one would dare lay a hand on Aidon's daughter, even without your reminder." The man chuckled. "I've taken enough grief from him in the past. But if she chooses to train, I would be more than happy to instruct." He bowed toward Katrin, toward her father. His voice was a serene chill, a blend of the ease she felt when she first met Leighton aboard *The Nostos* and an odd sense of knowing crept up Katrin's skin.

"That won't be necessary, Kristos, I will be training the princess myself." Ander winked at her.

"Is that so?" Katrin scoffed, rolling her eyes. "I'm pretty sure if someone should be training the other it should be me, considering I've bested you not once, but twice."

The men began to howl. Kristos the loudest of the group. "This small woman—no offense, Princess—beat you in a fight?" He was laughing so hard water welled in his eyes, the tattoo shuddering from the way his chest heaved as the booming sound left his mouth.

"She's a lot tougher than she looks," Ander muttered under his breath, barely loud enough to hear.

Katrin scrunched her nose at him, her amber flecked eyes narrowing. "I'll have you know I had him on his ass both times. Dare I say it was easy?"

"I still think you just wanted to be on top of me." Ander raised one eyebrow, shrugging his shoulders while he put his hands in his pockets.

Red swept across Katrin's face, that pulsing need clenching low in her stomach. She thought of the way he had stared at her broken body after he bathed her, the careful gleam of desire in his seatide eyes. Gods, she had to stop thinking about that, especially with this many people around them. But it was hard not to be enthralled by him. The whisper quiet way she could feel him all over her at once, even when he stood paces away. The way his voice lingered in the recesses of her mind, beckoning her closer. She glanced again at Ander, his devilish grin and fiery gaze burning straight through her.

"Ah-hem," her father coughed, breaking up the extremely awkward electricity buzzing through the room. "As much as it amuses me to hear how my lovely daughter can take on the prince, there are more pressing matters to discuss."

"And what might those matters be—other than the arrival of your daughter?" one of the other soldiers asked. This one was younger, around the same age as Katrin. He had a similar tattoo to Kristos, except his was only across his chest, the black ink a stark contrast to his pale olive skin.

"If Katrin is to fight for our cause and convince the people of Alentus and the Spartanis to as well, she must learn the truths of Cyther, all of them. I know this is a lot to ask of each and every one of you, the pain that speaking of that place may bring, but it is only through those stories we can truly make people believe." The soldiers were silent once more, eyeing each other to see who might speak first. Who may be bold enough to share their story, whatever that might hold.

The nauarch stepped up first. "I have spent the most time with Katrin—" He was the only one she had spent time with, but Katrin was not sure that really mattered. "I will tell her my story first, but I ask that I am allowed to do so privately."

Aidoneus nodded, as did Ander and Kristos. They stepped aside letting Leighton shift himself in front of Katrin. He held out his hand to her. "Follow me, Princess. I find it easiest to talk while my feet are buried in the sand."

Katrin looked at him with curiosity, the corner of her mouth ticking up. Whatever these men had to share was clearly a mix of trauma and pain. She knew how hard it was for her to speak of her own, so the princess appreciated his willingness to let her in. To give up a piece of himself, so that she could make better decisions for herself and eventually for her people. "It would be my pleasure, Leighton." She laid her hand in his as he guided them out of the underground room into the crisp coastal air.

"How much has the captain told you about me? How I came to be aboard his ship?"

"Thalia mentioned you knew Ander before he bought her in the markets of Lesathos; otherwise, I have heard nothing. I assumed you two had known each other from—well, from here I guess. Or wherever home is."

Leighton buried his now bare feet in the powder soft white sand as they sat along the waterline of the shore, his dark skin a stark contrast to the pearlescent beaches of Skiatha. "Home is quite far from here. A place I haven't seen since I was very young."

Katrin cocked her head to the side, empathy growing in her expression as pain grew in Leighton's. His hands gripped fistfuls of the sand, letting them trickle out through his fingers. Again and again he repeated this as he spoke.

"The coastal village where I was born in Votios was raided when I was around nine. My parents were both fishermen; the raiders were looking for warriors. Nonetheless, they were both violently slaughtered in their sleep." Katrin reached for the nuarach's hand, and although he flinched slightly, he let her keep her palm laying in his.

"My uncle, on the other hand, had been the leader of our village's small fleet. He was our chief, our king you could say, the best warrior I have ever seen fight—even to this day. But these men, they possessed something *else*. A persuasion of sorts. I did not know it then, but it came from a deep rooted and forbidden form of blood magic practiced in the deserts of Votios. All recollection of that sort of sorcery had ceased to exist after the Peloponnian War, or that was what we had been taught to believe. Yet these men arrived, with an oily way to their speech, promising riches and land until the moment they cuffed us as slaves.

"So there was my uncle—brave and fierce and strong—being bound and captured. My two older brothers and I, it seemed, were young enough to be thought malleable. My older sister—" Leighton's voice cracked as Katrin could see water begin to line the rim of his emerald eyes. "Her fate ultimately was worse than death, at least for a time. The men shoved all of us into a hold beneath their ship, about fifty from my village, I guess about twenty-five more from a village nearby. I thought that would be the worst of it, the smell of sweat and defecation, the thirst and hunger, lack of nourishment, the feeling of suffocation from being chained.

"We did not know where we would be sailing, the men never told us. Even when we arrived on that gods-forsaken isle, we did not know its name, nor the power that had lingered in the mountains. It wasn't until some of us escaped that we were told where we had been held. I warn you Katrin, where we are going is a place worse than any you may have seen or read about before. Cyther makes the tales of this isle surrounded in an all-engulfing flame seem like a child's bedtime story meant to soothe not frighten. But what we left behind—it is why all those men's faces went pale when your father asked for their stories. For sixteen years, I was held captive on that isle. I went from a young innocent boy to the warrior I am today. Yes—they trained us, hoping one day that we would side with their forces, that we would be enthralled by the lure that is Hades. The lure of a life everlasting.

"See, that is what he promised them. The sorcerers who shielded that isle from the rest of the world. The men who hailed from the deserts. To give the blood of life to the gods as a trade for the years they may live past their time. So they slaughtered the young maidens they took from not only our piece of Votios, but from across all of Odessia. And those whose maidenhead had no longer been intact—they used to warm their beds. Ileana, my sister, was eighteen when we were taken. A charming young woman with so much life left to live. She was a prized bride in our village, set to marry a chief from a nearby tribe. Because of that, she was gifted to their leader. I never saw her again. Never heard her sweet voice whisper bedtime stories in the dark. Never felt the clutch of an embrace since the day they pried her hands from around me and my brothers. I was told after a few years she slit her own throat, desperate to escape the life to which she was bound. That the leader of those men let her body rot in a ditch, never buried, never burned. A lifeless soul to wander the everlasting abyss in between."

Leighton stopped there for just a moment, looking out into the vast expanse of the sea before them. Katrin rested her head on his shoulder, still gripping his palm tight as he spoke. She understood—why Ileana had done it. When Katrin was swept away on the tides she had tried to do the same thing, yet she lived, while Leighton's sister lingered in death. Why the gods favor some and not others—a mystery she may never solve.

"The boys, the men, they sent us all to the mines beneath the mountain. There was no light there. No reprieve from the dust in our lungs and slashes at our backs. A black hued substance was held there in the rock. One we would pick away at day in and day out. They would position the pieces we hacked away into a dais every full moon. And every full moon a maiden was laid upon that dais, tied down with black rope as their throat and wrists and thighs were slit open, blood pouring over onto the rock. But it did not trickle down, instead it seeped into the black substance, turning it a golden hue. We saw it tested on others. Men and women who bore similar powers to those of the sorcerers we learned ruled Cyther. It stripped their power, fed off their will to live. If you ever encounter this, if someone ever tries to give you something made of what you may think is gold, do not accept.

"Finally, after sixteen years, a group defected; men who did not believe in blood magic, who learned their craft by the means of the earth, of the flowers that bloomed, of the animals that thrived in the mountains, not of death. They were able to smuggle a small band of us out. The men you met today. Myself, my uncle Kristos, and nine from our village."

Katrin lifted her chin toward him. Kristos was his uncle. But she had seen it, the same deep color in their eyes, the way Kristos's expression pained when Leighton offered to tell his story. "And what of your brothers?"

Leighton shifted his gaze away from her. "They did not make it. I am the last—I am the last of that line."

The tears Leighton shed began to dry against his heated skin. "I want them all dead. Everyday I think of the people we lost, their souls condemned. They never reached the hallowed halls of Aidesian, your father never greeted them as they passed into the serenity of the afterlife. The blood sacrifice captured their souls for Hades and Hades alone. To fuel his power. To fuel the power of the other Olympi kept locked away on that endless pit of an isle. You think the creatures that roam your father's dungeons are horrifying? You should see what lurks in Cyther, protecting those mountains. Protecting that rock. Protecting *him*."

Katrin's whole body stiffened while her mind filled with anger, confusion, and hatred. Pure unadulterated loathing toward these people. Ruthless men torturing innocent mortals, gifting their bodies away as if they meant nothing. "And what of my mother? If she truly sailed there, thinking it was a place of grace, of everlasting life? If she bore those golden cuffs that drained her very soul and muted her power?"

Leighton looked down at his hands, uneasy breathing coming from his throat. "If Kora was sent to Cyther—by her own choice or not—I don't know how to tell you this, Katrin. Your mother would be dead."

Although the words stabbed through her chest like a knife, a little piece of her had already known it to be true. There was nowhere in this realm or another that her parents could not sense each other. If Aidoneus could no longer feel Kora, then Leighton was right. Her mother was gone.

Chapter Thirty-Three

Katrin

After Leighton had told her about Cyther, they remained on the beach until the sun began to set, turning the sky a scarlet and saffron hue. It was the calming end to a conversation which had caused the nauarch so much pain. She could feel the guilt seeping from him, for his parents who were slaughtered, for his brothers who did not make it out of the mountain in Cyther, for Ileana.

Katrin would ask him more about her one day. To help him remember the good. The times when they lived in the serene coastal village of Votios. Whether she had played with him on the shores even though she was eleven years his senior. If she had told him stories as she tucked him in bed at night. Those memories, those thoughts, they were the only thing keeping the memories of the lost souls alive.

The next day, they all rose at the first light of dawn. The chill of autumn creeping farther in off the waters, causing the leaves in the trees to shake and float toward the ground. Katrin slipped into her leather trousers, adding a thick long-sleeved shirt and a vest within which she could sheath her sword. Well, technically Ander's sword. He allowed her to take the one she stole when she first arrived on *The Nostos*, the sword that depicted Odysseus's journey. Katrin still marveled at the intricate depictions carved into the steel, although now the images of the sirens caused a twitch in her neck.

Her father had said goodbye after dinner the night before, his duties in the underworld of Aidesian not allowing him much time in the mortal realm. But Katrin did not care. She only cared that she got to see him at all, even if it was just for a day or two. That a piece of home had been here with her. A reminder of why she had to fight these evil men who threatened to destroy everything she held dear.

The journey was long into the woods. Cypress trees and olive groves lined the dirt path as they walked farther and farther into the center of the isle. Katrin could have sworn a permanent fog lingered there, swirling just above the ground and casting an essence of mystery and dare she say fear. But Ander promised her there were no terrors hiding in the wood or the mountains. The only people who lived on Skiatha were the soldiers and their families. No one had breached the wards protecting the isle. No one could get to her. Nonetheless, she occasionally reached for her dagger when a twig snapped or birds rustled in the bushes.

It was silly, she knew that, not only were there no evil men lurking in the fog, she was surrounded by some of the most skilled warriors in the isles. Literally, these were the men of myths. Katrin would have felt better if she had not been attacked so recently. If every tiny sound in the darkness did not make her jump in fright. If the image of the ruddy faced man sending his foot into her stomach did not plague her when she closed her eyes.

By the time they stopped for lunch, Katrin was pleased the tempera-ture had cooled from the humid air. Even with the crisp breeze and the shade of the trees, sweat still slid down her skin. The leather trousers she put on this morning were starting to stick to her skin in a very uncomfortable way, squeaking with each step she took.

The second half of the day was not as bad. The winds picked up, drying the beads of sweat that had trailed down her back. Katrin stayed toward the front of the group of men, wanting to be near Leighton. The nauarch had not spoken since their talk on the beach the day before. She hated that he had relived his trauma for her. That she intruded on the memories of pain he had so that she could understand what these monsters were doing to innocent people. So she could see why they needed to fight. Why all the isles needed to fight.

Nearing the end of the day, Katrin's thighs began to ache. She ran every morning, and was used to long journeys on foot, but she had been confined to the ship for so long that her body now rejected the activity. She only hoped there would be a hot bath waiting for her wherever they were staying.

As Katrin looked over toward Thalia, she was jealous of Mykonos, who had spent the majority of the walk in a pack that the seer strapped to her own back. Katrin wondered why they had not taken horses, which would have taken significantly less time and would also not have made her feel like she would melt into the ground if she took one more step.

"We will stop here for the night and continue on in the morning. If we start again at dawn we should make it to the mountains by night-fall." Ander pointed at the large stone building that sat just off the trail through the woods. It was different from the houses that lined the coast of Skiatha. This was made of a darker stone, shiny and black like the night sky, the moonlight scattering off it back toward the trees. "It's one of the forts we have set up around the isle. There are around ten on Skiatha. If for some reason there is not enough time to escape, the people can flee to one of them. The forts hold enough weapons and goods in store to withstand a months-long siege. There is little known to man that could break these walls."

Katrin followed the captain inside, running her hand along the strange dark substance. Her skin prickled as she felt the stone. A sort of buzz, or heat coursing into her. This was not like the stone in Cyther of which Leighton had spoken. That one had absorbed power. This seemed to give it off. Like the building was alive, breathing its air into you to wake you from some sleepless slumber.

Each of the men followed behind, as well as Leighton and Thalia, carrying their packs and heading off in different directions, no doubt for the rooms they had stayed in many times before.

"Ander?" Katrin's voice was quiet as she contemplated whether to ask the question that had sat with her all day.

He turned back toward her. "Yes, Starling?"

"Do you think...well...do you think I could sleep in your room tonight?" Ander's brows shot up as he looked around to see if anyone else heard what Katrin had said. Luckily, the men and Thalia had all scattered faster than rats when they arrived to wash before their favorite chef whipped up dinner. The soldiers had told her all about the gruff old man who supposedly made the most delectable meats and pies. Maybe he could bake her into pie so she would feel less embarrassed.

"It's not what you think—well if you think what I was doing was propositioning you." Ander just blinked, no hint of a response other than a small tick up of his lip. A smile maybe, but possibly just a twitch. Gods, this man was hard to read. "It's just that I haven't had a single nightmare since you started staying in the cabin on the ship with me, and I think with the change of scenery, maybe I wouldn't know where I was if I woke up and—"

"I'll show you to my room then." Ander began to walk down the first corridor to a spiral staircase that led to the second floor. Small lanterns lined the circular path up into a receding darkness.

"I can sleep on a couch or the floor or wherever. I feel guilty I stole your bed on the ship and now—" Katrin needed to stop rambling. She would only embarrass herself more, if that was even possible.

"Whatever you would prefer, Katrin. But I hate to tell you, there's no couch in my room here, only a bed."

Katrin gulped, her insides instantly melting. That was not what she meant at all and yet that little flicker of desire swept right back in. Ander opened a small wooden door at the top of the staircase, entering into a simple room that replicated his quarters aboard *The Nostos*. A large plush bed lay in the center, covered in velvet comforters and pillows deep navy in color. A small desk sat on one side next to a rather large bookcase of worn spines and well read tomes, the opposite facing wall led out to a large balcony.

"Why don't you wash up, the bathing chamber is just through that door. I'll use one of the others and see you down at dinner." His demeanor was light as Katrin looked around the room, absorbing a little piece of who he was everytime he shared a space with her. Clearly this man loved to read, since she had not seen a single room that did not include a shelf or case of books. Even in his mother's little house on the coast, there had been a shelf filled with what Katrin imagined were tales of the Olympi or perhaps his sister's romance books.

"Ander," she called after him.

"Yes, Starling?" It was the second time he said those words since they arrived here, but it sent a tingle across her skin. The way the name rolled off his tongue and danced along her ears.

"Thank you."

Dinner had been exactly as Katrin expected. Delicious down to the very last morsel of that incredible flaky and nutty pastry the chef drizzled in honey. She licked each of her fingers raw, savoring every last morsel of dessert. And the wine—the rich and bold flavors, a bit of pepper and plum. The princess drank enough of the flavorful liquid that she felt giddy and emboldened.

"Ok, Starling, I think we should get you to your bed or you won't be able to make the rest of the journey tomorrow." Ander came up behind her chair, pulling it out slightly.

Katrin did not want to leave, she loved sitting with everyone, listening to their stories, hearing about their lives and dreams and loves. She could stay up all night just listening. But Ander was probably right. She was still sore and if she didn't give herself time to rest *she* would need to be carried in a little pack by someone, not the little white cat.

"You mean *your* bed, Captain." Katrin's voice was higher pitched than usual. She thought she had been whispering, but clearly she had not since her words got a snicker from Leighton.

"It's not what you think, I'm sleeping on the floor," Ander replied with a grimace. This earned a sly smile from Thalia. Katrin could have sworn she heard the seer mutter, "*I'm sure you are,*" under her breath.

"Ah yes, the captain will be on the floor. I wouldn't let him come anywhere near me like that—nope—not ever." Katrin crossed her hands in front of her body. Ander shook his head, dragging his hand through his hair. "Gods, Captain, you have no sense of humor!"

"That I don't." He rolled his eyes, and those sparkling green-blue pools hit her square in the heart. Her whole body heated at the sight of his gaze.

"Right, right. Well, I agree then, time for me to go up to bed. I will see you all bright and early." Katrin stood up from her chair, curtseying at the soldiers and her two friends, realizing too late that it was an odd thing to do.

Ander had walked halfway down the corridor by the time she left the table, scurrying after him. Her eyes trailing up his tight leather pants and the white linen shirt that was almost see through. Her mind was going places it should not.

"Hey! Wait up!" she yelled from behind him as he began to ascend the stairs, tripping over her feet.

Ander kicked up one brow. "Am I going to have to carry you up these stairs?"

"Oh gods, Ander, don't be so dramatic. I didn't even drink that much. I am just trying to have a good time before—before all the serious stuff hits."

"Right." His lips thinned and he averted his gaze, but Katrin felt like he had been staring at her. Staring at that hip hugging gold dress he had left on the bed for her, its supple silk soft against her skin, bringing out the light flecks of her eyes and the shimmering highlights in her hair. Alentian gold. Her favorite color.

"Do you like this dress on me?" Katrin did a little spin as she entered the room. Ander stood against the doorway, his arms folded across his chest. His gaze burned as he trailed his eyes up from her toes to the cord holding the panels of the dress together around her waist, to the deep vee of the neckline, the sun and moon pendant dangling between her breasts.

"It suits you," he grumbled.

It suits you. Really?

"Tell me a secret," Katrin giggled, her voice pitched from wine she had guzzled at dinner, as she plopped down on the giant bed. Her hands moved over the velvet comforter that was draped over the edge of the bed. "It's so soft!" Her eyes went wide and she smiled as she wrapped herself in it. "I could live in this blanket forever." Her words were slurred and sheepish. Katrin had not felt this happy, this alive, this at peace in such a long time. These feelings—she would let herself have them. If only for the night.

Ander shook his head at her, but inched closer to the bed. "You know, if you keep rolling around like that you are going to make yourself sick."

"No I won't! I never get sick!" She reached out and grabbed his hand, pulling him on to the plush bed next to her. "You know, you don't *have* to sleep on the floor. We are both adults. We can sleep in the same bed—especially one this large—" She threw her arms out to the side, almost whacking him across the face. "Without doing *things*."

Ander ran his hand over his face and then through his hair. His perfect, wavy, night-black hair. "I am perfectly aware of that fact," he purred.

Katrin's teeth pulled over her bottom lip. She rolled over so their bodies faced each other. "Tell me a secret, Ander." This time she was not giggling. This time her voice was soft and sultry.

His eyes began to swirl again, glowing like the high tides of the isles, newly swept into the harbor. "I can't say no to you," he whispered.

"Then tell me." Her breath caught in her chest, and instantly the dress she wore felt too tight to breathe in, her lungs constricting as if a hand grasped tightly around them.

His face turned serious. "That is the secret, Starling. I cannot say no to you." He had gotten closer to her, so close she could feel the soft puffs of his breath against her skin.

Katrin was not sure if it was all the wine going to her head, or the softness of the bed around her, or the way his breath heated her neck, but she leaned in and met his lips. For a second she thought he might pull back, and then she heard it. The little groan that escaped his throat as he leaned in and kissed her back.

It was different from the kiss he had placed on her cheek at the masquerade. That one had been soft and gentle and calm. This kiss—it felt the same way as when he looked at her after he bathed her. When her body had been bare in front of him, and he had been down on his knees. This kiss was fire and passion and desire.

Ander shifted against her, rolling Katrin onto her back, his body heavy against her as he braced one hand next to her head, the other sliding under her gown. She could feel his rough, calloused hands move up her thigh, his lips breaking from hers as he traced kisses along her jaw, down to her throat. A small moan escaped her mouth as his teeth grazed the soft skin above her collarbone. She arched her back up, needing him to be closer, needing to feel him against her.

Katrin hooked her legs up around him, her fingers lacing behind his neck, traveling into his hair. She needed more. More of his lemony scent, more of his heat against her. *More.*

He stopped for a moment, looking down at her, his lips ticking up in a feral grin. Ander looked at her. "Do you really want this?"

"Yes," she whispered as she pulled him closer still, "more than anything."

He clicked his tongue three times, "I'm going to need you to listen to me for a moment, *Starling*. If I am going to have you, I plan to take my time." He leaned down and placed a soft kiss on Katrin's cheek. His mouth tracing along to her ear where he whispered, "I'm going to need you to take this gown off so I can take a good look at you." His wet lips grazed her ear as he spoke. "Are you going to do as I say?"

She nodded, standing from the bed, the confidence from the wine coursing through her. Katrin's hands dragged up her body to the bodice, unlacing the cord that held the silken fabric together, all the while holding his piercing gaze. The sleeves billowed down her shoulders as she slid out of the golden gown, revealing her small peaked breasts barely hidden under her lacy undergarments, over her tanned stomach, down her legs where the heat of her core was on display beneath matching lace, before it slid onto the floor.

Ander sat on the bed, leaning back on his elbows, the vee of his white linen shirt unbuttoned, his tight black leather pants hugging his thighs, holding down the part of him Katrin wanted to see most. "Good girl."

She walked back toward the edge of his bed where his legs spread out slightly. Katrin settled between them as Ander slid his hands up her back, over the scars she held. But he did not flinch, bearing matching ones of his own she had seen. They shared that. The darkness and shame that came with being unable to forget what others had done to make them feel small and weak and helpless. But Katrin remembered the words Ander had spoken to her the first time they had seen each other in the groves. *You should never feel shame over the pain others inflict on you.* Her heart skipped. He understood her. Everything about her.

Katrin straddled her legs around him, easing them back down to the bed. For once she felt ready. She felt safe. Like the past was just that—the past—and she could finally be fully invested in the present.

Their kisses deepened as she began to shift her hips over him, as his fingers dug into her hips, holding her tight. Ander flipped them once again until he lingered on top of her trailing kisses down her chest, swirling his tongue around her peaked breasts as his hand found her center. "Mmmm, you're so wet for me aren't you?" A breath loosened out of Katrin's throat as she bucked against him. One hand grazed around her thigh, pushing her legs further apart while the other teased the outside of the lace that barely covered her.

The whole room began to blur as he grazed his lips along her hip bone, a soft breath tingling her skin. "Do you want me to take these little things off you?" he whispered, staring back up at Katrin through his dark eyelashes.

Once again the sight of the captain on his knees before her had her legs trembling. A low moan was all she could manage. But this time she felt no shame as he slid the lacey garment off, dropping it beside the bed. His gaze seemed to take in every inch of her naked body. Every dimple and scar reveled in it. "Beautiful." Ander's tongue grazed along his bottom lip.

He circled his thumb around her center, sliding one finger inside gently, coaxing her into a sweet abyss of darkness and pleasure. Katrin's breathing labored as she tried to grind herself against his palm. It wasn't enough. Even as his finger pulsed in and out of her.

He clicked his tongue again. "Oh no, Starling. I can't have you come before I've tasted you." Her breath caught in her throat as he trailed his lips across her stomach. Nibbling his way to her core. Gliding his tongue up her center as he kept the other finger inside her. Working her again and again as she writhed against him, tiny beads of sweat formed on her skin.

"Please," she groaned, "I need—I need—" It was there, just beyond her reach, the sweet release she craved all these weeks with him.

Ander swirled his tongue again, sucking gently as his finger stroked inside her. Until she was spent, until he pulled his finger out and licked what remained of her off of it. His brow kicked up. "Delicious."

Katrin did not know why, but her mind flashed to Kohl. His dark features, the goofy smile he would always give her on their runs in the morning. A smile much like Ander's right now. She had not thought of him in days. But now all she could see was the betrayal on his face when she came back that day from the cabin. The hurt and longing and utter cracking of his heart to see her in another man's clothes.

What would he think now? How quickly the tides had turned away from his favor. How fickle Katrin's words to him had been. *Even after the gods take us.* Those words meant nothing now. She had forgotten them. Forgotten him.

Her eyes widened. "I can't—I can't do this." Katrin's hands shook as she tried to shimmy away from Ander, pushing him off her with a greater force than she intended. Kohl was probably out searching the seas for her, while she was what—lying in another man's bed?

Kohl who she had decided not to return to. She was overreacting, she knew that, but also—maybe she was moving too quickly. Maybe she had gotten too wrapped up in emotion and not thought this through. Thought about who Ander really was and why she was here in the first place. Gods, why did she do the things she did?

"Do you want to talk about him?" Ander asked as he shifted away from her, hurt plastered across his face. Katrin could not blame him. She had all but thrown him off his bed.

Behind the hurt, though, was compassion and empathy. Ander was too good to her. Like he knew the way it felt to have this other love lingering in the back of one's mind. And even though it was entirely irrational in the moment, Katrin felt a pang of jealousy hit her square in the gut. Because he *had* been in love. There was still some woman out there he pined after, the reason he longed to return home. The love he sacrificed by trying to rescue her.

Katrin curled her legs up to a seated position, wrapping her arms around them. Staring for a second out the window into the ever-knowing black sky. "I just wonder sometimes if things would be different." Her voice was so soft it was almost a whisper. "If I had told Kohl about the nightmares earlier. If I had told him about all of my scars. If I had let him in from the start, maybe he would have understood. Maybe he wouldn't have broken earlier that night you took me. Maybe I wouldn't have stabbed him in the woods. Maybe I would never have needed to meet you—" Katrin regretted the words the moment they left her mouth.

Ander recoiled at her confession, his eyes turning a deep silver, not the lustful kind they had just been, but menacing. "You would still pick him. After everything I've told you, after *this*, it will always be him." The way he spoke, it was not a question, it was a confirmation.

"Ander, I didn't mean it that way." Katrin shook her head in her hands. "I don't know *how* I meant it. Don't you ever think of the woman back home that you loved once? What might have been if you hadn't come for me?"

His jaw ticked, lips thinning to a line. It still was not anger lingering in his emotions, what Katrin could feel radiating off him was more like betrayal. "I never said the woman I loved was back home, Starling. If you listened to a single thing I have told you since you came aboard my ship you would know that."

Katrin's face went sheet white. He did not mean—he could not mean—but she thought back through their time on *The Nostos*. Every delicate phrase he gave her day in and day out. The kiss he had given her when he said goodbye in Lesathos. The way he had wiped away the blood and bathed her after she was attacked. Gods, the way he looked at her right now, like someone had driven a bronze dagger through his chest.

"For me—you are the stars, the sun, the entire galaxy and I am the moon that will forever be enchanted by your light. But what am I to you? A distraction? Someone to keep you occupied until you return to that—that man who would turn on you so quickly?"

"I—I'm sorry," Katrin whispered, too stunned to say a single word more.

"I'm sorry too." Ander turned away from her. "I'll sleep downstairs. I've gotten quite used to not sleeping in my own bed since you." The words punched her in the gut. She had wounded him and he had come back at her in full stride.

Katrin could still feel her skin tingling, the bubbling nausea that crept up her throat. For letting him think what just happened meant nothing. For second guessing what she felt. For telling him the truth.

He loved her.

The man on the seas.

The pirate.

The Prince of the Lost Isles.

Alexander loved her.

CHAPTER THIRTY-FOUR

EMBER

The castle had been in disarray since Kohl had left, and Ember was questioning more than ever why exactly he put his father in charge. King Athanas had done approximately one thing the past week, staying cooped in his room smoking some vapid black drug from Anatole. The princess could smell it every time she walked by the guest wing, getting a face full of the thick smoke. She was not sure how he could continuously inhale it, even just the small secondhand effect had her gasping for fresh air.

It had been a week and Ember was growing tired. If the king had given her such a hard time about not knowing the politics of the isles enough to act as regent while Kohl was on the seas in search of her sister, the least that man could do was lead. Or take a meeting with anyone besides those lithe women that snuck into his room each night.

But now she paced back and forth in front of his door holding a piece of parchment. An urgent piece of parchment at that—given to her by Ajax that morning. An attack was imminent, and a defense strategy had to be set up. Yes, Ember could rely on the senators of the Spartanis to make these decisions, but something told her if she did, she would get an earful from the Viper whenever he dared to leave this room.

Ember sucked in a tight breath and knocked on the door three times. She should not be this nervous. It was her home, and she was Prytan now.

But no matter the place or title, King Athanas would always frighten her, if just a little bit.

"You may come in, Princess, I can hear your timid breathing through the door."

Gods, he was the worst human. Ember wished he would just pack up and go back to Morentius, where he could live with the other scary soldiers and their sharpened canines and viper venom-soaked weapons.

"Excuse me, Your Highness." Ember bowed as she entered the room—she was a lady after all, and had been taught the graces of one. Had once only been taught that not too long ago. "There is a missive from our spies in Xanthia. Nexian ships have been seen gathering in the northern part of the Mykandrian Sea. They are worried that King Nikolaos is trying to extend his blockade farther west."

Ember tried not to get too close to the Viper, who sat on his plush velvet pillows, teeth biting deep into some piece of fruit, a drop of its red juice sliding from his lip like blood. She swallowed and forced the bile that rose in her throat back down. It would not surprise her if this man did suck the blood of others, like those spineless creatures in the dungeons of Aidesian.

"Give me that," King Athanas hissed, pointing his long finger at the roll of parchment Ember held. "And who exactly gave *you* permission to read such a missive, Princess?"

Ember clenched her jaw, her amber eyes narrowing. It would not matter if she now wore the royal leathers of the Spartanis, the Viper would always refer to her as a princess. He was a complete power hungry ass.

"Well, Your Highness, as the newly inducted Prytan, I have become privy to any and all reports of threat. You will not forget that these do come from the spies of my soldiers, not yours." Ember let out a long hiss of a breath. Every time she spoke back to King Athanas it became just a little bit easier.

"Well until my son, *your king*, returns, I am still regent and I still hold the highest authority on these matters. I would like any report sent directly to me. *Unopened*."

Power hungry ass, indeed.

"Of course, Your Highness. The senators had hoped to meet and discuss options regarding the details the spies have outlined. Should I set a time for us to meet?"

"You can send them to my chambers, no need to join as you seem to already know everything in the letter. Hurry along now. I am sure there are plenty of better things you could be doing, like planning the dinner for my family this evening. That is the kind of thing a girl your age should be in charge of. Not the matters of men."

Ember muttered something vulgar under her breath, glad the king did not seem to notice. "I'll make sure we have something planned." She wondered what the Queen of Morentius would be like, to have agreed to marry such a vile man. She must be just as vapid and cold as the Viper. Although Kohl was kind most of the time really—for a time at least. Maybe that was a trait he had passed down from his mother. Maybe she was forced to marry this wretched man.

"Oh, and Ember? Make sure my daughter is seated next to the commander. She has a thing for the brooding blondes." The king cackled, knowing he had hit a nerve. He had seen the way Ajax looked at her, how she had looked back. This feeling of longing and forbidden lust or love or *something*.

"Of course, Your Highness." How many times would she have to repeat those words until Kohl returned with her sister

Ember hoped this princess was ugly. That her voice sounded wretched and her personality just as awful. She doubted it though. The looks at least. Kohl was objectively one of the most handsome men she knew, even the Viper was an extremely good looking older man if you could get past his personality. Ember sighed, exiting the guest chambers. She was screwed.

Farah Athanas was anything but ugly. The princess arrived with her mother around midday. Her flowing dark brown hair cascaded to the small of her back, half pinned up in waves with tiny gold clips. The

richness of her russet color skin looked like it would never age, and made her golden eyes stand out even more. Ember had always loved the way her eyes glowed like the sun, but next to Farah's they looked as muted as dried up mud.

The way she spoke was entrancing, a piercing song to the mind and heart. Even Ember, who had no inkling of feelings toward other women, was captivated by it. Men would fall to their knees for this woman. She just hoped one in particular would not.

Yet there he was, bowing in front of her, kissing her small outstretched hand, gaze tracing over every voluptuous curve her silky gown clung to. In this moment, Ember wished Ajax was more like the stiff and unfriendly soldiers and not such a gentleman. She could hear Farah's light giggle down the hallway as she spoke to each of the young guards in front of her. Ember stomped toward them, maybe a bit too aggressively for someone who was supposed to be a composed and dignified member of leadership.

"Princess, a pleasure to meet you." Ember did not know why she deepened her voice just a bit at the address.

Farah threw her arms around Ember, taking her into a warm embrace. "You must be the sister! It's so nice to finally meet you." Her voice was light and welcoming, a stark contrast to her father. "Kohl has told me so much about you."

Ember tried to force out a smile. Ajax snickered to her side, and she shot him a narrow glare. "Has he?" she drawled. Kohl was still on Ember's shit list. Until he brought her sister home, she could only see him as the man who had almost killed her.

"Yes, of course. He speaks very highly of you."

"I'm sure."

"And I hear congratulations are in order! You had a highly respected title thrust upon you recently. One that he believed was well deserved, even if my father thought otherwise." She rolled her eyes when mentioning her father.

Ember could not tell if she was actually nice or if she was just well-versed in politics and blowing smoke up other people's asses.

"Yes, well your father is not a fan of most people. Is your mother with you? King Athanas said to expect you both."

Farah's smile disappeared as she pretended to pick a piece of lint off her silken red gown. Ember had not noticed from a distance, but the gown had an intricate design stitched with a golden thread that made the whole thing shimmer.

"She's probably still at the ship bossing some poor men around to help her bring her trunks to the castle. I swear my mother brought every piece of clothing she owns. I know father didn't tell us how long we would be here for, but if you ask me it was a bit excessive."

Ember's brows shot up. "What do you mean, not sure how long you will be here for?"

"You never know with Papa. Sometimes he wants us around, sometimes he doesn't." The princess shrugged.

That was not exactly what Ember had meant. The royal families of other isles never stayed away from home for long. Especially during the times of suspected rebellion.

An uneasy feeling began to creep into her gut. Maybe Nexos was an even bigger threat than just the blockade. Maybe taking Katrin was only the beginning of some broader plot to cause unrest in the isles.

"Well you and the queen are welcome in our home for however long you need. I will have one of the guards show you to the guest wing, where your father is staying." Ember bowed, about to signal one of the young guards to take Farah when she spoke, turning to Ajax.

"Would you be able to show me? I would love a tour as well—that is if you are not too busy?" Farah smiled faintly at him, a glimmer of hope and desire that made Ember want to vomit shone in her bright golden eyes.

"I am sure the commander has much to do with your arrival..." Ember began.

"Nonsense, I would be happy to take you, Your Highness." Ajax bowed as well, lifting his arm so that the princess could loop hers around.

"Right, of course. Enjoy. I will see you both at dinner then," Ember said, but the two had already begun to stroll down the hallway. Ajax looked back just for a moment, giving her a look of—well, Ember was not quite sure what it was. She was going to be sick. But for now she was late to her training. Political training this time, trying to catch up on years of teachings she had neglected for parties and fineries. At least it was with Iason. At least she did not have to stare at Ajax's warm brown eyes and stupid grin like she did everyday in the ring.

Ember hurried off toward the library. She usually hated being in the dusty old room, preferring the small studies with their comfortable chairs and books on myths and fiction, but she loved spending time with Iason. She had grown up with him always being around. Her uncle had died quite some time ago, but Iason would always indulge Ember in stories of their past. The battles they fought side by side, the adventures they took on the great seas.

He had loved her uncle Machius more than anything, and took in Katrin and Ember as part of his family. Even though they had never married—could never marry—Iason had stayed loyal to Machius, to this family, to Alentus. He gave every bit of his heart and mind and soul to them.

But it had never been public. It never could be. Only those in the family knew what he really was to her uncle. To them all.

They began their lessons like they always did, reviewing political allies in the isles.

"Can you remember how each isle is tied to each other?" Iason would ask her.

To which Ember would always repeat as she did now, "Morentius is tied to Votios through King Athanas's marriage to Queen Zahra of Tyrair. It is also bound to the protection of Alentus now, through the future marriage of Katrin and Kohl. Well, I guess also because Kohl was unrightfully crowned King of my people." Ember tapped her fingers against the wooden table.

"Hush, now. The Wrecking is a binding tradition, you of all people know this." Iason pointed back down at the notes Ember had taken from her sister's desk. "Continue, before anyone overhears your treasonous words." His chastising was more lighthearted than the words he spoke.

"Alentus is the protector of the smaller nearby isles of Xanthia, Lesathos, Cantos, and Delphine through the treaty under us, the Spartanis. Although the smaller isles have their own rulers, they are more of an annex and live tied to the laws of Alentus. Nexos is backed by the Kingdom of Hespali in Voreia, and is bound by treaty to defend the Mykandrian Isles against outside threats. Though that is becoming increasingly ironic, since the only threat to the isles is Nexos itself."

"Well in that, Ember, you are correct. What else have we learned?"

Ember continued listing off specific traditions held in the isles. Then they came to the banners of each land. "Well ours is the fire-sun with a lightning strike down the center, colors turquoise and gold. Morentius is the viper, red and orange banners. Nexos is navy and silver, the wolf and the crescent moon. There was another one in Katrin's notes, black and gray or silver, it looks like two snakes intertwined in each other. I don't know where that belongs to, is it one of the kingdoms in Votios?"

Iason went ashen as he looked at the picture. "I—I don't think I have ever seen that one before. It must have just been a drawing of hers. Something from her imagination. I think we are all done with our lessons for today." Iason knew more, she could tell by the tremor in his voice as he spoke and the way his eyes shifted quickly from the image. Ember knew not to pry more now, but she would figure out what the senator was holding back from her.

Glancing out the window, the low light of the sun dipping over the mountains, Ember's mind went to Ajax. She had seemed to forget about him for all of a few hours, before that unnerving distraction came creeping back. Thoughts of how his time went with Farah, what they did, what they talked about. If he *liked* her.

"Can I ask you something?" Ember squirmed in her chair, biting at her lower lip.

"Of course, what's the matter, my sweet darling?" His gray flecked brows furrowed together, voice more somber.

"What was it like? Being with my uncle, but never knowing you could really *be* with him?" Ember began to pick at her nails, a nervous habit her mother always chided her for. One she had not done in years. Iason was the only one who could really understand her heartache, but also the feeling of not wanting this. She should not have feelings for him, Ajax was crass and full of himself and messed around with a number of women that Ember shuddered to think of—and most of all, the law did not allow it. But he was also thoughtful, and warm, and made her feel safe in a world that was so close to being broken.

Iason's features softened, reaching his hand over toward her's. "You know I have always considered you and your sister the closest thing I have to children. You have the same blood and the same fire and heart that my Machius did. But, my sweet darling, just because the law tells you that you cannot love does not mean you should not. It does not make the love you have for this person any less than what your mother has for your father or Kohl for Katrin. Because that's what this is—isn't it?"

Ember's head hung low, pieces of her golden blonde hair hanging in her face. "Maybe? I don't know...I just don't know why anyone would want a few moments with me when they could build a life with someone else. I always knew this would happen, that it came with the title, but it didn't really hit me until now. I will always be alone."

"You have grown into an incredible woman, Ember. Whoever this person is, they would be lucky to have whatever little piece of you they were able to capture. Because the fleeting moments or stolen kisses are not what you have to give. This," Iason placed his palm over her heart, "is worth any sacrifice. And, my sweet darling, you are never alone. Not while I am here."

A single tear escaped down her pale cheek, as she went to wipe it away.

"What is this old man teaching you that is making you so emotional? Politics was never that interesting when I learned them." Ember glanced over at the doorway and Ajax stood leaning against the frame. She could only hope he had not been standing there the whole time they were talking.

"Oh hush, you never listened in your lessons to begin with." Iason rolled his eyes. "The commander was quite the prankster when he was younger. It is a surprise he even has this title." He chuckled, a low booming laugh that reminded Ember of her father.

"You know I earned this title fair and square, Senator." And there it was again, Ajax's stupid, white, flashing grin so wide it showed the dimples in his cheeks. "Sorry to interrupt your clearly riveting studies, but the time seems to have slipped away from all of us this afternoon.

Dinner is approaching, and I'm sure our Prytan would like to bathe and change before then."

Ember slumped farther in her seat. She was a bit of a mess. From her physical training this morning to sitting around in the dusty library, she smelled of sweat and old books. Plus, she wanted to get out of these clothes and put something more delicate on. Something that could compete with Farah. Not that it *was* a competition.

"Right! Yes, I better get going." Ember hopped up from her chair. "Thank you, Iason. For everything." She leaned down and gave the old man a kiss on his cheek.

"Always, my sweet darling."

"What was that about?" Ajax asked as she walked over toward the door.

Ember rested her palm on his arm. "Nothing you need to concern yourself with, Commander. Just some advice from a wise old man."

Ember brushed out the long diaphanous turquoise dress she changed into. The thin material shimmered in the low light of the castle, flowing delicately with the puffs of wind that followed down the hallway. She kept her hair in curls, an array of little braids weaving through her half-pinned blonde locks. She had not dressed like this since being appointed Prytan of the Spartanis. Normally, she would not be allowed to, in light of her position, but King Athanas made it very clear that women had a certain place in the isles. As much as she despised his sentiment, Ember was grateful for the chance to wear one of her many custom gowns.

She felt beautiful, powerful even, and so much better than the Princess of Morentius—that is, until Farah walked in. Walked in on the arm of none other than the commander. They sat down at the table, right next to the place that had been set for Ember. Iason sat on the other side, giving her a knowing and empathetic look. Although she had not mentioned the commander by name, it was now pretty clear who she had spoken about to the senator earlier that day.

A few deep breaths and one dinner. That was all Ember had to worry about for now. But as the evening progressed, her patience wore thinner and thinner. The way Farah threw herself at Ajax was unbearable. Her light laughs and sing-song voice. How Farah touched his arm or leg or back every time she spoke to him, even leaning in for little whispers in his ear, to which he would smile and laugh himself. It was disgusting. It was going to make her sick! Ember threw back another glass of the amber liquid in front of her, ignoring the side eye she caught from Iason beside her.

"Are the soldiers in Morentius so drab that you must throw yourself at ours?" Ember scowled, the vein in her temple pulsing.

Farah's eyes narrowed. A deadly smile creeped across her lips, the same one the Viper had when he spoke down to people. "Ours are quite handsome, thank you, but I seem to prefer the way this one smiles at me when I speak." She slid her hand much too far up Ajax's leg. His whole body stiffened as Farah leaned up against him. But then he relaxed, covering her hand with his before he gently slid it back to the table.

"Yes, I am well aware of how captivating his smile can be," Ember murmured, earning a look from the commander she had not seen before. A brief twinkle in his light brown eyes, a softened twitch of the corner of his lip.

She was furious. And jealous. And apparently freezing. Even the blanket of the liquor Ember drank could not keep her from shivering. The autumn chill was returning, and it was piercing right through the thin material she wore, as were the words the princess spoke.

Ajax leaned over toward Ember and whispered, "Ember, do you need me to get you something to wear? You can have my jacket." Apparently, he had not whispered quietly enough, because King Athanas and his daughter both shot them a look. The king's—of warning. The princess's—of curiosity and a hint of jealousy.

Ember brushed his hand away. She would not give the Viper one more excuse to belittle her in her own home. "I'm fine. The night is almost over anyway. A glass of brandy should do the trick."

Ajax recoiled from her, his jaw tightening. He tightened his hand into a fist and released, shaking it off and reaching for his goblet of wine.

"If the princess refuses, you're always welcome to keep me warm, Commander. I get particularly chilly in bed." The words slid off her tongue like venom. Ajax gulped down the sip of wine he had lifted to his lips. A light blush crossed the bridge of his nose. Ember wanted to strangle Farah, tell her to keep her greasy little paws off of her man.

But Ajax was not *her* man. He never could be. Not unless she resigned from her position.

Ember was destined to live her life without love, despite what Iason had said. Even if it was not Farah—gods, she wished it was not Farah—Ajax would no doubt find some irresistible woman to take to bed, to have as his wife, to make happy and fill with the love she knew he had to give. She would never get that. His love. His affection. No more than what he was duty bound to give a higher ranking official. They were not wishful children anymore. Ember and Ajax could never be.

Chapter Thirty-Five

Kohl

They had only been at sea for a few weeks, and Kohl was already getting frustrated. Yes, they had a general direction to guide their sailing. And yes, Dolion, the odd and angry man, had a way to get them by all potential threats and blockades along the route to Skiatha. Still, something did not seem quite right. Like this man was a little pest eating away at Kohl's mind. He was keeping something from Kohl and he didn't know what it was.

The journey had been a rather calm one so far, something the newly crowned king rarely experienced when sailing the Mykandrian Sea. The winds had been blessed by the gods and they traveled swiftly over the crystal blue waters toward the ancient isle that should not have existed in this realm.

Kohl had spent most of his time in his quarters, writing in his log about the course they were taking. If they ever needed to return to Skiatha, he did not want to rely on that greasy man. There was something familiar about him that Kohl could not place. Not unsimilar to the distaste he had for those in his father's army. A presence that only the most seedy of men carried.

In the logs, he also documented anything he could discern about that curious device Dolion had given them. The spelled compass that seemed to faintly glow and warm at his touch. Sometimes so much so, he thought it would burn the first layer of his skin right off.

That was all Kohl did. Take notes, sleep, walk the deck, sleep, eat, fiddle with the device. The closer *The Hydra* got to Skiatha, the more the compass seemed to thrum with pleasure. A simple tune that repeated again and again in Kohl's mind.

Return to me, my King. Return to me.

The voice was not a familiar one, its low and soft whisper gracing his ears only in the darkness of night.

So when the voice stopped, when they were but a few day's sail from the Lost Isle, Kohl awoke startled from his dreams. At first the ship appeared to be silent. The only noise was a vibration on his bedside table. The compass no longer called to him, but instead shimmered a blinding gold light, like the fiery stars in the sky.

He heard it then. The footsteps padding above him. The cries from the corridor leading to the deck. More than should be at this time of night.

Only the captain and a small group of the crew should be out manning the course of the ship and the sails. The rest should be passed out in their quarters, bellies full of food and wine. Normally, Kohl heard the snores of the men through the ship's walls.

Kohl jumped out of his bed, slinging on his red linen shirt and black trousers. Careful to sheath one blade to his hip. It was not impossible that *The Nostos* had found them first—or perhaps some other pirate that dwelled off the coast of The Northern Lands they passed by. He could only hope the pirates could be tempted by coins and treasures rather than their usual lust for blood.

A little piece of Kohl hoped it was the Prince of the Lost Isles—that he would get a chance to slay him before they even had to reach Skiatha.

But as Kohl exited his quarters and reached the deck of *The Hydra* there was no other ship in sight.

Instead, all Kohl could see was an endless sea around them, darkened black by the starless night sky. The ship's deck had been flooded with the sea as *The Hydra* began to rock against newly formed waves. And men—he saw men, as they flung themselves from the rail of the ship into the endless sea.

"Calliope! Calliope, I am coming! Don't worry, my love, I will be with you soon." One of the soldiers yelled to the great unknown as he hung from the side of the ship, before stepping off and sinking below.

"Dion! Dion, where are you! I can't find you!" another screamed as he splashed in the water, a creature gripping him and dragging him beneath.

Kohl stood, mouth agape, as more and more men rushed to their deaths. Only a few did not. They stood equally frightened and confused. The soldiers of Morentius were not naive to death during battle. But this—this was an unwilling and unknowing sacrifice to the sea.

In the center of it all stood Dolion, his eyes wide and as dark as the sea. Kohl raced over to him as the screaming began to stop. He gripped the older man tight around his throat.

"What did you do? What did you do to my men?" the king seethed, his hand gripping so tightly Dolion could barely utter a word.

"Please. I did not cause this," he sputtered, gasping for breath beneath Kohl's firm palm. Kohl could see the faint glint of fear in his eyes. One that longed for the comfort of another, but not for death—his own or others. Kohl pushed the man away, as Dolion coughed, attempting to steady his breathing.

"The men—they said they heard voices before they jumped to the seas to perish. They spoke of their partners back home. What poison lingers in these depths?" Kohl gripped Dolion's arm. Only a small portion of them had survived. Kohl glanced around now counting six of his men and Dolion.

The ruddy older man lifted his brow, rubbing at his now bare throat. "A curious thing, the call of a siren. It bends the will of men and women alike, beckoning them to their death in the depths of the sea. It was said they were scorned by the goddess Demeter after Hades stole her daughter." Kohl's jaw clenched. Of course the seedy man would speak so freely of the Olympi.

"That doesn't explain why the men thought they were hearing people who are not aboard this ship." He should have just strangled the man, they would be better for it.

"A siren will only sing with the voice of one bound by marriage," Dolion smiled, a violent grin reaching from ear to ear, "or by Fate."

Kohl brushed his hand over his face, rustling it through his sleep-torn hair. "And those who were not affected by the lure of the wicked creatures?"

Dolion's eyes darkened to a deep ebony, the same look Kohl's father had when he spoke in anger. "Many things make you immune to the siren's call. Many things, Your Majesty." There it was again. The uneasy chill that crept up Kohl's skin like a spider.

He wished to be off this ship, glad to be away from the oily man who stood before him and Dolion's riddles. But first, they needed to finish the journey to Skiatha. To Katrin. Find *The Nostos* and the captain who took her.

One of the remaining soldiers came up behind Kohl. "Excuse me, Your Majesty, but it looks like a storm is quickly approaching. We will need to make haste if we plan to outrun it before we reach the Lost Isle. According to the charts Dolion procured, we have around two days until we reach port."

Kohl looked out to the west and indeed a storm was brewing. The skies had begun to cloud over a deep gray, the seas a swirling dark green now replacing the brief blackness of the siren's cove. Even from here Kohl could feel the winds pick up, the chill in the air heighten. The salty air around them thickened so much he could barely breathe.

Trickling in from the distance was a wave of fog, one they could not navigate through if it caught up to the ship. Magic compass or not, that kind of dense, blinding air would surely leave them crashing upon a rocky shore. Kohl couldn't help but wonder if this was where their luck ran its course. If the gods had indeed sought retribution for disturbing their peace. If the compass knew he was not its rightful owner.

"Keep course and travel as swiftly as we can to the east. We will sail through the night once more." The soldier nodded before returning to his post at the helm of the ship, charts in hand. Kohl gripped the compass tightly in his hand, even as the blinding light seared his skin.

Two more days. Two more days until he was with his betrothed once more. Two more days until the bastard prince was dealt with.

He was grateful, for whatever grace had allowed him to still stand aboard *The Hydra* rather than be swallowed by the deep unknown. But as the ship sailed farther from the storm, Kohl could not help but wonder what made him immune to the siren's song. Why had he not heard Katrin's voice beckon from the depth of the seas?

Chapter Thirty-Six

Katrin

Ander had been moody since the night they stayed at the fortress in the woods. Since then, he had not spoken to Katrin. Three days. Three days of utter silence. Not on the walk into the mountains. Not to show her the cabin she would stay in—a lavish one by barrack standards. Not even when the men and women would meet for dinner in the Castle Phyli—a large stone building carved straight into the side of the mountain.

It did not help that it had rained for the last three days. Not a heavy storm, but enough that caused the training pits outside to flood, and an uncomfortable second day walking through the woods. Shivering most of the journey into the mountains, Katrin's boots were soaked and squeaky, her leather trousers shrinking closer to her body. Her hair continuously plastered to her face despite starting out in a tight braid down her back.

If anyone asked her, it could not get worse than this. Katrin had tried to apologize once, the first night they had arrived at Castle Phyli. She had cornered Ander at dinner where he had elected to sit at the opposite end of the room. When she apologized to him, all the captain did was grunt, look away, continuing on with the conversation he had been having before she strolled over. If that was the way he wanted to handle things, Katrin would start ignoring him too.

The only bright spot had been her training with Leighton in the main hall of the castle. Since the captain was no longer speaking to her, he was also refusing to train her, or had simply not shown up to the sessions. In his place, the nauarch volunteered his time.

They brought in large leather mats that the men and women used for sparring in Skiatha to cushion the blow against the hard stone floors, but it hardly sufficed. Leighton had knocked Katrin off her feet quite a few times and she had the bruises on her tail bone and elbows to prove it. But she was improving, at least, that was what he told her.

"You have a center of balance, and quick reflexes, but the issue remains that you are too cocky." Leighton chuckled as he helped Katrin up yet again from falling flat on her ass.

"You do realize you are addressing a future queen, *Leighton*?" Katrin's eyes narrowed, but they were warm, and a little smile spread across her face. It was hard to be angry at the man, the lightness in the way he spoke, honest, upfront and kind, even after everything that had happened to him.

"The fact remains, *Princess*, you will find yourself continuously on your ass if you do not learn to read your opponents' moves rather than assume you can outsmart them." He held up his hands again in a starting stance.

"I will have you know, I learned to read my opponent by one of the finest soldiers in Morentius." Katrin wiped the dust off her leathers and black cotton shirt, and stood in an equal stance opposite the nauarch.

"Well therein lies your problem. Morentian soldiers are as cocky as they come. They rely much too heavily on the poison that laces their blades and brute force, rather than actual skill." She snorted. Somehow that did not surprise her, except Kohl was one of the best fighters she had seen and he never used the viper's venom on his blades.

Katrin jabbed twice with her right hand and threw a cross with her left, all meeting a block by Leighton's arms. "Good. Again." Two jabs, one cross. Block. "Again." Two jabs, one cross. Block.

The princess was trying to keep eye contact as she adjusted her footing. This is what Leighton had done each time before. Set her in a routine and then he would come back at her with a dodge instead of a block, followed by a hook, or a swipe out beneath her legs. It was an exercise, Katrin knew that, but she wanted to throw something else back at him, wanted to get one real hit in to show she could read his moves. But the distracting thought got her, and once again she ended up on the floor.

A slow clap came from the edge of the room. The other men and women training in the facility went silent. Ander stood leaning against the doorway to the main hall, dressed head to toe in black. Even from across the room, Katrin could see the silver storms in his eyes, the color of the endless raining sky outside.

"It's nice to see at least someone has a chance against you, Starling." Usually that word sounded sweet as it left his lips, but this time it hit harder than Leighton's punches.

"Oh, I'm sorry, are you speaking to me again or can you just not help being an insufferable ass?" Katrin could have sworn the captain's lip twitched up for just a second. Leighton's definitely did, an undeniable grin crossed from ear to ear. But when she turned back to Ander his jaw was clenched tight.

"Well, you are definitely in for an earful, Ander. I'll take that as my cue to leave."

Leighton went to step away, but Katrin threw her arm in front of him and cut him off. "Anything *the prince* needs to say to me, he can say in front of you," she spat, immediately sorry that her words seemed to strike not only Ander, but Leighton as well.

Katrin could see the captain's nostrils flare and his jaw tick as he leaned off the doorway and walked closer. Her eyes could not help but trail him as he sauntered over, the black leather tight around his muscles, his chest just poking out enough from his typical linen shirt. Memories of the other night at the fortress trickled back into her mind. No, she would not let herself think of that, the way he smelled of lemon and the sea, the way his lips tasted sweet like olive oil. She was furious at him and would stay that way, even if he dripped lust across the floor.

"You're going to make this difficult, aren't you?" Ander growled when he stepped up to her. Leighton's eyes shot wide and he backed up a step. The poor nauarch. Katrin should have let him leave.

"Make this difficult? Me? I made this very easy. I *apologized* to you and you just brushed me off. Went back to whatever insolent conversation you were having."

"Not that it matters, but I was in the middle of a very important discussion with one of my generals and I didn't think it was the time or place to discuss what happened. Especially when your emotions seemed heightened from all the wine I saw you drink."

"Oh sure, blame me. Because *I* was the one who ignored *you* the whole day after..."

Leighton began to shift uncomfortably on the side of the mat. "I think I am going to just leave you two...oh, what is that, Thalia? You need help with a shipment? Coming!" The nauarch backed away rather quickly. Fleeing from the embarrassment that was their fight.

Ander cracked his neck, running his hand through the back of his hair and sighed. "I told you that night, there was nothing to apologize for. It was merely a mistake."

Katrin's palms began to heat, light around her finger tips flickering. For a second she thought to stop herself, but when she looked at Ander she could not help but throw her arm back and land a punch right across his jaw.

Ander startled backward, his hand flying up to where Katrin had left her mark. A little trickle of blood trailed down from his lip. "What the fuck was that for?"

Katrin's eyes narrowed. She felt a little bad for drawing blood, but he just made her so unbelievably angry. "That's how you people solve things around here isn't it? You spar. At least that's what the soldiers told me."

It was true, some of the women who trained here told her at dinner that when there was a dispute between soldiers, they would take it to the mat. Better to get out their aggression in a controlled environment rather than let it fester and cause problems on the battlefield.

"I'm not fighting you, Aikaterine." Ander almost never called her that. It infuriated her even more, even though she'd always told him she hated his little nickname for her. At least, she hated it until she found out *why* he called her that. If the story had not been some fever-induced dream she had after she was attacked.

"Why not? Afraid I'll beat you again?" Katrin went to throw another punch, but Ander caught her by the wrist pulling her in closer.

"I assure you, Starling, you only beat me because I let you," he whispered into her ear, his voice low as his lips brushed her skin.

"Then prove it." Katrin pushed off his chest, holding up her arms in a ready stance.

Ander sighed, shaking his head, but mirrored her stance anyway. They began to circle the mat, sizing each other up. Honestly, she had gotten lucky the first two times. Well, the second time at least. Ander had lost his footing. The first time—the first time he asked her to come at him, basically just sat still in his chair.

Maybe it was a mistake to fight him. But at least this way she could see he felt something toward her. Even aggravation was better than disdain. Katrin threw the first punch, Ander blocked, throwing his own. She dodged back and reset her stance. Leighton had said to read your opponent. That her biggest weakness was that she couldn't anticipate the next move, that she already thought she would win and would lose herself in the attack. Katrin took in a slow, calming breath and began again. Jab, cross, hook, kick, reset. He would follow with the same moves. She knew he did not want to hurt her, Katrin was not sure that she could say that same thing.

"Why?" she panted through gritted teeth as they circled the mat once more. "Why do you think it was a mistake?"

Something flickered in Ander's eyes, something Katrin could not quite decipher. "Because you were confused. Because you still love *him*. Because you want *him*." He stopped for a moment, feet flat on the floor. His hand was shaking and it looked as if a light fog curled around his feet and fists. "Because I shouldn't have been selfish with you."

Katrin hated herself for it, hated that she used this confession to her advantage. She swung her legs behind his, taking him to the ground and pinning his back against the mat. "I don't know what I want. I told you that, and I'm sorry for it. Why can't that be enough right now? Can't we just be here in the moment?" Her breathing was labored as her chest dropped down to his, the sweat from her brow slipping down her cheek.

Ander hooked his arm through Katrin's, flipping them until his whole weight was pushed against her, pinning her arms down with his palms. "What if I want more?"

"I can't give you more. Not now. Not until—not until I figure out what is real." She searched his face for any sign of emotion, but all she saw was the darkening of the silver in his eyes, the sweat that had beaded on his skin rolling off his temples.

His chest heaved against hers in tandem breaths. "Fine."

"Fine?"

"Did you not understand what I said the other night?" he whispered between panting breaths, his brows scrunching together. "That I cannot say no to you?"

His eyes warmed back to their tidal blue-green, no longer the menacing silver of the storming skies. "Not *will not*, but physically, undeniably *cannot*. You say you are sorry, I believe you. Gods, Starling, I have no control when it comes to you. And I need control in my life. Especially now."

Katrin's face went sheet white, her whole body heating underneath Ander's as he continued to speak. "Do you know how hard it has been to be around you and not speak to you? How awful it is to see you smile and laugh with the others here knowing you regret me?"

That was what snapped her out of the daze his words had put her in. Katrin shoved against him, sliding back and standing up. "How dare you say that!"

Ander sat up on the ground, face buried in his hands. "Say what? That you regret me? Lie and tell me that's not true."

"I don't. I want to. I want to hate you. I want to scream and run back to the shore and tell you that it meant nothing. That I was drunk—that, like you said, it was a mistake. But I can't. I look at you and my world disappears into nothing but the damning echo of your heartbeat—how it calls to me even in a dreamless sleep." Katrin stepped closer to him now. "You say you can't say no to me. I can't *hear* no from you."

Ander's brow kicked up. "After all I've done to you?" And that's when Katrin saw it, the deep-seated pain in his eyes. That someone really had hurt him like this before. That it was another tiny piece of trauma they shared. She kneeled down in front of him, cupping his cheek in her small trembling hand.

"After all you've done *for* me."

Chapter Thirty-Seven

Ember

Potentially embarrassing herself at dinner was now the least of Ember's worries. King Athanas was getting increasingly reclusive since his wife and his daughter had arrived in Alentus. He still kept mostly to his quarters, smoking and tending to things Ember did not want to think about. Queen Zahra was always slipping in and out with whatever young woman she had decided they would entertain that day. Ember heard the little noises when she passed by and it sent a burning twinge right to her throat.

Today would be different. Today King Athanas had to pull himself together, leave his doting wife and drugs and scarcely dressed women to attend the meeting with the senators.

The Spartanis had been on edge since the Morentian queen and princess had stepped upon the shores of Alentus. With them, King Athanas had brought six of his war ships, all outfitted with a legion of soldiers and stores of weapons and armor. If Ember did not know any better she would say the Viper was attempting to occupy their lands. But that was a ridiculous notion, since Kohl had just been crowned King of Alentus and the ties between the isles were stronger than ever.

It did not help that the entire isle had been murmuring with worry and fear after King Nikolaos decided to make an appearance at the Acknowledgement. No matter that it had been weeks ago, the fact remained—he got in without people noticing, and disappeared with his family just as quickly.

Yes, the Bringer of Shadows had seemed frightening, any person in their right mind would be fearful of a man who could turn you to nothing more than a speck of black on the ground, a shadow of yourself. Yet, there was a stark sense of pain that had lingered in his words. Worry, regret, protectiveness. *You know very well where my eldest son is, Khalid.* The words repeated in her mind everyday since Nikolaos had spoken them.

Nikolaos the Second was rumored to have disappeared years ago. Most believed he was just staying hidden on Nexos. That his parents kept him locked away until he took the throne. But what if he was not just being protected by his parents? What if he was imprisoned somewhere or worse, dead? What if Nexos was trying to attack Alentus, not because they wanted to take Ember's home, but because they wanted to hurt King Athanas or because they wanted a trade? A prince for a princess. King Athanas was keeping too many secrets and Ember was going to find them out.

Ember sat in a chair toward the head of the table in one of their many studies, her knee bouncing uncontrollably as she bit the corners of her fingernails. They were all there—Remus, Linard, Asterios, Paris, Iason, Ajax. All except the Viper of Votios. Again. Iason laid his hand on hers, shaking his head. The old man had always been a stickler for Ember's worst habit. *It is not good for you to bite your nails. Do you know how much dirt resides underneath?* She swallowed, an acrid taste now coating her mouth.

Ajax sat across the table, his warm brown eyes narrowed, avoiding eye contact with her. Ember huffed a much too loud sigh and rolled her eyes. The commander had barely spoken to her since Farah had arrived at the castle. She often caught him sneaking in and out of her room at all hours, his dirty blonde hair disheveled, shirt unbuttoned just enough that you could see the muscles rippling beneath.

A constant reminder that she would never have his affection gnawed away at her insides. Made her feel as though someone was dragging a knife slowly up her chest until it pierced her heart, reveling in the blood that trickled out. Ember would never be enough for him. For anyone.

"Where exactly is King Athanas? This is the second time he has been late to an official meeting. He can't expect to skirt his duties all day while fucking whatever vapid woman his wife convinces to join." The words came out before she had really thought them through. Technically King Athanas was Crown Regent, and it was distasteful to disrespect someone in authority, especially as a dignified member of the court.

"Maybe if you got fucked yourself, girl, you would understand what all the hype was about." The Viper's languid voice trickled in from the doorway. He stood dressed in a red silken shirt and black leather trousers, a sword slung across his hip, painted in the venom of the creature he held so dear.

Heat built in Ember's cheeks. Not because she was embarrassed he heard what she said, but because she knew the king was right. She could see Ajax shift uncomfortably in his seat, his jaw stiff, lightly tanned hands gripping the corner of the table.

At least he was showing some reaction to her, even if it was clearly disdain. Ember had been so rash and naive to think the commander might actually reciprocate her feelings.

"King Athanas, a pleasure to have you join us." Iason winked at Ember, taking the attention away from the Viper's words. There was not another moment she would be more grateful to Iason for. "Let's turn our attention to more pressing matters than the love life of our Prytan."

"Or lack of one..." Ember muttered under her breath, crossing her arms in front of her chest, the tight navy leathers she now so often wore squeaking at the movement. She could have sworn the commander's lip twitched up slightly. Ember blinked, and any semblance of a smile disappeared.

Iason continued. "It has come to our attention that you have ordered a meeting of the representatives from the surrounding isles without a vote from the senate. Is there a reason you bypassed our laws, Khalid?"

King Athanas flopped down in the chair at the head of the table, his eyes deepened to only the pupil and lip curled in a snarl. A chair that was meant for a Drakos, adorned with carvings of the Triad mountains, and the river that led into Aidesian. One side of the arms depicting the night sky and the storm that could be unleashed. The other the fiery sun, flowers in bloom.

"Yes, well I would have if the matter was not urgent. Would anyone here have disputed the request when we have a dire need to bring the smaller isles together? Would anyone here leave those isles unprotected, while Nexos sails their fleet in for destruction?"

"I am not implying anything of the sort. But laws are laws, even for a king." Iason held the Viper's stare.

"I'll take that under advisement for the next time." King Athanas leaned into the table, propping his elbows up and clasping his hands. "I have new reports that Nexos plans to attack within the month."

"A month!" Ember yelped, her hand clasping over her mouth.

King Athanas merely lifted a brow at the outburst. "Their fleet is strong. However, I have it on good authority that they are waiting for someone before they launch the attack."

Ember began to bite her nails again. A month was not enough time to prepare their forces. To train the reserves from the smaller isles. There had been minor skirmishes here and there, attacks from pirates, but never a full scale assault on the isles. They would not be ready. *She* would not be ready.

Iason's clear voice broke the perpetuating silence in her mind. "Who exactly are they waiting for?"

"I am told it is the Prince of the Lost Isles. No doubt the deal they brokered when taking our dear Aikaterine included coming to the aid of Nexos in their rebellion against the rest of Mykandria. We can only hope that my son returns with his future bride before then."

Chapter Thirty-Eight

Katrin

T he bow and arrow had never been Katrin's weapon of choice. For some reason she just could not get the hang of it, always missing her target. Throw a punch. Throw a dagger. Wield a sword. Those the princess could all do with a level of precision unheard of for her age. But pulling back a threaded string and letting a quiver soar—impossible. Which is how she landed herself in yet another training lesson, this one with Thalia.

This was not to say she wasn't grateful for training—sparring in the ring and learning proper swordsmanship was what brought her back from the darkness all those years ago. Now—her body had felt rejuvenated by the daily exhaustion as she pushed her physical limits in the mountains. She relished the feeling. Each day on Skiatha she learned more about the Olympi, more of this cause, and with the passing time, felt a deeper desire to be part of it. Even if it meant putting up with archery for the time being.

The Skiathan soldiers had explained that the seer was the best archer of all the men and women who fought to protect this isle. Katrin wondered how a chaste maiden from Delphine came to excel at such a skill, but quickly shoved the thought away as a thin arrow whirled by her ear, landing in the dead center of a target.

Katrin scanned the area for Thalia, or Mykonos, or any sign that the seer had shown up on time for their training. She was a notoriously late individual, abiding by her own rules of civility. There was no sign of the lithe woman and her moon-white hair, nor the little creature that clung to her side.

Two more arrows flew by, landing on each side of Katrin's boots. She knew no evil resided in these woods, or on this isle, but still the princess's heart began to race. Not knowing where the potential threat came from unnerved her to a degree she couldn't explain. It made her insides sour and a sickening heat flowed through her veins. She could hear the thumping of her blood through her heart reverberating in her ears.

A laugh came from behind her. "Thalia tends to do this to unsuspecting people who come to learn from her." Katrin jumped at the words. She had not heard the nauarch approach through the brush either. "She says it's because it is funny, but in reality she just wants to show off." Leighton's voice boomed from the base of one of the many cypress trees that laced through the woods, where she had not even seen him. Her guard was down here, not something one would want as they approached a potential war.

"And yet, I don't see Thalia anywhere?" Katrin chuckled back, attempting to mask her unease. She could see it though, that the lithe seer would play tricks on unsuspecting soldiers to show off a talent many men had failed to acquire. Thalia was quick and sly and feral, just like the creature her *psychí* became.

"Lesson one—" a light voice came from nowhere and yet everywhere all at once as the princess heard a soft thud land behind her. A little tap followed after. Katrin whipped around to see the moon white haired seer crouching on the ground, an arrow strung up in hand, the little cat flipping its tail back and forth beside her. "—expect the enemy to strike from anywhere."

"Gods, Thalia! You don't just creep up on people like that. Especially when you're armed." Katrin tried to calm the incessant pounding of her heartbeat with deep breaths.

Thalia snickered. "That is kind of the point, Princess. Lesson two—don't question the teacher." Thalia stood, turning the bow around so it hung from her back on an attached bag of arrows.

"And how many lessons exactly are we learning today? I did think it was meant to be just archery."

Leighton shook his head in his palm. "Lesson two, Princess. Forgetting so quickly, are we?"

Thalia looked frightening in all black, a shimmering blue and purple scaled corset hugging her waist. Katrin had never seen the seer so prepared for battle before. Usually she was in simple cotton trousers and a tunic, that is, when she was not wearing one of her elaborate gowns. But this—this was deadly.

Leighton shook his head at Katrin as she fumbled to catch the wooden bow and a quiver of arrows that he tossed to her. The bow was beautiful, made of a pale, worn wood with ancient markings carved in the center. She ran her fingers over the markings, a heat trailing up her arms as she outlined each one.

"What are these?" The princess recognized some of the symbols—from Ander's sword, the maps, from the delicate comb she had held onto so dearly, never realizing its significance.

Katrin could hear a low thrumming in her ears as the symbols began to glow. At least she thought they were glowing. But as soon as she blinked, the dim sparkle around them faded.

The seer eyed her with curiosity. "The *Elliniká Glóssa* did not use the same characters we write with now. It had its own unique script, one I am afraid is a lost art."

"Would you be able to teach me? What each of them means, how to write them?" Katrin circled one particular character over and over. It looked like an upside down horseshoe that flared out slightly from each side.

Thalia sighed a low long breath. "I can, Princess, but right now we have more pressing things to learn." She pointed at the long wooden bow.

Katrin would have done anything not to pick it up, to avoid learning how to use one more weapon. To keep Thalia and Leighton, who stood by and watched their exchange, from seeing how utterly terrible she was at the sport. She fought out an uneasy grimace. "Right—archery first."

"Ok now, I am going to need you to stand upright like this," Thalia moved Katrin's body with her delicate hands so she was standing, feet staggered, arms up in a t-shape, her right arm pulling back to the string. "Good. Make sure your stance is firm, but relaxed."

Katrin bobbed her head back, brows scrunching toward each other. "Isn't that a contradiction? Firm but relaxed?"

Thalia rolled her violet eyes. "You get my point. Now you are going to want to aim the bow down and nock the arrow like so." Thalia demonstrated with her own bow. "You'll want to have your second finger above the arrow, your middle and ring fingers below when you pull back. Now lift the bow back up to aim straight at the circle we have painted on the tree." Katrin followed along closely. "Good. Then you'll just want to pull back using the line along your ear as a guide, and let the arrow fly."

The seer released the arrow, and it flew through the air, hitting the target dead center. Katrin tried next and hers barely went halfway to her target. Thalia cringed at the poor showing of skill. "Lift your elbow up just slightly, that will take off some pressure, transferring it to your shoulder. It will make it easier to aim with distance."

So the princess tried yet again. Over and over until her quiver was empty and she needed to collect the arrows from the ground below. Not a single one had hit the target, not even hit the tree. A low sigh escaped Katrin's lungs. She could have sworn even Mykonos snickered at her.

As Katrin retrieved the evidence of her lack of skill and promise for archery, the little white creature pranced around the woods, pawing at various insects and chasing small furry animals from their homes. She climbed up branches to watch tiny winged insects flutter about. Jumping from the trees to catch them in her paws.

Katrin found it distracting and a bit amusing to see Mykonos so carefree and wild. Yes—she would sometimes drop a mouse or two at the door to their quarters on *The Nostos*, but otherwise she mostly slept or watched the sea pass by on deck, letting the rays of the sun warm her, lulling her into a dreamland. But here, she was truly in her element.

"Princess, you really should be focusing on the target, not Myko, considering you've missed every one."

Katrin's head shrunk into her shoulders as her lips formed a tight line. She hated being bad at anything, and archery—gods, she was worse than bad. The princess was abysmal.

"I know, but she's so cute. Watch! She can catch that winged insect in her paws. How is that even possible? It's so fast I can barely see it." Katrin was in awe of the little creature.

Thalia smiled brightly. It was a reflection of her, Katrin guessed, the wild curiosity the cat had in that moment. "She's used to being cooped up on that ship for months. When we take our short stays in Skiatha, she revels in exploring the woods. It's a release of kinds—for the both of us."

The princess understood how Mykonos felt—how Thalia felt. Being cooped up on *The Nostos* for so long had begun to make her stir crazy. She was glad to be here, in the woodsy air surrounded by earth and mountains and trails to stretch her legs and run. To smell the musky scents of tilled dirt and cut grass and evergreens as she wound through the paths, letting all her tension go.

"Enough of the sentimental talk, you two, Ander had strict orders that Katrin needed to focus during today's lesson. Apparently her lack of, dare I say, seriousness during our session yesterday has him worried."

Katrin rolled her eyes. The captain was such a thorn in her side when it came to anything fun. But at least he was speaking to her again, no more of that strange silence and disdain he had the first few days.

So she tried. Again. And again. And again. But not once could she even make it in the general range of the painted target.

Katrin gritted her teeth. Just one. All she had to make was one hit and they could go inside and call the day at least somewhat successful, but she could not even do that.

A glow so bright it was almost the shade of Thalia's hair began to simmer over Katrin's skin. It did not matter how many times she tried to listen to directions of Thalia and even Leighton's slight tweaks, she could not hit a single target.

It was beginning to get ridiculous. She was a princess, skilled in battle and hand-to-hand combat, yet this little piece of wood and string would break her. What would her parents think? What would her people think if she could not do something as simple as hit the target?

"Princess!" Thalia began to scream. "Katrin! You—" But Katrin did not let her finish the thought. Her whole body was burning with such an intense heat that she bolted. Away from the woods, away from the nagging feeling that she was not fit for the role she would one day play in Alentus. All she left in her wake was a trail of scorched earth.

White-flecked pupils stared back at Katrin in the looking glass. She had not been keeping track of the days that had passed. Not anymore at least. But now she could feel it, the overwhelming sense of power that grew in her chest and limbs, threatening to snuff her out. Twenty-five years leading up to this moment, and she had no way of dampening back the light that coursed in her bloodstream. She was a star ready to burst. A supernova set to destroy everything around her.

Just breathe, her mother always said when she was younger and a trickle of her power would slip through. *In, two, three, four. Out, two, three, four.* But thinking of Kora only made her think of where she was now. What might be happening to her on Cyther.

Katrin clenched her eyes closed, gripping the sides of the dresser that the looking glass sat upon so hard that her nails dug into the wood.

"Starling, are you in there?" she heard Ander yell just before he barrelled in through her door.

"Deep breaths." His voice quickly calmed. "You'll be alright." Katrin felt his hands cover both of hers, his body firm against her back, causing her very heart to tighten.

She felt something else too, the thickening of air around her as it dampened the light that burned her skin, that must be burning his if he stood flush with her body.

Still Katrin refused to open her eyes, to face the reality of what was happening. "You're safe," Ander whispered, this time his lips almost grazing her ear. Instead of the usual warm puffs of air that came from his mouth, his breath was icy, trickling over every inch of her.

The air thickened even more, it felt damp and soothing and ticklish along her now cooling skin. Her chest began to move at a more normal speed, and she fluttered her eyes open, adjusting to the darker tone of the room. It no longer burned with the light and fury of a star in the night sky.

"Thank you," Katrin said, her voice still breathy. She slowly released the grip on the dresser, where handprints now lay singed into the faded wood.

"I guess congratulations are in order." Ander faked a slight grin, but his brows were still threaded closely together.

"There's nothing to congratulate me on. I—I can't control it. There's too much built up anger and resentment for what is happening on Cyther. The only person who ever helped me was my mother." Her head hung low. "And you know what's happening to her—what *happened* to her. What good is being a god if I can't even help the people I love?" Katrin did not mean to crack at that moment. Did not mean for the words to flow out of her with tears streaming so hard her eyes felt raw and burned.

Ander turned somber, his hand reaching out for hers. "You are helping the people you love, Starling. More than you even understand. You are fighting for the cause, for peace, for the little bit of good that is left in this world. You are *elpís*, you are hope. And Kora—Kora is not dead, I promise you that."

Katrin's eyes began to itch as the salty tears continued cascading over her cheeks. She felt the captain's thumb grazing below her eye, wiping away the little drops of agony she had let loose.

He should not have promised that. Could not promise that. Katrin had seen the golden bangles upon her mother's wrist, and had felt a strange lure and pulse coming from them. Now she knew why, what they did, what pain they could cause.

The princess collapsed to the floor, her body convulsing so uncontrollably she thought she might actually die from the pain. "Even if that's true, Ander, how can I really help if I can't use the only thing I have without burning down everything around me? I've only ever seen flickers of the starlight, once in the alley with those men, and once—well once when I was very angry at you."

"Is that so?" Ander seemed to grin, an odd response to knowing she wanted to singe him to ash. But the smile was a distraction, one that caused her trembling hands and heaving shoulders to still.

"You can ask Thalia about that one...I think I scared Mykonos right out of her slumber in your quarters." Katrin's face scrunched. She stared up at Ander's sea-torn eyes and her breathing began to regulate. The princess needed to focus on him, on something other than the feeling of utter helplessness that clawed in her mind.

"I see. I guess that explains the burn marks on my favorite chair," he chuckled.

Katrin squeezed her eyes shut once more. "Sorry." She was almost embarrassed remembering the moment—almost.

"Well that is pretty easy to fix—the power that is, not the chair. Unfortunately, that was an heirloom of my family. Don't fret, we just need to find your point of focus. Something that grounds you."

"Like a mantra?" Katrin asked. She had used those before to calm her anger, to lull mind back into focus.

"No, this has to be much more personal. Something that could lead you through the darkest of nights. The only thing that will always give you a glimmer of hope, even when all feels like it's lost. Your northern star."

"Like home?"

"Yes, Starling. Something that makes you feel home."

An odd feeling washed over her. A memory maybe, or a familiarity with the words she spoke. Something clawed at the recesses in her mind, but she could not make it out, could not remember why her heart tugged just a little at what he said. *Northern star.*

"How do you know so much about controlling powers?"

A vein in Ander's neck twitched, his mouth shifting to the side for a moment. "I had a friend once. God born, like you. He struggled with letting his emotions get the best of him. Got too cocky in his ability and wielded power with no restraint. When you do that—one of two things happens, you either burn out or the power begins to take over. You no longer control it, it controls you. He retreated into a very dark place for a while, until—well until he had a reason to fight back. Until he had some—something to fight for." His expression went glassy as he stared out the window.

"And this friend of yours? Where is he now?"

"Lost—he is lost at sea." Ander's eyes darkened a mix of swirling blue and silver as he clenched his fists so tightly Katrin thought he might pierce his own skin.

"I am sorry to hear that," she replied, laying her palm against his back, feeling as his muscles tensed beneath her. He reached for her hand, intertwining his fingers in hers.

"I am sorry too."

CHAPTER THIRTY-NINE

KOHL

They were close. Kohl could feel it in the depth of his bones, like a song crying out for his ears only. Skiatha and The Prince of the Lost Isles. He would leave them all in ruin.

A tug continued pulling low in his gut. Of regret. Of desperation. For his father's men who had not stood a chance against the vicious creatures of the deep.

Kohl was still grateful for whatever force allowed him to remain on the ship, to avoid a fate many sailors must face when traveling by those jagged shores. For allowing him to make it this far, this close to finding Katrin, whatever state she may be in. He kept the compass tucked away in his pocket, away from prying eyes and sticky fingers. Its low hum and light heat grazing against his hip, a continuous reminder of the power thrumming in the small device. The wonder it could cause when little bits were released. A shroud to encompass *The Hydra* as it sailed through the wards and the veil surrounding the isle that should not exist.

Thick fog lifted from the sea below them, burning off as the day dragged on. Kohl remained on deck as the view before them came into focus. There was only sea by endless sea. A glassy crystalline turquoise blue. The calming color of the seas he would see around Alentus, not what he expected here. Twinkling light radiating off the waves as they peaked and rolled toward nothingness.

It could not be.

They were close.

They were close.

There should be land ahead, or at least some indication that land was soon approaching. A bird in the sky, a flutter of an insect. Yet, for as far as Kohl's eyes could see, it was just the same rolling crystalline tide.

Until a shimmer caught his eye to the east. Kohl scrunched his ebony eyes, shielding the sun from them with his rough hands. Another flicker, a film of sorts mirroring the sea behind them.

The ward.

The veil.

Skiatha.

Kohl palmed the compass, flicking the golden instrument open. The arrow inside whirled with a vengeance. Around and around and around until it began to glow. A faint white at first, then deeper and deeper until it was almost a midnight blue. The color one would expect the darkest corners of the sea to hold.

Slowly, the film began to shimmer, bend and fade. Slowly, Kohl could make out a darker sea, one encompassed by a peninsula, tucking it away from travelers, merchants and the people of Mykandria. But still no isle. No Skiatha. No Prince. No Katrin. The king's hand clenched around the small compass so tightly his knuckles were drained of all color. If Dolion had lied...

Kohl's nose twitched at a smoky scent that engulfed his nostrils. It smelled like something putrid, like rotten flesh roasting over a flame. His palm began to burn. Not with anger Kohl realized, but actually *burn*. Like the metal object had been dipped in fire then laid across his skin. He dropped the device, the compass snapping in two. Kohl looked at his palm, a swirling X now branded on his flesh.

"A price must be paid, to use power so old it is no longer spoken of." The ruddy man's oily voice crept up Kohl's spine. "A price must be paid for using that which was never yours."

Kohl whipped around, extending his arm and closing his uninjured palm around Dolion's throat. How many times would he threaten to strangle this man before he actually did the deed?

"It will heal, Your Majesty," he coughed out as he attempted a wheezing breath.

Kohl narrowed his gaze, the vein in his temple pulsing so violently he could almost hear the blood as it flowed through. "You lied to me," he snarled through gritted teeth.

"I did no such thing," Dolion rasped out. "Did we not sneak through the straits surrounding Nexos? Did the veil not drop for you? Have the wards not fallen and let you pass?"

Kohl peered around, the soldiers aboard were loyal. They would not stop him if he grasped tighter until no life was left in the ruddy man's eyes. But if he had lied, Kohl would need to know how to get home, or where the man had even taken them. He had earlier notes, but since the cursed siren attack his mind had been too scattered to focus on where the ship had drifted.

The king could see as the filmy veil closed behind them, locking *The Hydra* in wherever this place may be.

"Welcome to The Manos Sea, Your Majesty. We are not far from where you wish to be." Releasing his grip around Dolion's throat, Kohl dropped him. He landed with a thud against the wooden deck, scampering backward toward the two broken halves of the compass. "You will not need this anymore. The price has been paid, and we will travel swiftly on this side of the wards. Poseidon will it."

Again he mentioned an Olympi. Again Kohl's head pounded in a shrill throb, a blackness seeping in behind his eyes, blurring his vision. "Give me that." Kohl snatched the pieces of the compass out of Dolion's hand. He would not give the man any advantage.

"The mark will heal. It is *his* brand. It binds us all." Dolion lifted the cuff of his shirt, revealing the same symbol seared into his wrist. Kohl recognized it, but it didn't make sense. It looked too much like one from a book he once read. A book that had since been banned from the Morentian Libraries and burned. But if they were one in the same—it was impossible.

They were struck by a forceful gale that carried them quickly over the seas. Howling with ferocity, it whipped at the darkened sails of *The*

Hydra. A storm was brewing. One for the ages. And Kohl was not ready to be encompassed by it just yet.

"What do we do now? There is no isle in sight. Not even a speck out on the horizon. You promised we would be there by the end of today." Kohl grabbed at a piece of cloth.

"Don't worry, Your Majesty. The prince will soon be in sight." Dolion grinned, his smile feral as the seas that thrashed beneath them. He passed Kohl an elongated barrel-shaped tool that he pulled out of a pouch on his hip. "When it is time, look through this."

CHAPTER FORTY

KATRIN

For days, Katrin tried to figure out how to fire that gods-forsaken bow and arrow, and not once was she able to hit her target. Given she had gotten closer, striking the trees nearby rather than the one with the blue painted circle. It was better than the first day, when the arrow barely stayed in the air halfway to the trees.

Ander caught her practicing, no longer under the constant bickering and guidance of Thalia and Leighton. He was dressed in his usual fitted black leather trousers and buttoned linen shirt. Today a single silver chain hung around his neck. The pendant was engraved with some symbol Katrin could not discern. A letter perhaps, the same style that decorated their weapons. The characters of the *Elliniká Glóssa*.

She pulled back on the bow string, letting another arrow fly toward the trees. This one closer still to that painted circle.

"You know, if you keep your elbow up more it will help steady your aim." His voice carried on the swift wind that began to wrap its way through the trees.

Katrin rolled her eyes, grabbing for another wooden arrow in the quiver slung across her back. "So I've heard." But she listened anyway, creating a T with her body, pulling her arm back, using the line by her ear as a guide.

The arrow whizzed ahead. At first it looked like it might skim right past her mark, but the wind picked up and seemed to alter its course, the arrow striking the tree just inside the mark. Katrin squealed.

"See, I told you." Ander strolled up behind her. "Elbow up always helps." He flashed a bright smile, softening his tanned skin and thick brows.

"It's the first one I've made."

Ander's smile turned to a grimace. "Well, I'm still proud, I guess. You're going to need some more practice though, if you ever hope to leave this place."

Katrin swatted him across the arm. "I thought I wasn't your prisoner, Captain?"

His calloused hand crept up to her cheek, brushing his fingers over her parted lips. "You never were. And never will be." His soft voice caressed the depths of her mind, sending heat to places he had been before. The delicate words lulled the wicked self-deprecation that so often crowded her mind.

But she couldn't feel this way. At least not now. It complicated too many things. Ander told her as much that day on the training mat. He needed control in his life and so did she. As much as she felt a preternatural draw toward him, his lemon and salt scent, his captivating eyes, she could not be his. Not with Kohl waiting for her. Not when the fate of her people—the fate of Katrin herself—hung by a single thread.

Katrin plopped down on the hard forest floor, snatching a vat of water from her leather pouch. "So, to what do I owe the pleasure of your company, *Prince*?" Her eyes crinkled and nose scrunched.

"I came to tell you that we will need to start heading back to the coast. So it's a good thing you got at least one successful shot out of this thing." He pointed to the wooden bow now lying beside them.

Katrin chucked a small rock at him. The captain let out a light laugh that seemed to wrap around her very bones, igniting her soul. "And where exactly are we going?"

Ander's eyes sparkled the most brilliant color she had ever seen. It reminded her of the Alentian shores on the brightest of summer days. Pure, magnificent turquoise.

"Home, Starling. We are finally going home."

It felt strange to be back aboard *The Nostos*. As Katrin ran her hand along the faded rails of the ship she felt safe. At peace with her decision to stay. Like this place, with these people, was where she was meant to be.

The salty smell of the sea and low tide filled her lungs as the ship began its journey back to Mykandria. At least, that was where Katrin thought they were going. Ander had not specified where home was, but they had discussed rallying both the smaller isles and Alentus.

He had to have been from nearby with his parents trading with hers all those years ago. Maybe it was Xanthia or Cantos. Both isles were known for their less seedy merchant trade compared to Lesathos. It was probably Cantos, the isle of gemstones and craftsmanship. Only a skilled artisan could have made that delicate comb she loved so dearly, that intricate sword hanging at her hip. It did not matter where he was from. What mattered was whether she would ever see her sister again. See *her* home. See her people.

On the horizon, the skies began to darken. Katrin could only hope a storm wouldn't deter their course. But the swirling wake in the tide and the looming clouds ahead did not seem reassuring. She retreated below deck, where all but Kristos and a few men, who stayed above to steer the ship and man the sails, stood around the heavy wooden table that lay in what they were now deeming the war room.

Charts lay scattered across, covering every inch of space on the table. Ander was pointing at an area north of Nexos, part of the continent above. From what Katrin could remember, it looked like the location of the port entrance to the Kingdom of Hespali. He must have been showing where they needed to avoid. No doubt the birthplace of Giselle, Queen and Goddess of Nexos, was allied with the man in Voreia who was capturing and slaughtering women in Cyther.

"We will start by taking port at home. Gather supplies and see if my parents are willing to give us aid. Then continue on to the other isles and, of course, Alentus. With Katrin on our side they could be our biggest ally." He shuffled more of the charts around, places she did not recognize flagged with tiny pins.

Katrin squinted at the small markings that seemed to drift around each chart. "You keep saying home. Where is home, Ander?" She didn't understand why no one spoke of the destination. Katrin could see Thalia bite her lip, Leighton shifting his weight from knee to knee, avoiding eye contact with her.

Ander rapped his fingers over the dark wooden table, his thick brows scrunching together. The captain's breathing seemed to become forced, letting out a long sigh. "Home—yes. I was hoping to discuss this in private tonight, but—"

A shudder ran through the room, a force so powerful it rattled the wooden planks of the *The Nostos*. Katrin could feel it charge up her skin, a tremor of magic sparking in the distance. Something was coming for them. Something dark. Something that was able to break through the ward woven by gods.

Katrin locked eyes with Ander, whose lips thinned and jaw clenched, his fingers looked like they were digging into the sides of his chair. Was it anger? Or terror? Or both?

The captain pushed back from his chair. "Weapons at the ready, men, we aren't expecting anyone to cross the border of the wards." His voice was ice, a tone Katrin hadn't heard from his lips before. He reached for the crossed swords mounted on the wall, the ones that resembled the banner that flew on the navy and silver flags of *The Nostos*.

Ander's eyes flashed a deep silver, the color of the storming skies above. Katrin almost thought she saw a field of fog flicker between his fingers, but it was gone as quickly as it came. Her power on the other hand, welled deep in her gut. The spark of a bolt of lightning, the starlight drained from the skies above, the shroud of darkness from the underworld circling her entirely.

They sprinted up from below, arrows and swords in hand. Ander made it to the deck first, followed by Leighton, then Thalia, then the remaining crew. Last was Katrin, weaponless except the dagger at her thigh that seemed to radiate heat as she stood on the slippery deck.

Katrin's breath hitched as she stared at that ship heading toward them. The dark sails she knew so well. The red and orange flags it flew, a viper stitched in the center. *The Hydra*. She couldn't believe what she was seeing. How could he break through the wards? Kohl wasn't born of the gods, no magic flowed through his veins, and yet there he was, sailing full speed down wind.

Chapter Forty-One

Kohl

Kohl could see them now. He didn't even need the spyglass Dolion had given him. At first, it was just a handful of people manning the ship. A few men tending to the navy sails attached to two masts, a taller man at the helm of the ship. They were in the thick of a storm that seemed to start and end with the outline of *The Nostos*.

Then the rest came. First a young man around his age, who must have been the captain—*the pirate*—who took his beloved. Then another man with darker skin, shouting orders at the crew. His second. The third was a thin woman with long white hair and a demon looking creature attached to her hip. Then more of the crew followed, weapons at the ready.

The last person came out from below the ship. Kohl knew exactly who she was. The dark brown hair plastered to her face. The angry stance she held when she saw the ship before them. When she *recognized* what ship it was.

Katrin was not bound, not caged, not a prisoner. And Kohl, Kohl screamed at the betrayal he saw before him.

"We need to be on that ship now!" he yelled to the soldier manning the ship's wheel. The seas under them continued their violent thrashing against the side of what should have been the fastest ship in the isles.

"Yes, Your Highness. If we hold a steady course to the port side of their ship we should be able to latch on to board," the stocky man replied, his grip firm on the wheel.

The rain began to pick up, its droplets like small knives lashing against Kohl's fuming skin. She was not in distress. She was not a victim. She was not taken; she had left. Or maybe she was brainwashed, or they threatened her life, or his, or her sister's. That made more sense than what was laid out before him. Katrin had not left of her own free will. Did not help this pirate and his men while they tortured and rampaged the eastern shores and seas of Mykandria.

The thunder that began to roll in from the distance sounded overhead as they inched closer to the enemy's ship. The Prince of the Lost Isles would meet his end today.

Lightning began to strike along the sides of each ship as they drew near. The gods were angry. Lightning, the symbol of Alentus. One of many powers Kohl's betrothed would possess now, since her twenty-fifth birthday had passed. Katrin would not have been able to control it yet, and Kohl wondered what other powers she would be trying to tame.

"Your Highness, we are close enough to drop the platform! Men are at the ready," the stocky soldier yelled out again.

"Prepare to fight on my command. Our only priority is to get Princess Aikaterine back on this ship and safely home to Alentus." Kohl unsheathed his long blade from his back and waited to jump over to *The Nostos*.

Dolion approached his side. "And as we agreed, Your Highness, the prince is mine."

Kohl's eyes narrowed at the ruddy man. The same offputting feeling crept up his spine as he sliced his blade across Dolion's throat. He was a loose end—that's what Kohl's father would say. "Throw his body overboard," he yelled to one of the soldiers. "I don't want his blood staining the ship."

He could see Katrin now, more clearly despite the downpour of rain and salty sea burning his eyes. Could see her shock and confusion, but also a light. A glimmer of happiness as she saw Kohl for the first time in months. But then—then he saw the man that stood beside her. His dark black hair matted from the rain, eyes matching the storm brewing above, harsh jaw and an air of confidence that only came from one place. From one person.

Chapter Forty-Two

Katrin

"Of course it would be you!" Katrin's lungs tightened at Kohl's scream as he jumped from the platform now connecting the two ships, his boots landing with a thud. His sword was drawn as Kohl flipped the hilt around and around in his palm. "Oh, won't my father be excited to learn where you've been hiding the past few years," he hissed.

Ander took a step between him and Katrin, shielding her from his line of sight. "I'm sure he will be quite upset to know I'm not where he left me." She didn't understand. Did these two know each other? Why did King Athanas have anything to do with Ander, or where he would be?

"Can someone explain what is going on? Kohl? Ander?" Katrin flashed between the two men. What if Ander was right? What if Kohl knew what his father had been up to this whole time? She could feel the bile rising in her throat, the tangy taste of regret and disgust on her tongue.

Kohl began to laugh. A deep and ferocious chuckle that made the hairs on Katrin's arms stand up. "Ander! Is that what you're calling yourself these days?" He took a step closer to Katrin and the prince, Kohl's sword pointing directly at him. At the way he held his arm in front of Katrin, like Kohl would ever really harm her. "What other lies have you spewed, Nik? This man is Nikolaos Alexander Kirassos, *Prince* of Nexos. Nexos, the same people that took you five years ago. The same people who tried to kill you so they could conquer the isles unopposed. Did it not seem odd that it happened again? Right as we were to be married? Right before the Acknowledgment?"

Ander turned and looked at Katrin, his eyes washing over in a silvery gaze. Katrin's heart sank as her eyes locked with the captain's. No—not just a captain. Prince Alexander. Prince *Nikolaos* Alexander. How could she not have seen it before? She cocked her head to the side, really taking him in. The deep black hair, the olive skin, eyes the color of the sea beneath them. King Nikolaos's features, only younger. She was a fool.

Her eyes narrowed, burning hot as the fire of the stars rising inside her. Ander—Alexander—had taught her how to control the fire inside her, but never when she had been this caught off guard. Never when her emotions had been all consuming. Never when *he* caused them.

"You!" she screamed. "It was you all along!" Her blood boiled as she pulled the dagger from her thigh and shoved him straight in the chest with her other fist. Alexander stood—just stood there, not fighting back an inch—until she had him pressed against the edge of the rail, dagger firmly planted against his neck.

The brand on his neck—on Thalia's neck—not the mark of their captor. It was *their* symbol. She had heard his voice in her kidnapped daze. It was not because he had tried to rescue her. It was because he was the reason she was taken in the first place. A six letter nameless ship. *The Nostos.*

"Starling—" his gaze wandered to hers looking with utter pleading, willing her to see past her emotion, "Starling, please."

Everything from the past two months started flooding in her head. How he spoke about his family, how he couldn't return home, the masquerade, him rescuing her from those men on Lesathos, her *father* meeting them in Skiatha. Oh gods—*everything* that happened in Skiatha. Had it all been fake? An illusion in her mind? King Nikolaos could manipulate the minds of people, had that trait passed down to his son? Had her father even been there at all?

Leighton lunged for her. "Katrin, it's not what it looks like. Let him explain." Her other hand outstretched, a bolt of light flashing from her palm and hitting the nauarch straight in the chest. Leighton stumbled backward, collapsing on the ground.

"Katrin, what are you doing? You have to trust us!" Thalia screamed, now clutching Leighton's limp body. He was still breathing, but the bolt would knock him out until she had answers.

"Take a step closer, *Seer*, and you'll meet the same fate as him," Katrin seethed, her other hand still pressing the blade firmly to the captain's neck, her elbow pinned into his shoulder.

The power was settling low in her stomach. She could not think straight. All she could see was the blinding light and the man who stood emotionless before her. She was a goddess who was no longer in control.

Out of the corner of her eye she saw the *psychí* transform. No longer a small lithe cat, Mykonos was instead an all white mountain lion, no doubt twice Katrin's size. The creature's fangs glistened in the moonlight as she growled, her yellow eyes fierce and deadly.

"Thalia, keep that thing in line or the same goes for her!" Katrin's voice was lower, coming from deep within her soul. All the nights Mykonos spent curled up next to Katrin as she wept, as she confided in her—in the seer as well—it had just been a ploy for information. To gain Katrin's trust before they all betrayed her.

She turned back to the captain. "Prince of the Lost Isles, really? Are you or are you not the Prince of Nexos?" The blade pressed harder now as blood trickled down. He refused to say a word. "Answer me!"

He was silent, eyes locking still on hers. But they were not the eyes she remembered from years ago; she knew that man's face, the hatred that encompassed his whole being, but that didn't mean Ander did not give the order to take her. She had suppressed and resurfaced those days so many times maybe she had truly forgotten or maybe she had avoided what was right in front of her.

"I am," he whispered, his throat bobbing against the blade. She could see the words racing in his mind, but she would not let him manipulate her again. Not let him weave stories and illusions into her mind. "You have to understand—"

"Don't say another word, you traitor! I trusted you! I trusted all of you!"

"Starling, please—I love you. I was going to—"

"Love? Love!" Katrin let out a deep, maddening laugh. "Someone as ruined as you could never love." This man. This liar. Her betrayer and her ruin. Katrin pushed off him, turning and running her nails along the rail of the ship. Sparks started to fleck off them as the clouds above collected, snuffing each twinkling star above them. Their power drained from the sky into her.

"You will burn for this," she spat at him as she pushed off the rail and the power of the stars struck the stern of *The Nostos* like a bolt of lightning, setting it ablaze. "I guess we'll see what gods favor *you* now." Katrin walked back and leaned toward Ander, Alexander, Nik, whatever he called himself. "I take back what I said. I regret all of it. Especially you."

The rain started pouring once more, but the fire still burned. The blaze grew too big and too fast, fueled by the heavy winds racing by. A low lying fog began creeping in from the distance, snuffing out the view east of the ship.

Kohl ran up, grabbing her hand pulling her back toward the platform that connected them to *The Hydra*. "We have to go! Now!" For a second she couldn't move, staring at the three people she had considered her friends—one who she might have considered as more. The crew that stood around them, their faces in a permanent state of shock. But as the fog inched closer, she began to run.

As she ran, Katrin tried to ignore the weight of what was happening. Tried to ignore the feelings she had formed that somehow still lingered. Tried to ignore the gnawing feeling that the only person she could trust was herself.

The Hydra began to sail away, toward the calming seas, toward home. Katrin stood at the stern of the ship, watching as her heart broke. As those she'd called friends disappeared. As the man she started to love burned. As *The Nostos* began to sink.

Chapter Forty-Three

Katrin

The slow pace of *The Hydra* sailing back to Alentus was absolute torture. A glass of blood-red wine sloshed back and forth, the stem rolling between Katrin's fingers. It was her sixth that day. Bottles she had emptied were her only companions these days, stolen from the storage room when she dared to leave her quarters. The bold liquid meeting her lips was the only thing allowing her to fade off into a dreamless sleep. One where her mistakes and regrets were not all consuming.

Still, all the lies haunted her. Why create this fabrication of a threat if it did not exist? If it did exist, then Kohl lied to her. Kohl who never let a false word trail from his lips. Who was she supposed to trust? The man she spent her whole life growing to love? The pirate—prince—who helped her finally open up about her past? Neither?

Kohl tried to visit her those first few days. Knocked on the door, delivered food, spoke through the creaking wood locked shut. *"Why did you stay, Aikaterine? Why did you not come back to us?"*

Why did it take so long to look for me, she wanted to ask. But she never did. Katrin just clutched her arms around her knees, leaning against the other side of that door, letting the ruby liquid flow down her throat. He always left the food. She barely ate it, just enough that she didn't hurl the crimson contents of her stomach back up.

Even books weren't helping. They only reminded her of that day on *The Nostos* when Ander lingered by the door, his shoulders sagging in defeat. How he left her myths of the Olympi. To comfort her? To confuse her? Her reality melded together.

Slap, slap, slap; the waves crashed against the hull. Darkness seeped in through the small windows on the side of the ship. Not a candle to deter it. She preferred to sit in the shadows. They let her fester in her failures. It would only be moments now. A few more sips. Blanket curled around her waist, eyelids heavy, the room blurred and once again Katrin was asleep.

Salty air danced through the window. Cypress trees, daisies, crisp coastal wind. Home. Katrin was finally home. She rose from the rug where she'd drifted off, stumbling a bit as she found her grounding. Relief swept over Katrin, then resolve, then pure terror. She wasn't ready to talk to anyone—except perhaps Ember. Even then, she wasn't sure how to explain everything that happened the last few months. How she eventually willingly stayed away from her responsibilities to the isle, left her sister to fend for herself against King Athanas and his strict values.

Golden rays hit her eyes and Katrin flung her arm across her forehead. It was the first time she stepped outside since boarding *The Hydra*.

"You're awake," a familiar whisper came from behind her.

"Of course I'm awake," Katrin snapped.

Kohl tried to come over to her, wrap his arms around hers, but she recoiled at the movement. No—she could not be around anyone right now. Especially him. He stepped back a pace, wringing his hands together.

"We docked a few hours ago. I wanted to wait for you to arise on your own. I didn't want to startle you." Ebony eyes raked over her. His voice was strained, purple bags puffed under his eyes, wrinkles snaking their way out from them. Kohl's shoulders dropped forward, his knuckles scraped and bloodied. He looked awful.

Katrin didn't even respond. She turned on her heels, storming off the ship, down the dock, up the path to the castle, and straight to her room. Ignoring every gasp and clap and gossip filling the halls as she passed. When she locked the door to her chambers, she sunk down on the bed. *Her* bed, turquoise velvet blankets engulfing her, warming her heart for just one moment. Low light flickered in through the windows, casting shadows on the worn pale wooden floors. The hearth crackled with a fire, counteracting the breeze drifting in through the gossamer curtains.

Silent. Her mind was finally silent.

Rap, rap, rap. Katrin blinked her eyes open to the sound of the faint tapping at her door.

"Katrin?" the faint voice choked through the crack in the wood.

She shimmied off the bed, padding over to unhook the several locks that were added since she was last in Alentus.

"Oh, Katrin! It's really you!" Her sister flung her arms around Katrin in a gut-wrenching embrace, Ember's sobs deafening against her shoulder. Behind Ember stood the commander, who only nodded, a curt smile tugging at his lips.

Katrin brought her hand to her sister's head, stroking her straw locks like Kora used to do when they were children. "Everything is alright now, Ember. I'm home. I'm home and I am not leaving you again."

She meant it. This would be the last time she was taken from these shores. Katrin would sooner die than endure another moment knowing she was lost without a path home. Be so far from the people who truly mattered in her life. A bubbling of regret filled her lungs. She *willingly* stayed with *The Nostos* to fight this non-existent war. Never again.

"Oh gods, Katrin. There is so much I need to tell you!" Ember stepped back from their embrace.

"There's so much I need to tell you too." She cupped her sister's face, her thumb grazing against a faint scar by Ember's temple. "You tell me first though."

Ember winced, her breath hitching. "You may want to sit down for this."

So they sat and Katrin willed herself out of the fog that had consumed her for the last week, because she had to. For Ember's sake.

Katrin could not bear to be around other people anymore. Not while they coddled her like a fragile glass doll, afraid she would step off the balcony and down the cliffs below. Or worse, when they expected her to smile and curtsy and proceed as if she had not been absent for months.

The only person she allowed in her wing of the castle was Ember. Her sister had been the only person who truly fought for her the entire time. The only person Katrin knew with her whole breaking heart she could trust.

All Katrin knew was that she was unbearably tired. But when Katrin would try to go to sleep, it only evaded her. For weeks on *The Hydra* she had been in and out of a drunken daze, sleeping, but not truly resting—or healing.

Now even that was impossible.

Tonics did not help. Books did not help. Wine no longer helped. Katrin was in a state of perpetual spiraling, the little bits of spark she had seen return during her time on *The Nostos* and in Skiatha snuffing out with each successive day. In the few moments where she somehow drifted into a hazy sleep, she was met by his face. Ander's face. The lines that formed around his lips as he clenched his jaw. The bob of his throat as she held her dagger against it. Brows scrunched above the anxious longing and regret in his crystalized eyes. Katrin could not stand this image. Could not stand to see *him*, his lies, his half-truths, his smile, his lips, his breath hot against her skin.

I never said the woman I loved was back home, Starling.

You always have a choice with me.

You were my northern star...the thing I knew would lead me home.

Every moment that passed remembering the way he touched her, kissed her, held her when she was breaking convinced her even further. It was all an illusion. A fabrication in her mind. One that Ander put there to torment her.

Katrin reached for the vial of ink on her desk, smoothing out a wrinkled piece of parchment from the drawer.

Dear ~~Ander Alexander~~ Nikolaos,

I don't even know how to start this. I feel as if I have written it again and again in my mind during the weeks I spent on The Hydra sailing back to Alentus, back to my home. Gods, I don't even know what to call you. Ander just doesn't seem right anymore.

When I think of that name, I think of the small boy who gifted me the beautiful sea glass comb and played with me on the shores of my isle. When I think of that name I think of the prince who carried me to safety, bloody, beaten, and unconscious. Who bathed me and nursed me until my scars faded to nothing more than memory. The man who helped bring me back from the darkest places of my mind and taught me the strength my power holds. To always trust myself even when that overwhelming feeling of darkness calls.

But you weren't him. You are not Ander. You never really were. Not since you were a child. And even then, was it all for show? Playing nice with the younger princess, while your parents brokered deals with mine? Were you always the manipulative prince your father made you into? Did you always loathe me? Loathe me enough to do all this?

You are not Ander. You are Prince Nikolaos Alexander Kirassos II. Heir to the throne of Nexos. God of Shield and Storm. Abductor. Liar. Betrayer.

I know you will never read this, but I fear if I don't write it down it will eat me from the inside out and I can not have one more thing picking away at my mind. I trusted you. Only you, with all my secrets. All my scars. Bared my heart, my mind, and my soul and the blackness that filled each one. You made me feel like someone knew me. Truly knew me, and yet would stay. Was not afraid of the weight tying down my limbs, threatening to sink me to the bottom of the seas to drown.

Was any of it real? Was I just a means to an end? Did you gain my trust and break me once more for sport? Did you ever truly feel the way you whispered to me that night in the mountains? How did you do it? How did you get inside my head? I don't think I'll ever forgive you. For infiltrating my darkest thoughts. For making me see things that never were. For pretending.

You are nothing, like I was nothing to you.

-~~Katrin~~ *The woman whose will you shattered*

Katrin thought the time she spent in Skiatha healed a piece of her that had been broken for so long. That she finally put the puzzle pieces of her scattered mind in place. That *he* helped her heal those wounds that ran deeper than flesh and bone and blood. A lie. Her curse. A life set to repeat itself again and again until she was nothing more than a shell.

She tore the piece of parchment from her desk walking over to the fireplace that burned in her living chambers. Katrin placed the corner of the parchment over the flame, watching as the fire ate the words she poured out. Hoping the smoke would engulf her anger and betrayal with it on the wind. But it did not.

So Katrin ran. Out of her chambers and into the darkness of the night sky. No moonlight to guide her. Past the barracks and out of the castle's gates. Away from the sloshing sounds of waves against the shoreline. Into the groves that led to the Triad Mountains.

And she ran and ran and ran. From the thoughts, the fear, the pain. Until she slammed into a tree. Until she leaned up against it, the bark clawing at her back. At the scars that did not heal. The scars that could never heal. God born or not, these were sliced so deep in her, in her very soul.

And she wept. Wept for the past. Wept for the present. Wept for the future she would no longer have. Before she dried her tears on her sleeve and began running once more.

Chapter Forty-Four

Kohl

Nik—Alexander—whatever he called himself, he was a dead man. For how he kept Katrin from him. It didn't matter that Katrin had spoken no more than a few words to him since he rescued her from *The Nostos*, from the clutches of that vicious prince. Or that she'd looked confused when Kohl first boarded the ship; that she'd looked like she belonged.

Kohl had not heard the words she spoke to the Prince of Nexos over the clapping of thunder, the strike of lightning, and the power of the endless starry sky that flowed from her to the ship and the seas below. Katrin was his. She would always be his. He just had to convince her of the same.

The silence of the forest shook him out of his thoughts. Katrin had taken off running again. She was always fast, but this was something else. Kohl tried to keep pace with her, but he truthfully stopped going on runs when he'd lost her. Tears stained her cheeks and yet she flew through the wood like a mountain lion, leaping over branches and roots. No target in mind, just the instinct to escape.

He dug deep, using whatever strength was left in his legs to propel toward her. Snapping of twigs caused Katrin to cock her head back over her shoulder. She knew someone was following her—knew and did not care. It was reckless and he had to stop her.

Inches, he was only inches from her now. Kohl reached out his hand, locking it around her wrist. "Katrin, stop!" He pulled her around until she was facing him, inches from his heaving chest. "You have to stop running, Aikaterine. From me. From everything."

"I don't want to talk to you! I don't want to talk to anyone." She tried to pull away, but his grip, even wrapped and injured, was too strong for her.

"I am your king and you *will* speak to me," Kohl hissed. He had enough of it. Her brooding and hiding and self-deprecation. She was home. She should be happy.

"How could I forget?" Katrin seethed. "Tell me one thing, Kohl, did you even try to postpone the Acknowledgement? Or did you see the opportunity to take what was not yours and lunge? You are just like your father. You'd burn everyone around you all in the name of peace."

"I am nothing like my father. I did this for you. For us!" It felt like fire was exploding in his veins once more. Black snaked around his finger tips and he clenched them into fists, the burn on his palm pulsing in pain.

Katrin's lip twitched up in a snarl. "You almost killed my sister and now, what—you are going to try to kill me too?"

A long sigh left Kohl's lips. His tension slowly retreated. He had to stay calm. "I would never hurt you, Aikaterine. "

Glassy-eyed, brows furrowing, Katrin finally looked directly at him. "How can I believe that? How can I trust you?"

"I don't know," Kohl whispered. He took his good hand and clutched hers, bringing it to his heart. "But this has always been yours. Long before the prophecy was fulfilled. I know this isn't how you pictured things—how either of us wanted our marriage to start. But even if you loathe me, I will always love you. Even after the gods take us. For the good of the isles, for the good of Alentus, can you not pretend you could love me once again too?"

Kohl inhaled a sharp breath, holding back the pools of liquid that formed behind his eyes. He would not shed a tear, not until she wrote him off entirely. Not until she said no.

Chapter Forty-Five

Katrin

Katrin had just married the love of her life. At least, that is what she would have said only a few months before. How everything could change that quickly was something her mind could not process right now. Right now she had to present a certain image to her people. Standing in front of her guests with smiles and polite waves. A woman of grace and respect. The Queen of Alentus. Her rightful title at last.

Maybe she would grow to love Kohl again. Despite the lies, the treachery, the plotting and destruction. Maybe redemption lay at the end of their path—or the beginning. But forgiveness was not an easy thing to come by in the isles, and trust even harder. That's what it came down to. For her sister, for her people, for her home, she married Kohl. If Katrin was honest with herself, she didn't think she *could* ever trust him again.

The wedding had been short, a series of formalities and boxes to check. It was not the lavish event that her mother and King Athanas had planned all those months ago. Vows were not exchanged except those promising loyalty to the other gods of the realm.

Katrin had worn a simple gown, made of white silk and turquoise, embroidered flowers along the hem. Kohl had selected the traditional formal attire of Alentus, a navy tunic and dress pants made of a thick cotton material, the banner of the isle patched on his chest. He donned the crown of Alentus, with its spikes exploding into stars around the fiery sun. *Her* crown by birthright. Instead Katrin was given a smaller circlet, engraved with the constellations that appeared around the summer solstice. A single lightning bolt struck through the center.

Kohl and Katrin exchanged simple thin silver bands, since she had refused the gold one presented to her earlier, as did she refuse the gold cuffs that King Athanas had presented as a wedding gift.

She knew he was getting increasingly angry at her dismissive attitude toward Morentian traditions and colors, but this was Alentus. Her home. Her colors. Her traditions. And even though she was back and Kohl seemed to be acting like himself again, she couldn't help but remember the warning she'd received from Leighton in Skiatha. The treacherous rock hidden by gold, able to drain a god's power right out from within.

She could not risk it. *Would not* risk it.

The people in the crowd before her cheered, for the return of their queen, for this blessing from the gods. But they had also cheered when Kohl had been crowned, when he defeated her sister by knocking her over the head with an almost lethal blow.

If there was one thing above all else she would never forgive him for, it was that. He had not protected the things that meant the most in the world to her. But neither had Katrin. She chose not to return. Chose to help a man that only ever lied to her over her own blood. She would not make that mistake ever again.

Today Katrin would go through the formalities. Wave graciously at her people like the newly crowned queen she was. Make small talk with whatever leaders of other kingdoms King Anthanas had decided to invite. Act the dutiful wife and consort beside Kohl, despite not being able to stand him at the moment. He had been right, tensions were too high in the isles, and they needed to show a unified front—*in public*.

But later, she would need to sit him down for a discussion on what this all meant. How they would live. How they would learn to trust one another again. She would have to be honest with him about everything. The scars. What happened in Skiatha. What the crew on *The Nostos* had expected his father was aiding, or at least knew about. If Kohl himself had known too. How, if it was true, they would work to stop it before Odessia crumbled beneath the wrath of an Olympi reborn.

King Athanas approached the dais, where Katrin and Kohl now stood hand in hand. He was accompanied by three others. A tall soldier, the top of his face masked by his helmet. The second, an older man, looking to be around the same age as her father, his sandy blonde hair tied back with a leather string, his fingers adorned with golden rings and gems the size of Katrin's eyes.

The last was a beautiful woman, somewhere between the age of Kohl and his father. Her skin was a deep umber, features delicate and lips plump. And her eyes. They were familiar. A glittering emerald that was so striking they could pierce your very soul. King Athanas smiled at the two newlyweds. Waving his hand to the side to display his guests. "Aikaterine, Kohl, I would like you to meet our allies from the north. King Edmund Briarre of Harrenfort and his lovely Queen Consort Ileana."

A coppery tang filled Katrin's mouth. Ileana. The eyes. Leighton's eyes. His sister was not dead. She knew Leighton had not lied. Had felt his pain radiating deep inside herself as he told his story, peering out at the Skiathan waters. But what did that mean?

"A pleasure to meet you both." The King of Herrenfort gave a curt bow. "I am looking forward to expanding our alliance with Alentus."

Kohl extended his calloused hand to the king. "Edmund. Ah yes, you are the one who gave my father his prized possession." Katrin peered at Kohl. *His prized possession?*

"I don't know if I would call *The Hydra* my prized possession, but it is high on the list." King Athanas chuckled. So this was the man from Voreia who gifted one of the fastest ships in the Mykandrian.

Katrin could barely hear as the men spoke back and forth. Her stare was locked directly on the queen. *I was told after a few years she slit her own throat, desperate to escape the life she was bound to.* Katrin's gaze drifted up to her neck, covered by a thick gold choker adorned with sparkling jewels the color of a blackened abyss.

"Of course, *The Hydra* is nothing in comparison to its parents, *The Typhon* and *The Echidna*." The silent masked soldier now spoke. "The olde myths were always a favorite of my king."

Katrin knew that voice, though she couldn't quite piece it together. The graveley rasp the soldier made as he breathed. The way words slid off his tongue like thick, hot oil. "What exactly is a hydra?" Katrin asked. "You don't know?" The masked soldier grinned. "In ancient times, the people believed there lived a beast beneath the waters—a many-headed snake, its bodies twisted around each other." The man blinked and when his eyes opened they turned a deep crimson red. But when he blinked once more they turned back.

Katrin went ashen. It could not be. But it was. She was frozen in her spot, the scars along her wrists and back burning with an uncontrollable icey fire.

But then the screaming started. Katrin whipped around, trying to find its source. The Spartanis began to shift, protecting the leaders of the isles. No—protecting King Athanas and King Edmund. Protecting their people.

Where was Ember? Where was the commander? Katrin began to wonder as she glanced through the courtyard. But the only people she truly recognized were the five senators. Then the rumbling began, a stomping of footsteps coming from the mountains through the gates. From the dais in the courtyard you could only see the faint outline of what was heading toward them. An army. The Spartanis—they had to do something.

Katrin could see her sister from across the courtyard, her short sword now drawn. "Soldiers, on orders, prepare for an attack! Hold your mark!" she yelled out to the men dressed in Alentian blue. Only the senators seemed to look concerned, to be wary of who may be inching closer toward them. Grabbing Ember's arm, Iason whispered something that Katrin could not make out. The dark banners were approaching quickly, their symbol still hidden by the distance.

That was when she saw it, as the men dressed as the Spartanis—or possibly even the Spartanis themselves—unsheathed their weapons. Two snakes intertwined, engraved on every blade. Ander and Leighton and Thalia and her father—it had really been her father. They had all known. They had warned her and she chose not to trust them. And now not only had Katrin been betrayed, but her people as well.

She went ashen as members of the guard turned on one another, on the senators, and slit their throats. Hot thick crimson now splattered in uneven patterns on her white gown. Her hands trembled, and a sinking feeling of fear she had never experienced sent chills up her spine. Katrin needed to get out. Needed to get her sister and get out, or they would be next.

Where was she? Ember had been on the opposite end of the courtyard. She would be safe for now. Ember had learned to hold her own and Iason would be with her. He would protect her no matter what had been promised to those men who defected from their positions. He was like a father to them. Katrin raced through the now upheaved crowd, trying to find the yellow braids Ember had pinned back. The next scream she heard was too familiar. A piercing, blood curdling shriek. *Ember.*

Chapter Forty-Six

Katrin

Katrin could see her sister across the courtyard. See as Iason lept in front of her, as the sword that was meant for Ember pierced through his heart. The most respected member of the Spartanis, a man who should have been considered family, struck down by one of his own.

Now she really needed to rescue her sister. Needed to get them both out—to where, she was not sure. Katrin knew the mountains better than anyone, where hidden caves lay off the trails. Yet Kohl knew them too. Would he send these soldiers after her for slaughter? Ander had been right. Kohl had to have known what his father had been planning. He had taken her home, her people, and now he would take her life.

Katrin sprinted across the courtyard until she reached her sister, frozen in her place. "We have to go, Ember! We have to get out!"

Ember did not move. She only whispered under breath, "He told me to run."

Katrin practically dragged her sister out into the halls heading toward the staircase that would lead them to the castle's gate. The four remaining senators would not be able to hold off the members of the Spartanis who had turned for long. That was, if they were even still standing.

Eventually they would need to fight, and if they needed to fight then Katrin would have to find more weapons than her dagger and Ember's sword.

They would need to make it down to the barracks. There was a small storage shed there that housed at least basic weaponry they could steal.

Katrin whipped around the corner, her sister still in tow, when she slammed into someone. *Ajax.* She had not seen the commander in the courtyard when the attack began. Friend or foe? Which would it be?

Ajax glanced around, pulling Katrin and Ember into a nearby room. His voice was hushed and his breathing labored. "My Queen, Prytan, are you both alright?" Katrin nodded. Should she say more? Was the commander a defector too? He was always loyal to the Drakos family. To Ember. But Katrin would have said that about all the Spartanis before today.

"What is that?" Ember pointed at the canvas bag Ajax had slung over his shoulder. It looked heavy by the way his body tilted to that side.

"It's everything we need. I grabbed as many weapons as I could carry." He scanned the area around them, making sure no one had seen them tuck away into the small reading room by the back entrance to the castle, before dropping the bag on the floor. A long sword, twin blades, a baldric filled with daggers, and a bow and arrow. "There are more soldiers coming up from the docks. I have a way to get us out, if you trust me. But we are going to need to fight our way there."

Friend? Or Foe?

Ember's emotions finally unfroze. Her brows furrowed together, her features softening. She placed one hand over the commander's heart. "I'll always trust you, Ajax. With my life."

Katrin knew that the two of them could never be together. That it was against the laws of Alentus for the Prytan to marry, but it was a shame. She could see the way the commander and her sister looked at each other, with such unrequited longing. That look—it had been the same one Ander had given her at the masquerade.

"I have a ship in the harbor ready to take us. The crew aboard is aware of *who* they will be helping." Katrin could have sworn Ajax smirked for a second at her. "I know neither of you have killed before, but you will need to. If we are going to make it to the ship, lives will be lost and I will not have it be either of yours." Katrin only nodded, though her thoughts flashed to the night in Lesathos. A slit throat. The fog that had blanketed the scene.

Ajax nodded back. "Are you both ready? I need you to run as fast as you can to the docks and not look back. It is not a question of if we will be spotted, but when."

Ajax slid the two twin swords into a holster on his back, handing the bow and arrow to Ember and the long sword to Katrin. She tightened her dagger around her thigh, sheathing the long sword on her back with its leather holster, looking at the former Commander and Prytan of the Spartanis. The Spartanis that had betrayed their people. The Spartanis that had fallen. "For Alentus."

"For Alentus," they both repeated.

Ajax peered into the hallway, checking both directions. "It's clear."

So they began to run. Down the steps to the back gates of the castle. Around the winding path to the rocky trail taking them down to the docks. When they left the cover of the trees lining the perimeter of the castle, Katrin saw them. The bands of soldiers wearing that dark black and silver symbol of the north. Twined snakes ensnared in each other. The brand her friends wore. The symbol of her captor.

She knew she should not do it. Not only would she bring attention to them as they escaped, but using that much power would burn her out. At least for a period of time. But Katrin lost control, forgetting everything Ander had taught her. As her palms began to glow. As she turned and sent starlit fire at the soldiers. For what those people had done to her—had done to all of them. For herself. For Ander. For Thalia. For Leighton. For Alentus. And when the fire reached them, the soldiers were reduced to ash.

Katrin was shaking, her breathing labored. Ten more people she could add to the list of lives she had taken and not regretted. A hand grabbed hers. "We need to go, Katrin," her sister whispered. Now it was Ember who wished to drag her away from the trauma if necessary.

Like Katrin had expected, the flame drew the attention of more soldiers of the north. They began to descend the stairs toward them. So Ajax and Ember and Katrin took off once more. They were close, so close to reaching the docks. They would just need to make it over and down the last cliff walk. That was when she saw it, over the rocks, bobbing against the dock below. *The Nostos*. Their way out. She was not sure how *The Nostos* was whole. When she had seen the ship last it had been in flames, burning to ash over the Mykandrian Sea. Whoever made it possible, she was grateful.

They ran closer and closer to the shore, away from the soldiers of Harrenfort. Ajax had gotten them out, his hand never leaving her sister's as they wove down the winding, crumbling cliffs. Katrin did not understand how he had known to find them. Had known the attack would be coming. How his spies had remained loyal even when most of the Spartanis had turned.

In the distance she could see Thalia fighting with the other members of *The Nostos'* crew against a unit of northern soldiers. Men lay slaughtered and bloody on the docks as she noticed another familiar creature. Thalia's *psychí* in her snowy mountain lion form, ripping limbs from the attackers, tossing them into the harbor below.

As the soldiers inched closer, Katrin drew her dagger from her thigh, the long sword from her back. She could hear a deep voice coming from the ship, ordering the archers aboard to send their arrows as a shield for the three of them approaching. *Leighton*. Giving them the only chance they might have to break through the lines of soldiers that were trying to regroup between the docks and the shores of Alentus.

Katrin's powers may have been drained, but she would wield her blades until she fell. To save her sister, to try to save herself. Ember gave her a knowing look, grabbing her bow from her back and knocking an arrow.

"I'll cover you from behind. There looks to be a break in the line to the left. Ajax you signal to the ship we need cover from the front. See if they can get that *animal* to make a path to the port side of the ship." Katrin stared at her sister in awe, a similar look crossed the commander's face. In only a few months her sister had grown into a fierce warrior. One without fear. One with passion and promise.

"On your order, Drakos." Ajax turned and took off in front of them. He made some hand signal that Katrin was sure was one of the Spartanis, but maybe all warriors in the isles knew them.

As they approached the shoreline, closing in on the docks, some of the soldiers turned to face them. Ember began firing off arrow after arrow, hitting her mark each time, as Katrin began to fight through the line. "My queen, stay close!" Ajax screamed ahead of her, meeting every blade that came close with his own.

Katrin was almost at the ship when she heard a scream come from behind her and saw as a soldier sliced his sword across the back of her sister's knees. Ember crumbled on contact. Her heart began to race even more. They were so close, she would not let her sister fall. Not today. Katrin began running toward her sister when a lithe hand grabbed her.

"Don't worry, Katrin," Thalia's voice yelled over the fighting. A flash of white flew by her, aiming straight toward the soldier about to land his sword across Ember's neck.

Fear grew in her sister's eyes, not a fear of death, but of the creature barreling toward her, streaks of red lining its white fur. Ember held up her sword with the last bit of energy she had to block the soldier's blade. But the animal was faster, its elongated teeth ripping into the man's throat, claws digging into his leathers. When Mykonos landed, the soldier lay in tatters.

"We got her!" Katrin could hear Leighton now, as he and Ajax ran toward them, lifting Ember and racing back toward the plank that led up to *The Nostos*. "Come, Katrin, we need to get aboard now!"

The wind was strong, they could make it off the dock. *The Hydra* was fast, but *The Nostos* would have a head start. Where they would go she was not sure. They would not make it all the way back to Skiatha, not without stopping for supplies and they could not afford being hunted down in Lesathos or one of the other isles.

"Where is he? Where is Alexander?" Katrin pleaded as Leighton pulled each of them on board.

"Is he not with you?" Leighton asked.

"I'm sorry, Leighton. Alexander didn't make it out. They took him to the dungeons. I couldn't—I couldn't save them both." Ajax grabbed his shoulder.

Leighton. Ajax *knew* the nauarch?

"It's ok, Jax, she was our priority." *Jax? Priority?* "Man the sails! We need to be off this dock now! Archers, hold your stances, we need time!" Leighton shouted his orders to the crew as they began to push back off the dock, the navy sails unfurling from the two masts on the ship, catching the western wind that would lead them out of the cove.

"No! No, we have to go back for him!" Katrin screamed, hoisting herself up onto the rail to jump off. Strong arms wrapped around her, dragging her back onto *The Nostos*. He had told her the truth. This whole time. She should have trusted him, but instead she was fickle with her loyalty. He protected her for years, with no recognition. Saved her twice. She needed to save *him* now. "Let me go!"

"I'm sorry, Katrin," Leighton whispered. "I'm so, so sorry. It's what he would want."

Standing at the stern of the ship, Katrin could not move, watching her home fade in the distance. She needed answers. From Ajax. From Leighton. From Thalia. *From Ander*, but she would not get those.

Salty air began to whip at her face, stinging against the small cuts and scrapes on her skin. Her breathing began to steady as a single tear grazed down her cheek. A tear for her people. For her home. For *him*.

"I'll come back for you, Ander. I promise," Katrin whispered to the howling winds. And in her mind she could have sworn she heard him whisper back. *I know, Starling. I know.*

It was then that Katrin realized the red-eyed man was right. Ander was her curse, but he was also her salvation. He had sacrificed it all to save her. Had given himself up so that a little piece of hope could still linger in the isles. For a better world. For peace.

But war was coming, and once again Katrin found herself on the seas.

Bonus Chapter: The God of Shield and Storm

Alexander

*D*rip, *drip drip*. Salty water trickled down from the ceiling landing on his head. Darkness surrounded him, but he paid it no mind. Usually the silence and unknowing blackness made him feel at home. He experienced a unique warmth of sorts when the shadows and fog wrapped around his body.

But this—this was a different kind of darkness. This darkness made his bones shiver and burn at the same time. It tasted like decay and copper and something old he could not place.

A soft voice caressed his mind. *I'll come back for you, Ander. I promise.* Katrin had gotten out. She had made it to *The Nostos*. That was all the prince cared about. Anything that came after his reckless decision to save the princess from King Edmund and his men he could deal with. He had survived their torture once, and for her—for her he would die in her place if it meant she could breathe even one more breath.

His mind drifted back five years earlier, how it still haunted him. How he had woken in the night with a feral tug low in his gut. How he had heard a woman's screams in his mind. It was not that he had never sunk into the mind of another before by accident, but this voice—it was familiar, though deeper and raspier than he remembered.

He had been too late to protect her then, draining himself of his unformed power while hastening across the seas to the Alentian shores. Had thought for a moment that it had been a trap when he was shackled with similar cuffs now seared into his wrists. But then he had seen her, bloody and damp from the rain, passed out from a knock to the head, lying on the deck of the ship.

For weeks he tried to escape the chains and bars that kept him hostage in the brig of the ship. Tried to get to her in the locked cabin. Tried to shut out the pleading she made the first few days. They had brought him once—only once—to see her. Threatened to slit her throat if he did not follow their rules. If he did not relinquish the power that would soon be fully realized in him to the golden shackles.

Then she had gone silent and a pain that felt as if someone ripped a sword down his chest gripped him. Alexander thought she was gone—that the man from the north had finally made due on his promise. But then he heard them, the calls that were all too familiar. The low and vile coaxing of men and women alike to their death in the deep abyss below.

The golden cuffs that dug into him kept him locked in his place, but he heard it anyway. *Her voice.* Luring him out to the thrashing waves. He knew she would hear them too, and could not stand to see her ripped from him by the taloned creatures beneath.

Alexander had sent out the last trickle of his not entirely formed power to his father. Prayed to Poseidon, the olde God of the Seas. *Save her. Protect her. I beg you, take from me what you wish, but do not take her from this earth.*

So for two more years he fought against the men until he grew strong enough to break free. He left the ship stricken in ruins, the men shredded at the bottom of the seas. But he would do it all again for her. Always for her.

A shadowy figure began to appear on the other side of the wrought metal bars holding a flamed torch. His broad frame and narcissistic gait meant only one thing. *Kohl.*

They had never seen eye to eye, not even when they were children. But Kohl had claimed to love Katrin and she seemed to love him too, despite everything he had done. They had married, even after—even after everything that happened in Skiatha, happened on the ship. Alexander couldn't blame her, he should have been honest from the start. That was all she had ever asked of him.

The king stepped fully into Alexander's frame of sight. He would never forgive Kohl for betraying Katrin. He *knew*. Knew everything, and yet did not stop his father.

Kohl flipped a long thin blade around in his hand, his lip curved up to display newly shaven canines, sharp as the viper he bore on his chest. Alexander was not sure if it was from the lack of food and water, or the pounding in his head, but Kohl's eyes appeared black as obsidian, the whites completely sucked out. And when Kohl placed his hand on the opposing side of the bars, a matching mark to the one on the back of Alexander's neck glared at him.

The raspy voice filled the dungeon, echoing off its deprecating walls. "Well, well, well, Alexander. What are we going to do with you?"

Bonus Chapter: Welcome to Hades

Alexander

Hazy smoke of tobacco swirled around the club, coming from every direction except for the small alcove where Alexander sat. Its rich, woody aroma clung to crimson velvet curtains hanging from the ceiling that were tied back by black cords. Some of the alcoves, however, had their curtains drawn, their occupants indulging in fantasies far beyond what he wished to experience at this moment.

For now, all Alexander wanted was reprieve—from her smile, her snarky banter, the way her skin sparkled in the amber light of dawn. How might her skin feel against his, how might her lips might taste as they met his own? It was undeniable torture and he had let himself sink right into the abyss of longing and hope. Not any longer.

Katrin did not want him, did not want to be here, and he had done nearly everything to convince her otherwise. She wished to return home to that lying snake of a prince. She claimed he knew nothing of his father's dealings, but how could he not? It caused Alexander's very blood to boil and the clouds to thunder just thinking of her with Kohl, but it was just as torturous to see her fade away. That beautiful star from his childhood turned so cold and lonely. If letting her go would bring back just the smallest bit of that light he would have to do it. Alexander would watch from afar, protect from afar, like he had been doing all these years.

Small moans trickled into his ears from the red-head that writhed up against his leg. She was attractive by most standards, full lips, curves you could latch onto in the night, sparkling jade eyes—but it was a lost cause. Abandoning himself to the pleasures of the club was supposed to keep his mind at ease, but he couldn't seem to move past the fact that this woman was not *her*. He was ruined and he hadn't even kissed Katrin yet.

"Are you not enjoying yourself tonight?" the lilting voice of the red-head rasped against his ear.

Alexander went to reply, to tell her to find some other more well-suited man to finish her off when golden silk and chocolate hair caught the corner of his eye. It should have been surprising to see her here, to know she disobeyed his direct orders, but Katrin's blatant disregard for anything he said was one of her charms. Gods, she looked absolutely exquisite in the dress he saw earlier draped on his bed. Even more so with the golden pendant hanging just between her breasts, luring mens eyes from across the club. But with a sweep of the room, it was not their eyes she locked onto, but his—staring, observing, an almost lustful glimmer in those darkened orbs. A feral smirk ticked up on his lips, he could not help himself, not when he knew what lingering thoughts swept inside her mind.

If this was to be the last night he saw the captivating princess, Alexander was glad a smile lit her face. Glad that warmth glowed in those amber flecked orbs as Katrin took in her surroundings. Ah—and there it was—the person who brought her here. Thalia snatched two goblets of wine from a small table, passing it to Katrin before grabbing her arm and dragging them to the middle of the room to dance.

The music turned to a deep melody and Katrin twirled with a sort of reckless abandon he had never seen in her before. This wild young woman was so full of life, even when the world around her crumbled—pretending for only a night that she was not a princess taken so far from home, but a mysterious woman of the night. He could watch her for hours on end, this fantastical image burning into his memory.

Swatting off the red-head, Alexander moved to the dance floor, sneaking up behind Katrin and wrapping his arm firmly around her waist. Gods, it was foolish to let himself get this close to her, to let himself have the smallest taste of what could be before he sent her off. But he couldn't help himself. He needed her—needed the whiffs of lilies and mint, needed the tingling of his skin as her fingers grazed his—even if it was only for this one fleeting moment. Another memory he would cling to.

"You didn't think I'd let the most ravishing woman wander about alone all evening, did you?" he purred into her ear, lips just grazing her flesh. "Care for a dance?"

Twirling Katrin around, Alexander softened his grip, moving her into a waltz he had learned as a young boy. The dance matched the haunting melody that floated from the musicians in the corner—almost as entrancing as the woman he led around the room. This was it—all he would give himself, all he would indulge in, the fantasy of her choosing him over Kohl. It would be enough for him, this solitary dance, any piece of her was enough.

The reverberating string melody came to a close and just then did Katrin look up at him through that gilded mask. Without thought Alexander leaned down, brushing a soft kiss against her cheek. He wanted to do so much more but her happiness was worth his heartbreak. Unable to bear looking at the one woman he could have loved, Alexander turned and began to walk away. "Thank you, Starling, for the dance. You can leave—you can go home."

Sinking into the crowd, Alexander could not help but wish she would change her mind. That he would return to *The Nostos* and Katrin would be there waiting for him, would tell him she could not leave—that she chose *him*. But then he heard her start to run.

ACKNOWLEDGEMENTS

Words cannot describe the feelings I have as I write the Acknowledgements portion of my first book. Ten years ago, when I was in college, I sat down and wrote my first trilogy. Although I wouldn't share that very awfully written work with anyone today, I accomplished the first step to my dream. Then, self-doubt and unkind words from others set in and I gave up on my passion. In the spring of 2023, right before I moved out to the suburbs, I had a dream—I kid you not an actual dream—of a fiery young brunette sword fighting with a captivating pirate during a storm. When I woke up, the idea for A Wrecking of Salt and Fire came to me. What started as a Helen of Troy retelling inspired by the Iliad and Pirates of the Caribbean, turned into so much more. Now that it is out in the world, I can only hope but do it justice. Now bear with me—Acknowledgements are hard to write because it is hard to pin down a few lines of how important the following people were to my dream.

I want to start by saying thank you to you, the reader, for taking a chance on me and on Katrin and Ember's story. It is a wild feeling to know that a piece of me—my heartbreak, my love, my struggles—is out there in the world. I always told myself if just one person related to the characters or if this book helped them heal even the tiniest bit, I would say I had found success. So I hope it did. I hope you read their stories and know that you are not alone in this world.

Nicole, Liz, and Meredith, my original readers. I'm sorry the version you read was so riddled with errors and awkward spice, but thank you for loving it anyway. This one is better. I swear.

To my beta readers Danny, Christin, Sim, Taylor, and Emily—there are not words to describe how forever grateful I am to you all. From the actual critiquing portion, to the unhinged theories, and the unwavering support when I feel like a complete imposter in this industry. I could not have made it through Book One without you all.

Ciara—my amazing editor. You helped craft this debut baby of mine into the work it is today and I cannot wait to work with you on A Spell of Bones and Madness and continue Katrin and Ember's stories. I promise I'll try to remember what you've taught me! Bring on the voice memos! An extra thank you for helping to coordinate my ARC team and discord. Being an indie author, and especially a first time indie author has been—to say the least—a trying time. Doing that all while working full time, renovating a house, and planning a wedding—almost impossible without someone there to support you and help when the crazy gets a little crazier. I could not have made a better decision when choosing you to help me make this dream a reality.

David—the most incredible cover artist I have ever met. You took a really non-descriptive, basic jumble of an idea and somehow worked your magic to create this epic cover. Thank you for designing the reason I'm pretty sure 90% of people ended up buying the book! I cannot wait to see what you have in store for A Spell of Bones and Madness.

To my parents—you both have always been these incredibly supportive people who would sacrifice anything for their children and I will never have a way to repay you for that. Thank you for always believing in my wildest dreams. And mom—thank you for reading my manuscript with an open mind and not using an entire box of red pens. I cried a little when you told me you actually liked it. Also, thank you for skipping the second scene in the castle at Skiatha, or at least not telling me you read it.

Myko and Cobes, my snuggle buddies, my floofy floofs, my writing partners in crime—thank you for always bringing a smile to my face.

And last, but never least—to my future husband, Josh, where would I be without you? I think I sat, staring at the computer screen for an hour, unable to write this part. The dedication pretty much sums up how I feel. You let me be a gremlin, huddled under a blanket, clacking away at my laptop for over a year and a half with little to no complaints. You made dinners when I needed to get in extra writing, and sat with me on the couch even when I was lost in my book and forgot to respond to the questions you asked me—and then asked me again. You are my lighthouse, you are my northern star. I love you until the world fades and we are nothing but dust in the night sky.

KICKSTARTER
ACKNOWLEDGEMENTS

T hank you to this incredible group of people who helped make my dream a reality and believed in me enough so I could bring this book to life.

Cortney Babcock, Nikki T, Yara Dijkstra, Ian Kirkwood, McKenna Hubbard, Annarose Willhite, Rebecca J, Alexandra Corrsin, Lori Brown, Nicole Fitzgerald, Alex C, Giulia Santucci, Elizabeth Lentz, Elizabeth W, Rosa Thill, Bella Nile, Lorena Skates, PunkARTchick "Ruthenia", Ann Flanagan, Qavee, Robert C. Worstell, Mary Ann Santay, Mandi, Laurie Condos, Tary Taylor, Sarah, Alyse Palsulich, E.S. Abbott, Allison Venner, Brittany Roberts, A Mowat, Alicia Banac-Aricayos, K.M. Davidson, Alyssa Kinser, Alexandra Simpkins, Liza Clarke, Catherine Levinson, Ali Christina, GT, Kiki Smart, Dragon Moms Book Club, David DeHaan, Laura Nelson, Luckie, Stephanie Crachiolo, Eric Mancia, Samantha Newberry, Nikkii Thompson, Adrianna Ferrannini, Amy Kitterman, Raven, Lisa Healy, Mel Lemon, Matthew Condos, Rachel Shear, Angela Morse, Faith Christiansen, Katherine Shipman, Ashley Kashner, Willa Layne, Krystal Ketterman, Samantha Rozy, Trisha Vergeire, Christine Hatter, Jodie E. Parks, KJ Bradford, Emily West, Morgan G, Chloe Hoop, Martha Mendez-Machado, Rachel Walker, Chrissy Cullen, Victoria P, April L. Miller, Gwendolyn Lee, Katherine

Malloy, Helena, Caitlin A, Savannah Gwynn, Gee Rothvoss, Anna Walton, Elise Crowley, Ashley E, Chance Hightower, Krista Westermayer, Sim Kay, Nicholas Paynter, Jenny Oliver, Holly Colvin, Aisha H, Andrew M, Robin Hart, Amanda Balter, Gabrielle Landi, Jamie Dockendorff, Kyle J Cisco, Amber Monroe, Pari Zeba, Alexis, Niki Kuhlman, S.D. Huston, S Simmons, K.J. Cloutier, Meggy Klepto, Ashley Belanger, Meagan L, Dorothy Tecuminngs, Cat Dean, Sophia Heald, Vannessa Goodwin, Shala Michan, Diane, Kristina R, Abigail Manning, Heyley Ingram, Maria Wilson, Kelli Swett, Simon, Jordan Johnson, Valeria Zayas, Celia Rodriguez, E. Kim, Doris, Maria M, Fira Richardson, Levi Harrell, Kate Carney, Bridget Young, Beth D, Hallie Maynard, Alyssa Pressley, Lex Aulum.

ABOUT THE AUTHOR

E.K. Condos is a fantasy and romance independent author who debuted her first novel in 2024. She currently lives in the suburbs of Boston with her husband, their Australian Shepard Cobalt, and their Turkish Angora Mykonos. When she is not writing, her hobbies include boating off the coast of Cape Cod and skiing the Northeast.

For information on upcoming works, follow on instagram.

@authoremilyk

authorekcondos.com

Made in the USA
Middletown, DE
23 August 2024

59051671R00215